It seemed _____ _____ his cabin, with a _____ _____ his deep voice _____ _____ _____. But today there was a difference.

Today, there was a bond between them, invisible and undefined but as real as the crazy lurch of her pulse when she saw him walk toward her across the barnyard. Suddenly there was more meaning to the looks they exchanged, greater depth to the feelings that flowed between them, more awareness of each other.

Merrie leaned back in the rocker and closed her eyes. She thought of him so often. What did he mean to her? What was the feeling that shot through her like an electric current when he was near? Why was she feeling so lonely, so sad because his being with her would not last, because inevitably her husband would return?

WILD VALLEY—

a strong, proud, savage place where men and women lived and loved with a passion as hard and as driving as the raw forces of nature around them. . . .

Wild Valley

(Orig. Title: The Cup of Strength)

by
Charlotte Paul

ace books
A Division of Charter Communications Inc.
A GROSSET & DUNLAP COMPANY
360 Park Avenue South
New York, New York 10010

WILD VALLEY

An ACE Book,
by arrangement with Random House, Inc.

First Ace Printing: July 1978

Published simultaneously in Canada

Printed in U.S.A.

To Smoky

Author's Note

When my novel, *Gold Mountain,* was published, I explained in a forward that, although it was fiction, incidents and characters were drawn from events which actually took place in the Snoqualmie Valley of Washington State many years ago, and from people who really lived here. In re-creating as faithfully as I knew how the true setting and spirit of the period, I tried to write a book that was far more "real" than any history would have been.

The same may be said of this book. It is in no sense a sequel to *Gold Mountain,* but those who remember it will be in familiar territory and may even recognize some old friends.

As before, I am indebted to many of the elder citizens of the Snoqualmie Valley, whose memories and observations have filled so many pages in my notebooks: To Brooke Carmichael, for his descriptions of logging with oxen sixty years ago; to Arthur Morgan, whose personal experiences in everything from farming in Dakota County, Minnesota, in the 1880's, to life as a buck private in the Army in Montana in the early 1890's, to homesteading and ox logging in the state of Washington from 1895 on, all of which are woven into the fabric of this book. I am also indebted to Otto Reinig, who has accepted patiently the role I assigned him years ago—that of the man I turn to when no one else knows the answer. Although he is not a Snoqualmie Valley pioneer, Jim Stevens is a veteran both of logging and of writing. I render him sincere thanks for his unselfish help with many technical details.

And finally, I am indebted to the late Alex Gardiner, to whom I gave the title of "technical adviser." The title was a joke, but the job wasn't. To him, every detail *did* make a difference. He was born in England in 1882, was brought to the Snoqualmie Valley when he wasn't yet two years old and lived here continuously for the rest of his life. He knew the Valley when riverboats were the only means of public transportation; he was a boy when the first wagon road was cut through the Snoqualmie Pass of the Cascades, and a railroad was built from Seattle to the towns at the foot of this pass. He saw homesteaders turn to logging, and logging methods advance from oxen to horses to donkey engines. His mind was keen and so was his sense of humor; his recollections of the events of sixty to seventy years ago had depth as well as color. Though he was a bear for facts, he was sensitive to, and tolerant of, human weakness, and abidingly confident of human strength.

Of the thirteen men and women whose help I acknowledged in the foreword to *Gold Mountain*, only five are alive today. Alex Gardiner died the week after he had finished his job as my "technical adviser." No reference had been too small to be scrutinized, and yet, in his final appraisal, he didn't judge WILD VALLEY by its factual accuracy at all. He said simply, "It's a fine story. It's a good book." I couldn't have asked for more.

Charlotte Paul
Snoqualmie, Washington

Wild Valley

1

TWO MEN SAW the strange girl riding into the country alongside of Martin Kittinger. It was almost as if their words had conjured her up, for they had been arguing ever since supper about which one of them most needed a wife, or rather, if either of them needed a wife at all.

One was Brother Bill, the itinerant Methodist minister who had been comforting the faithful and harassing the wicked of the Snoqualmie Valley for some eleven or twelve years. "I've made up my mind to leave the circuit and take the church in Gold Mountain," he was saying, "but that doesn't mean I'm looking for a wife."

The second man was Jeff Smith. Jeff was only twenty-seven years old, but he owned most of the timber as far as he and Brother Bill could see in any direction, as well as the logging camp hidden in the woods behind them. "Look, Bill, you're thirty-five, and people are beginning to believe you'll stay single the rest of your life. That's no good. A bachelor preacher was all right ten years ago, when there weren't ten families between Snoqualmie Falls and the Pass, and church services were held in the schoolhouse every other month. But this is 1893. We've gone beyond the homestead days, we've got towns now. When a congregation grows to the point that it can support a permanent minister, it wants a married man. You know that better than I do."

"The Gold Mountain congregation has grown to the point of needing a church building," Bill retorted. "As long as I'm a fair-to-middling carpenter, they won't complain because I haven't got a wife."

And at just that point Kittinger and the girl came into view.

Jeff and Bill, sitting side by side on the stoop of Jeff's cabin, fell into silence. Brother Bill's homely face was marked too deeply by weather and worry for a man of thirty-five. As he watched the slow approach of the rig, the lines around his mouth and eyes deepened and his dark eyes grew thoughtful, for the sudden appearance of the girl raised a question he yearned to ask but did not dare to answer.

Jeff was as curious about the strange girl as Bill was, but Jeff was a different sort of man. He was younger than the preacher, and taller. Twenty-four hours high and only thirty minutes wide, as the camp bull cook put it. Physically he was as weather-beaten as Bill, for he had lived outside under rain and sun since the day he was born. His hands were rough, his face brown except for the lines fanning out from his eyes, lines etched by squinting against the sun and by frequent laughter. His gray eyes were peaceful, full of humor. Bill's instinct was to question the unusual, Jeff's was to accept it. And unusual indeed was the sight of a strange girl riding a hired buggy along this lonely road at a time of day when the chickens on the farms were settling in the trees, and in the camps the stove loggers had swapped their last story and were heading for the bunks.

Jeff recognized Martin Kittinger easily; neither fading daylight nor a distance of fifty yards could blur the angular outline of the wiry little Englishman's figure. Besides, Jeff had been born here on the homestead, in the very cabin where he and Brother Bill had just consumed a fine bachelors' supper of fried venison, fried potatoes and baked beans. He knew everyone: the old-timers, who had settled when his father did, but outlasted him; the prospectors, who had only recently heard that the hills above the Snoqualmie Valley were full of gold, copper, silver, and if some big men in Seattle were staking claims and forming companies, why shouldn't they get rich, too? The loggers, drawn to the new operations near Gold Mountain and Three Forks by rumors that in Snoqualmie Valley camps the food was good and plenty of it. Jeff knew most of the drummers, too, and the city-bred fishermen and hunters who had waited for a railroad to be built before they ventured so far from Seattle. Kittinger was neither pioneer nor tenderfoot, but he had been repairing saddles in Gold Mountain when Jeff first went to school. Whether haggling over a price or issuing advice in his clipped and reedy voice, he had been a functional part of Jeff's world for so long that Jeff would have known him any place.

But the girl—Jeff could make out very little about the girl. Only that she was young, for she wore neither shawl nor hat, as an older woman would have done. Something else gave her youth away, even at a distance. He puzzled over it for a second, letting his instinct lead his reason to the answer.

It was the way she moved. Instead of sitting still and looking straight ahead, mindful, as a grown woman would be, of her corsets and the bumpy road, she kept turning and looking. Like a child. First, to the right, at Mount Si, a great purple-black rock rising more than four thousand feet toward the sky. Next, to her left, at the swift, cold Snoqualmie River. Then, like an anxious deer, she would lift her head, peering across the river where the hop fields rolled off toward the horizon and the four cupolas of Bengstons' Inn could be seen dimly against the gathering dusk.

She was young, she was eager. But, Jeff thought, she must be cold-blooded. The evening was warm for November, yet she was covered by a lap robe all the way up to her chin.

The rig creaked toward them down the dirt road, and came up even with the cabin. Kittinger waved, but didn't rein in. The rig rolled past and into the timber which covered the mountain's slopes almost to the bank of the river.

Jeff leaned back against the doorjamb and crossed his arms. "Well, Brother Bill, that might be the solution to your problem."

Bill said flatly, "I never had any solution come right up to me unasked, even that close. My life has been full of questions, but the answers have always been hid and hid good."

"You wouldn't know an answer when you saw it. If it were to come easy, like a girl passing right by your doorstep, you'd distrust it."

"Jeff, I've been offered the appointment I wanted, I'm going to take it. Even the presiding elder seems to be pleased with me." Bill's plain face was puzzled. "For once in my life I don't have a problem. Why are you trying to give me one?"

Jeff grinned. "I'm not. I'm just looking into the future. Ten years ago you swore you'd rather give up the ministry than quit traveling the circuit. You said that when the fight was over, and the church built, and the congregation began paying the preacher in cash instead of old clothes and cold meals, it was time you moved on and left the job to a settled man. Bill, you're about to become a settled man. You know what the next step is bound to be. The minute you've built that church, the good people of Gold Mountain are going to turn on you and say, 'We want a preacher who's a married man. We want a preacher's wife to play the organ, and teach Sunday School, and keep the parsonage up for missionary meetings.' "

"Maybe it won't come to that," Bill mused, looking down at his hands. "In the past I've never received more than three hundred seventy-five dollars for a year's work. I've had to sleep in whatever shelter I could find, all but beg for food, and the one new suit of clothes I've had in ten years was a present from my brother in Portland. I stayed single for one good reason—I couldn't ask a woman to live like a beggar. But in Gold Mountain I'm to have a steady salary and a church of my own. I might be thinking about marrying long before the congregation gets around to saying I have to."

Jeff grinned. "That's what I suspected. Forgive me for suggesting that, therefore, you have a problem." He nodded toward the dust which Kittinger's rig had stirred up. "No disrespect to the lady," he continued in a philosophical tone, "for I don't know her and neither do you. But here now, let's pretend. We don't know who the girl is. She might be cross-eyed and haggle-toothed, and the way she was all wrapped up in that blanket she could be concealing a sorry-looking parcel of skin and bones. We can't even tell why she's come to the Snoqualmie Valley, least of all why she and that hard-headed little Englishman are riding down this road when there's almost no place you can't get to on a better one."

Bill said gruffly, "If I could talk as fast as you, I'd give a better sermon than I have so far."

Jeff laughed. "There's a skid greaser in my camp can preach better than you. You think too much and worry the words to death. But don't try to change the subject. Like I said, let's pretend. Let's say the girl is young, pretty and single. She loves mountains, she can stand rain eight months out of the year, and she's here to stay."

Bill nodded grimly. "Let's quit pretending and

face the facts. Whoever that girl is who just rode by, cross-eyed, haggle-toothed, or whatever—if she's looking for a husband, she can still do a lot better than me."

"Seriously, Bill," said Jeff, and the jesting went out of his voice, "why don't you look for a wife?"

"And why beholdest thou the mote that is in thy brother's eye . . ."

". . . But considereth not the beam that is in thine own eye . . ."

Jeff saw he had startled Bill, who seldom found anyone even among the faithful who could finish a Biblical quotation for him. He smiled. "My sire was Harvey Barrington Smith of Kentucky," he said, with a ring of pride he could never quite keep out of his voice when he spoke of his father. "He taught me a good many things you could approve of."

"I remember your father," Bill said stiffly, "but let's get back to the beam in thine own eye. You're getting toward thirty years old. You've got too much money and too much good looks for a single man. Why don't *you* find a wife?"

Jeff hesitated for a moment, and then said slowly, "I've known many women. Some physically beautiful, others beautiful in a different, deeper way. They all had qualities I could admire and they were all generous. I can truthfully say that every woman who has come to my bed did so willingly and every one of them is a friend of mine today. But a wife?" He looked down at his hands, studied the tip of the forefinger he had lost to a circular saw, turned the hands over, palms up.

Calluses, the marks of a man who swings a double-bitted ax for a living. Burns, the scars—in his case—of bachelorhood, for in all the years he'd cooked for himself he'd never quite outwitted a hot frying pan. Why hadn't he married? Because, though he worked from sunup to sunset, as wedded to logging as he ever could be to a woman, he felt free? Because, though he was often lonely, and alone at night sometimes felt it from the surface of his body right through to the marrow, he loved the empty cabin, the shelf of books, the stillness, and was afraid to give them up?

"Our situations are different," Jeff said slowly, "and our desires, our needs, are different. You've been wandering all your life, you're weary of it, you want to settle down. I think you should. One church, one town, one woman. But I don't want such ties."

"You have strong ties, you've had them for years. The timber you own, the logging camp you built, the crews you've got working. Jeff, you're more tied down than you would be by a wife and six children."

Jeff shook his head. "I can sell the timber, abandon the camp, dismiss the logging crews. It's true—I haven't. But I've always known I could."

"You could have built a fine home. . . ."

"That would be a commitment, a promise to myself that I am going to stay in one place. I like to be free."

"Why?" Bill asked simply.

Jeff thought, why, indeed. He'd talked of heading for British Columbia with the prospector whose cabin was just to the north, but he hadn't done it. He hadn't returned to his father's home in Kentucky nor shipped out of Seattle on a frigate, nor even left the Snoqualmie Valley for any length of time. Being unshackled, free to go, he had stayed. Year after year, he had continued logging as he had when his father was alive, though he had refused to expand or modernize the operation— for this, like building a fine house, would be a binding tie. Strange, Jeff mused, that Bill thinks permanence will bring him peace, when I've found peace in being forever temporary. . . .

"I'm not married because I'm lazy," Jeff said aloud, avoiding Brother Bill's probing glance. "Nothing to choose from in Gold Mountain, and I can't be bothered to go all the way to Seattle."

"You're afraid of women, same as I am."

Jeff felt himself recoil, and then the earnestness on Bill's plain face struck him funny and he began to laugh. "You're probably right," he said, "but being a bachelor is no problem to me, and it is to you, or will be, even if you won't admit it."

Jeff stood up suddenly. "Looks like Kittinger and his passenger are coming back this way. They couldn't have got much farther than the next cabin, Lord Henry's place."

"Lord Henry?"

Jeff said dryly, "You wouldn't know him. He's not a godly man." Jeff narrowed his eyes. "It's Kitt, all right, and the girl still with him. I could have told them old Henry wasn't at home."

Bill drew his feet together, braced his hands on his knees, pushed, and slowly rose. "You've seen

Martin Kittinger before. What's there about him tonight that makes you jump to your feet?"

"Curiosity."

Bill snorted. "A man of twenty-seven who's too lazy to get married doesn't need that much curiosity."

"Kitt is reining in . . ."

"Halloo!" Kittinger was on his feet and waving both arms. The horse started forward, Kitt dropped to the seat, pulled in hard on the reins. "Halloo!" he called again. "Say there, Jeff!"

Jeff turned to Brother Bill. "See, Bill, she must have caught a glimpse of you when they first went past."

Bill scowled. "Don't make light . . ."

Jeff was already walking down the path toward the road. Still frowning, Bill followed.

Jeff got to the buckboard first. He had admitted to curiosity, but courtesy ran even deeper and he hadn't let himself look at the girl until he reached the rig and was standing right at her feet. Even then he tried to look past her, at Kittinger.

Kittinger's sharp features ordinarily gave the impression of being firmly united in disdain or craftiness or both; now they looked thoroughly disorganized. Flushed from the tip of his thin nose to the large ears which supported his cap, Kitt said, "Glad you were home, Jeff." Invisible hands might have been strangling him as he added, "Because this little lady—this little lady is in trouble." Then, for the first time, Jeff let himself look at the girl.

Yes, she was young, very young indeed. Her

coppery dark hair fell to her shoulders and was held back from her face by a wide blue ribbon. Her skin looked soft as a child's; her mouth, which was a little too wide to be pretty, was curled into a trusting smile. But it was her eyes which made Jeff forget his manners so completely that he said nothing, either to Kittinger or to the girl, but just kept on looking. They were curious, wide, smiling, beautiful eyes, not the kind Jeff had ever seen before. They were blue-green as sea water. And they shone like sunlight.

Brother Bill came up behind him. "Good evening, Mr. Kittinger," he said formally. Jeff echoed hurriedly, "Yes, good evening, Kitt." The girl was looking at him so confidently that he could not help but smile. "In trouble?" he asked gently. "You don't look like—what kind of trouble?"

Kittinger rushed in. "Jeff, Brother Bill, I'd like you to meet Merrie Dooley. That is, Mrs. Jim Cowen."

A married woman—Jeff said, "My pleasure, Mrs. Cowen . . ." but he dared not glance at Brother Bill and he was just as much afraid to face the girl. Married—but she couldn't be more than sixteen or seventeen. And she looked so—Jeff's mind struggled to define the impression she made. There was a glow to her, as intangible, but as real, as the scent of dry pine needles when the sun is on them. She looked as if she did not know what it was to be lonely, and for just an instant the loneliness Jeff had learned to cherish seemed to him unbearable.

Kittinger was saying, "Mrs. Cowen come in on

the evening train. I was driving her to Lord Henry's place. He's her uncle. That is, her husband's uncle . . ."

Jeff nodded. It was curious—poor Kitt's face was more fiery with every word he said. Yet the girl, wrapped to the chin, was neither red-faced nor fidgety. "So you are Lord Henry's niece by marriage," Jeff said politely, though the fact that the eccentric old Englishman had any kinfolk at all was a complete surprise. He'd almost forgotten that his neighbor's name was Cowen. But it was, of course. George Edward Henry Cowen. "Mr. Cowen went off prospecting. I saw him this morning when I was heading out for camp."

Kittinger's voice was beseeching. "You figure he'll be back tonight?"

Jeff shook his head. "The way his pack mule was loaded down, I wouldn't look for him for a good long time. There's been a lot of talk about gold along the North Fork, you know that, Kitt. And you know how Henry . . ." He stopped abruptly. He had a fanatical belief in family pride; any truthful description of Henry would rightly be offensive to his niece. Jeff put his hand on Brother Bill's shoulder. "Bill and I will be glad to help out, if you'll just tell us what the trouble is."

Now Kittinger was truly in agony. "Well, Mrs. Cowen had thought of staying for a while in her uncle's home, but her calculations—that is, maybe it was the long ride . . ."

The girl spoke up at last. "I'm going to have a baby," she said simply. "It was supposed to arrive next month, but the way I feel, I'm afraid it's going to come—quite a bit sooner."

There was no embarrassment to it. Just a statement of fact, given in a clear, friendly voice. Kittinger was well past speech, but he made up for it by nodding vigorously. Brother Bill sucked in his breath so sharply it sounded as if he were choking. As for myself, Jeff thought, I wish I'd gone along with Lord Henry. . . . All three of us scared to death, but look at her. She's smiling. Three strange men, a clearing in the wilderness miles from town, she's about to give birth to a child, and she isn't scared at all. If anything, Jeff realized suddenly, she looks terribly pleased with herself. . . . All at once the situation lost its strangeness. "Sooner?" Jeff asked gently. "How soon?"

The girl said apologetically, "I'd better not try to ride back to Gold Mountain with Mr. Kittinger. The road is awfully bumpy."

"You mean . . ."

She glanced past him, toward his cabin, and nodded. My bachelor quarters, Jeff thought, the stronghold of my loneliness. For an instant of bottomless silence he looked at the girl, and she looked back at him. Then he grinned. "*I* was born here," he said. "Here, Mrs. Cowen, I'll help you down, and into the house, and then I'll ride for the doctor."

"I'd send Doc Adams when I get back to Gold Mountain," Kittinger offered, "but I happen to know he drove a logger to the hospital at Gilman."

The girl said quickly, "I'm awfully sorry, putting you to so much trouble. I helped my aunt once. Maybe I could . . ."

Despite his efforts to be a gentleman, Jeff stared. "You mean you would try to—to be unattended?"

"There's lots of things you can do, if you really have to."

It wasn't bravado, it wasn't bragging. . . . She means it, Jeff thought wonderingly. What are the things she's had to do that have stripped her of fear and yet left her soft and childlike? Brother Bill and Kittinger were staring at her, too. "What are we standing around for?" Jeff said abruptly. "Kitt, you drive on to Bengstons' Inn. Nils and Katherine may have their hands full, but they might be able to send Julie over to help out. As for a doctor, Mark Smith's wife has brought a hundred babies into the world. I'll ride over and get her. Brother Bill, you stay right here." Jeff stepped closer to the rig, and held up both arms. "Mrs. Cowen," he said politely, "let me assist you into the house."

The instant she moved to uncover herself, Jeff realized he had been dreading the moment she would throw off the lap robe. Offering to lift her down from the buggy had been an exercise of courtesy, which he had tensed himself to perform. But she dropped the robe as simply as she had said, "I'm going to have a baby." Without the least self-consciousness she leaned forward and put her hands on his shoulders. With a shock Jeff noted that she was not grotesque. Even when he touched her, carried her in his arms, held her until she had found her balance and could stand on her own feet, he had no feeling that he was doing something strange or unseemly. "Walk carefully," he said. "Don't trip over the roots."

She nodded. Her face went pale and her hand tightened convulsively on his arm.

"You're in pain . . ."

She nodded again, but almost immediately she smiled, the color was back in her face, and he could feel her fingers relax their hold on his arm. "They just started before we got here," she said matter-of-factly. "But this is my first baby. It will be a long time yet." As if to prove it, she withdrew her hand from his arm and began walking alone up the path toward the cabin.

"What am I doing, sitting here," Kittinger exclaimed, "with a good two miles between me and where I want to go?"

He lifted the reins, slapped them lightly along the horse's back, and the rig jerked forward.

Jeff turned to follow the girl, but Brother Bill reached out quickly and held him. "I'll go fetch Mark Smith's wife," he said urgently. "You stay here with—Mrs. Cowen."

"She's told us it will be a long time. I'll be back with Mrs. Smith before anything happens."

"But if you're not . . ." Bill's voice shook. "Look, Jeff, I'd be no help to her, if she needed me."

Jeff hesitated. "It was the seemliness of it. A lady, being left alone with one of us bachelors. I thought, you being a preacher . . ."

Bill said gruffly, "I don't know much about seemliness, and care less about what people say, if I can answer to my own conscience. But I'm awkward, Jeff, especially with women.''

Jeff grinned wryly. ''I always thought I was handy, until right now. All right, Bill, go ahead. Take my horse.''

Bill nodded. Relief brought color back to his face. This, too, had been a battle, Jeff realized with a stab of fellow feeling. I am afraid—is it my duty to do that which I am afraid of? Is being afraid a sin in itself? Brother Bill was almost ten years older than he and a man of the cloth to boot, but Jeff reached out impulsively and thumped his bony shoulder in a fatherly way. ''You might say a couple of prayers,'' he said softly, ''if you can do it with a horse at full gallop.''

Bill gave him an answering smile that seemed, to Jeff, to be equally compounded of relief and gratitude. And then the preacher loped across the field toward the horse barn, and Jeff turned toward the cabin.

Kittinger was on his way to Bengstons', the nearest neighbors. Julie Bengston was only fifteen but she was uncommonly wise, and better yet, Jeff reflected, being half-Indian she never talks unless she has something to say. Bill would soon be headed for Smiths', so if all went well both midwife and helper should be back here at the cabin in an hour's time. Meanwhile, there was the girl to take care of, the girl with the blue-green eyes and an air of being a little old lady and a child all at once. She needed him—that was the feeling that grew on him as he followed her up the path to the cabin.

She stopped in the doorway, catching her

breath. Leaning heavily against the doorjamb, she surveyed the room that was Jeff's parlor, kitchen and study.

"There's a bedroom," he said hurriedly. "Sit down, while I make the bed up fresh."

She obeyed, selecting the bench in front of the fireplace, though there had been no fire in it all day. For the first time Jeff allowed himself to look squarely at her figure. She was wearing a coat, a neat dark blue serge with buttons down the front, and below it, a dark blue skirt. Except for the baby's bulk, which she was clasping now as if she were holding a bundle in her lap, she was thin. Her bare hands, stretched protectively across the unborn child, were slender, with long fingers. She was shivering. The coat wasn't keeping her warm, Jeff realized with new wisdom, because she had undoubtedly bought it months or years before and now she couldn't button it. She must have warmer clothing. . . . Jeff exclaimed, "Your grip! Did you have one?"

"It was in the back of the buggy." She looked up at him and smiled. "I was so excited about the baby, I forgot it."

Excited—Jeff thought, excited and *pleased*. He smiled back. "Never mind. I've got everything you and"—he started to say "midwife" and decided it sounded too personal—"everything you and Mrs. Smith will need. My mother's things. A little yellow by now . . ."

She seemed to wince. The brightness went out of her face for an instant and her lips were pressed together hard.

"More pain?"

She nodded, then took a deep breath and began to breathe rapidly, as if she had been under water and just come up for air. All the half-scientific, half-superstitious tales about childbirth that Jeff had ever heard whirled crazily through his mind. If the baby came quickly, what could he do? He looked at her pale, drawn face and felt sure his own was as white as hers. Then, all at once, her face brightened, her whole body relaxed, and she was smiling at him again, those wide, odd-colored eyes as gay as her mouth.

Jeff sighed tremendously. "Look here, Mrs. Cowen," he breathed, "you've got to get to bed."

"If you're so scared already," she asked, "how are you going to feel later on?"

"I'll find out when the time comes," Jeff said grimly, and hurried into the bedroom. He tore the bed apart, remade it with soft cotton flannel sheets dried in the sun, piled an extra comforter on it, and went back to the living room.

"I've been thinking," she said, frowning earnestly, "that it would be easy to fix this place up real nice. I'll do it, just as soon as I . . ." Suddenly she blushed. It was the first sign of self-consciousness he had seen in her. "I know," she said, "you're looking just like my Uncle Mike. I should do one thing at a time, I know."

Jeff offered her his arm, elbow politely crooked, eyes turned the other way so as to let her get off the bench as slowly and awkwardly as she need. She got up, took his arm, and he walked her across the room to the bedroom door.

"There are things . . ." Jeff tripped over the next word, cleared his throat, and went on purposefully, "ladies' things, in the cupboard by the bed."

She went in. Jeff closed the door firmly, so she would surely hear the latch click shut.

Instantly it opened. The girl looked up at him and whispered, "Are you going to stay here or are you going away?"

Jeff felt a sudden constriction in his throat. "I'll stay," he said solemnly, "just as long as you need me."

She smiled and closed the door.

Jeff stood for an instant, shaken by his own words. She does need help at a time like this. . . . And then, all at once, he thought, where is her husband? Where is Mr. Cowen, when his child is about to be born? She needs me—Jeff frowned at his own egotism. She needs the man she loves, why isn't he with her? The thought confused and troubled him. Trying to escape it, he went into action. First, the kerosene lamps, for the half-light was fading rapidly. Then he prodded the fire he had banked earlier in the big black cookstove, and filled the teakettle. He built another fire in the hearth, for warmth. Then he went to the bedroom door and knocked lightly.

"Would you like some tea?"

"Yes, very much . . ." Her voice was clear and cheerful.

Jeff measured tea into his mother's old china pot, took down cup, saucer and sugar bowl. Still the question harassed him. Perhaps the husband was dead. Perhaps, though she called herself Mrs.

Cowen . . . Jeff poured boiling water into the teapot, and set the teakettle back on the stove so hard the brass lid rattled. A grief-stricken widow? An immoral young woman about to have a child out of wedlock? Neither was possible. Jeff filled a teacup and carried it into the bedroom.

Only her head showed above the comforter. He balanced the cup of tea, dropped sugar into it, stirred it, held the cup to her mouth. Yet all the time, he wanted to ask her, "Where is your husband? Why isn't he with you?"

She finished her tea, and was smiling up at him, when the question finally fought its way to the tip of his tongue and was out. "Mrs. Cowen, where is your husband?"

Perhaps another pain hit her, this one sharper than the others. The merriness went out of her face, she looked weary to the point of faintness. "I couldn't find him," she said simply. Then she turned over, facing the wall.

Jeff went out of the bedroom, hating himself, and closed the door carefully, so she would surely hear it click.

II

Merrie lay very still, looking up at the ceiling. She was thinking—it's such an empty room. A bed, a chest of drawers, a cupboard, one chair, and nothing at all on the floor or walls. Not at all what any room of Merrie's had ever looked like, for she collected everything and never threw anything away. Not even a clock, Merrie noted, deciding impulsively that she loved clocks, especially those which ticked loudly. It would be like having someone in the room. Her watch—no, it was gone, the big silver watch that had once belonged to her father, but the events of the past were hopelessly jumbled with the pain and excitement of the present, and past and present whirled around in her mind so fast she couldn't remember just where, or when, she had lost it. Something to do with Jim . . . No matter, she told herself hurriedly, shrinking from the memory, no need to know what time it is. She had learned a good deal about childbirth after she went to live with Aunt Sal and Uncle Mike in Dakota and she knew instinctively that her pains were not as sharp as they would be and that there was considerable time between them. It might be hours. . . .

A deep sigh went through her, and she closed her eyes. In the next room the man they had called Jeff was moving about carefully. This was something she could safely put her mind to. A sudden crackling—he had laid dry wood on the fire. A hollow sucking sound, like someone breathing in hard, then the splash of water—he must be working the pump she had seen at the end of the sink. A soft click of heavy metal against metal—the stove lid, probably. He had lifted it off, dropped in a stick or two of wood, gently set it down again. Merrie had performed all these tasks so often that every muffled sound translated itself instantly into a mental picture of the task itself. Only in her mind's eye, it wasn't the man she saw at work; it was herself, Merrie Dooley.

"The little Dooley girl . . ." That's what everyone had called her. The people who came to tell her how her father had died. The people who said Mike and Sal Bruner had a fine helper in their orphaned niece. Jim's parents, and even, before they were married, Jim himself . . . But here she was, back again, to the things she didn't want to think about. If she let them loose they would crowd out of her mind the one reason she had for being happy. She was going to have a baby. Even the pain didn't matter, it was something she knew about and expected. She, the little Dooley girl, was going to have a baby of her own. That was the real, solid truth she must cling to now.

A baby . . . The memory of her first meeting with her aunt and uncle freed itself suddenly from the turmoil of past events. Years before, when she was only six years old . . .

The place was her mother's sitting room in the house she could scarcely remember now, the red brick house on a narrow street in Chicago. Her mother was dead. The neighbors had been dressing and feeding Merrie as if she had never done these things for herself. Merrie resented it, and resented the way they kept saying her mother had gone to sleep. Her mother had been ailing for many years, almost as long as Merrie could remember. Merrie had nursed her, she had helped dress her for the casket, she had seen the box lowered into the ground. How silly the grownups were, saying again and again in bright voices, "Your mother has gone to sleep. . . ." Her mother was *dead*. She told them so, and they looked sorry for her, so she didn't say it loud again, only silently, to herself.

But her father's death six months before—that was different, that she couldn't believe in though she had all but seen it happen. She had been playing in the street when the team he was driving shied and bolted. She had heard the men cry "Runaway!" and had seen the wagon overturn as the horses lunged crazily around the corner.

Someone had picked up the body of Joseph Dooley, carried it down the street and up the narrow wooden staircase to the flat where the Dooleys lived. Merrie had been in the silent crowd that followed him, and Merrie had been in the sitting room when someone, another teamster perhaps, another big Irishman like Joseph Dooley, had talked with her mother. Even after the funeral, Merrie had spoken as if her father were still alive. Even when Uncle Mike and Aunt Sal came down some time later from Dakota to get her.

Merrie's first impression as a little girl was that her uncle was very big and her aunt was very round. "So you're Merrie Dooley," the big man called Uncle Mike had said solemnly. "A little bit of Irish there someplace, isn't there?"

Merrie nodded slowly. "Papa is Irish as a boiled potato." Papa had been dead for almost a year— she had known it, it was just that she had never stopped speaking about him as if he were in the next room.

Uncle Mike's face had a funny look to it, but he nodded gravely. "I'm German, you know, but there must have been some Irish in my mother, because she named me Mike."

"Papa named me Merrie because I was born on Christmas Day."

"Merrie, pull that rocking chair over here for your Aunt Sal. You and I will sit down on the sofa here and we'll all three talk."

What a sober little group they had been. Aunt Sal sitting so straight in the rocker, her feet planted squarely as if it were important to keep the chair from creaking. Her Uncle Mike sitting up just as straight in a worn black suit, big, rough hands cupped over his knees. Merrie studied the pair. She knew from their faces that her aunt and uncle considered the moment terribly important. It was necessary to be solemn, that was part of the importance of it. So Merrie sat up stiff as a board, smoothed down her petticoats, and put her hands on her knees, as her uncle had done.

"Now, Merrie," her uncle had said, "You know that your Aunt Sal and I are going to take you to our farm in Dakota."

Merrie nodded. "I'm an orphan."

Aunt Sal's face had looked still funnier, but Uncle Mike agreed with a matter-of-fact nod. "Yes, you're an orphan. The hardest part of that is going to come right at first. Our farm will seem strange. Everything will be different from Chicago. And no matter how hard we try, your Aunt Sal and I won't be like your mother and father, not to you, anyway. Sometimes you'll have to be a lot braver than you've ever been before."

He stopped, looking intently into her face. Merrie returned his gaze just as steadily, because she was sure that was what was expected of her. For a moment neither of them moved. Aunt Sal, still as a statue, seemed to be holding her breath. The thought struck Merrie that her uncle didn't know what more to say to her. She should help him with the conversation. "Uncle Mike," she asked pleasantly, "does your wife have any babies?"

Aunt Sal gasped and began rocking briskly. Uncle Mike's solemn expression did not crack.

"Aunt Sal is my wife," he said gently, indicating the little round woman in the rocking chair, "and we have five children. All but one are too big to be called babies."

"My mother only had one, me," Merrie had offered. "Something happened to her inside machinery. I've decided to have twelve."

Her aunt murmured, "That's a good many. . . ."

Seeing that her aunt and uncle seemed interested in her remarks, Merrie continued more confidentially. "I haven't decided yet whether to get a father for them, though. I'd have to get someone who liked a lot of children."

Aunt Sal had stopped rocking, and Merrie saw her frown at Uncle Mike in a way he seemed to understand instantly. But Uncle Mike hadn't frowned. Instead he asked, "Weren't *you* glad to have a father?"

Merrie nodded.

Her uncle turned to her aunt. "How do *your* children feel about it?"

Aunt Sal's eyes seemed to be fastened on Uncle Mike's forehead. She took a deep breath and said, "They tell me they prefer having a father to—to not having one."

Merrie sighed happily. "I like children," she said, smiling, even if it did show the gap where the two teeth had been. "I'll be glad to take care of yours. Have you got one called Joseph?"

Her aunt shook her head. "Your father's name . . ."

"Never mind," Merrie had reassured her, "maybe you'll get some more. If one of them is a boy, we'll call him Joseph."

And as she had hoped, Aunt Sal had gotten some more. First, twin girls. Merrie had been seven when they arrived, and a scrawny seven at that, but she had had as much to do with the delivery as the doctor and her uncle's notions of propriety would allow. When the last hour approached and she was sent from the room, Merrie had attacked the farmhouse with broom and scrub pail. She swept furiously and at random, stirring up a storm of dust; then she mopped the kitchen floor, and when Uncle Mike came in she was filling up the wooden bathtub, and all five Bruner children, naked and docile, were lined up on the bench along the kitchen wall. "We've got to look nice," Merrie explained, selecting the smallest Bruner and immersing him energetically.

Uncle Mike had laughed and said something about "Merrie's children . . ." Merrie smiled at the memory. It was true, she had mothered them fiercely, including the two who were older and bigger than she was. They all came to her when they couldn't get a button through a buttonhole, and her word had been final as to when it was time to get out the long underwear. Aunt Sal had had to force her to go to school even for the six months a year the little one-room schoolhouse was open. The only part of school she liked were the stories, which she brought home and retold to the younger children, though her memory was so inaccurate and her imagination was so good that by the time she got through, the original tale was lost under the mountain of her own inventions.

Four years after the twins were born there had been another baby, and that had been Joseph. He would be six years old now. . . . Merrie opened her eyes, looked around this strange, bare bedroom and listened for the sound of the strange man as he moved around the next room. It would be Joseph's birthday next month, and here she was, two thousand miles away. She would name her baby Joseph—no, she couldn't. Jim had forbidden it. "My son will have some Irish blood," he had shouted at her, "but I can keep him from bearing a common Irish name."

It had been one of the worst fits of temper Merrie had ever seen and even now, when she was trying so hard not to think about it, she could see Jim's face contorted by the force of it. Such a handsome face. "Too beautiful," Uncle Mike had once said before he knew there was something between them. Large dark eyes, curly dark hair, a high narrow forehead and skin that kept its fine white look even when he worked out of doors. He would look at her so hard it frightened her, grope for her, whisper, "Merrie, I need you . . ." and her heart would turn over.

There had been violence in his lovemaking from the first, even on the hot summer night, weeks before their wedding, when she had submitted to an act she remembered afterwards mostly for the pain.

A brook cut across the back field of the Bruner farm in Dakota. Its green banks dipped below the surface of the meadow, invisible from the farmhouse, a damp sweet-smelling refuge when she wanted to get away from the energetic squabbles of her younger cousins. So one evening when she and Jim wanted to escape the heat and the children's noisy game of Run, Sheep, Run, Merrie whispered, "Come with me. I'll show you my secret hiding place."

She ran ahead of him, sure of her footing in spite of the opaque darkness, calling over her shoulder "Catch me if you can. . . ." When she reached the little stream, she descended its bank like a child on a schoolyard slide. Jim dropped beside her, panting, and they knelt by the brook, cupped the cool water with their hands and splashed their faces until their clothes were soaked and rivulets ran down their cheeks and dripped from their chins.

With a happy sigh, Merrie fell back on the grass and looked straight up at the blue-black sky. It was a moment of simple, childlike happiness. The indefinable uneasiness about her feelings for Jim and his feelings for her was left behind, back with the dusty heat and the shrill voices of the children.

The moment ended suddenly. Jim's body was on top of her, his legs locked against her sides, his hips pinning her to the ground. She gasped, "Jim! Please, Jim. . ." His response was to tighten his hold on her wrists and lower his head until his mouth found hers, and his lips and tongue became as demanding as the urgent pressure of his body.

They had kissed before, passionate but furtive embraces just out of sight of Uncle Mike Bruner's disapproving eyes. The kisses had never failed to excite her, so that when Jim broke away abruptly, as he always had, and strode off without the smallest show of affection or regret at leaving her, her body ached with unfulfilled needs. Tonight in the sheltering darkness, feeling the weight of a man's body for the first time in her life, Merrie was both excited and repelled.

Somewhere in the secret regions of her body desire was throbbing like a pulse beat. She sensed the inevitability of what was happening; she was at the top of a long, steep slide, going down, down, faster and faster, powerless to slow or stop the downward rush. Jim's hips were forcing her legs apart as his tongue moved hungrily inside her mouth. And she was responding, though she was frightened by his violent thrusts and outraged by the roughness of his hands.

She resisted, she cried out, but as if they were independent of her, her hands fastened on the firm flesh of his hips and her back arched as his tongue moved from her mouth down her neck to her breasts. There was pain, and they merged in a blinding moment with Jim's last brutal thrust and his hoarse, wordless cry. Then he was lying on the ground with his back turned, as distant as if they had never touched. He had awakened her. He had hurt her. To some extent he had filled her need in the act of fulfilling his own. But she knew then, with a flash of prophetic insight, that she had other needs he hadn't touched at all, and probably never would. He could arouse passion, but he could not truly share it. Giving herself to him was an act of debasement.

Merrie rose slowly, straightened her clothes and walked alone across the meadow toward the friendly lights of the Bruner's farm.

Merrie closed her eyes, as if to banish the unhappy memory. Bits of orange light, like stars falling apart, danced against her eyelids. Her hands were clenched into fists; she became aware of it and consciously relaxed them, spreading the fingers out wide, palms down flat against the comforter. There was no use trying to forget. Every happy memory she might set her mind to would trick her and lead her back to Jim. Jim was real, her husband, the baby's father, and she would some day have to face him again. She would not be here now, in a stranger's cabin, if she had not gone out looking for him. It had been natural for the man called Jeff to ask her about her husband. It was something he had a right to know, something she would have to learn to answer.

Impulsively Merrie called, "Mr.—Mr. Jeff?"

There were two quick steps, three, as if he had run across the room, the click as his hand hurriedly grasped the doorknob and turned it. Then, for all that speed, he opened the door cautiously and walked in so slowly Merrie felt the need to reassure him. "I'm awake," she said, "and don't look so worried. There's still quite a bit of time."

He stood between the bed and the window, with the light at his back; Merrie could see his face only dimly.

"Shall I light the lamp?"

He had the deepest voice she had ever heard. Merrie said quickly, "Not right away. The reason I called . . ." The impulse to make up for her rudeness was fast losing out against the wish not to talk about Jim, not even to think about him. The man wasn't pressing her. How to explain, where to begin . . . Merrie said suddenly, "I don't know what to call you."

The man said, "My full name is Jefferson Davis Smith. My father came from Kentucky."

It sounded like the beginning of a story. Merrie was distracted instantly from her pain, even from the original reason for calling him into the room. "It's a very dignified name. I like it a lot. I'll bet your father was an officer in the Civil War."

The man laughed softly. Merrie decided that his voice, laughing or speaking, was as gentle as it was deep. "My father *should* have been an officer in the Civil War. But he was right here on the homestead when war broke out, a man nearly sixty, and crippled on top of that."

"Crippled? Oh, I'm sorry . . ."

"Injured, I should have said. During the Indian Wars, the winter of 1855 and '56. He was a member of the WTV. Washington Territorial Volunteers."

"I wish you'd . . ." She broke off, gasping with the sharpest pain she'd experienced so far. It wasn't like the earlier pains, which seemed to collect slowly, giving her time to prepare. This one hit without warning.

"Mrs. Cowen . . ."

He was leaning over her. She couldn't see him

34

distinctly. He was a tall, faceless shadow, with a voice. "What can I do?"

Merrie shook her head speechlessly. This pain was lasting longer. From now on every one would be worse, there would be less time between them. . . . The worst passed. For a moment relief was almost as overwhelming as the pain had been.

"What can I do?" Jeff repeated anxiously.

"Would you stay," Merrie asked, "just stay and talk to me?"

"Of course . . ." With a series of quick, soundless movements, Jeff picked up the chair with one hand, placed it next to the bed, sat down. "The question," he said gallantly, "is whether an ignorant logger like myself can carry on a conversation interesting to a lady."

Merrie smiled weakly. "Not conversation. Could you tell me a story?"

"My imagination is a poor, puny little thing. What kind of a story?"

"A true story."

"A true story?" Jeff's deep voice echoed. "But they are always sad."

"Then a story that *sounds* true. Or, better still, tell me more about your family."

Jeff spread his hands on his knees and looked down at the floor. "I am my family," he said slowly, "for my father left Kentucky many years before I was born, and he never went back. I may have a hundred cousins, uncles and aunts, but I've never seen them.

"My father had an older brother, Abner, and he was the cause of my father's leaving Kentucky.

They didn't get along, but Abner, being older, always seemed to have the best of it. My father was a wanderer. In a fit of restlessness, made worse by a quarrel with his brother Abner, he joined a wagon train for the Oregon Territory. But the restlessness stayed with him. He wandered from Oregon City to California, then to Nevada, then north again to Seattle. He was well-read, he wasn't lazy, but he had no respect for the kind of work men did here forty years ago, so he never stayed at one job long. Hunting, shooting, riding horses, that's what he did best. He might have made a fine Army officer, but he couldn't find a war that suited him. He thought he had when the Indian Wars broke out in Washington in '55. That's what brought him to the Snoqualmie Valley.

"He was in a party of fifteen men, Washington Territorial Volunteers, who came to this valley in the winter of '56 to prepare for attack from the Yakima Indians, who were expected to come over the mountains and join forces with the Indians on the coast. They built five forts, crude cabins of peeled hemlock logs with neither floors nor windows, one or two with underground tunnels from the fort to the riverbank, which were to be used for escape. If there had been any action, if the Yakimas had crossed the mountains and invaded the valley, I think my father would have fought bravely and then, if he had lived, he would have returned happily to Kentucky. But there was never any fighting. My father was injured in a bad fall, not from a horse, but down a steep bank when he was on patrol at night. His broken hip was set improperly and healed crooked. When he walked, he seemed to drag half his body. He was too proud. He would not return to Kentucky, not even to Seattle, when the militia disbanded. He stayed right here in the Snoqualmie Valley, and took out a homestead claim only a few miles from the fort where he had been stationed.''

Jeff stopped. Merrie's eyes were closed. He leaned forward and asked softly, ''Are you asleep?''

Her eyes opened wide. ''Don't leave me,'' she whispered, and he realized that she hadn't been drowsing, but fighting pain. ''Tell me some more, please. . . .''

''Are you sure?''

''Oh, yes, please . . . Stay with me, and talk. . . .''

''As I said, my father was proud,'' Jeff continued quickly. ''He wrote home faithfully but every letter, though it was addressed to his parents, was really meant for his brother Abner, and he never let them know he had been crippled. In time, this brought an even bigger hurt to his pride. Abner married, and soon after wrote my father that his wife's sister was eager to move west and would make a fine wife and that my father should correspond with her. My father refused, but Abner was not accustomed to respecting his younger brother's wishes. Six months later he arrived, right here in Gold Mountain. He wasn't alone. He'd brought his own bride, and her sister Lucy, the girl who became my mother.

''It must have been a terrible moment for my

father when Abner and the two girls drove up in front of his cabin and he had to limp down the path to meet them. He must have hated his brother, hated the younger girl Lucy, as he dragged his twisted body toward the rig, trying hard to hold his shoulders straight and his head high.

"I know what changed his mind about the girl, because he told me years later. When he reached the buggy Abner was staring at him with a white face, Abner's bride was twittering, 'Oh, you poor man, whatever happened to your leg . . .' but my mother, who was neither very pretty nor very young, asked him politely to help her down from the seat and next thing was telling him which trunk was hers so he could carry it into the house.

"And he did. Somehow he lifted it down by himself, got it onto his back, carried it what must have seemed miles up the path to the cabin, with Abner standing by watching him do it. All my mother said was a real polite 'Thank you.' Two weeks later they were married, and my Uncle Abner and his wife returned to Kentucky."

Jeff's voice faded as he saw Merrie's hands tighten into fists. "Pain?" he asked, and she nodded. "Do you want me to leave?"

"No," she gasped, "no . . . Tell me some more. . . ."

"There is a little more," Jeff said, "very little. I was the only child born to them. When I was nineteen years old, my mother went back to Kentucky to visit her family. While she was there, my Uncle Abner died, and that seemed to remove the evil spell my father had been under. He listened to my mother's pleas, planned to sell his holdings here and return to Kentucky. He found a buyer, in fact he was on his way to town to sign the papers when he took another fall. If he had lived, he would have had to walk with crutches. I wrote my mother immediately, and she started out for Washington by train. She took some kind of fever on the train, and died some place in Kansas or Oklahoma. My father lived long enough to hear the news, and then he just turned over and closed his eyes, and gave up.

"The relatives in Kentucky wanted me to go ahead with the sale and go back to live with them. I didn't want to. I felt cold toward relatives I'd never seen, perhaps because my father had thought so little of them. I stayed right here, in this cabin, the cabin where I was born."

Merrie turned her head so as to look up into his face. "You've lived here, all alone, ever since?"

Jeff smiled. "For eight years. That's what I meant when I said, 'I am my family.' "

Questions came to Merrie's mind but were scattered by a sharp warning of a new wave of pain. "When I called to you, and asked you to come in, there was one thing I wanted to say." She spoke quickly, racing against the moment she knew was coming. "I wanted to answer your question about my husband, to explain. You wondered why he isn't with me."

Jeff said quietly, "Yes, I wondered. However, you aren't obliged to explain anything to me."

"But I want to!"

"Later, then," said the gentle voice. "Not now."

Merrie sighed. "All right, afterward."

Jeff straightened up. The dark, comforting shadow seemed to slide away from her, across the room, to the door.

"Don't go away!"

The dark figure stopped.

I must have shouted, Merrie thought. "Could you stay?" she asked in a small voice.

The man sat down on the chair near the window. "I'll be glad to."

Merrie thought of the women she had seen in labor. "I'll try not to—to make a fuss."

"Once I had to cut a man's leg off, to save his life. It was a logging camp, and there was nothing to ease his pain. You go ahead and yell and holler all you want to, Mrs. Cowen. It might help you and it won't do me one bit of harm."

"But you'll stay . . ."

"Mrs. Smith should be getting here soon. I won't leave the room until she does."

"That's good," Merrie whispered. "I'm not like you. I don't like to be alone."

III

As a boy of ten, Brother Bill had raced to warn
settlers of an Indian attack. It seemed to him that
since that time he had gone out on every conceiv-
able errand and faced every possible emergency.
Forest fires, christenings, marriages, Sunday services, help for the logger injured in the deep woods
or comfort for the old woman afraid to die without
the preacher at hand. But never, until tonight, had
he been forced to make a choice between staying
to deliver a baby or riding to fetch the midwife.

The road was only a narrow cut through virgin
timber. Cedars and firs crowded the ruts on each
side and seemed to overlap above his head, shut-
ting out the last light of day. When they got to a
clearing . . . The big bay horse threw his head up,
pulled on the reins, snorted anxiously. He's got
more patience than I have, Bill thought. Or is it a
cougar? There might easily be one nearby,
perched somewhere to the windward of a deer,
waiting. The horse would sense the cat's nearness
without seeing a movement or hearing more than

the distant snap of a twig. Not that the big cat would attack a man, regardless of the tales city people passed along in all seriousness. In the northwestern wilderness man's worst enemies were yellow jackets and skunks. Cougar, bear, bobcats . . . Brother Bill smiled ruefully and thought, they don't frighten me. It's people I need courage to face.

The big horse stumbled. Bill reined in quickly, the horse found his footing. It was dark and the Smith place was a good half-mile away. I should have brought a lantern, Bill thought, and a gun. But under the circumstances . . .

The good Lord had certainly handed out a fine set of circumstances to a couple of bachelors. Brother Bill could not think about the details, but he prayed silently that he would get back with Mark Smith's wife in time. If he didn't . . . It hardly seemed decent, and yet, he thought suddenly, she is so young. Not much older than my daughter would be, if I had married when the presiding elder first suggested it was the thing to do. Her very youthfulness made it seem permissible to think about her. Bill recalled her way of talking, in a clear, straight-out voice, looking right at you. He remembered her smile. . . . Whatever she's done, he thought, whatever has happened to her, she can't be bad.

The road left the woods. There was a meadow ahead of him, then the river, and directly across the river, the Smith homestead. Jeff kept a boat tied to this side of the river, for he often took this route to get to the town of Gold Mountain. Nearing

the riverbank, Brother Bill could discern the dark
shape of the farmhouse. Still nearer, he saw that
lamps were still lighted, probably in the kitchen.
Unless Min Smith was sick in bed or had gone
visiting . . .

With help so near, Bill's anxiety began to get the
better of him. He jumped to the ground and ran the
last few yards to the riverbank, reins in one shaking hand. The boat was gone. He narrowed his
eyes, wishing he could concentrate hard enough to
make the darkness split apart and show him if it
was on the other side. Yes, it was, moored to an
overhanging vine maple, the current pulling it out
from the bank and banging it gently against a derelict log. Someone had crossed over and hadn't
come back this way.

Bill's head cleared, as it always did when fast
action was called for and no battles of right versus
wrong or desire versus conscience were involved.
Jeff's horse could probably swim the river, though
this stretch of water was deep and doubly dangerous at night. But in that case he'd be wet through
and he didn't want to waste time while the friendly
Smiths tried to find clothing big enough for him.
He could swim the river himself—he'd done it
more times than he could count, but to keep his
clothes dry he'd have to leave them on this bank
and he'd be no sight for Mrs. Smith to see when he
got to the other side. . . .

I wonder what the presiding elder would do, Bill
thought, allowing himself an instant of malice, and
whether he would recommend that a minister of
the gospel arrive on the doorstep as naked as

Adam. . . . He made up his mind. He tied Jeff's horse to an alder. Then he undressed hurriedly, dived off the bank into the river, and swam across. He was chilled through and winded when he pulled himself out on the opposite side, but far more important than these discomforts was the comforting fact that it was good and dark.

He untied the boat, pushed off. Rowing as if the reward were to be nothing less than eternal salvation, he crossed the river again. He tied the boat, clawed his way up the mudbank to his clothes, dressed, and panting now, climbed down the bank, into the boat, and began rowing back.

No one need to know how many times I've crossed this water for the sake of propriety, he thought. I'll run to the farmhouse, get Mrs. Smith, row her back across the river, and (thank the good Lord she is a small woman) she can ride to Jeff's on the back of the big bay. . . .

The moment Brother Bill could see his job through to the end, he felt confident that he would bring the midwife to the girl in plenty of time. Jeff had said to pray, if he could do it with the horse at a full gallop. Well, he couldn't let the horse gallop, but he could pray. That's what he was doing when the boat hit the bank, when he leapt out, pulled it ashore, and with strength and wind he didn't know he had, ran across the field toward the house.

2

SOMETIMES SHE WAS asleep, sometimes awake, but awake she was suffused by such deep drowsiness, and asleep she sped through such lively dreams that Merrie could not distinguish the dreamlike people of reality from the vividly real people who weren't there at all. Neither time nor place could fetter her. She was in Jeff's cabin one moment, in her Aunt Sal's kitchen in Dakota the next, a child, a married woman, a child again.

Once she asked, "Is this a dream?" The man standing in the corner turned, and she saw it was Jim. "Yes, this is a dream," he said, and moved toward her. She screamed—surely it was a real scream, not the choking, muffled sound in a dream, for it wakened her. She opened her eyes and there was a man, as she had known there would be. But it wasn't Jim, it was Jeff.

"I'm right here," he was saying, "I haven't left, and I won't."

Relieved, she closed her eyes.

Only minutes later—or was it hours, or days?—she asked again. She was back in Jeff's cabin. Darkness filled the corners of the room, but the lamp on the chest of drawers cast a circle of warm yellow light. Right next to the bed stood a little woman with a wrinkled face and pointed nose and a white bundle in her arms. "This is no dream," the woman chirped, like a biddy rounding up chicks. "This is a boy, a fine healthy boy," and she leaned forward and settled the bundle into the crook of Merrie's arm.

Merrie turned her head slowly. Deep in the wrappings of soft, yellowed linen was a baby, red-faced, wrinkled, altogether real. Merrie touched him, and such a feeling of exultation went through her that she closed her eyes and pressed her lips together to keep from crying out. She pulled the bundle closer to her. Minutes later she opened her eyes. The little woman with the pointed nose hadn't moved, but her dried-apple face was still further puckered by a wide smile.

"Go back to sleep," she said. "I won't take him away."

The next time Merrie awoke the lamp was out. The pink-gold light of daybreak was coming through the window. Sitting on the floor near the window, her back braced against the wall, knees drawn up under her chin, was a young girl Merrie had never seen before.

A movement no greater than the turning of her head brought the girl to her feet. She moved across the room soundlessly. "I'm Julie."

She's as dark as an Indian, Merrie noted curiously; her hair is straight and black, but her eyes are blue. "Julie . . ."

"Julie Bengston," the girl said with a strangely contained quality to her voice. "Nils Bengston is my father."

Curiosity, as Merrie had heard her Uncle Mike remark, was one of her better faults, and for a second her normal instinct to ask people personal questions nearly took control. But the cocoon of her private happiness was too warm to break out of. Her curiosity about Julie lasted only until she glanced down at her baby, when it was drowned in the flood of a stronger, newer feeling.

"Are you going to go back to sleep?"

The question established, finally, the boundary between dream and reality. Merrie sighed with pleasure. "I feel awfully tired, but I'm going to try and stay awake."

"Then I'll tell them they can come in."

"Them?"

"My father, and the others." Julie went to the door and called to someone apparently waiting right outside. "Teacher? She's awake now."

"Good," a woman's voice replied. "I'll stir up Nils and Jeff."

"Stir up?" This was a man's voice, and a loud one. "I might of closed my eyes but I'm no more asleep than you are. Lead me in, Kate. I want to meet the baby's mama."

They entered the bedroom single file. First, a little woman with deep blue eyes and red hair braided into a crown on top of her head. She walked with a short, firm step and she was smiling the way Aunt Sal did when all six children were ready for Sunday School on time. Close behind her was a man so big Merrie had a childish impulse to hide under the covers. Actually he was no taller than Jeff, but he had such a mane of sun-streaked yellow hair, such a square jaw and strong neck and heavy shoulders, that he looked like a giant. After the first instant, he wasn't frightening at all. His grin was friendly; despite his size he was trying to walk on tiptoe, and was so awkward about it that Merrie forgot to be afraid of him.

Last in line was Jeff. Tall, thin, quiet Jeff Smith. Yesterday he had been the stranger. Today, in the midst of strangers, his dark eyes, his gentle voice, and the sense of great inner strength, were all that was familiar to her. Merrie looked up anxiously, turning to an old friend.

Her feeling reached him, for he nodded reassuringly. These people are all right, you can trust them. . . . Merrie got the message as surely as Jeff had caught hers. Then all at once he became quite formal. "Mrs. Cowen," he said, "may I present my good neighbors to the west, Mr. and Mrs. Nils Bengston."

The smile on the little woman's face widened. She's much younger that I thought at first, Merrie reflected; she even has freckles across her nose. The big man surged forward. Merrie thought, he'd just as soon throw me up in the air as shake my hand. . . .

His wife did not seem terrified by the mass of him. Placing one small hand against his chest she said crisply, "Don't press so, Nils. If you lean forward one bit more you'll fall flat on your face."

Still grinning, Nils Bengston backed up. But his bright blue eyes didn't waiver. "You look fine, Mrs. Cowen," he said in a voice too big for the room. "And with that baby in your arms you look proud as a peacock with two tails."

Mrs. Bengston was studying her, head tilted to one side. "Yes, you do, and no wonder. You've got a fine, healthy son. But you look tired, too, and we mustn't stay too long. Here, Julie . . ." She turned, drew the girl forward with one arm and hugged her affectionately. Julie is taller than she is, Merrie noted, and so dark, and so different. A banty hen with a full-size chick.

"This is Julie, our only daughter," the little woman was saying, "but you've already met . . ."

"You've heard of us," Nils Bengston broke in. "Bengstons' Inn. Bengstons' hop ranch?"

It sounded like a question, but Merrie guessed that this giant of a man wouldn't believe his ears if she gave him the wrong answer. She smiled apologetically. "I should have, I'm sorry . . ."

Incredulity made Nils Bengston's voice both louder and higher. "Bengstons' Inn on the bank of the Snoqualmie River? Bengstons' hop ranch, used to be the biggest hop ranch in the world?" He shook his head. "You don't come from Seattle," he said flatly. "In fact, I don't see how you can come from any place in Washington."

His wife said pleasantly, "There are forty-three other states, and a good many other inns, too." She turned to Merrie. "Wouldn't you like something to eat, dear? Aren't you hungry?"

After that, the little woman with the red hair was in command. Julie cooked breakfast, with Jeff fetching and carrying for her. Nils fed the stock and his wife took charge of Merrie and the baby.

"Now," said Mrs. Bengston, hands on her hips, "there's going to be a nice warm bath for you, a change for the baby, and though Jeff did a good job of making that bed, I'm going to do it over again, but don't tell him." She left the room, was back in seconds with a gray granite basin of warm water and a cake of yellow soap. "Jeff has lived alone too long," she said, looking critically at the rough-cut square in her hand. "His books are expensive and his soap is cheap."

Merrie laughed. It had been a long time since she'd really laughed, free as the wind. She laughed until there were tears in her eyes, partly because it was a relief to feel like it, partly because she was too weak to stop.

The little woman looked at her curiously.

"I'm sorry," Merrie gasped. "I was thinking of the soap I used to make. Lard, ashes, lye and rose water, but I never could remember to put in all four in the same batch. . . ." She gulped down a fresh burst of laughter. "It really isn't that funny."

The woman smiled. "You're lovely when you laugh. Why try to stop?"

Because Jim hates the sound of it . . . The sudden and unwanted thought of Jim caught her with laughter in her throat. It died there, hardened into a lump. She turned her head quickly to face the wall.

"Why, Mrs. Cowen . . ." the woman said softly.

I'm not turning away from *you*, Merrie thought, any more than yesterday I meant to turn away from the man called Jeff. It's just that all at once I'm thinking of Jim, and I don't want you to see my face. . . .

The woman sat down on the edge of the bed. "My name is Katherine."

Merrie realized with a sense of gratitude that she was going to pretend to have noticed nothing. "Before I married Nils four years ago, I was a schoolteacher."

Merrie swallowed hard, and turned back to face Katherine Bengston. "That's why Julie called you Teacher?"

The woman nodded. "I'm not Julie's mother. Her mother was an Indian, daughter of the chief of the Snoqualmies. But I was her teacher, and so that is her name for me. Nils and I have two children. Boys."

The bad moment was lost in the distance. Merrie smiled happily. "My Aunt Sal had six children, most of them boys. I took care of them."

Katherine Bengston smiled. There was a second's silence, then she leaned down impulsively and smoothed Merrie's hair back from her forehead. "Tell me, Mrs. Cowen," she asked gently, "how old are you?"

"Seventeen. I'll be eighteen on Christmas Day."

Now Mrs. Bengston's head was cocked to one side, in the same posture she had fallen into when she first came into the room with her husband Nils and Jeff. She's studying me again, Merrie thought.

"Really, I'm only seventeen," Merrie said hastily. "I suppose you think I'm older."

Katherine Bengston's smile deepened. "No, that wasn't what I was thinking."

"What *were* you thinking?"

"That you were telling the truth about your age, but that I didn't, when I was seventeen."

"Why not?"

"I wanted to be a schoolteacher. But no one wanted a schoolteacher who was seventeen years old." Now there was a funny little lift to her chin, like that of a defiant child. "So I—so I changed my age, you might say."

Again Merrie noted the freckles, scattered liberally across the tip-tilted nose, and the wide blue eyes, and all at once Katherine Bengston seemed no older than herself. "My name is Merrie Dooley. Please don't call me Mrs. Cowen."

She hadn't meant it to sound as if she were denying her married name. But that's the way it came out. She was trying to flee from Jim and the misery of her short married life to the days when she was the little Dooley girl who laughed a lot. She looked up at Katherine silently, begging her not to notice.

Katherine said matter-of-factly, "I was just going to ask if I could call you by your first name. I'm nine years older than you are, but please call me Katherine or you'll make me feel much older than that." She stood up. "Now, let's have that bath, before the water cools."

Daylight was warming the windowpanes. The smells of boiling coffee and frying ham blended into a single early-morning fragrance. Katherine worked quickly, talking little. Soon the crumpled sheets were drawn tight, the hot and lumpy pillow was fresh and smooth. Merrie closed her eyes and listened to the sounds from the next room. The voices of the men, the clatter of stove lids and frying pans and crockery, the explosive snap of the hearth fire eating into a cedar log. Katherine left her, and was soon back with a plate of food and a mug of coffee. Right behind her was Nils, with a cradle in his hands.

"You know what that fool Jeff was doing all night, instead of getting some sleep?" Nils said, balancing the cradle on one big palm. "He was out in the barn, colder than a lead ox heading into a blizzard, fashioning this baby bed out of some fine, clear-grain cedar." He grinned at Merrie. "And then he got too bashful to bring it in and give it to you."

The cradle's sides slanted at an angle like a tiny hayrick; it stood a half foot off the floor on wide half moons of cedar placed crossways at the head and foot. Every edge had been rounded, every board rubbed smooth.

"Julie made the mattress and bedding," Nils said proudly. "I hope Jeff don't look too hard for the stuff she used."

Merrie looked at him speechlessly. "I want to thank you," she said at last, "and I want to thank Jeff."

Nils snorted. "I guess he knew you would, that's why he took off for camp in such a hurry. You might as well know that about Jeff. He can handle the meanest loggers on the coast, and do it three at a time, but he can't find anything to say to a girl.''

Merrie exclaimed, ''Why he seemed . . .'' She stopped abruptly. What was the feeling Jeff had given her? At the wagon, when it was clear that she, a strange girl, was going to come right into his home to have a baby. ''*I* was born here,'' he had said, and held up his arms to help her down. When loneliness had suddenly caught up with her, and she had been afraid. ''I'll stay,'' he had promised, ''just as long as you need me. . . .''

''Nils, set that cradle down,'' Katherine was saying. ''I'd like to put the baby in it.''

An hour later, breakfast eaten and the cabin tidied, Katherine and Nils came into the bedroom to say good-bye. Julie would nurse her for a week, they said, and then they would move her and the baby to their hotel. A dozen objections rose in Merrie's mind. She was a stranger, no charge of theirs, and there was so much about her they didn't know. That she was literally penniless. That if her husband was not here in the Snoqualmie Valley, she had run out of places in which to look for him. That her husband's uncle had been her last hope—and what hope was that, if he was as poor as she, and a bit crazy as well? So much to tell them, so many problems to be solved. But she was spent. ''What will Jeff do?'' she asked weakly. ''This is his room, isn't it?''

Nils laughed robustly. ''Jeff? That one doesn't waste much time sleeping, anyway. He reads all night.''

''He'll be all right,'' Katherine said reassuringly. "And Julie will be in here with you. . . ."

Julie appeared with the sound of her name. She was carrying a rolled-up mat such as Merrie had never seen before. "Made of cattail reeds," the girl explained. "You pull the thread down the center, and split the reed, and then weave them. I made this myself." It was the most she had talked all morning, and the words were accompanied by a smile.

"You see," Katherine said, patting Merrie's shoulder, "Julie will be comfortable, too. There is nothing to worry about."

The Bengstons were almost out the door when Nils turned back. "Say," he exclaimed, "we're a fine pair, Kate. We didn't even ask the baby's name."

Merrie stammered, "I haven't—I mean, I know some names I like, but I don't know . . ."

Katherine took a firm grip on her husband's arm. "The baby came sooner than was expected, Nils. She needs time to make up her mind." Katherine waved to Merrie and pulled Nils forward.

Merrie was half asleep, but through the growing drowsiness she sensed that they stopped in the next room and whispered together. She couldn't be sure. Sleep was a warm tide flowing around and under her, and she sank into it gratefully. The sounds of reality, muted and blended, slid down the walls of the trough of sleep in which she lay. The crackling of the cattail mat as Julie spread it out in the corner. Footsteps on the bare wood floor, whispering voices, the click of the latch as the door was opened. The last Merrie heard was

Nils' voice, protesting hoarsely, "But how did she get here?"

I'll tell you, Merrie's mind cried out, I'll tell you everything, if you won't call me foolish or feel sorry for me. And then the wave of sleep closed over her.

II

It was July, 1892, and heat lay heavy on the Bruner homestead outside of Providence, North Dakota. At the long table in the summer kitchen the Bruner family lingered over the midday meal of cold beans, pickles, buttermilk, and the biscuits left over from first breakfast.

Even Merrie, whom Uncle Mike called "the git-git-goingest sixteen-year-old in Mansfield County," was lazily turning her empty glass between her palms, studying the patterns the tiny curds of butter had made as they slid through the film of buttermilk on the inside. Ordinarily she would have been marshaling the Bruner children past the washstand to make sure they wiped the dinner off their faces. But it was hot, and besides, Aunt Sal and Uncle Mike were having a discussion, or what Uncle Mike called a discussion, which meant a talk he initiated after he had come to an irrevocable decision as to how it was to end. Today, it had to do with her.

"You danced a little too much with that young Brusik scoundrel." Uncle Mike meant Merrie, and they all knew it, but as usual he addressed his criticism of Merrie to Aunt Sal, as if it were necessary for her to translate into some special sixteen-year-old language a man of forty-odd couldn't be expected to know. "John Anderson was there. He is a steady young man. Why didn't you dance with him?"

"I did. And with several others."

"Yes, she did," Aunt Sal concurred, nodding vigorously. "Merrie never lacks for beaux."

"That's just *it!*" Uncle Mike exploded, changing his course of argument. "There are too many!"

Aunt Sal pursed her lips. "Too many? A moment ago the trouble was too few."

"It's too few when it gets down to young Brusik," Uncle Mike said positively. "I don't trust him. Young Anderson, he is all right."

"Merrie is just having fun," Aunt Sal said. "She isn't serious about anyone, and everyone likes her."

"Didn't I say that?" Uncle Mike retorted. He turned to Merrie and shook a stubby finger at her. "You put too much heart into getting every Tom, Dick and Harry to like you. But the heart is also meant to tell you who is the right man for *you*. What happens, I wonder, when some young man asks you to marry him?"

Merrie smiled. "I have two offers already, Uncle Mike. Last night, at the barn dance. I was going to tell you."

"Two in one night!" Uncle Mike's ruddy, kindly German face showed that he did not know whether to be proud or suspicious. "Young Brusik was one of them?"

Merrie nodded, trying to keep the laughter out of her eyes. "John Anderson was the other."

"So!" Uncle Mike rubbed his chin hard. "What were your answers?"

"I said no."

"Why did you say no?"

"Because I don't love either one of them, Uncle Mike."

"So," Uncle Mike repeated, more softly this time. "It's a wonder you didn't say yes to both of them anyway, just to keep from hurting their feelings, and we'd have a bigamist in the family."

"Truly, Uncle Mike," Merrie said earnestly, "I don't hide anything from you."

"No, no, girl," Mike Bruner said, dropping his big work-worn hand over hers. The storm was past, the discussion over. "I know that, Merrie Dooley. You are a good girl." Now he was thinking out loud, and Merrie knew enough not to intrude. "It's just that the young men you favor all seem to look more like Brusiks than they do like Andersons. . . ."

Aunt Sal sighed. Bracing the palms of her hands on the table, she readied for the mighty effort of getting up. "It's hot," she said, blotting her upper lip with the corner of her apron, "and still we eat." All at once she squinted, focusing her gaze on something well beyond the fringe of the dusty barnyard. "Looks like someone's riding over from Cowens'," she said. "Oh, Mike, I know it's something bad."

The Bruner children jumped off the benches and

scattered into the barnyard. Merrie jumped even faster than they did, and ran to the kitchen door. Aunt Sal's guess was probably right. The Cowen homestead was at the end of the double rut they called a road, there was no other farm beyond them. Though they had been neighbors for many years, the Cowens were not sociable, nor crazy enough to go riding horseback at high noon of such a hot day, unless there was reason. Mr. Cowen? No, he would send one of his sons. The eldest, then, Jim—that was it, for the figure seemed to be too big for one of the younger boys.

Jim was four years older than she was, and handsome. There was such a flock of girls in and around Providence who turned pink when he smiled at them and pale when he frowned that Merrie had never expected to be noticed. Briefly she and Jim had been in the same classroom. At harvest time he was among the men who worked first one farm, then another, and Merrie was one of the cooks who moved from farm to farm in order to feed them. This was their closest contact. From it no friendship had grown, nor liking, nor dislike. Jim simply didn't see her. He came in with the rest, washed the dust from his face, pushed his dark hair back with wet palms, glanced noncommittally at the spread of food and sat down. He ate rapidly, in complete, unsmiling silence. When the others wiped their mouths with the backs of their hands, lit their pipes, and began exchanging opinions about the weather, the railroad and President Harrison, he went out into the barnyard, alone. Smoking, thinking, staring out over the endless plain?

Merrie had never known nor had time to ponder.

But her curiosity was aroused now. It was Jim, all right, keeping the horse at a gallop and riding at midday without a hat, which was the same as asking for sunstroke. Merrie ran out and joined the waiting circle of Bruners. Jim reined in hard. "My father is sick," he said. "He was pumping water for the horses. All at once he fell to the ground. Mother and I dragged him into the house. His eyes are open, but he can't speak. He can't move. I'm headed for Providence, to get the doctor."

Uncle Mike nodded curtly. "Don't keep that horse at a run, or you'll end up walking." He turned to the circle of his own children. "Joe, you and Will harness the mare to the light cart. Merrie, you help your aunt get some things together. Jennie, you take charge of the young ones while we're gone." He picked the wide-brimmed straw hat off his own head, handed it up to Jim. "And you, Jim Cowen, keep your head covered in this heat, if you want to be of any use to your father. Go ahead now. We'll be at your place before you've reached Providence."

Uncle Mike was talkative when there were reins in his hands and a pleasant ride ahead, but both he and Aunt Sal kept their thoughts to themselves now. All the way to Cowens' the only breaks in the silence were for their recollections of the past.

"I'll never forget the first time I saw the Cowens," Aunt Sal mused. "Mrs. Cowen reminded me of a little brown chipmunk. Darting around that squatter's cabin with such bright eyes and such a chirping voice. I just couldn't get used to the voices, always going up when you expected them to go down."

"He's done well," Uncle Mike put in soberly. "Starting out with an unproved claim, a two-room cabin, empty pockets and six people to feed and clothe. Today he's got as fine a farmhouse as any in Dakota, and a hundred and sixty acres of good wheat land."

Aunt Sal added, "And he never went back on his promise. . . ."

Merrie had often heard the story behind this promise. Charles Cowen had been born in the north of England. He began work in the mines when he was ten years old, and for twenty-five years went down into the earth before the sun had risen and came up again only after dusk. It was the posters in the railroad station that had opened his eyes, the story went, and Merrie knew it was true because she had seen the one the Cowens brought with them to the United States. During harvest time, some years before, when the dinner dishes were clean and the men had returned to the field, Merrie had gone into the Cowen parlor and had seen the big placard, nailed up like a tattered battle flag. The big print stood out, incongruous and meaningful, against the maroon and lavender pattern of the parlor wallpaper.

"Through tickets to the states of Kansas, Nebraska and Colorado. The population of the United States numbers at present about FIFTY MILLIONS, having increased about TEN MILLIONS since 1870. Cheap and fertile lands are open for settlement in sufficient quantities to furnish freehold farms for all applicants. Free schools and church privileges . . .''

In her reedy voice Mrs. Cowen had added more to the story. "One night Charles came out of the mine," she said, "and looked about him at the dark sooty world, which was as dark and sooty as when he had left it in the morning. 'I'll never go down in that damned hole again,' he told his friends, right there and then. 'I'm going home as fast as I can and tell my wife to make ready to go to America.' The next morning he began selling everything we had. The stone house where his father and grandfather had lived, all the clothes but what I could squeeze into three valises. Everything," Mrs. Cowen repeated, nodding for emphasis, "but his stubborn nature, and you couldn't get a price for that in the north of England."

The day the Cowens boarded the train for Liverpool, Charles Cowen had ripped the poster off the wall and stuffed it into the inside pocket of his greatcoat. "The portions of the States to which attention is particularly invited are the sections traversed by the Union Pacific and the Kansas Pacific Railways and their branches . . ." That was the call Jim's father had worn over his heart all the way across the Atlantic. But there were posters on the steamer, too. They had been printed and distributed by a different railroad company and they didn't mention Kansas and Nebraska and Colorado; they said the land of opportunity was Dakota. Charles Cowen had never ceased to treasure the poster that had brought him out of the mines forever, but by the time the Cowens disembarked in Canada, Dakota was their goal. They took another steamer up the St. Lawrence River to Quebec, a train to Sarnia on Lake Huron, a lake boat to Duluth, and another train to Dakota. They bought the claim that lay next to Bruners', paying the squatter who had failed to prove it up "ten pounds cash and a treasury of promises," as Mrs. Cowen had expressed it. He had kept those promises, and even through hard times he kept the first big promise to himself. He had been a kindly man, Merrie thought, and a handsome one, despite the grayness of his skin. And now we are all three thinking about him as if he were dead.

When they reached the Cowen farm, they found little to do. Charles Cowen lay on the parlor sofa, little Mrs. Cowen, crumpled and brown, sitting beside him and staring at him uncomprehendingly. Merrie busied herself finding something to eat for the Cowen boys, and soon the doctor arrived, riding at a hard clip with his medical bag hanging from the pommel. He did not explain why Jim had not returned with him, but with a friendly smile for Merrie went right into the parlor.

"I'm afraid," Aunt Sal whispered, "that there is nothing he can do, either."

And that was true. In less than an hour Charles Cowen was dead.

"A blessing," the doctor said when he came back to the kitchen, "but of course she can't understand that." Mrs. Cowen's sobs were high and uncontrolled. The doctor inclined his head toward the parlor. "She'll need someone, for a while."

The realization struck Merrie that Jim had still

not returned from Providence, though he could have been home for an hour.

"We'll stay until dark," Uncle Mike assured the doctor, "and we'll leave Merrie here until Mrs. Cowen gets back on her feet. Merrie has a knack with children, and she's a good nurse."

The doctor smiled. "I know that. Remember when I came to your house for the birth of Joseph, and I was suffering with a cold in my chest? Merrie was no more than eleven years old then, if that, but she made a mustard plaster and there was no stopping her, she slapped it onto me. Maybe you've forgotten."

Uncle Mike grinned. "I remember. Merrie takes care of everybody."

"She just about took care of me for good," the doctor grumbled. "May God protect me from another one of her mustard plasters."

The doctor promised to notify the undertaker in Providence, and then he mounted the big mare and turned her head toward town. Still Jim had not returned. Neither her aunt nor uncle noticed it. Merrie said nothing.

Later in the day the undertaker came, black coat buttoned tightly across his chest so as to cover as much as possible of his bib overalls. He and Uncle Mike lifted the body of Charles Cowen into the back of the wagon, while Merrie held Mrs. Cowen in her arms and hoped it would be done quickly. The undertaker, understanding, slapped the reins hard over the backs of his horses and the wagon was gone in an instant, down the dusty road and out of sight.

Suppertime came, the sun began to drop rapidly across the pale blue western sky. Now at last Uncle Mike noticed Jim's absence. "That young Cowen never came back, did he?"

"He must have known his father was dying," Aunt Sal said. "He's off by himself someplace, poor boy."

"Boy! Uncle Mike scoffed. "When I was twenty, I was a man, and I was expected to act like one."

"Some people are stronger than others," Aunt Sal said gently. "Jim was always moody."

Uncle Mike said stubbornly, "His place is with his mother at a time like this." Then he added irrelevantly, "I don't know what there is about him, reminds me of young Brusik." He turned to Merrie. "We'd best be going home now, girl. You want something, send one of the younger boys after me."

One of the younger boys . . . Merrie saw that her Uncle had made up his mind about Jim. "I'll get along fine."

"Mrs. Cowen is better now," Aunt Sal said, "but keep her company, Merrie darling. As for the children . . ." Her plump hand patted Merrie affectionately. "You'll know what to do."

Though some of the Cowen youngsters were almost as old as she was, they were easy to care for, and with the body of her husband gone from the house, Mrs. Cowen became as docile as a sick child. She didn't ask for Jim. Strange, Merrie thought. Neither have the younger boys. Her curiosity was aroused. Were they used to such disappearances? "Moody," her aunt had said. Then he must be unhappy—and Merrie, who had scarcely been aware of Jim Cowen up to that moment, began to be sorry for him. Once that feeling had stirred, she could not get him off her mind.

The children were asleep. Mrs. Cowen was lying in the big oak bed, still as a doll Merrie might have dressed and placed there, but her eyes were wide open. Merrie made up the sofa in the same room, and whispered, "I'll sleep in here with you. Call me if you want me. . . ." The little eyes blinked. Then she went into the kitchen to blow out the lamps. Jim was standing at the window, looking out.

He turned, and his face was so twisted by emotion that for an instant he looked almost ugly. Merrie was confused. He appeared angry, not unhappy, and instead of speaking he stared at her darkly, as if she should explain why she was there. "Your father . . ."

"I know all about that."

Merrie caught her breath. "Do you want—I mean, your mother is still awake, if you want to talk with her."

"Has she asked for me?"

Merrie's impulse was to lie. Jim's mother should have asked for him, what harm to tell him she had? Her glance wavered while she tried to make up her mind. Before she could choose between truth and kindness, Jim was answering his own question.

"No, she hasn't. I didn't think so." He turned abruptly toward the stair which led to the boys' sleeping rooms in the loft.

The words tapped Merrie's bottomless reservoir of sympathy for another person's troubles. If his face had revealed anger when it should have shown grief, there must be a reason; he looked so tormented, so utterly lonely. "Are you hungry?" she asked quickly. "I'll fix you something."

Jim shook his head. "There's nothing you can do for me," he said disdainfully. "Just leave me alone." And he disappeared up the stair.

Merrie felt her cheeks grow hot. He had no right to talk to her that way, and she would tell him so. She had put up with his rudeness long enough, and she was angry. . . . She cupped her hand around the top of the lamp's slender globe and blew out the flame. Then she crept into the bedroom and quietly closed the door.

For a long time she sat in the chair by the window, looking out across the dark fields as if she could force the beloved shape of the Bruner farmhouse to become visible in the distance. She was troubled without knowing why, except that more and more Jim's presence had the power to upset her. From now on, she was going to ignore him. If he stomped through the kitchen, she would pretend she didn't notice. He could stomp right out again, it wouldn't matter to her. . . .

It was a brave resolution, but it hadn't worked. She went on cooking his meals, washing his clothes, and worrying about his stormy moods. Turning her back to him didn't relieve her of the excitement she felt whenever he came into the room. Again and again she was sure he caught her watching him.

Then there was a change. Jim seldom spoke to her, but whenever he came into the room she could feel he was looking at her. The first time, it startled her. It was such an intense, secretive gaze. Her natural friendliness bubbled up and, resolutions to the contrary, she smiled.

There was no friendly grin in return, only a narrowing of the dark eyes.

Merrie thought impishly, "Well, aren't we the sober one!" and followed an impulse. Looking straight at him, she made a face.

He frowned, walked out of the room, and slammed the door behind him so hard that the tin dipper was jarred off its nail and clattered to the floor.

"Damn you! Damn you!" Merrie repeated the most shocking words she knew in a futile effort to drown her true feelings in a tide of righteous anger. "I hate you, Jim Cowen. I hate you, *hate you*. . ." But she was already crying, because she knew it wasn't true.

Mrs. Cowen grew stronger, and one afternoon announced that she had to go into Providence. "Jim will drive me," she said. "Would you find him, Merrie, and tell him to harness up?"

Merrie found Jim in a box stall in the barn, pitching straw down from the mow to make a bed for a new calf. Bits of straw were in his hair and the air was dusty and sweet.

Merrie came in. "Jim," she called, "your mother wants you to drive her to town."

Jim didn't seem to hear, so she went into the stall, closed the door behind her and repeated,

"Jim, your mother sent me to tell you . . ."

"That she wants me to drive her to Providence. I heard." He set the pitchfork against the wall, and began to brush the straw dust from his trousers and shirt sleeves. "And what does she intend to do in town?"

"She mentioned seeing the lawyer."

"Sure she did, sure she did!" Jim blurted out, his face distorted by anger. "To find out what's in the will. I'd say she got over Father's death pretty fast, wouldn't you? I'd say the widow did a good job, forgetting her grief so soon, wouldn't you?"

He was shouting at her. Merrie stared at him numbly. He was moving toward her. He was going to hit her, she was sure of it, but she couldn't move. And then suddenly, he collapsed and covered his face with his hands.

Merrie had never seen a man cry. Once or twice one of the Bruner boys had, just a little, but they did it as if the tears were wrung out of them; they fought crying, and hid themselves until they could show dry eyes and steady chins. But this was different, and terrible. Jim didn't fight the sobs, he rode them, letting them carry him up and down on one wave after another of sorrow and self-pity.

But she hadn't recognized the self-pity then. Instead she heard the sorrow, and stepped forward to put her arms around him. "Don't feel so bad," she murmured. "Jim, Jim . . ." He did not pull away. Minutes passed. Her hand went to his hair. The fingers smoothed it down, picked off bits of straw, smoothed it again. "It's all right," she said, "all right . . ." Gradually he quieted. She waited until he was still, until she heard him sigh and felt his body relax against her. "You'd better go up to the house now," she said gently. "Your mother is waiting." She released him and stepped back to let him pass.

She expected him to stride by without a word. Instead he threw both arms around her and pulled her forward so roughly she lost balance. He held her up, his arms tightened around her, and he kissed her.

He kissed her on the mouth, as she had never been kissed before. "I need you, Merrie," he whispered. "I don't have anyone else but you. . . ."

Merrie could not have pulled free without fighting him, and she was too surprised to try. He likes me after all, she thought foolishly. What would all those older girls think if they knew. . . .

As suddenly as he had reached for her, Jim let her go. The stall door slammed behind him, he was gone.

Merrie stared at the damp spots on the breast of her shirtwaist—Jim's tears. Her cheek was wet where his face had rested against hers; she dried it absent-mindedly, with the back of her hand. Jim had gone toward the horse barn. For an instant she thought of following him; why, she didn't know. But that was crazy. . . . In confusion, she turned the other way and walked slowly to the farmhouse.

When they left for town, Mrs. Cowen waved to her pleasantly, but Jim looked straight ahead and cut off his mother's parting words by whipping the horse into a trot. Back from town, he stayed in the barn, and even at the supper table he managed not to look at her. Merrie had never experienced the kind of nameless misery he was causing her. She slept poorly and awoke with an ache in her throat. To her surprise, Mrs. Cowen was already in the kitchen, busily mixing biscuits.

"Good morning, my dear," she said. "I just made up my mind that I'd been leaning on you long enough. I should have let you go home days ago."

"I'll gladly stay. . . ."

"That's just it, you'd gladly do everything for me I should force myself to do. You're bad for me." But her voice was kind, and she was smiling. She began beating the dough briskly.

Merrie heard someone come into the kitchen behind her. It was Jim—she sensed it, and with a painful effort kept herself from turning.

Mrs. Cowen's glance told her she was right. "This has been an unhappy place for a girl as full of life as you are," the little woman said cryptically.

Merrie drew a deep breath. "If you really don't need me, I will go home," she said. Why was the blood pounding so hard in her throat? What reason was there to raise her voice as if she were flinging it over her shoulder? "I'll give the house a good going over today, and I'll leave tomorrow."

Behind her, the door slammed.

Mrs. Cowen looked up quickly, turned her bright dark eyes on Merrie. Merrie felt her cheeks redden. "I've been deaf and blind the last two weeks," Jim's mother said. "Has he hurt you?"

Because she had come close, Merrie gasped, "No, not at all!"

"I'll speak to him."

"No!"

For a moment they looked at each other, and neither spoke nor moved. Merrie prayed her face was not as flushed as it felt, nor her voice nearly as desperate as it had sounded to her.

Mrs. Cowen sighed. "It will be better when Jim has a farm of his own," she said. "And now, my dear, wherever have you been hiding the sugar? I like my breakfast biscuits sweet."

It seemed that the whole day would go by without a word from Jim. He came into the kitchen only twice, only for breakfast, later to tell his mother he was riding into Providence and would not be back until late. Merrie thought, perhaps he will be the one to drive me home in the morning. But why did she want that? He *had* hurt her, just as his mother had guessed. He had stirred up emotions she couldn't understand, then left her confused and ashamed. "I need you, Merrie," he had whispered. "I don't have anyone else but you. . . ." It's true, she reasoned. His mother doesn't care for him. Naturally he is unhappy, and lonely, and bitter. If someone loved him . . .

For an instant Merrie wanted to go home. Not tomorrow morning, now. She longed to drop the broom in the middle of the kitchen floor, to run out the back door, and race, race like the wind, until she could see the gray square of the Bruner farmhouse growing big and solid against the horizon, and she would be safe. . . .

The impulse lasted only a second. Like an ocean breaker, crashing against the shore, receding suddenly, leaving as a backwash only a sense of shame. Merrie gripped the broom handle tightly. What was there to run away from?

It was dark when Jim returned. Merrie was alone in the kitchen, banking the fire for the night. She looked up, prepared for his scowl, or for the intent, inward look that meant he wasn't seeing her at all. But he was smiling. His dark eyes, so often cold, were resting on her hopefully. "Oh, Merrie, you're here," he said. "I was afraid you would have gone away."

Merrie stared at him foolishly. The barricades she had been building within herself all day crumbled before the feelings that smile of Jim's startled into life.

"I want to ask you something," he said eagerly. "Come outside."

"No." Merrie glanced toward the door of Mrs. Cowen's bedroom. "I was going in to bed."

Jim stepped forward and grasped her hands. *"Please,"* he whispered, the smile gone now, the dark eyes frankly pleading with her. "Only for a minute . . ."

She let him pull her through the door. It banged behind her and she stopped, her back to the wall of the house. Jim, still holding her hands, loomed over her in the dark. The night air was still and warm. Jim dropped her hands, grasped her elbows roughly. "Merrie," he said, low and quiet, "will you marry me?"

For an instant Merrie thought she would fall, and she had never fainted in her life. She felt weak, too weak to breathe.

Jim had let go of her elbows and put his arms around her. The feeling that had engulfed her that day in the barn came back in a rush. He was going to kiss her, she wanted him to kiss her. . . . She had the sensation of being outside herself, watching. She saw herself look up at Jim, she saw the kiss, even as she felt it. It was a strange feeling, splitting her in two. Jim kissed her again. Suddenly his arms tightened. He was so much stronger than he looked. "Merrie," he asked hoarsely, "you do love me, don't you?"

His embrace was rough and yet it was he who seemed to be clinging to her for support. Love him? He needed love. This new feeling going through her like a fever, surely it was love. If not, why had she been unhappy today? Do I love you, do I love you . . . Of course she did. "Yes, Jim," whispered the Merrie in his arms, while the other Merrie, looking on, hesitated and wondered.

"You'll marry me?"

Merrie protested, "Jim, I don't know." Instantly she was afraid she might have hurt him. "I love you, yes," she added quickly. "I'm sure I do." But did she, when there were times she saw an ugliness in him that frightened and repelled her? Loving and hating should be farther apart. With Jim, they often assailed her at the same time. *Love* him?

"Marry me," he whispered urgently. "You know I don't have anyone. . . ."

Marriage . . . Merrie's heart was beating so hard it wasn't letting her think. Of course she wanted to get married. Children, a home of her own, that's what she had wanted all her life. She was old enough and she loved Jim. . . .

"Merrie . . ."

"We haven't seen much of each other," she said, trying to pull away. "And you know so many other girls."

"No one! No one knows me as well as you do, not even my mother. I couldn't be happy with anyone else. You understand me, Merrie, listen to me. . . ." His hold tightened, his lips moved across her cheek, searching for her mouth. She turned her head. "No, no . . ." he said huskily. One hand pressed hard against the small of her back, the other grasped her chin and forced her to turn back. "Don't ever pull away from me," he said against her mouth. "Let me kiss you, let me love you. . . ."

She closed her eyes. . . . "Answer me," he begged her at last, his face against her cheek. She was trembling. Her body, shaking and weak, was frighteningly aware of his body—the sharp knee, the long hard thighs, the arms, the hands, the soft throat, the rough skin along the jaw line . . . He was trembling, too. "Answer me," he repeated. "You will marry me. . . ."

"I've got to think," Merrie whispered.

"Think now," he said. "This is when you know. When you feel, as you are feeling now . . . Merrie, I'll give you a home of your own. Do you hear that, a home of *your own*. Isn't that what you want, more than anything else?"

Merrie nodded. "All my life," she said. "Aunt Sal and Uncle Mike have been wonderful to me, but it's true, their home isn't mine, really. I've only borrowed it. Even in Chicago, with my own father and mother, we lived in a rented flat. I always knew that it wasn't really ours. It belonged to the little lame man that was the landlord, and if I made too much noise or we couldn't pay the rent every month, he could throw us out. That home was borrowed, too."

It was more than she had said to Jim at one time since she'd come to Cowens' to care for his mother, more than she'd ever revealed to anyone about the yearning she bore like a birthmark. But with the darkness pressing them together, with his arms around her . . . Invisible in the darkness was the climbing rosebush that covered the trellis by the back door. The sweet-spice odor of the flowers lay on the warm air, entering her nostrils with every breath she drew. Without thinking, only feeling, Merrie raised her arms, clasped her hands together at the back of Jim's neck, and drew his head down for another kiss.

His body shook with a sudden spasm. "Dear God," he whispered, dropping his arms to his sides, "I was afraid you'd turn me down."

The other Merrie, the invisible and voiceless, saw her arms tighten around him and her hands caress his dark hair. What to say? What to do? The emotions were too big and too new. Merrie clutched at a feeling that was old and tried. "Don't worry about anything," she said soothingly. "Everything's going to be all right. . . ."

It was a simple wedding. Partly because cash crops had been poor that year and Uncle Mike had little to spend. Partly because Jim's father had been so recently buried. But mostly because Uncle Mike and Aunt Sal had given their permission reluctantly.

There had been angry scenes, the worst when Merrie first broke the news. Her uncle stared unbelievingly, then banged the table with both fists and shouted, "And why isn't the young man here to tell me this himself?"

Jim was afraid they would disapprove, he had the idea they didn't like him, he thought it would be easier for Merrie to speak to them first. Then he would talk to them himself, he really meant to. . . . Uncle Mike stormed, Aunt Sal placated, in the end they agreed to the marriage.

"It's not that we're against Jim," her aunt told her. "It's just that it all came up so sudden. . . ."

But that was skirting the truth, Merrie knew. Jim was right, they didn't like him, for all Aunt Sal's loyal effort to hide it. The week before the wedding she devoted herself to making Merrie a new dress, though Merrie knew it was a pinch to find money for the material. Uncle Mike arranged to bring Preacher Albrecht out from town, which meant a few dollars more, and they did their best to prepare a good spread for the neighbors who would come to the ceremony. Through it all, Aunt Sal looked troubled, but unchanged toward Merrie. It was Uncle Mike who could not smile at her, though she saw him try. Some tie between herself and her uncle had been broken, and she did not know how to mend it.

After the ceremony, Uncle Mike kissed her

brusquely on the cheek, but he didn't say a word. Later, after the guests had left and the preacher had been paid, it was time for Merrie and Jim to ride toward Cowens'. Jim carried her valises out to the buggy. The children went through a last round of tearful and giggling good-byes. Merrie kissed her aunt and uncle, there were many last-minute words hastily said and scarcely heard by any of them, and finally Merrie turned to go out the door and join her husband.

At that very last minute, Merrie was overcome by the magnitude of the step she had taken. She stopped in the doorway, fear tightening in her stomach like a clenched fist. Her mind cried out silently, "What have I done?" She wheeled around. Uncle Mike and Aunt Sal were right behind her, they were alone together.

"Good luck," Uncle Mike said gruffly.

"Uncle Mike," Merrie breathed, "Aunt Sal, I want to thank you for everything you've done for me. I tried to do the right thing. . . ."

Uncle Mike's square face was set. He shook his head slowly. "There's nothing more we can do for you now."

Aunt Sal tried to speak and couldn't. Tears were pouring down her round cheeks and she was shaking with sobs. Uncle Mike put his arm around her. Merrie felt her own throat would burst. "Auntie . . ." she whispered. "Uncle . . ." And then she turned and ran out the door.

The next day Jim told her his plan. His father had willed him a homestead of one hundred and sixty acres. He was going to farm it, build a house on it, be the biggest homesteader in all Dakota. There were a great many laws and rules and regulations, Jim's explanations were wordy; Merrie's attention wavered and she found it hard to understand everything he was saying. But through the muddle of legal talk, one fact stood out as clear as blood on snow: The homestead his father had laid claim to in Jim's name had not yet been proved up. To inherit it, the law decreed, Jim had to be twenty-one years old or the head of a family. Jim was twenty years old.

Their marriage had been hasty, but it had secured for Jim Cowen one hundred and sixty acres of the best wheat land on the Dakota plain.

3

IT WAS JUNE, 1893. Driving home from Providence with supplies in the back of the wagon and three weeks' mail on the seat beside him, Jim Cowen let the mule set his own pace and picked up the St. Paul daily newspaper. "General" Coxey had been arrested for trespassing on the White House lawn. Mints in India had been closed to the coinage of silver. The newly installed Democratic president was already figuring on calling a special session of Congress in the hope that something could be done to pull the country out of panic. But the news which caught Jim Cowen's eye was something much closer to home. The first Great Northern passenger train to go all the way through to the Pacific Coast was to leave St. Paul in two weeks.

It would be no ordinary train, the papers said. Not only was it the very first to be launched on the westbound run, but it was expected to reach Seattle in seventy-two hours; there was talk that across the plains she might hit fifty miles an hour. It was no ordinary train on the inside, either. Day coaches were of standard pattern, to be sure, and so was the baggage car. But in the elegant sleeper "Seattle," the oak paneling was polished until it seemed threaded with gold, the seats were covered with velvet plush, and damask hung at every window.

But the Buffet Car! Nothing like it had ever sped across the Dakotas. It was sixty feet long, finished in old gold and polished oak. It contained a large sitting room, with a dozen easy chairs of willow upholstered with easy cushions. A refreshment stand had been placed beside each chair, whereon were to be deposited the dainty edibles which came from the buffet in the corner. There was a barber shop, offering shaves, shampoos and haircuts. At one end of the car stood a writing desk with the best of writing papers and pens, next to it a library table covered with the latest periodicals and newspapers. At the other end of the car was the library, where, one reporter insisted, there were French novels on the shelves as well as soberer works. And finally, there were the luxurious, private, tête-à-tête rooms, each cubicle separated from the next by delicate screens of scrollwork and velvet. Excellent retreats for important persons who want to carry on important conversations . . .

Merrie knew, the moment Jim came into the cabin, that he had gone off into a mood. He dropped newspapers and mail on the table, threw her a sightless glance and stomped out toward the woodshed. There was no need. She had chopped wood and filled the wood box herself, if he had only noticed.

She glanced at the untidy stack of newspapers, most of them folded crookedly and inside out. Something he had been reading, she guessed. If she was careful not to laugh at anything—laughing was a habit of hers which annoyed Jim more than any other—and didn't question him, it might pass quickly. She picked up the coffee mill, slid back the top and filled the wooden box with the beans she had roasted that morning in an iron skillet on top of the stove. Just a few beans at a time. It wouldn't take much more than the sound of coffee beans clattering to the floor to bring Jim storming in from the shed. "What are you doing now?" he'd demand. "Breaking something? Cutting yourself? Dropping things?" The beans were safely inside. Merrie gave the handle of the coffee mill a hard turn. What was the use of getting all quivery, she thought, when nothing had happened?

Jim came back into the cabin, arms loaded, and for the first time looked at the wood box. In a flash Merrie saw that this, a box already full, would be the needle that lanced the boil of his temper. Whatever was behind his mood, whether he felt he had failed or that someone had failed him, he would have no relief until he could find someone to blame. She tensed, hearing his outburst even before it came.

"Why did you let me get more wood? Or didn't you see me come in?"

It was childish, it was unjust. But if she let him know that she could see him as he really was, he would surely hate her. She set the coffee mill down carefully, and waited.

Without leaning down to shorten its fall, Jim dropped his load. Sticks banged against the side of the cookstove, thudded on the floor, sent flying much of the wood she had stacked neatly in the box. He turned to Merrie. "I hate this place," he said bitterly. "I'm going to get out."

Merrie drew in her breath hard. Jim had said "I . . ." He was staring at her, daring her to protest. She clenched her jaw and held her tongue.

With one long stride he moved from stove to table and sat down on the bench opposite her. "There's no money in farming," he began. "There might have been, when my father came over from England, but there's no future in it now."

Only months before, Jim was going to have the biggest wheat farm in the Dakotas, the finest horses, and a farmhouse that would make his father's home look small. Merrie looked at Jim curiously, wondering what notion had taken him now. True, they had nothing more than a cabin for themselves and lean-tos for the stock. But it was their first year. They hadn't been on the homestead long enough to bring in a harvest. Leave? They were little more than squatters. No deed, no cash crop, nothing more than a pair of work mules and a one-room cabin. Why leave, when they had no more than started?

Jim leaned across the table and grasped her hands.

"Merrie, we're going to Washington."

"We . . ." The black mood was over. For an

instant the significance of what he had said was swept aside by an overwhelming sense of relief. Anger was gone from his face, his dark eyes were eager. Responding blindly, Merrie returned the pressure of his hands.

"Out in Washington, they're giving timber away. I could prove up a homestead out there and I'd have one hundred and sixty acres of the biggest trees in the United States. All mine, free."

Washington . . . The meaning of Jim's words broke through. "Leave here?" Merrie whispered. She felt panicky. All at once there was a sick feeling in the pit of her stomach, an ache in her throat. She couldn't think where Washington was, but it must be far away, a thousand, two thousand miles to the west.

"There's still free land in Washington," Jim was saying. "All the best hasn't been snatched up by someone else. There are mountains and lakes and salt water . . ." He threw a disdainful glance through the window at the country outside. "Out there your eyes don't get tired of looking across empty plains."

"Leave here?" Merrie repeated dumbly. Her hands felt cold. Jim's, holding hers, were warm and damp to the touch. "But this land is 'free,' too and you have told me often that it's some of the best wheat country in the state."

Jim shrugged impatiently and dropped her hands.

She was spoiling his good mood. . . . Merrie said quickly, "I'm just surprised, that's all. I have heard a lot of talk about Washington lately, and

I've seen the posters at the depot in Providence, but I had never thought we'd go—go away.''

She had placated him. He rewarded her with a sudden boyish smile. "We'll sell the homestead," he said, "take the train to Seattle, go across Puget Sound to a place called Port Townsend, stake out a claim . . .''

There wouldn't be a scene, if she kept still. That fear subsided; the bigger fear, of leaving the known for the unknown, settled into a hard knot in the center of her being. He must not know it was there.

Silence was dangerous. Merrie prodded her mind for the right thing to say, and a memory stirred. Jim's mother had once mentioned a relative, her husband's brother, who had emigrated to Washington even before it became a state. "Don't you have an uncle out there?" she asked, trying to echo Jim's enthusiasm. Instantly she was sorry she had spoken. Jim's face clouded. "I mean, is he in that place, Port Townsend . . .?''

"No," Jim said curtly. "He's a prospector. He took out a claim in the Snoqualmie Valley.''

"Where is that? Near Port Townsend?''

Jim frowned. "I don't know. My Uncle Henry doesn't interest himself in me. He's been gone from Dakota since I was fourteen years old, and I don't intend to go looking for him.''

"I just thought you'd want to . . .'' Merrie's voice faded out to nothing. ". . . to be close by someone you know . . .''

Jim's dark eyes were scornful. "Not I," he said coldly. "I'm not a tabby cat, that sits by the fire.

You're thinking of yourself, aren't you? You're afraid."

"Yes," Merrie said, her voice falling to a whisper. "I want to stay in one place. I want to build something, make something better. I want what you promised me—a home of my own."

She waited, too miserable to be frightened, for the outburst that was sure to follow. For minutes that might have been measured by the heavy beating of her heart, Jim looked at her, his mouth twitching at one corner.

Let him shout at me, she thought, let him compare me with a tabby cat, or laugh at me, or disdain me, but I had to say it and I will not take it back.

Jim got up quickly, came around the table, with a firm hand drew her to her feet. His arms went around her. "Merrie," he said urgently, "Merrie . . ."

She lifted her face for his kiss, more aware than ever of how deeply she resented his way of exploiting their lovemaking in order to get what he wanted. Whatever respect or liking she had felt for him before their marriage was gone for good, and still he could excite her as he was now, by holding her so close she could feel his heartbeat and every curve and hollow of his body.

"I haven't forgotten that promise," he said. "I want to go to Washington because out there I can build you a finer home than I can here. And I can build it sooner."

"I don't want a fine home," Merrie protested. "I don't mind waiting, if we can stay here."

Jim's arms tightened convulsively. "You're

coming with me to Washington," he said, "or you stay here, alone."

In silence, they stood together, Merrie locked in Jim's embrace. Merrie could see the posters in the Providence railroad station. "Free land—direct, fast route to the land of opportunity . . ." They had meant nothing to her, but to Jim, whose father had crossed an ocean and half a continent because of a railroad poster? "Dakota fever," that's what it had been called in earlier days, when the railroads first pushed westward across the central plains. Now it was Washington fever. Was it surprising that Charles Cowen's son had been infected?

"I am a failure here," Jim burst out. "In Washington I'll begin all over again." His voice softened, *"We'll* begin all over again. Go with me, Merrie. I need you."

He had touched the tender spot. He needs me. . . . Merrie looked up into his face. Eyes filled with tears, she nodded. "Yes, Jim," she said brokenly, "I'll go with you to Washington."

He kissed her then. "Merrie," he said huskily, "thank you for giving me one more chance. . . ." He kissed her again, fell on his knees beside her. "Let me love you, Merrie," he whispered, "let me love you. . . ."

II

They had two weeks in which to tear up the roots of a lifetime. The homestead Charles Cowen had planned as his son's future was nothing but an unproved claim, and had to be sold cheap. One hundred and sixty dollars for one hundred and sixty acres and not a penny for the crop, which stood green in the fields.

"Land is worthless," Uncle Mike remarked. "It's the man who works it that gives it value."

Jim had put little into it, and took little out. Even the livestock—the milch cow Uncle Mike had given them as a wedding present, a dozen chickens from a farmer's wife Merrie had helped during threshing, some feeder pigs, a few geese Jim had received in trade for the use of his mules—they had all been sold for half what Jim should have asked.

Jim didn't even protest when the man who sold them the mule team took the animals back.

"Our agreement was ten dollars each and your

promise to pay off the rest with your first crop," the man said. "But you ain't waiting for no crop, and with you heading west, I'd be a fool to go on waiting for my money. Here's five dollars for good luck, and I'll take back my mules."

Jim shrugged, dropped the five dollars into his pocket and walked into the cabin. Merrie lingered in the barnyard, and she swallowed hard as she watched the man lead the jack and the jenny down the dusty lane. She was glad Uncle Mike was not here to see it.

The first through train to Seattle was to leave St. Paul on June 18. Providence was not a regular stop, but the stationmaster could flag the train for passengers.

"You and I, Merrie . . ." Jim exclaimed, throwing the words like a challenge, "you and I are going to be on that train. We'll make them stop her in Providence, just for us. The whole town will turn out, believe me. They'll see us get on."

The practical in Merrie came forward timidly. "Aren't there going to be emigrant cars? The ones with stoves at the end, so we can take our own food and cook hot meals? It wouldn't cost nearly so much."

Jim looked at her disdainfully. "I wouldn't go any other way," he said, "than first class."

There was little time for good-byes. The people of Providence had known Merrie since the day she arrived with her aunt and uncle from Chicago, "the little Dooley orphan with the odd-colored eyes." But Jim had been offish with Merrie's friends and so no one in town got around to organizing the traditional drop-in party.

At last the day came. June 18, 1893. At a quarter to eight that evening the great Brooks Consolidated engine jerked the cars into movement and the first through train to Seattle pulled out of the station in St. Paul. It was due in Providence at nine, and just as Jim had predicted, the whole town knew the depot master was going to flag her and the whole town was there to see her come in. They, too, had read about the golden oak and the velvet plush and the French novels.

These same people, who had known Merrie all her life, were watching her curiously and keeping their distance. Everything stood between them. The fact that she was wearing her best dress—her wedding dress—and a bonnet. The valises on the platform beside them. Jim's new hat and checkered vest, items everyone in Providence had fingered at the general store but never once thought of buying. Even the presence of Uncle Mike and Aunt Sal, standing by with stern faces and nothing to say, did not establish a link with the people she and Jim seemed to be scorning through this spectacular departure.

"We stand out so," Merrie whispered unhappily. "I wish we had gone to St. Paul to catch the train."

Jim said curtly, "I wanted to get on here. Right here, in Providence, where everyone could see."

Merrie looked away quickly, hoping her aunt and uncle had not heard. They hadn't, for like everyone else on the platform, they were looking east down the tracks. The train was coming in.

There wasn't time to cry, nor to pour out, in last-minute confession, all the things she had wanted to tell her aunt but had not dared to say. There was scarcely time to kiss Uncle Mike, then Aunt Sal, before Jim was pushing her up the steep iron steps of the Pullman car, and a man's high nasal voice was calling, "Allaboard!"

Uncle Mike's face was flushed but grim, Aunt Sal was trying to smile. Looking down on their upturned faces, Merrie thought her heart would break. The train lurched forward, the locomotive belched a shower of soot, the people of Providence blinked, stepped back from the train, and began to wave. Merrie looked back through the half-open door. The figures of her aunt and uncle grew smaller with every turn of the wheels until, even squinting, Merrie could not distinguish them from the crowd. That was my last chance, Merrie thought, and I lost it.

How silly was this empty, hopeless feeling, she told herself hastily. Last chance for what?

But she knew, that was the trouble, and no amount of pride or stubbornness or loyalty to Jim could conceal the truth. She had known for some time that she was going to have a baby. She wanted a child more than anything else in the world, and gentle, round-faced Aunt Sal was surely someone in whom she could confide. But she hadn't, not even in that last instant before the train pulled out, when the desire to tell had all but choked her. Why hadn't she, with all the chance she'd had, unless it was because she knew but did not want to see that Aunt Sal and Uncle Mike did not trust Jim and would not be happy that she was going to have Jim's baby? Nothing more wonderful could happen to me, Merrie thought, and I couldn't tell the two people who would have cared the most.

"Come *on*." Jim's voice was commanding. "And for God's sake, don't cry. Everyone in the car is staring at you."

Merrie blinked hard. No tears, except two which squeezed out of the corners of her eyes, rolled down her face and dropped onto the collar of her wedding dress. She blotted her cheeks hastily with the back of her hand, and followed Jim into the world of golden oak and velvet plush.

III

The train was cheered in every town and village between St. Paul and Seattle, and despite a delay in Montana arrived in full glory at a quarter to four the afternoon of June 22. Passengers who had been doffing hats and waving handkerchiefs to the crowds for four memorable days, stepped out into a dismal one-story building which needed a three-story flagpole in order to rise above the surrounding factories and warehouses. But a flag waved from the flagpole, the waiting crowd was the most admiring so far, and the loudest, and in no time passengers were confessing their impressions to newspaper reporters. Breath-taking speeds of thirty to forty miles an hour had been reached along the Red River Valley. At one point along the Columbia, the train was believed to have hit sixty miles an hour. . . .

Gradually reporters knotted around the Great Northern executives and other dignitaries on the passenger list. "How has the panic affected things back east? Will you stay in Seattle for the Jim Hill Carnival on the Fourth?''

Merrie grasped Jim's arm. "A carnival!" she whispered excitedly. "Did you hear that?"

Jim's smile, warm as the sun when he stepped off the train, had hardened into the thin-lipped, set expression she knew so well. He liked the excitement at Providence, she reflected, but resents it here because others are the center of it. He feels slighted. Merrie was torn as always between pity and impatience.

"Look at the posters," she said quickly, trying to distract him. "After today you can buy a ticket to St. Paul for only twenty-five dollars, and eighteen dollars, second class."

"We're not going back!"

"I didn't mean . . ." Merrie shook her head helplessly. "I was just reading what it said on that poster. There's another one, about the Jim Hill Carnival."

"I didn't come out here to go to carnivals," Jim said. "I'm going to Port Townsend first thing in the morning. And I don't want you out in the street while I'm gone. Now, let's get out of here."

It was only a short walk from the depot between Marion and Columbia Streets to the hotel on Pioneer Place. They made it in silence. Once Merrie had tried to soften Jim's moods, but she had learned they were like fevers that had to run their course. With little or no reason behind them, they spread out formlessly, seeking a reason, needing an irritant around which the infection of bad temper could collect. If she spoke up, even in sympathy, his mood took shape instantly around her protest. *She* was to blame. . . . And so she walked along quickly, said nothing, and tensed herself for what was to follow.

Because she knew the anger would have to come to a head and burst. He would shout at her, fling senseless accusations at her, and then, when he had driven her to the very depths of her feeling for him, to disgust, and pity, and dismay, his mood would change. She dreaded this almost as much. For then he would be remorseful. He would throw his arms around her and beg her hoarsely, "Tell me you love me, Merrie, tell me. I need you . . ."

"Watch where you're going," Jim said brusquely. "You want people to know you're from the country?"

It happened just as she knew it would. Jim's anger exploded the moment they were in their hotel room and the door was closed behind them.

"Who told you to smile at everyone? 'Oh, good morning, Mr. Smith . . .' " He raised his voice mockingly, " 'How are *you* today, Mr. Smith. . . .' You had to make friends with everyone on the train. They were important people, they might not have wanted to talk to you. You didn't think of that, did you? *Did* you?"

Later, regrets and self-reproach. "I'm no good," he whispered, clinging to her passionately. "But I need you. Forgive me for the terrible things I said to you. I didn't mean what I said. Listen to me, Merrie, I didn't mean them. . . ."

Merrie held him, and promised everything would be all right.

In the morning he left for Port Townsend. But now he was in a confident mood. He talked about the timber claims he would take out, the giant firs that would be his, the money he would make.

"You're going alone?" Merrie asked.

"I'll be back for you in a week."

"But I don't know *anyone* in Seattle!"

"There isn't enough money left to buy two tickets to Port Townsend."

Merrie stared at him unbelievingly. Their entire grubstake—the sale of their claim, the cabin, the livestock—she had never asked how much there was, but surely it could not be gone? "The hotel room," she said weakly. "They'll want to be paid."

Jim turned away from her. "I'll leave enough money for food. They won't turn out a woman."

Only when he was at the very threshold did he turn back.

"Don't doubt me, Merrie," he said, against her cheek. "There's timber over there for the asking. I've looked into it, I know. I'll be back before your money's gone." Seconds later he was at the door, valise in hand. "Stay in your room," he said, "don't make a spectacle of yourself . . ." and the door closed behind him.

For ten days Merrie obeyed him. She went out only to eat, ever so sparingly, at the café near the hotel. She wrote letters to Aunt Sal, describing each lonely day in carefully selected half-truths. Her extravagance was the pennies spent for newspapers. Day after day she sat at the window, looking out over Pioneer Place, and read about the events scheduled for the Jim Hill Carnival.

At the end of the week, Jim had not returned, nor had he written. She was not frightened, for Jim always spoke loosely about time. But she was disappointed, because she had hoped he would be back in time for the carnival and in such good spirits he would take her to see it. Parades, football and baseball games, even a balloon ascension . . . For more than a week Merrie's world had been confined to the view across Pioneer Place. Surely if Jim did not return by the opening of the celebration, July 3, surely, it would do no harm . . .

Merrie was awakened at daybreak the morning of July 3 by the sound of booming cannon. She opened her eyes wide, shocked into wakefulness. The dream world vanished all too quickly, she was back in the hotel room in Seattle, Jim was gone.

Those were the guns of U.S. warship *Monterey,* proclaiming the opening of the two-day celebration. . . . Merrie sat up quickly, shook her heavy chestnut-colored hair back from her face. "Keep to your room," had been Jim's last words, "don't make a spectacle of yourself. . . ." But would she be a spectacle? She threw back the covers, tested the coldness of the floor with one bare foot, and then, more bravely, with the other. She crossed the room quickly to the chest of drawers, stood up very straight, shoulders back, chin up, and looked into the long mirror. A spectacle? She wasn't large at all, she decided. If Aunt Sal hadn't guessed she was carrying a baby, how would anyone else? What thickness there was to her waistline would be well hidden if she wore her blue serge coat and kept it buttoned.

Merrie enjoyed two happy days. She toured the warship *Monterey*. She boarded the Yesler Avenue streetcar, the first such vehicle she had ever been on, and rode to Leschi Park where Madame Leland made the crowds gasp with her balloon ascension and parachute drop. There was a parade the morning of the Fourth, with hundreds of marshals marching down Front Street, their uniforms brightened by sashes of buff and gold, rosettes on their hats, and red, white and blue batons in their hands. Later eighty bicycles swept by in a parade of their own. Japanese lanterns, glowing softly, swung from wheels and handlebars, and the riders shot off firecrackers as they passed.

Directly across the square from the hotel was the Palace of Industry, a massive gray stone building draped with flags and bunting. Within were exhibits of all the wonders of Washington, but it was nightfall which made the building a palace, for then the lights went on. The walls above the second-story verandas were encrusted with electric bulbs. White brilliants outlined a locomotive and tender, smaller bulbs of different colors flashed on and off so that the wheels seemed to be revolving.

Merrie sat in her chair by the window and for an hour or more looked out across the square at the glittering, moving pictures of light. For two days she had been exhilarated by a sense of freedom she had lost since her marriage to Jim. She felt ashamed of such a feeling, but it was real—she had actually been glad that Jim had not come back when he had promised. Merrie sighed. The celebration was past. Jim might return tomorrow, the next day, even tonight. But the money was gone, she could wait no longer. Merrie made her decision easily, for it was so obvious. In the morning she would go out and look for a job.

IV

The sister at Providence Hospital had a round, pink face and penetrating blue eyes. They looked into Merrie's eyes silently, but at last the mouth turned up in a smile. "You are applying for a job? What kind of a job?"

Merrie shook her head. "I don't know." It was the plain truth. She had worked since she was a little girl, for her aunt, for neighbors, but she had never been paid. What could she do for wages? That was the question, and it hadn't been answered in a morning of job-hunting in Seattle.

Perhaps she hadn't gone about it the right way. Drawn by window displays like a child to a parade, she had walked from one department store to another. Whenever the goods in the window caught her eye, she went inside. At the Bon Marche, it had been the elegant Alexandre five-hook kid gloves, only a dollar a pair. At W.P. Boyd and Co., it was the ladies' French jersey ribbed vests in white, cream, blue, pink and black. At

MacDougall and Southwick, she had been arrested by the parasols, all colors of the rainbow and some costing as little as $1.75.

How wonderful to handle such objects! But in each store the manager eyed her skeptically, asked "Previous experience?" and after a word or two about the panic and bad times advised her to look elsewhere.

At the last store the manager proved to be a graying, kindly woman. "We do need a clerk," she told Merrie, "but, my dear, you shouldn't be on your feet that much. Do you really need to work?"

Flushing, Merrie thanked her and left the store. Jim had been right, she had made a spectacle of herself. How foolish was the confidence with which she had left the hotel this morning! Who would hire a girl whose pregnancy was already straining the seams of her carefully buttoned blue serge coat?

"But you must have had some idea of what you could do," the sister insisted, "or you wouldn't have come in, would you?"

Merrie blurted out the truth. "It was the children. There must be young patients here? There must be newborn babies?"

The sister smiled. "Oh, yes, indeed there are."

"Could I help take care of them?"

The sister's bright eyes grew thoughtful. Merrie submitted, with a sense of relief, to a long, silent study. At last the sister asked, "When is your baby expected?"

"Not until December."

"Then you would want to work only until that time?"

"I . . ." Merrie was jarred for the second time today by the realization of her ignorance of the wage-earning world. Who would hire a girl for a few weeks or months? "No," she answered truthfully, "just until my husband gets back."

The sister's encouraging smile broke with surprise. "Your husband?" she repeated. "Oh, I see."

Merrie felt her cheeks grow warm. "You don't believe me."

The sister said solemnly, "Forgive me. So many come here, and they always talk about their husbands, right at first." She stood up, came around her desk and rested her hand gently on Merrie's arm. "You are welcome here, in any case. Now, let's go talk to Sister Theresa and let her show you the nursery."

Merrie worked at Providence Hospital from five in the morning until three in the afternoon, sometimes in the kitchen but more often, to her great joy, in the children's ward. Days passed, then weeks. There was one letter from Jim, one check.

"This town is not what I expected. But I have another plan that is sure to work out. . . ." He wrote little more, and the sum of money enclosed was so small Merrie was convinced he would be back in only a few days. But that week ended, another came and passed.

At the hospital no one asked about her husband. They were too kind to challenge his existence, Merrie had neither the means nor the heart to try to prove it.

By mid-September, Merrie had grown large, and the walk up the hill to the hospital left her out of breath and with a strangely light-headed feeling.

"Trolley rides and steep hills are too hard on you now," Sister Theresa said one day. "Besides, a good deal of your wages must be going to pay the hotel. There is a room for you here."

Merrie said quickly, "Oh, I can't leave the hotel. My husband wouldn't know where to find me."

The sister looked sympathetic. "Perhaps you could leave a letter for him at the hotel, telling him where you are?"

"No," Merrie protested, "no . . ." Jim had not provided for her. But she knew, though she could not make herself reveal it to the sister, that he would resent everything she had done to feed and clothe herself. The anger would be less bitter—if he returned in a triumphant mood, it might be averted altogether—if she were waiting for him just where he left her, and if by getting him to talk about himself she managed to say little or nothing about what she had been doing.

"Sister," she said, "I should tell you one thing. If I don't come to work some morning, it will mean my husband has returned."

Merrie got it out as quickly as she could, and waited unhappily for Sister Theresa's displeasure. The sister had every reason to be angry with her for accepting help for so long and then planning to leave without notice. She must wonder why the return of a husband would call for such thoughtlessness. But Sister Theresa's answer, when at last it came, was gentle. "You must think about your baby," she said softly. "You have a deep obligation to your baby." And then she turned and sped down the hallway, the folds of her black habit lifting slightly with a whispering sound.

That night Jim returned from Port Townsend.

Merrie had undressed for bed and was standing at the window, brushing her hair, when she heard the key in the lock. She knew instantly it was Jim. This was the moment she had been anticipating for two and a half months. She should be exultantly happy, she should run to him, welcome him. . . . But instead, she stood still as stone, clutching the hairbrush nervously, waiting in fear and confusion to see what his mood might be.

The door slammed back against the wall. Jim stood in the open doorway, staring at her. He looked thin, sick, and murderously angry.

"Jim!" Merrie said in an agonized whisper. She couldn't move.

"Where have you been?" he asked thickly.

His appearance was shocking. His hair was long, his face emaciated. His suit—his best suit, on which he had spent so much of their grub-stake—was dirty and torn.

"I said, 'Where have you been?'"

He must have come in while she was at the hospital, and gone out again. She said haltingly, "I have a job . . ."

He was too angry to hear her. *"Where have you been?"* It was a scream, high-pitched, insane, splitting his voice. He took a step toward her, stopped, his body suddenly shaken by racking, silent sobs. Merrie ran forward and caught him.

"Merrie, Merrie," he moaned, "I lost everything."

"You're sick," she said, "you need rest. Here,

let me help you get to bed.''

She undressed Jim, bathed him, covered him with a warm quilt. ''You have a deep obligation to your baby,'' Sister Theresa had thought fit to remind her. And to this child, Merrie reflected, looking down at the thin, crumpled form of her husband. She went to the chest of drawers and turned down the lamp.

Jim's voice came out of the darkness. ''Come here to me.''

Merrie caught her breath. ''I'm going to sit up for a while. By the window. I always do . . .''

''Merrie, please . . .''

She hesitated an instant, eyes closed, fists clenched. If you love him, you must go to him, she told herself, and if you don't, you cannot abandon him now.

''Merrie . . .''

She felt her way across the dark room to the bed and lay down beside him. The hungry kisses, the urgently searching fingers, the mouth on her breast—once these components of the love act had affected her so strongly that she could forget, until it ended abruptly, that stroking her, touching her, even entering her were to achieve his own selfish release, and when she, too, reached the final explosive moment it wasn't because he had wanted her to share it, nor that he had enjoyed it more when she did. How different now! How long had it been since *she* had really desired *him*? When had she become dutiful, instead of caring?

In the morning there were no scenes, no anger or shouting. Jim sat on the edge of the bed, hands between his knees, head down, and told her what had happened.

It was another story of failure, played this time against the setting of a town that was failing, too. Once there had been seven thousand people in Port Townsend. There had been six banks, three street railways, canneries, nail works, foundries, sawmills. The panic had dealt the mortal blow. The real estate business had collapsed, people were leaving by the hundreds, the half-completed drydock had been towed away, the nail works equipment had been sold for junk, cobwebs gathered in the corners of the new, fine, three-story business buildings. Through this drama of the death of a town Jim's personal defeat was woven like a black and rotting thread. All that free timber? He hadn't taken out a claim, there were easier ways to make money than breaking your back to prove up a homestead. Had he looked for work? Yes—he'd sent her a check, hadn't he? He had been willing, but in a place like Port Townsend he hadn't had a chance.

Much of what he said did not make sense, but Merrie was grateful for Jim's docility, short-lived as it might be and born as it was of sickness and failure, and she listened patiently. Her mind wandered to Sister Theresa and the children at the hospital, to Aunt Sal and Uncle Mike, who still did not know she was carrying a child. A change in Jim's tone of voice jerked Merrie back to full attention. He had stopped talking about his months in Port Townsend. Leaving that broken dream behind, his voice was rising excitedly as he began creating a new illusion.

To the east of Seattle was a place called Kirkland, the "little Pittsburgh of the West." Still farther east, toward the Snoqualmie Valley, the coal town of Gilman. That's where the money was now, in coal and steel. He was going to Gilman and work in the mines.

He was no longer sitting on the edge of the bed, throwing his confession of defeat over his shoulder. He was on his feet, facing her. "It's what I should have done in the first place. The Cowens were always miners."

For an instant Merrie doubted his seriousness. But his eyes were bright, his voice confident. The best wheat farmer in Dakota, the biggest timber owner in Washington, and now, the richest miner in Gilman—Merrie could not restrain a sigh. "Oh, Jim," she murmured, "your father . . ."

"My father could have made far more money in the mines in Wisconsin or Canada or Michigan than he did on the farm, but he was too stubborn to do it."

The picture of Jim's father flashed across her mind, so very like Jim except that he was taller, heavier, more manly. How often Jim must have heard his mother tell about the night Charles Cowen came out of the mine for the last time and swore never to go back.

"Your father hated the mines," Merrie said. "He vowed . . ."

Jim said curtly, "But I didn't."

For all the tradition of his kin in the north of England, Jim knew nothing about mining. This decision, Merrie knew, was nothing more than salve for the wounds of his defeat in Port Townsend. But he was determined, and the more she said against it the more sure he was to go. Merrie was seized by a sense of foreboding. The baby was due in less than four months. If Jim left again . . . "Jim," she said urgently, "this time, take me with you."

He frowned. "A mining town is no place for a woman."

She could work now, and for several more weeks. But then? Merrie crossed the floor to Jim, grasped his hands in her own. "Please, Jim," she pleaded, "there must be other women in Gilman."

He shook his head. "I don't know," he said evasively. "If there is a suitable place, I'll come back for you in a week."

Merrie shook him gently. "Jim, look at me!"

He turned his head reluctantly.

"The baby . . ."

Jim jerked away from her and walked across the room to the window. "Why do you suppose I'm going to work in the mines?" he shouted. "I hate mining as much as my father did. But I've got to, for you and your baby!"

"You could find work in Seattle."

"They're digging a hundred thousand tons of coal a year at Gilman. I can make money faster, and more of it."

"I wasn't thinking of money," Merrie said. She was beginning to feel light-headed and ill. "I was thinking of being left alone."

"I told you I'd come back for you!" Jim flung at her.

But you won't! You didn't before, you won't

now. . . . The protest formed in Merrie's troubled mind, but went unspoken. The giddiness was the worst she had experienced in all her pregnancy; she was beginning to feel really ill. It was fear; she recognized it, tried to fight it down. Because of her job at the hospital, she had not been lonely or frightened while Jim was in Port Townsend. But soon, very soon, she would be helpless. She couldn't return to her aunt in Dakota; they hadn't the money for a ticket and her pulse quickened at the thought of Jim's temper if she even suggested it. Her thoughts raced about, hemmed in on every side by the barriers of hopelessness. One last escape opened up. "You said Gilman was on the road to the Snoqualmie Valley. Your uncle lives there, in the Valley. I could stay at his place, while you are at Gilman."

"I know nothing about my uncle;" Jim retorted. "I care nothing for my uncle and would not know him if he walked into this room."

This was untrue, for Jim himself had said he was fourteen years old when his Uncle Henry left for the West. Surely he could not have forgotten him so completely. Merrie shook her head helplessly. "If I stayed at your uncle's place, Gilman wouldn't be so far away."

Jim snorted. "For all I know, the Snoqualmie Valley is a hundred miles the other side of Gilman. Why have you taken this silly notion? Why go searching out my uncle?"

"Because," Merrie said weakly, shivering with a sudden onslaught of nausea, "because he's—he's family."

Jim shrugged and turned his back. A cold silence fell over the room as he washed, shaved, carefully dampened and combed that hair that had grown too long, and sponged the mud off the trousers and coat of the only suit he had. Merrie did not ask what had happened to his valise and all that was in it. When he turned to leave, she did not ask where he was going or when he was coming back. It seemed to her that this had all happened before, and it was as useless to struggle against it as it would be to shed tears when the sun went down. She knew before he told her that he was leaving for Gilman right now, and alone.

At the door Jim said, "This time, everything is going to be different."

Merrie nodded dumbly. When he reached for her suddenly, clung to her, and murmured, "Merrie, Merrie, I need you . . ." she whispered, as she had a thousand time, "Everything is going to be all right, Jim, everything is going to be all right. . . ."

In a moment he released her. Mouth twitching, he said hoarsely, "Stay here. Wait. I'll be back. . . ."

Again Merrie nodded. The door closed behind him.

She went to the window and sat down. If she watched the street below, she might be able to pick out Jim's figure. He wasn't coming back, she would never see him again. . . . She accepted these thoughts with a strange sense of detachment. Nevertheless it seemed important that she catch sight of him. She narrowed her eyes, squinting against the sunlight. Like a magic incantation, she whispered, "If I could see him . . ." as if that last glimpse were absolutely necessary. As if her one chance of saving herself from despair were to see Jim, hurrying away from her. In growing desperation, she strained to focus, forcing her eyes to select the one familiar figure in a street crowded with strangers. Minutes passed. The magic failed. He had gone, she had not seen him leave. Merrie covered her face with her hands, and began to cry.

V

The man behind the desk in the Cascade Development Company's dingy coal-streaked office was clearly both embarrassed and amused by her presence. The baby was due in less than a month; if Merrie had wondered what kind of a picture she made, the grinning, pointing boys at the Gilman depot would have enlightened her. But neither their laughter nor this man's careless effort to conceal what he was thinking were important now. She had one concern only, and that was to find Jim.

"He wrote me that he was working here," Merrie insisted. She drew Jim's letter from her reticule, as if such physical evidence would arouse the man's memory.

"When was that?" the man asked, his rough voice coated with a thin film of patience.

"Two months ago," Merrie replied truthfully, feeling her cheeks grow warm. She had not meant to tell him she had heard nothing from her husband in two months.

The man looked at her sharply. "You are Mrs. Cowen?"

Merrie exclaimed, "Of course . . ." and then blushed and bit her lip.

The man opened a drawer in his desk, frowned at the contents. "I figured you'd show up sooner or later." He reached into the drawer, pulled out a bundle of letters held together with a piece of dirty string. "You write these?" he asked, tossing the bundle onto the desk.

Her letters to Jim. Faithfully, like a wife whose husband has not abandoned her, she had written him every other day. Dull letters, hopeless letters, for all her efforts to write as if this separation were something they had planned together. Pretense was easy when she wrote to Aunt Sal, for she alone knew it was all pretending. But the make-believe in her letters to Jim had mocked her even as she was writing it, for however gaily she referred to his "trip to Gilman" or to joining him when he "had found suitable quarters," she knew Jim would recognize this play-acting for what it was. And still she had written, each letter a bit more desperate than the last.

"Yes," she said, "I wrote them."

The man's manner changed. "I'm sorry." He sighed, shook his head. "You see now why I was so sure no Jim Cowen had come into this office. I've been saving these letters personally."

"You don't suppose . . ." Merrie cleared her throat, lifted her chin and said more firmly, "You don't suppose he could have gone to work here under some other name?"

The man shrugged. "I don't question men who come in here about is that their real name. It don't work, with miners."

"You don't remember him, perhaps from someplace else in town? A little taller than I am, dark curly hair, brown eyes."

The man sighed loudly. "Lady, you seen what this town is like? You seen all the people?"

Merrie nodded like a child accepting a just scolding. She had seen, indeed. The crowd at the depot had been so thick she could scarcely push through it. It appeared that everyone in Gilman turned out to meet the train. Many were in work clothes gritty with coal dust, for the big mines were in the hills directly above the town.

"Yes," Merrie admitted, "I saw." The man was growing impatient. She stood up slowly. "Thank you for your time."

His impatience dissolved. "I'm *real* sorry." He rose, ran his forefinger nervously around the rim of his celluloid collar. "There's one spot in town where everybody goes. It's no place for a lady, but the owner knows more than anyone else in Gilman about who comes to town. The saloon down at the bottom of the hill, near the depot. Eric's.

A tavern, filled with men . . . The picture of the boys at the depot, snickering and pointing, flashed across Merrie's mind. "Do you really think he might be able to tell me something?"

The man nodded. "I'd take you down there myself, but I can't leave the office."

"Then I'll go alone."

The saloon was a great, dark cavern, filled with

men, with smoke, with the smell of wet dirt and stale beer. Merrie hesitated. At the nearest table four men stopped talking, turned to appraise her silently.

"Eric?" she asked.

"Back there," one of them answered. "At the far end, behind the bar."

Merrie walked resolutely the full length of the big room. Let them laugh or point. . . . But they didn't. Her progress past table after table of hard-faced, rough-talking miners was marked by a wide path of respectful silence. At the end of the bar a big man with shaved head and a bright red scar across one cheek was drying his hands on his apron.

Merrie stepped up to the bar exactly as she would have approached a grocery counter if she wanted a sack of sugar. "Are you Mr. Eric?" she asked politely.

"I'm Eric, ma'am," the bartender said.

"I am looking for a Mr. James Cowen. Do you know anyone by that name?"

Eric hesitated. "Let me think. . . ." Reflection produced deep wrinkles from his heavy black eyebrows all the way up into his bristly scalp. "When would he have been hereabouts?"

"Any time during the past two months."

Watching the barkeep's face anxiously, Merrie described Jim.

The big man pondered the matter silently for some time, rubbing his hands on his apron with slow, deliberate motions, though they were long since dry. "Don't know that name," he said at last, "though it seems like I seen someone in here three, four weeks ago, answers that description. If that's him, he didn't stay for long."

"Did he say where he was going from here?"

Eric shook his head. "I'm sorry, ma'am." His pale blue eyes rested on her sympathetically. "Mostly they don't say, and I don't ask."

Merrie hadn't really expected to find Jim here. Invading the tavern had been a last effort to ignore the crushing truth—Jim had lied to her, Jim had left her, and her search for him had come to a dead end. She had tried to believe that he was right here in Gilman, that he wanted to be found as much as she wanted to find him—the loss of this last reckless hope left her weak. She clutched the rounded edge of the bar and closed her eyes.

"Lady, let me give you something. . . ."

Merrie opened her eyes, looked into Eric's battered face and managed to smile. "No, thank you, I'm better already."

Eric leaned over the bar. His eyes were wise and sad. "You got relations," he asked softly, "somewheres you can go to?"

Merrie looked at him helplessly. Aunt Sal and Uncle Mike in Dakota. That was impossible. The sisters at Providence Hospital—they were only three hours away by train, but that distance seemed as great as the two thousand miles separating her from her aunt and uncle.

All at once Merrie knew what she must do. Relations—there was Jim's uncle, of course. Being in Gilman, she must be near his home in the Snoqualmie Valley. Hope was reborn with the thought that Jim might be living with his uncle. Whatever he had said about him before, Jim might easily have changed his mind if things had gone badly for him in Gilman. . . .

"I am going on to the Snoqualmie Valley," Merrie said, grasping this rash hope as one gropes to keep from falling. "To my husband's folks. Could you tell me when the next train leaves from here?"

"Could be the same one you came in on," Eric said, "if they had a lot of stuff to unload and if you can make it back to the depot in a hurry. Otherwise, you got to wait until tomorrow."

Merrie thanked him and left hurriedly, glad she had been cautious enough to deposit her valises at the depot. The crowds inside the tavern had overflowed into the street. In her haste Merrie did not see that the men were standing in a tight circle around a fist fight. Her mind was on her goal— first, the train, and next, the home of Jim's uncle. Blindly she pushed through the knot of men. A strong hand fell on her arm, jerked her back. Only a foot away a pair of miners, stripped to the waist, were charging each other like crazed bulls.

Merrie gasped, "Oh, excuse me. . . ." Laughter followed her as she retreated from the fight, turned, and ran down the wooden sidewalk toward the depot. The train was still there. . . . The heel of her shoe caught between the rough planks. For a terrifying moment she fought to keep her balance, and then she fell.

All eyes were on the fight. The crowd of spectators was growing, audience and fighters were moving in a solid mass from the front door of the

tavern to the middle of the street. Slowly Merrie
got to her feet. She wasn't hurt. On the contrary,
she felt strangely light-headed and carefree. The
train—she ran the last few steps to the ticket
office.

"I want to buy a ticket to the Snoqualmie Valley," she gasped. "I'm not too late, am I?"

The ticket agent looked at her skeptically. A
half-hour earlier she had asked him to keep her
suitcases for her, explaining breathlessly that she
was meeting her husband here and he'd be back for
them later. He obviously considered it odd that
she should be leaving alone, and in such a hurry.
"Where at in the Snoqualmie Valley?" he
drawled. "Black River? Three Forks? Gold
Mountain?"

This was an unexpected difficulty. On the few
occasions when Jim's uncle had been mentioned,
Merrie had always pictured his home, "the
Snoqualmie Valley," as a town just like Providence. One town, one general store, one depot. If
she must choose from three towns?

There was another problem, or at least the possibility of a problem so tremendous she couldn't
let herself dwell on it. Some indefinable change
was taking place in her body. Perhaps because of
her fall, the weight of the baby seemed to have
shifted and a new feeling was spreading through
her, threatening to engulf her.

"Quick," she breathed to the blinking ticket
agent, not knowing herself whether she was talking about the train or the baby. "I want to go
to . . ." Jim had always spoken of his uncle as if he

119

lived on the edge of the last wilderness. "I want to go to the end of the line," she gasped. "To Gold Mountain."

Ticket in hand, she grabbed the valises as the agent shoved them through the door, and dragged them outside to the station platform. Breathing hard, she made her way clumsily up the steep iron steps into the passenger car, dropped into the front seat and closed her eyes. Seconds later the locomotive emitted a hysterical blast, the cars trembled, submitted, and rolled forward.

The Snoqualmie Valley, to which this last impulse had committed her, lay ahead, but she did not even open her eyes. Strange and different as this unknown land might be, it could not be as terrifying as the thoughts in her head. She had not found Jim, in the one place she had reason to believe he would be. And she was running short of time. She could have misjudged it; the baby might come sooner than was expected.

Gilman was out of sight. The train labored up the hill, struggled along tracks hemmed in by purple dark forest. "Black River!" Another depot, another crowd of grinning settlers waiting for the mail. The train continued along the slope, with a turbulent river beating against the rocks in the chasm below. It emerged from the deep woods; at the left a tremendous waterfall broke from the valley above like a gust of wind bursting without warning from a peaceful sky. The roadbed leveled out, followed the bank of the now wide and peaceful river.

"Three Forks!" the conductor yelled, and the

locomotive gave its shrill assent. As in Black River, the locomotive rolled to a jarring halt, there was a wait while passengers spilled out of the coaches and melted into the noisy crowd on the platform. Merrie rested her forehead against the window and closed her eyes. The next stop . . .

Fields, forest, a wide, gray river, and to the left a mountain dark against the evening sky.

"Gold Mountain!"

The end of the line. . . . Merrie stood up carefully. Bracing herself, she began to reach for her valises.

"Here," the conductor said brusquely, "let me handle these things." And then he added, with a twinkle in his eye, "And you're still carrying more than I am."

Merrie smiled wanly. There was no insult in the man, his round face was pink with fatherly concern.

"You staying in Gold Mountain?" he asked, emboldened by her smile.

Merrie nodded.

"With someone?" the little man insisted.

"My husband's uncle," Merrie said. "Mr. Henry Cowen."

The conductor's face underwent lightning change.

"Do you know him?" Merrie asked uncertainly.

The man nodded diagonally in a way that could mean yes or no. "You get to know everyone in town," he said vaguely. "But you got quite a ways to go to his place. He don't live right in Gold Mountain. He lives on his claim, three, four miles north of town, right under that their mountain. That's Mount Si," he added reverently. He cleared his throat. "There's a couple hotels in Gold Mountain."

Merrie shook her head. "I'd like to go right out to Mr. Cowen's place."

The little man looked troubled. "All right then," he said, "it's none of my business, of course. You go see Kittinger, Martin Kittinger. Livery stable right there . . ." and he pointed to one of the frame buildings which lined the dirt road near the depot. "He'll help you, if anyone can. Here, you leave your grips on the platform. Let Kitt come and get them."

The liveryman was less evasive than the conductor had been. "You want to go out to old Henry Cowen's place?" he asked, eyeing her sharply. "Wouldn't you be better off staying right here in town?"

Merrie hardly heard his objections. Even when his wife, a woman as gentle as Kitt was shrill, joined in begging her not to attempt the trip, Merrie held to the idea. The outside world seemed to be receding pleasantly. Mountains, rivers, trees, people, voices, trains, horses, carriages . . . Merrie's heart and mind looked inward at the much greater reality. There was no doubt now, she was going to have her baby soon. She hadn't enough money to stay in a hotel, and she was driven by an instinct she could not define, a desire to get "home," even if that home belonged to an uncle she had never seen.

The terror that had overtaken her briefly at Gilman was gone now. Her body was in the grip of strange sensations, but the sharper these physical feelings, the deeper her sense of contentment. The Kittingers were watching her anxiously. Merrie smiled. "You see," she explained, "I'm going to have a baby." With that she turned and walked to the horse and buggy standing in front of the stable.

Kitt hesitated, threw a helpless look at his wife, and hurried after Merrie to help her into the rig.

The town of Gold Mountain was hardly behind them when Merrie felt the first distinct labor pain. She recognized it instantly, and grew calm. Kittinger, on the other hand, was uneasy—she could guess it from his silence and occasional frowning glances thrown her way. If she told him pains had started, he would surely rein in and ride back to town, no matter how much she objected. A great sense of peacefulness settled over her, erasing all thoughts of Jim. There was no bitter past, no frightening future, just the warm and exciting present in which she, the little Dooley girl, was going to have a baby of her own.

She sensed that Kittinger's nervousness was growing with every turn of the wheels. It was as if he knew about her pains, but was afraid to mention them out loud for fear of making them worse. The road took them through a woods, emerged to follow the course of the river. Past a cabin in a clearing, where two men sat on the front stoop, silently watching. By the time Martin Kittinger reined the horse in at the cabin he claimed was "Lord Henry's place," Merrie could think of little but the baby.

The liveryman jumped down, ran to the cabin, was back in an instant, red-faced, and excited. "I was afraid of that!" he groaned. "Gone from here. And by the looks of it, he intends to stay out for quite a while."

"There was a cabin right back there," Merrie said, gritting her teeth against a sudden pain. "Mr. Kittinger, you'd better take me there, as fast as you can."

"What a fine surprise," Kittinger said tensely, "for that pair of bachelors."

The hours slipped by quickly after that. From within her personal world of pain and contentment, Merrie looked out with ever-growing confusion. The dark, frowning man named Brother Bill. The tall, thin man they called Jeff. Jefferson Davis Smith, he told her sometime later, in a voice deeper than any she had ever heard. The voice stayed with her through it all. As she lay in a strange bed, trying not to cry out, and drank from the cup of hot tea he held to her lips. As the room grew darker, and the pain coursed through her in such red, burning waves, she could not see his face even when she opened her eyes. She called out, and the voice arswered, "Here I am." When the pains followed each other so quickly that she could not catch her breath between them, she clutched the edge of the bed with one hand and the other hand flew to her mouth.

"Don't," the voice said softly. "Listen to me, Mrs. Cowen. I don't mind hollering. I've heard lots of it. Here's my hands. Now hold onto them, good and tight. And then go ahead and holler, just as loud as you can."

Merrie found his hands, gripped them with all her strength. "Will you stay?" she managed to gasp.

"I'll stay," Jeff's deep voice assured her. "But don't you worry, ma'am. I'll be looking the other way. Now go ahead and yell."

4

GRAY DAYLIGHT SEEPED through the window and settled over the room like mist. Jeff opened his eyes, listening even before he was fully awake for some sound from the bedroom. They must be sleeping, Merrie in his bed, the baby in the cradle beside her, Julie on her grass pallet on the floor. He sat up slowly, looked longingly at the empty coffeepot on the cold stove, and decided that it would waken them if he started a fire. Besides, he was late now. A good thing he owned the logging camp, or he'd be looking for a job, for ever since he had given the big, loud-ticking alarm clock to Merrie, he hadn't awakened until the logging crews were well into the morning's work. He'd leave the cabin quietly and ask the cook for coffee when he got to camp.

There were two routes to camp. One ran along the bank of the Snoqualmie to the booming grounds. Here logs were rolled down a chute into the water. "Boom stick" logs, chained end to end, formed the corral for the free, unconnected logs; later the full boom of logs would be floated down-river to the mill. From this riverbank above the booming grounds Jeff could ride inland, following the skid road to the spot in the woods where trees were being cut, and from there to camp. But there was a shorter route, from his cabin straight into the woods. The moment Jeff was in the saddle, the gelding threw up his head and trotted toward the woods. Jeff reined him around toward the river and the long way. He was late, but he would be a little later, for his mind was full. There were specific problems calling for specific action. There were feelings, much more difficult to define, which he must recognize for what they were. Jeff had never known peace more complete than that which came to him when he rode through the woods alone. He would take as long as possible to get to camp.

For the most part the river path clung to a narrow treeless strip between the woods and the cold, fast-flowing Snoqualmie. Mount Si rose awesomely at Jeff's right. White clouds, ruffled and nestling as broody hens, had settled down on the dark green forest at the mountain's base. The great gray crags above the timber line shot up through the clouds to be warmed to a glowing pink by the afternoon sun. Four thousand feet up, the topmost ridges and peaks glistened with a fresh capping of snow.

Looking up toward the mountain, Jeff thought of the man for whom it was named. Uncle Si, old Josiah Merritt, an early settler whose homestead, when Jeff was a little boy, had been a mile or so to the south, near enough to make the beloved Si the Smiths' closest neighbor. Uncle Si hadn't been rich, or powerful, or even lucky. Many settlers knew him best as the man who had played the fiddle for dances since the first day there had been enough white people in the Valley to get together for a party. He had played many a time from nine o'clock at night until six o'clock in the morning, when the dancers would eat a big breakfast together and then scatter to every corner of the Valley to do their morning chores.

Famous? Yes, he probably would be, as long as the mountain was called "Si" and people wondered why. More famous, perhaps, than Nils Bengston, who had once owned the biggest hop ranch in the world, a man who had been rich, and powerful, and lucky. Nothing had been named after Nils except those things he had managed to acquire for himself. Nothing has been named after me, either, Jeff added with a smile, nor is it likely to be. "That bachelor, owns all that timber up the North Fork, keeps pretty much to himself. . . ." That's the way folks described him now. Twenty, thirty years from now? He might be as queer a bird as his neighbor, "Lord Henry," who disappeared into the mountains for weeks at a time without a soul in Gold Mountain bothering to worry whether he'd come back.

The booming grounds were right around the bend. By the sound of it, the man had just brought down a load of logs. Jeff could hear the shouts of the bull puncher, directing the oxen with bursts of profanity that blew downriver like gusts of hot wind. Only Dave Riley was so proficient in the use of language the big patient animals understood.

Rounding the bend, Jeff saw that it was Dave, all right. The swearingest man in camp, and one of the most valuable. He was standing next to the lead ox, goad stick over his shoulder, letting his tone of voice and choice of words do the job for him. Twelve oxen were in the string, each pair joined by a heavy hardwood yoke and tied to the next pair by two chains, each link big enough to cover halfway the palm of a man's hand. There was sullen strength in the creatures. And beauty, Jeff thought, admiring the massive shoulders and the smooth, round, upsweeping horns.

Jeff called out, "Hallo, Dave," and nodded a greeting to the rest of the skidding crew. There were six of them altogether, including the grease monkey, a pimply-faced youth standing by with a bucket of dogfish oil in one hand and in the other a swabbing stick with which to grease the skids. Jeff rode in to speak to the bull puncher. It was time to meet the first problem.

The oxen were lined up parallel to the river, so that the logs they had dragged were in position to be rolled down the bank into the water. "Get them rolling jacks under her," Dave ordered, indicating the first log with a commanding gesture of his thumb. He strolled away from the bank and took up a position next to Jeff's horse. Eyes still on the skidding crew, he barked, "Morning, Jeff."

"Everything all right, Dave?"

Dave shifted his goad stick to the crook of one

elbow, slipped his thumbs under his galluses, spat sideways, and nodded. Shrugging his shoulder both upward and forward, he wiped his mouth carefully on his heavy woolen undershirt. It was chilly, but it would have to be downright cold before Dave would add anything to his uniform. His work pants, stagged two inches above his ankles so as to clear the tops of his boots, maintained a precarious position around his middle—courtesy of a pair of worn Irish-green "Police and Fireman's" suspenders. By Dave's lights, it was too warm for the wool shirts the other men were wearing, but Dave had never seen a day, winter or summer, when he would go without his hat. Like most loggers' hats, it was a dark felt with a battered crown and a brim turned down behind to keep fir needles and rain water from going down the back of his neck. Sweat and time had made it impossible to guess whether it was a dirty brown or a faded black, but once it had been a little "Boss Raw Edge," price five dollars, standard equipment in the woods just as much as the little cans of "Scandinavian dynamite" which every snuff-loving logger carried in his pocket.

The "dogger," with steel pinch bar and wooden maul, was prying out the iron rings, or "dogs," through which the drag chain ran, connecting one log of the turn with the next one.

"Easy there!" Dave blasted suddenly, his eye on the heavy cable that encircled the log. "Watch that choker chain!"

The log was free. With a cracking sound it rumbled down the bank into the river. Dave frowned as the log bounced on the water, then rose, rolled over gently, and came to rest against the boom. The crew turned to the next log.

Dave looked up at Jeff. "Yeh," he said, "everything's all right, now that I gave that new man to Mike."

"Tony Marko?"

"Yeh, Tony Marko," Dave agreed, sarcasm erupting in the emphasis he placed on the name.

Mike Jessup was the head faller; he and his crew would be working deep in the woods, at the far end of the skid road, cutting the giant firs and cedars which Dave and his men and oxen brought down to the river. Mike was as rough-cut and as seasoned as Dave. It was strange, Jeff thought, that Mike would have more patience with an apprentice than Dave would.

"What's the matter with Tony?" It was a question Jeff had put to himself many times since the day the young man had walked into camp and asked for a job. Jeff had needed men. Despite his resolution not to expand, early spring had caught him dreaming about cutting more, selling more. Even as he was protesting to men like Dave Riley and Mike Jessup "We'll keep this operation small. I don't want to own anything I can't get rid of in a week's time," he had let the dream become a fact, and when Tony appeared, the crews were short and Jeff was in no mood to be fussy about a man's qualifications.

"Know anything about logging?" he had asked, taking in Tony's youth and good looks and immediately thinking of him as a boy.

"I can learn."

Jeff had been struck by a fiery quality in the boy. A kind of repressed anger in his dark eyes and in his speech, as if he were trying to prove something and dared the world to stop him.

"Logging is heavy work," Jeff said. "More than that, it's dangerous, especially when you're green."

"I'm not afraid!"

He spoke as if Jeff had accused him of cowardice. "That's fine," Jeff said quietly, "but daring alone won't protect you. When you're matching yourself against a big tree, the fear of the Lord is often the beginning of wisdom."

"I told you I want a job."

His youth aroused Jeff's sympathy. "Where do you come from?" he asked in the same tone he would have used if Tony had been his own son. "Where did you work last?"

The boy stiffened and his dark eyes blazed. "Does that matter to you? I didn't claim to know anything about logging."

Jeff was startled. This was the kind of hands-off answer he would have expected from an older man; in fact, if Tony had been older, he would not have put such a question to him. But the impression persisted that this was a boy, not a man. A troubled boy. "You can talk to Dave Riley, the head bull puncher, when he comes in from the woods," Jeff had said, with just enough coldness to remind Tony who the owner was. "If he's willing to give you a try, you've got a job."

That had been eight, ten weeks earlier, and now

Dave was relieved to be rid of the boy and Jeff was still asking himself—What's the matter with Tony Marko?

"The trouble with Tony," Dave was saying, "is he wants to run before he learns to walk. He can't wait to be the best logger in the whole damn outfit. It don't matter to him that the rest of us were bucking and falling before he knew how to button his own pants."

"He's a boy."

Dave shrugged. "All right, then give him a boy's job. Let him grease skids, or be flunky for the cook. But he don't want that. He wants a man's job. Then let him act like a man."

"We're still short of help, or I'd throw him out. Maybe I will, anyway."

Dave spat carefully. "Let's see what Mike can make of him."

Jeff looked at Dave curiously. The bull puncher didn't want Tony on his own crew, but hard-bitten old bluenose that he was, he didn't like to see the kid lose his job. "I'll check with Mike," Jeff said, nodded good-bye and turned to follow the skid road into the woods.

So much for the problem of Tony Marko. Jeff set it aside and proceeded, reluctantly, to the bigger question. What was the future of the Smith Logging Company? Deliberately he rephrased the question, forcing himself to move closer to the heart of the matter. The real point was—what did he, Jeff Smith, want to make of the future? Was he to drift peacefully from year to year, containing the operation within the old-fashioned framework he had set up eight years before? Or was he to anticipate the future, let his dreams push him toward new equipment, new methods, new markets—and entanglements he did not want?

It was a longer ride to the spot where timber was being cut than it had been even a year or two before, and it would get longer, Jeff reflected. Twenty years earlier, settlers could cut virgin timber in their back yards. And they had, more to make room for gardens and pasture than for the value of the wood itself. Gradually the edge of heavy timber was receding. Uncle Si's homestead between town and the Smith holdings had once included a stand of the finest cedar. Now it was a spread of stump land, where a farmer from Nebraska was pasturing his herd of dairy cattle. The same gradual change was taking place on Jeff's own land. Each season, the area where the timber was cut was farther from the river, deeper in the woods. The skid road was longer, the effort to bring the logs out more costly.

Some day, Jeff thought, I'll build a railroad. It should connect up with the regular line into Seattle, so that logs could be shipped direct from Smith's camp on the North Fork of the Snoqualmie to the mills in the city. The little sawmill in Three Forks could handle everything they were cutting now. But, Jeff mused, if we enlarge our operation . . .

An old worry returned to shatter the vision. If he borrowed money, made improvements, exchanging his freedom for a bigger camp and a better operation—how long would the timber last?

Jeff had been nagged by this question almost from the day he bought ox teams and set up a real camp. If he expanded operations too fast, he might end up with a fine little railroad, some of the best logging equipment in the West, and nothing to work but a section and a half of worthless stumps. This fear had often driven him to calculating how much they were wasting. Every logged-over area was littered with logs left to rot on the ground, victims of their effort to get the big trees out. "No market for that small stuff," Mike Jessup, his head faller, replied whenever Jeff said it was a shame to discard so much wood.

The stumps of the big trees bothered Jeff, too. They stood higher than a house, and many of them were twelve to fourteen feet through. Enough timber in each to build a shed or to cover a house with good thick shakes.

The men laughed at Jeff when he expressed such thoughts.

"There's enough trees in Washington and Oregon to last until your great-grandchildren have great-grandchildren," Mike Jessup assured him.

But what then? Jeff had wanted to ask, but hadn't, because Mike would have put him down as a fool and a dreamer. Besides, he knew, as well as Mike and Dave Riley and the rest, that trees had to be cut high. Those big cedars and firs were wide at the base; their trunks curved for a good ten feet above the ground. If they were cut close to the ground, the wide, curving butt ends would catch on the skids and give both men and ox teams a fight to the death when they tried to drag them down the skid road. Some day, Jeff dreamed, we'll find some use for those stumps. Better yet, we'll figure out a better way to log.

He and Mike Jessup had already talked about the new donkey engines some of the camps were using, though Dave Riley scoffed at the idea that any such "tin can with a stovepipe" would replace his oxen. But the tin cans worked. Logs could be coupled to a cable and dragged by a donkey engine down the very skid road the oxen were now following. Jeff had heard of one operation where logs were hauled this way for more than a mile. Of course, if he built the railroad, track could be run into the woods right to the spot where they were cutting. . . . Move in a little farther, lay a little more track. Then the donkey engine would pull logs to a platform beside the track. You'd set up a gin pole, rig a line to it from another donkey, and let steam lift the logs onto the railroad cars. There would be no need for the long skid road, for booming logs into the river. There would be no need for men like Dave Riley, unless they could learn to do something else. . . .

Jeff shook his head and pushed the future out of his mind. He might dream, occasionally, of logging railroads and donkey engines. But pursue the dream—for what purpose? He rode on to the hole in the woods where Mike and his crew were cutting.

There were three men, besides Mike. They were working on a fir Jeff estimated at a glance might run some thirty feet around. The fallers had already cut deep chinks into the trees, some nine or ten feet off the ground. Into these holes they had wedged springboards; now they were balancing themselves on these precarious platforms, swinging their double-bitted axes to chop the undercut. Wood chips like thick, narrow shingles had piled up against the base of the tree, enough to fill a wagon. The damp air was pungent with the sweet-sharp odor of fresh sap.

This part of falling was where the science came in, for the placement and angle of the undercut would determine which way the tree would fall. A good faller liked to think he could drop a five-hundred-year-old tree as accurately as a skilled bass fisherman plunks a lure between lily pads. The job was almost done. After a few strokes more, the men would throw down their axes, pick up the ten-foot crosscut, and saw through the trunk. Then they'd know whether Mike Jessup's boast was right, that he would put his gold watch on the ground one inch from where the tree was to fall and drop that tree so his precious watch wouldn't suffer a scratch. He had never been challenged.

Jeff's glance traveled over the scene, seeking out the slim figure of Tony Marko. Shorty Andersen, the old Dane, Jim Cox, Finn Tiola and Mike. They were shy a man. But this was to have been Tony's first day with the falling crew. Where was he?

The undercut complete, the men stopped to rest. Mike Jessup jumped down and loped across the clearing.

Mike wasn't big, loud, or colorful, like Dave Riley. He stood less than six feet tall, he was

square, barrel-chested, strong as an ox and sometimes not much more talkative. If there was any
man in camp who might be tagged a "typical"
logger, that man was Mike. The irony of it was that
Mike was the only one who hadn't been a logger all
his life. He'd been a mule skinner for the U.S.
Army, and had spent years in Montana and Wyoming helping the government keep an eye out for
hostile Indians.

The usual crumpled felt hat protected his bald
head; a gray woolen undershirt protruded through
random holes in his outer shirt. The one adorn-
ment to his square face was a mustache, which was
blond, soft, and drooped over the ends of his
mouth. He pulled on one end of it as he looked up
at Jeff and said, "I took one man back to camp
already this morning."

"Tony Marko?"

Mike nodded. "He got in the way, limb knocked
him cold."

"How badly was he hurt?"

Mike shrugged. "Fool kid wanted to go back to
work the minute he come to. I wouldn't let him."

Jeff said grimly, "I'll bet he gave you an argument."

"Oh, sure," Mike agreed, "but I can handle
him."

"The minute you can't, you let me know."

"If I can't, I'll knock his block off, then I'll let
you know."

Jeff grinned. "So that's the way you feel about
him. Funny thing, that's the way he affects me,
too."

"Just sometimes," Mike replied. "Then other times, I think there's a lot to the kid, something worth working on. But he takes chances. That's his trouble. . . ."

So even Mike Jessup had been asking the question—What's the trouble with Tony Marko? Jeff sighed. "I'll talk to him. Everything all right, otherwise?"

Mike said dourly, "As long as she don't snow."

Jeff chuckled. Mike was plagued by memories of lonely Wyoming outposts in the wintertime, where buffalo-skin overcoats were regular Army issue even for the greenest private. "You know as well as I do we never have so much snow we can't log."

"I don't know about that 'never,' " Mike said, shaking his head. He wheeled around as if he were going to rejoin the crew, seemed to think better of it, and turned back. "Say, Jeff," he began, in a conversational tone, "say, everything going along all right down at your place?"

Jeff felt his face freeze. "Mind telling me what you're talking about?"

Mike was fifteen years older than Jeff. A trace of fatherly patience crept into his voice. "Look, you ought to know everybody in camp is talking about the girl and her baby. They heard Martin Kittinger drove her to your place, but that's all they know, so naturally they make up a whole lot more. Some of the tales are pretty wild."

"You can tell them . . ." Jeff stopped. His first impulse had been to explain the situation truthfully. His second was to protect the wide-eyed girl named Merrie Dooley Cowen, for he knew the truth would expose her to all kinds of sly or pitying looks. A seventeen-year-old girl had come looking for her husband, on the very eve of the birth of their child. She had been reduced to seeking out an old reprobate like Lord Henry, who had not expected her nor even known that she was married to his nephew. In desperation, she had turned to him, Jeff Smith, a bachelor, and was even now sleeping in his bed. . . . No, the truth was cruel. "You can tell them," Jeff said stiffly, "that my house guest happens to be a blood relative from Kentucky. Her husband is in the Army, just recently transferred from Seattle to Fort Keogh, Montana, and she is remaining with me until she is strong enough to rejoin him." The invention came easily, for Jeff disdained anyone, everyone, who pried into his personal affairs. "Furthermore," he went on, glaring at Mike, "you can tell them that Julie Bengston is my guest's constant attendant and if they have any more questions, they can submit them to me, privately, in the yard behind the bunkhouse!"

"Well," Mike said appreciatively, "well, I will that!" He wheeled around and in a slow, deliberate gait walked back to the base of the big tree.

And you can tell them, Jeff added silently, that some men don't fall in love until they're twenty-seven.

II

The buildings in the logging camp were made of
rough cedar slabs an inch thick, split by hand with
froe and wooden mallet, planed with a drawknife,
nailed together by men who were loggers, not car-
penters. There were two bunkhouses, a barn and
blacksmith's shop, the cookhouse which was
kitchen and dining room combined, and two small
shacks made of cedar slabs with the bark left on,
one the cook's domain and the other a combination
of business office and company store. Fresh cut,
the handmade lumber had a golden-red sheen to it,
but rain had beaten the color out. Now the walls
were gray as wet granite and the roofs were green
with moss.

The more weathered the buildings became, the
closer the surrounding forest seemed to be; it was
as if houses, like animals, could assume the colora-
tion of their surroundings. It had been hard work
to build the camp, for in those days Jeff had been
land poor and had had to do most of the construc-

tion himself. Despite this, it was a better camp than most. The buildings didn't leak, they had plank floors when many others had dirt, and there was a kept-up, civilized look to the place. But leave it untenanted, let the sword ferns grow and the alder sprout and the vicious devil's-club take root and spread—if you did that, Jeff had often reflected, it would be swallowed up. It was the abundant rain that made the trees grow big, but rain was the ally of weeds and brush and Douglas fir seedlings that grew in dense stands in any untended clearing. If I should sell out, Jeff thought to himself, and head for Canada or the Yukon or some other distant place as I've so often talked of doing, how long before this camp would disappear under the young forest brush? Five years, ten years, and you'd never find even the big bunkhouses unless you stumbled against them.

Jeff rode to the barn, turned his horse over to the big Norwegian who served as blacksmith and stableman, and headed for the bunkhouse and a chore he disliked—his talk with Tony Marko.

At night the bunkhouse was a warm and noisy place. There would be a hot fire in the little round-bellied wood stove in the center of the room. Twenty to twenty-five men would be lounging on the double-decked beds along the walls, or straddling the benches which formed a square around the stove. There would be card games, laughter, wet socks hanging from the rafters, and boots, dozens of pairs of boots, around the stove to dry.

But at midday the room was cold and the bunks deserted, except for the one in the far corner where Tony Marko lay with his face to the wall. Jeff stamped his feet, closed the door with a bang. Tony didn't move.

Jeff sensed that he was awake. "Tony?"

He lay still, but a muffled voice retorted, "What do you want?"

Jeff strode across the room. Rudeness was typical of the boy. But it was always pointless, a general striking out against the world rather than a personal affront. Like the snarl of a wounded animal, Jeff had thought several times, and could not bring himself to cut the boy down to size. "Turn over," he ordered. "I want to see where you were hit."

Tony didn't stir.

"I said, turn over." Jeff's voice had dropped to a terrible quietness.

Tony lay facing the wall. Jeff stood over him, waiting. His command hung in the air; invisible but strong, the boy's defiance came out to meet it. A minute passed in which neither of them spoke nor moved. Then Tony broke. With a quick, angry movement he rolled over and looked up into Jeff's face.

For Tony, this was defeat. For Jeff, it was no victory, for he had no desire to match himself against this young hothead. "Small scalp cut," he said, appraising Tony with an expert but impersonal eye. "Bad bruise on your forehead. Your head aches?"

"Yes."

"I should think it would." Jeff studied Tony's face. It was too pale; there were hollows around the dark eyes, as if he had not been sleeping well. "Feel feverish?"

Tony answered brusquely, "No."

"I could take you to Gold Mountain on the chance of finding Doc Adams, but I think a four-mile ride in a wagon would do you more harm than the doctor would do you good. You stay right here."

"What else can I do?"

It was an irritating reply. The boy was suffering with some inner conflict, made worse, probably, by this morning's failure in the woods. But he wasn't going to bear it alone. He was going to throw it at Jeff, at the world. Jeff said coldly, "What else can you do? You can pack up whatever you came with and move on."

Tony tried to get up. Jeff watched silently, torn between sympathy and resentment, as the boy pushed himself to a sitting position, grimaced with pain, gave up, and lay back slowly, one hand shading his eyes. "I'm staying," he said weakly.

He's a troublemaker, this is the time to get rid of him—the thought flashed across Jeff's mind. He rejected it. Tony was one of fifty men, the greenest and least important of the lot. It was ridiculous to treat him as if he were dangerous. "All right. But while you're lying here, I'd like you to get something into your head. You aren't a good logger when you take chances."

Bruised and cut as he was, Tony spat back, "It's my life, not yours."

"If that were true," Jeff said curtly, "I wouldn't be wasting my breath on you. But it isn't. When you take a risk, you're creating danger, not only for yourself but for every other man on the crew. That isn't fair. You've got to think of the others."

Tony was silent.

Jeff looked down at him thoughtfully. "Tony," he said finally, "do you really want to be a logger?" He asked on impulse, half expecting Tony to ignore the question. Tony's reaction surprised him.

His hands dropped from his face, he looked up at Jeff squarely. In a voice thick with emotion he said, "I'm going to have my own logging company. It's going to be one of the biggest in the state."

Dave Riley's comment—he wants to run before he has learned to walk—came back to Jeff, along with many observations of his own. He didn't voice them because they were sensible, and Tony's goal was not. If another young man, even a man who knew as little about logging as Tony, had said, "I'm going to own one of the biggest logging outfits in Washington," without the fanatic ring that was in Tony's voice or the blank, too-bright look in Tony's eyes, he would not sound so—Jeff thought uneasily, so crazy. Nils Bengston had not been much older than Tony when he made up his mind to own the biggest hop ranch in the world. But Nils was a different sort of man. If he had talked wild, he had dealt practically. He looked reality in the face. Tony didn't. Perhaps, Jeff thought, Tony can't.

"I'll come back later," he said quietly, and left the bunkhouse.

III

It was the end of the day. The men had come in from the woods, rinsed dirt, sawdust and sweat from their arms and faces, stomped into the cookhouse as the cook banged an empty dishpan with a big spoon and bellowed, in best logging-camp tradition, "Come and get it while it's hot, keep a comin', don't stop!"

An intense quiet fell in the dining room as the men ate. Nothing interrupted the ritual—no conversation, no laughter, only the thump of crockery set down heavily on a wood table and an occasional demand for the beans. Warmed and well fed, the men relaxed, unbuttoned the top button of their trousers, and strolled back toward the bunkhouse.

Dave Riley and Mike Jessup, seated at either side of Jeff, were the last to leave the table.

Dave went through the preliminaries slowly, pushing the bench back, yawning, lifting both arms toward the ceiling in a mighty stretch.

"What's this I hear," he asked lazily, "about how we're going to quit logging with oxen?"

Jeff's mind had been a long ways from logging. It had been on Merrie; at this time of day, when he would soon be riding back to his cabin, his thoughts were full of her. "Just what have you heard?"

Dave shrugged, looked up at the ceiling. "What you told me yourself. A lot of talk, some time back, about big changes."

Jeff grinned. "That's what it was, just talk."

"You're keeping the oxen?" the bull puncher asked, all too casually. "Not bringing in horses?"

Jeff shook his head. "I'm not changing anything."

Dave relaxed his scrutiny of the ceiling. "That's all right then. You keep the bulls. Horses eat too much for the strength they get from it. An ox is good for you, live or dead."

Jeff knew what he meant. If a horse broke his leg, you shot him and accepted a total loss. But an injured ox was meat on the hoof; if you had to shoot him, you were putting food on the table. One of the loggers' standard jokes was to exclaim, when the beef roast was served, "If I break another tooth on another consarn yoke buckle, I'm going to run that cook right outa camp!"

"To tell you the truth, Dave, if I ever replace the oxen, it would be with donkey engines."

Dave looked at him accusingly. "You just said you're not changing anything."

"I meant it." Jeff smiled at the bull puncher's anxious red face. "If you hear talk from me about building a bigger camp, or hiring more men, or buying new equipment, don't pay it any heed. You know as well as I do that two hours later I'll forget everything I said."

Mike Jessup looked at him shrewdly. "Jeff, it might be the thing to do, to make this into a real camp."

"It might be."

"Then what are you waiting for?"

Jeff's long fingers pulled thoughtfully at his lower lip. "I don't know, Mike," he said slowly. "I guess I'm waiting to *want* to do it."

The three men fell silent. The subject was of interest to them all. There was much more to be said about it, but Jeff had driven it into a dead end.

Dave got nosily to his feet. "Well, I'm ready for my bunk. You staying in camp tonight, Jeff?"

It was a natural question, for until Merrie's arrival Jeff often slept in the shack which served as his office. Tonight the query seemed to have an edge to it. Jeff stood up. "I'm going back to my cabin," he said, looking Dave squarely in the eye.

Dave shrugged. "Sure."

Mike Jessup rose and began to follow Dave out of the dining room.

Jeff said curtly, "Hold up, Mike."

Mike halted and turned back.

"You remember what I asked you to tell the men?"

Mike frowned. "I was going to tell the men? . . . What was I going to tell them, Jeff?"

"About the girl who's staying in my cabin."

Mike's weathered face showed honest astonishment. "I didn't know you was serious."

"I was."

"Now look, Jeff . . ." Mike's gesture expressed both disbelief and a desire to appease. "You didn't have to take what I said to heart. The men have been talking a little. Don't they always? They got to have something to do besides play cards."

"You tell them what I said," Jeff repeated, "and just as close to what I said as you can remember."

Mike blinked. "Sure, I remember."

"All right," Jeff said gruffly, "go and tell them now."

Now, at last, the day was really over, and he could go home. Home . . . Since the death of his parents, Jeff had never thought of his homestead cabin as home. It was a retreat, a shelter. But a home? He was surprised that the word had come to his mind.

He started toward the door, stopped. There was one more thing he had to do before he could leave camp.

He sat down, and waited. The cook's flunky came out from the kitchen, a lard bucket of hot soapy water in hand. He cleared away the dishes, scrubbed the tables, returned to the kitchen and came back with a broom. He swept absent-mindedly, throwing curious glances in Jeff's direction. Their eyes met. The flunky squirmed under Jeff's look, muttered, "Good night, Mr. Smith," and fled to the kitchen.

Fifteen minutes had passed. . . . Jeff rose, pushed back his empty coffee cup and walked across the yard to the bunkhouse.

It was noisy inside. Voices, laughter, the thudding sound of cord wood being fed into the stove, of heavy boots dropped to the floor. Jeff opened the door.

Every sound broke off, every movement was suspended. The men in their bunks lay still, eyes on Jeff. Others were on the benches around the stove. One man was doing his washing in a kerosene tin, another was whittling, a third was shuffling a deck of cards, a fourth was stoking the stove. All were frozen into position, as still and voiceless as the underwear and socks hanging from the rafters overhead. The room smelled of wood smoke and steamy wet woolens, and of the wicks burning in pots of dogfish oil.

Jeff sought out Mike Jessup. He was standing near his own bunk at the opposite side of the room. "Mike?"

Mike stepped forward. "Yes, Jeff?"

"You give everyone here the message I sent?"

Mike nodded. "Sure did."

Jeff looked around the room, his eyes traveling slowly from one man to another. No one moved, but their thoughts were on their faces. They were curious, they were watchful, but more than that, they were surprised. Jeff saw that Mike Jessup was surprised, too. And no wonder, Jeff thought. Why am I so intense about this? What am I trying to prove?

"O.K.," he said softly, "then there's nobody here with some questions they want answered?"

The silence continued unbroken. Eyes blinked, or turned to peer sideways at the next man, but no one spoke. Jeff wheeled around abruptly, went out, and closed the bunkhouse door with a bang.

IV

Nils had come to take Merrie, Julie and the baby to the hotel. It had been agreed long since that Merrie was to stay out the winter at Bengstons' Inn. Jeff himself had agreed that it was the sensible plan, had helped to persuade Merrie that it was the thing to do. But now, at the actual moment of her departure, he was filled by a sense of desolation.

He glanced at the baby, sleeping in the crib he had fashioned. At the cookstove and kitchen table, both laden with foods only a woman would cook. At the open bedroom door, through which he could see Merrie and Julie clearing out the chest of drawers, filling the wicker valises with square, neat piles of feminine belongings.

Merrie ran past him, intent on some chore.

"Take your time," Jeff said, so curtly Merrie stopped in her headlong rush and turned back to look at him. What have I done wrong?—he could see the question on her face. The mouth, quivering on the edge of a smile, but not sure. The wide, sea-green eyes, fixed solemnly on his face.

"I mean, Nils isn't in a hurry," Jeff said quickly, ashamed of worrying her. "And you haven't been up and about for very long."

Her smile broke through. "Oh, is that all?" she said. "I feel fine. I could run all the way to the hotel." Laughing, she disappeared into the bedroom.

Jeff had hoped Merrie wouldn't notice his mood. Now he was pained because she hadn't.

It was only a few minutes' work to load into the rig everything Merrie had brought with her to the Snoqualmie Valley and everything she had acquired since. Jeff glanced at the meager pile of possessions and hurriedly turned away; in such a pathetic collection Merrie's aloneness was cruelly revealed, it didn't seem fair to look at it.

Yet Merrie herself was cheerful as her name. She bustled around the cabin in an activity she called "setting things to rights." The tea-kettle at the back of the stove, though Jeff had always left it on the hearth. The sugar in a bowl on the table, though Jeff had always stored it in a can on the shelf. It hadn't taken her long, Jeff reflected, to replace his bachelor habits with her own not quite efficient notions of the way things ought to be. He smiled at her, and she responded instantly. But in an absent-minded way, as if he had interrupted her when she was counting the kernels of wheat in a feed bin. Her face was flushed, a few locks of shiny chestnut-colored hair had pulled loose from the blue ribbon and fell across her cheek. "Well," she breathed, hands on her hips, "I think everything is . . ."

"Set to rights," Jeff said with her.

Merrie laughed. "Julie has the baby, Nils took out the cradle . . ."

"*I* took out the cradle," Jeff corrected. "The grips are in the buggy, everything else has been loaded in, you're ready to go."

"I'm ready to go," Merrie repeated. But she didn't move. Her hands slid from the housewifely pose on her hips and fell helplessly to her sides. Her eyes lost their twinkling gaiety and moved solemnly about the room from one object to another. "We must get back to the hotel," she said, not looking at Jeff.

Jeff nodded. Back to the hotel . . . She had never once been in the hotel, but here she was, already eager for the burden of a new responsibility. "Plenty of time," Jeff said.

"Oh, but there are always a lot of chores in the evening." It sounded like a mother's patient explanation to a slow-witted child. But still she didn't take a step toward the front door.

Jeff looked at her thoughtfully. "Merrie," he said, "what is it you wanted to tell me?"

The worry line between her eyebrows disappeared and she uttered a deep, trembling sigh. "About my husband. I told you I would. I never did."

Jeff said hurriedly, "There's no need to."

"Yes, there is," Merrie said earnestly. "I came out of nowhere, you took me in. . . ."

"You are under no obligation to explain anything!" In his own ears Jeff's voice sounded like that of his father when he had felt it necessary to remind someone that he was Harvey Barrington

Smith from Kentucky. "I mean," Jeff added more softly, "that I'm glad if I could help you, and I would have helped you whoever, or whatever, your husband might be. You don't owe me anything, not even an explanation." Jeff reflected that being a watered-down Southern gentleman was a burdensome duty at times. What silliness made him think it *was* his duty? Why refuse to let Merrie tell him about her husband, when there was nothing he wanted more to hear?

"I think he must be in Gilman," Merrie said so quickly the words ran together. "He left me to go to Gilman, to work in the coal mines. I should have stayed longer, and really looked for him. But I didn't. When the man in the coal-mine office told me he'd never worked there, I gave up. Maybe, if I'd tried harder . . ."

The words were pouring out of her like a confession. "There's no reason to blame yourself," Jeff said quickly.

"But I do," Merrie said, her voice dropping, "I really do. Maybe I could have found him. It was the way I felt that made me hurry away. I knew the baby was coming. I kept thinking over and over, I've got to get home, and the nearest thing to home I could imagine was with my husband's uncle." She stopped, her face flushed. A wistful smile broke through her earnestness. "I guess that was pretty silly, wasn't it?"

Jeff took her gently by the shoulders. "You did everything that you could," he said. "No one else would have done as well."

"Jim *might* have been going by another name,"

Merrie said. "He might even . . ." Her voice broke off, she swallowed hard, and finished shakily, "Might have lied to me in his letter, about where he was working. But he was in Gilman, because that's where his letter had been mailed."

It was hard for her to say such things, Jeff could see, though he could not be sure what element of the situation hurt her most. The fact that her husband had abandoned her? Her conviction that she should have found him? A feeling of disloyalty . . . Jeff shook his head. "Look," he said, his hands tightening ever so slightly on Merrie's shoulders, "the worst medicine in the world is looking back."

"If I only *knew*."

Jeff looked into her face, searching for the truth about her feelings for her husband. No doubt that her concern was genuine, but was it any different from her compassion for any human being she perceived to be in some kind of trouble? She was turning to him for reassurance, clearly believing that he, too, was worried about Jim's disappearance. If she knew he hoped Jim Cowen would stay lost forever? That his hands, resting on her shoulders in what pretended to be an affectionate older brother's way of comforting her, were actually clinging to her, feeling her warmth and softness, reminding him that he hadn't touched her since he carried her into the cabin the day Kittinger left her at his door?

"Brother Bill is about to head for Gilman," he said at last. "It was a regular stop on his circuit before he decided to take the church in Gold Mountain, and he is holding services there until they find someone to take his place. Bill knows everyone in Gilman. I'll ask him to see what he can find out."

"Would he do it?" she asked. "Would it be too much to ask?"

Jeff shook his head. "Certainly not. Brother Bill is very much interested in you. In fact, he admires you. I know he'd be more than willing to help you locate your husband."

She repeated softly, "If I only knew . . ."

"Don't fret," Jeff said. "We'll find him for you."

Merrie smiled wistfully. "You're being very gentlemanly, pretending it's a misunderstanding, nothing more. Jeff, the truth is, my husband left me deliberately."

"Something could have happened to him."

"Yes," she said, "for a while I almost believed that. But I know, and you know, that if he had been badly hurt, or killed, I'd have heard of it."

"Not necessarily."

"But probably." Merrie's face was pale, her voice earnest as a child's. "It doesn't help me to pretend. Jim went off without me, he didn't come back. Finding him won't change that."

Jeff said brusquely, "Then why do you want to find him?"

"Because . . ." She shook her head, looked down, whispered, "Because he might—need me."

"Need you," Jeff exploded. "What right . . ." He dropped his hands from her shoulders and walked away from her. He was getting altogether too involved in matters which didn't concern him.

Where was the feeling of detachment he always prized? He changed the subject. "Brother Bill understood you wanted the christening to follow the regular service this coming Sunday."

Merrie answered in a small voice, "Yes, I do."

Instantly Jeff was ashamed of his outburst. He turned back to her, and said gently, "Then you'll have to make up your mind about the baby's name."

"Yes."

She looked up at him helplessly. Moments passed.

"Merrie, I didn't mean you must decide right now."

Her chin lifted. "I have decided," she said firmly. "I am going to name my baby Joseph, after my father."

Jeff did not know what battle had ended with this decision, but he sensed that in some way her husband Jim was involved and that Merrie had gathered, with great pain, enough strength to defy him.

He was on the edge of territory he had no right to invade. A Southern gentleman, he reminded himself, even a watered-down Southern gentleman who was beginning to dislike the part, would not press her further. He put an arm around her, turned her toward the door, and said, "Remember those evening chores at the hotel. I'll bet the Bengston boys are driving their mother crazy, asking when you're going to get there." Handing back her privacy was like helping her into a coat.

Merrie smiled. "Thank you, Jeff. You're as kind as my Uncle Mike."

It was her greatest compliment. Jeff wished fervently that it hadn't made his heart sink. He opened the cabin door, and together they walked down the path to the road. All the way Jeff was thinking—she is confused, she doesn't know what her feelings for her husband are. But I do. I hate him. May the good Lord see to it that I never have to meet him face to face.

5

ANOTHER RIDE IN a wagon. Another change, wrenching her from the familiar and thrusting her into the unknown . . . When Nils Bengston slapped the reins over the horse's rump and the buggy rolled forward, Merrie could not bear to look back. She had lived in Jeff Smith's cabin for a scant three weeks, but leaving it, she felt homeless and uprooted.

"Nice day for a drive," Nils suggested amiably.

Merrie huddled over the baby in her arms. "Yes, nice day . . ." But she looked straight ahead.

When the rutted wagon road turned north along the riverbank, she knew the cabin must be out of sight. Inexplicably she felt better. She even turned slightly to look back at the mountain, secure in her knowledge that the wound of loneliness would not be reopened by a last glimpse of Jeff's familiar figure.

Slowly the lost feeling receded. When Nils said,

"Sure is lucky for us that you came along. Work at the hotel is getting to be too much for Julie and Katherine . . ." the sun broke through. "Don't you worry," Merrie reassured the big man. "I'll take care of things." After that, she could hardly wait to reach the Inn.

Bengstons' Inn was built on high ground above the river, in a clearing just below the spot where the three forks met to form the Snoqualmie. It stood three stories high. Round turrets rose above the four corners of the building, each topped by an ornately carved cupola and each cupola different from the others. Glass windows had been a luxury when the Inn was built, but the first-floor windows at Bengstons' were big as doors and were framed by leaded panes of many-colored glass.

Merrie's eyes widened as the carved filigree and wrought iron and colored glass came clearly into view. "It's so fancy!"

"Biggest, best, most expensive house in the state of Washington," Nils admitted.

As they pulled into the courtyard, two little boys as blond as Nils spilled out of the back door and raced toward the buggy. Katherine Bengston and Julie followed.

"Is that the girl who's going to take care of us, Mama, is that the girl?" the larger towhead sang as his smaller brother danced around him chanting, "New baby, new baby." Katherine tried to hush them, Julie and Nils were laughing. To Merrie, the yard seemed to be full of people all talking at once. Her throat tightened in a sudden excess of happiness. She was down from the wagon before anyone could reach out to help her.

The sturdy, pink-faced Bengstons looked like small Bruners, Aunt Sal and Uncle Mike's children whom she had mothered for so long. Merrie held the baby Joseph tightly in one arm, with the other drew both little boys against her shoulder.

In the weeks that followed, Merrie found in the hotel almost everything she needed to be happy. She was with people, often a good many people, whose wants she could fulfill. There were the children to care for, her own baby and the Bengston boys. With much affection and very little system, Merrie marshaled them through each day. She scrubbed them until they were pink and shining. She knit sweaters for them, which were warm although they didn't fit. She told them stories, scolded them, gave them chores to do. From breakfast until bedtime they followed her, or sat in her lap, or if this space was already occupied, leaned against her.

The children saw nothing unusual in the fact that baby Joseph seemed to have no father. Guests of the hotel, the drummers, the cattlemen and loggers, the sportsmen from Seattle, accepted her just as the children did. As for the Bengstons themselves—Merrie felt sure they had come to some conclusion about Jim which made it unnecessary to question her. They didn't say what it was, and Merrie was grateful to them.

During the day it wasn't hard to put thoughts of Jim out of her mind. Children to be fed, clothes to be washed, butter to be churned, coffee to be roasted. Nut meats for Saturday's baking, patches for Nils' overalls, cloth to cover the fresh hoops of cheese. The faster her hands moved, the more peaceful her mind.

But at night, when she must reluctantly set down the last chore, and shivering with awareness of the loneliness to come, slowly climb the stairs to her room . . . Then Jim returned in a rush. Sometimes she would undress quickly, praying that the pleasant drowsiness she had felt downstairs would not wear off before she fell asleep. Or she would prepare herself for bed with painstaking care, performing each step of the pointless ritual with the same fierce concentration she poured into the chores of the day. But it was no use. Whatever her plan to trick herself into sleep, she would lie in bed for an hour or more, her body aching with fatigue, her eyes wide open. From all corners of the dark room, memories of Jim came forward, leering and gesticulating, piercing the wall of forgetfulness she had been building up during the day.

She saw him, she heard him, she felt him. She lay in bed, stiff and cold, begging him to go away.

Where was he, when would she see him again? If he sought and found her, if she found him, what then? His excuses would be no weaker than those she had accepted before. He could not shame her more than he already had, and she had never turned against him. But now there was Joseph. Jim's child, to be sure, but a child he had not wanted. If Jim returned . . .

At last she would fall asleep. And then would come the dream. . . . Jim had come back. He was in the hotel. She must take Joseph and hide, but she could not find him. She ran from one room to another, afraid to call out, for Jim would hear. Every room was empty. Cold, brilliantly lighted, empty. The sound of Jim's footsteps grew louder. She ran from the first floor to the second, from the second to the third. All at once, she was in a tiny room under one of the cupolas, and the baby was in her arms. She struggled to lock the door. But there was no lock. Even the doorknob was gone, the door hung uselessly on rusty hinges. Behind her a cold wind blew through an open window, the door banged rhythmically, in time with the louder and louder sound of Jim's steps. She hugged the baby to her, crouched against the wall, the door opened, Jim was in the room. . . .

There the nightmare ended. She would sit up in bed, trembling violently, searching the shadows for Jim. Half awake, she would throw back the covers and stumble across the room to Joseph's cradle. Reality returned when she touched him. The sound of his breathing, the warmth of his body, drove back the dream. Truly exhausted, she would return to her bed, lie down, turn her face to the wall, and sleep.

II

As the winter set in, travelers were few and the rooms at the Inn were frequently empty. "This is the time of year we catch our wind," Nils said. "Snow's too deep for anyone to come through the Pass, so we won't see any cattlemen from the east side for a while. Most drummers have finished their rounds for the year and won't be back till spring. Local people staying closer to home. Slow down. You couldn't hunt for work any harder if it was made of gold."

It was true. Winter had thinned the ranks of people Merrie could do something for, but she made up for it by doubling her attentions to those who remained. A hunter from Seattle remarked at dinner that he liked crullers with his breakfast. Merrie was in the kitchen until midnight, frying enough doughnuts to feed the Valley. A salesman who couldn't get anyone else in the hotel to listen to him boast about his successes found in Merrie a wide-eyed, believing audience. If a hotel guest had holes in his socks, Merrie mended them, reinforcing the holes so thoroughly the patches bulged out like welts.

Nils asked wryly, "What do you think you're running, Merrie, a hotel or an orphanage? You treat our guests like kids. Someday one of them is going to forget himself and treat you like a woman."

The incident of the seed salesman proved him right.

Most drummers made the rounds of the Valley once or twice a year, in the early spring and in the fall. Egon Bradshaw was new in the area and two months late in completing his calls. He was a young man, he talked rapidly, strutted when he walked, and dressed like a dandy. In the downstairs hallway, his fast gait invariably slowed to a stop when he passed the big gilt-framed mirror opposite the staircase. He threw several quick sideways glances at his reflection, gave his fine brocade vest a pat or two, then cleared his throat and hurried on.

Drummer Bradshaw was the first to ignore the wide gold wedding band on Merrie's finger. He stared at her throughout his first meal in the hotel and afterward followed her into the kitchen. Katherine and Julie were in the room, but their presence didn't deter him.

"I'll bet you don't get out much," he said to Merrie, and then, with many references to what the girls thought of him in Seattle, he outlined the ways in which he was going to keep her from being bored while he was in the Valley. To begin with, there was a dance in Gold Mountain tonight. . . .

Merrie washed dishes in frantic haste, her head bent over the sink. She should be indignant, but his boasting sounded pathetic. She should say, "Mr.

Bradshaw, I am married . . ." but she recoiled from the questions, spoken or unspoken, which logically followed such a reply. Married? To whom? How is a man to know you are someone's wife if there's no sign of a husband?

"Well, how about it? Don't you like to dance?"

She loved to dance. She hadn't for months. No, it was years. Not since the barn dance when dark-eyed Chris Brusik had lifted her off the floor in the giddy turns of a polka and Uncle Mike had scolded her for paying less attention to blond John Anderson. This man reminded her of Chris. Or did she imagine it simply because he talked of dancing? Without looking up, Merrie said, "No, I don't care for dancing."

"I don't believe it," the drummer retorted. "Why, you just about dance when you walk. What's the matter, won't the boss let you have a night out?"

This question was directed at Katherine. Merrie looked up and their glances met. "Tomorrow is going to be a very busy day," Merrie said, her eyes begging Katherine's help.

"Yes, it is," Katherine agreed with a vigorous nod. "However . . ." She paused, and then said brightly, "You may be mistaken, Mr. Bradshaw. Maybe the boss *would* let her have a night out. We just won't know 'til we ask, will we?" She wiggled her index finger in Merrie's direction. "Come along, Merrie. He's in the sitting room going over the ledger."

In muted voices, Katherine, Nils, and Merrie debated the issue of the drummer's invitation. Katherine held that Merrie should get out and meet people. Nils retorted that anyone worth meeting would be bound to patronize Bengstons' Hotel. Merrie admitted that she loved to dance but she was married, and Nils, with a wink at Katherine, asked what being married had to do with the two step.

At length the door to the kitchen opened and Egon Bradshaw's head appeared. "I give you five more minutes to make up your mind, whichever one of you is doing the deciding. There's another girl that's holding her breath waiting for me to ask *her*."

Merrie said solemnly, "Thank you very much for your invitation, Mr. Bradshaw. We accept with pleasure."

"We do?" The drummer's voice was a startled squeak.

"Nice of you to ask," Nils boomed. "I'll go harness up while the ladies get their dancing shoes."

"I see," Bradshaw murmured, nodding thoughtfully. "Yes, I see. Just one little question, if I may. Do I get to sit next to Merrie or is she going to ride up front with you?"

"She's going to ride up front with *you*, Bradshaw. You're driving. Me and Katherine are riding in the back of the rig where we can keep an eye on you without getting a crook in our necks."

"And how about at the dance?"

"At the dance?" Nils repeated as if the smaller man had introduced an issue totally foreign to the subject at hand. "Oh, you don't have to worry none about the dance. Not as long as you stay inside the hall."

III

As Nils often said, Merrie wouldn't look any harder for work if it were made of gold. She was as much afraid of being idle during the day as she was of being alone at night. So when Katherine became ill, Merrie embraced the emergency as if Nils and the doctor were bystanders.

"Nothing really serious," white-haired Doc Adams from Gold Mountain decided. "But she's going to need a lot of nursing care and a lot of rest. It's a pity, we ought to have a hospital in Gold Mountain. Of course, I could take her down to Gilman."

Nils looked troubled but Merrie spoke up promptly, "Katherine would be unhappy in the Gilman hospital. She'd get well much faster if she stayed right here at home. I'll take care of her."

The doctor looked at her curiously. "You ever had any nursing experience?"

"I took care of my aunt when her youngest children were born and I took care of all the children. This last summer I worked at Providence Hospital.''

''As a nurse?''

Merrie's confidence was unshaken. ''Not a regular nurse. But I can do everything anyone else could do for Katherine.''

The doctor smiled and turned to Nils. ''Well, what do you think?''

Nils ran both hands through his mane of sun-streaked hair. ''It's true, Kate would bawl me out for the rest of my life if I let you take her to Gilman. And Merrie, here, is a working fool.''

''Fine,'' Merrie said instantly. ''Now, Nils, you're to move out of your bedroom. I'll fix up the north room for you. Julie, run get me some linen. Dr. Adams, you wait right here for a moment while I get paper and pencil. I'm going to write down everything I'm to do for Katherine. Nils, I'll take over Katherine's work, like ordering for the hotel. If you'll just let me know whenever you're driving to town, so I can figure out what supplies we need .''

''Oh, Lord,'' Nils said, ''oh, Lord . . .'' He folded his arms across his chest, threw back his big blond head, and burst out laughing. ''One strong-minded female in the house wasn't enough for me,'' he exploded, ''I had to go out and rope another one!''

Merrie's nursing care was unrelenting. Though she did not relinquish any of her other chores, she was on duty in the sickroom all day and most of the night. Dr. Adams' first skepticism faded quickly. After his second visit to the Inn, he said, ''Merrie,

I hope you won't be too disappointed when Katherine gets well."

Merrie was disconcerted. "You're teasing me."

"No," the old doctor said, "I'm not at all. I'm expressing admiration, in the sour way an old man does."

Katherine was strong enough to be sitting up in a kitchen chair the day two loggers from Jeff Smith's camp came to the Inn. Nils had driven the team to Gold Mountain for a load of supplies and so it was Merrie who rented them a room.

The smaller of the two gave his name as Jack McChesney. The larger man, his face as red as his friend's, was Red McArvan.

"You're from the Smith camp," Merrie said eagerly. She had thought of Jeff often; in this country of new sights and strange people, he seemed like kinfolk. "How is Jeff? It's been a long time since he came by this way."

- The two Irishmen seemed impatient with the question. "He's same as ever. Works all day, reads all night, keeps to himself." The big logger dropped his arm around the shorter man. "Come on, old friend, let's get up to our room." As loving as brothers after a long separation, they walked up the stairs.

In the kitchen, Katherine frowned when Merrie told her of the new arrivals. "McChesney, McArvan," she repeated. "Loggers from Jeff's camp? But this is Friday."

"Is there something wrong? Shouldn't I have given them a room?"

"Yes, of course, you should. But Friday. Strange they aren't working . . ."

All morning the hotel was as peaceful as a mountain lake on a hot day. The only guests were the two loggers, and they might have been sleeping for all the sound they made. Katherine was rocking contentedly in the corner of the kitchen, the children playing at her feet. Julie was doing the outside chores, and Merrie was flying from sink to table to cupboard in an effort to do three or four things at the same time.

All at once the stillness was shattered by shouts from upstairs.

Katherine and Merrie flew startled looks at each other. Merrie dropped the knife she had been sharpening. Katherine stood up. One behind the other, they tiptoed down the corridor to the foot of the wide, curving staircase which led to the hotel rooms on the second floor.

"I'll kill you, Mac, I'll kill you!" This was the voice of the smaller man, McChesney.

"Like to try it, Shorty?" This was McArvan.

Katherine's small face was pale. "They've been drinking," she said weakly, the covey of freckles across her nose suddenly standing out sharply against her white skin.

Merrie had no idea what to do, but Katherine's helplessness made her feel wise and self-possessed. "I'll look," she whispered. "You go back to the kitchen," and she advanced resolutely up the stairs.

A torrent of sound broke as she reached the top. The two men were in the middle of the hallway, facing each other like stupefied but angry bulls. McArvan leaned over McChesney as if poised to fall forward and crush him. McChesney, arms stiff and fists clenched, peered up furiously into McArvan's face.

Neither of them saw Merrie approach. With two of them shouting simultaneously, there wasn't a chance that either man could make sense of what the other was saying. Nevertheless, each seemed to understand that every word he drowned out with an insult of his own, was an insult just as vile.

"See here," Merrie began confidently, "you two were friends a few hours ago. If you'll quiet down . . ."

The two of them became aware of her. The double torrent of invective halted as they slowly turned their heads.

Merrie took heart. "I'm sure you can settle your differences some other way."

Their red eyes rested on her groggily. They shook their heads in mutual agreement that she wasn't there. Before she could draw breath for another peacemaking effort, they were at each other again, louder, more profane than before.

"Merrie, come down!" Katherine's anxious voice reached her through the tumult. Merrie turned to see that Nils' wife was halfway up the stairs.

Merrie ran down. "You go back and stay with the children," she commanded, slipping an arm around Katherine and helping her down the steps and along the lower corridor to the kitchen. Katherine sank into a chair. "I wish Nils were here," she said with a wan smile, "or that I were feeling like myself—one of the two."

"Don't you worry," Merrie told her, with a

show of assurance that was somewhat less than sincere.

"They're awfully strong," Katherine said, "and awfully drunk. Don't do something foolish."

"I won't," Merrie replied, though she had no idea what she would do. With Katherine and the two children secure, she hurried back to the front hall, just in time to see the two loggers stumbling down the stairs with pistols in their hands.

"Settle it, settle it!" McChesney was crying, and McArvan was echoing him with even louder boasts.

Their faces were red and wild with anger. At the foot of the stairs, they hesitated, leaning on each other for support. As if trained to move in unison, they turned toward Merrie and pointed the guns at her.

"Duel," McArvan announced thickly. "Kill him."

"Kill *me*!" the smaller man hooted. "I'll kill *him*!"

Merrie backed away, bolted down the hallway and through the door into the kitchen. Katherine was guarding a corner of the room, Joseph in his cradle and both little Bengston boys behind her.

"I think they're going to kill each other," Merrie said helplessly. With Katherine and the children here, there was only one person unaccounted for. "They'll start shooting when they go outside. I've got to find Julie."

"I *wish* I felt more like myself," Katherine repeated, with an impatient movement remarkably like stamping her foot. Merrie ran out the back door and down the steps to the barnyard. "Julie! Julie, come here quickly!"

The girl's short, square figure appeared in the open door of the stable. A man followed her into the barnyard. Merrie caught her breath; it was Jeff Smith.

She felt weak with relief. "Two men in the hotel are going to shoot at each other," she called as Jeff loped across the barnyard. "Julie, run for the house, quick!"

"They've got guns," Merrie cried, the words falling over each other. "Right this minute they're probably going out the front door. They're going to have a duel."

"In that case," Jeff said quietly, "let's *all* of us run for the kitchen."

"We've got to stop them!"

"Yes," Jeff agreed calmly, "but we can't do it at the back door if they're going out the front." He put a firm hand on Merrie's arm and hurried her into the house.

"Jeff," Merrie breathed, "it's two men from your camp. Jack McChesney and Red McArvan."

Jeff nodded. "I know. That's why I'm here. I've been looking for them."

By now he had steered her into the kitchen. "Hello, Katherine," he said with the touch of formality in his manner which set him apart in Merrie's mind from every other man she had known. "You're looking very well."

"Jeff, they're going to *duel*," Merrie broke in excitedly. "*Now!*"

"So this time it's a duel, eh?"

He was entirely too detached to suit Merrie. "We've got to keep them from fighting!"

Jeff shook his head. "I don't think so. I believe it's much wiser to let them go ahead."

Merrie was indignant. Jeff, whom she remembered as the gentlest man she'd ever known . . . "I didn't think *you* would stand back and let two people get killed!"

Jeff appeared to be amused rather than hurt. "Let's think it through," he said. Though she stiffened against it, he guided her across the room and with utmost courtesy pushed her down in a chair.

"We can't sit around and talk. They'll start shooting any minute."

"I doubt it," Jeff said dryly. "Now, these two men have been good friends for a long, long time," he began, while Merrie squirmed in her chair. "They've had a misunderstanding, but it would be too bad if it broke up their friendship, for six days a week they have to work together. If I know the two of them, they've been bragging. They've talked each other into this duel. If we stop it, each man will say the other was afraid to fight, and they'll never be friends again."

"They won't be anyway if one of them is dead," Merrie said heatedly, trying to get out of her chair.

Jeff's strong hand held her still. "You're absolutely right," he said, grinning down at her. "That's why I'm going to take the bullets out of their guns."

Merrie looked up unbelievingly.

"I'll offer to referee the duel, and of course part of the referee's job is to check the weapons before the fight. You wait and see. They'll have their duel, and a half-hour from now they'll be better friends than they've ever been."

Merrie began to laugh. Hurriedly Jeff clamped his hand over her mouth. "Sshh . . ." he cautioned, his gray eyes bright with laughter, "if they think we're making fun of them, they'll shoot *us*. Now I'll go out and talk to them."

"I'm coming with you."

Jeff raised both eyebrows. "Aren't you afraid?"

"Not when you're here."

He laughed softly. "Were you afraid before I got here?"

"Yes!"

He shook his head. "I don't believe it. In any case, wait here until I call. I'd just as soon have those guns in my own hands before you join the party."

In a few moments, Jeff summoned her from the hallway. He was standing between the two loggers like a rock against which angry seas are breaking. The pistols were in his hands.

"I'll get you with one shot, Jack McChesney," the redhead threatened, and the other growled, "Duel, settle it, duel . . ."

But there was a change in them. Their voices, once loud and dangerous, were now only loud. They seemed to be shouting less to scare the other fellow than to convince themselves.

All at once they ran out of words. Red McArvan looked uncertainly at Jeff, knotted his fists and stroked the air a few times in the general direction of McChesney.

"Not afraid of you," McChesney muttered, leaning forward unsteadily. "Not afraid to shoot."

"All right, gentleman," Jeff said solemnly, "we will proceed to the road in front of the Inn."

Neither combatant moved. McChesney's mumbling flow of threats died to a whisper.

"If you will carry the pistols, please, Mrs. Cowen," Jeff said ceremoniously. Merrie stepped forward and accepted the guns. Jeff grasped McChesney by the left elbow, McArvan by the right, and piloted them across the entrance hallway, through the vestibule, and down the front steps to the road.

On Jeff's instructions Merrie returned the pistols to him. Jeff paced off the arena and marked the duelists' positions in the dirt with the toe of his boot. Then he gave the pistols a long and thorough inspection. Satisfied at last, he returned the guns to their owners.

"Back to back," he instructed them, but neither of them seemed to hear. McChesney was shivering violently, McArvan was staring across the field toward the river, as if the idea of running for his life were struggling to the top of his mind. Jeff put his hands on their shoulders and turned them around so that they faced in opposite directions, McChesney's shoulders resting against McArvan's shoulder blades.

"Walk to your positions, turn, and fire!" he called out, and stepped back to the side of the road.

The two men who had sworn to fight to the death seemed to be supporting each other. If McArvan stepped forward suddenly, McChesney would surely fall flat on his back. They had looked big and rough when they were shouting at each other on the stairs. Now the heavy woolen underwear looked too big for them, the galluses which held up their work trousers threatened to slide off their shoulders. Merrie noticed for the first time that they were in their stocking feet. Patches of none too clean skin showed through the holes in their socks.

"Walk forward, turn, and fire!" Jeff bellowed.

The two were startled into action. McArvan stepped forward experimentally, tottered, caught himself, and continued unsteadily toward the position marked for him by an X in the dirt. McChesney, his big face gray as his undershirt, stumbled down the road in the opposite direction.

"Ready, aim, fire!" Jeff ordered.

The two men, numb with fear, pivoted slowly. For a second they stared at each other, pistols bobbing in hands that had lost strength to pull the triggers. The view of the other man pointing a gun at him brought McArvan to life. He straightened his arm, took aim. Scared into action, McChesney followed suit. The expectation of sudden death cramped their faces as they took one last look at each other, closed their eyes, and fired.

The pistols clicked flatly. No explosion. The men opened their eyes, stared, fired again. Again the result was nothing more than the dull sound of the hammer hitting against an empty chamber.

McChesney's face was flooded with incredulity, then relief. "Red, you're all right!" he cried, dropping his gun and running toward his friend.

"Yes, you're all right . . ." was McArvan's senseless but happy answer, tears spilling out of his red-rimmed eyes. The two men fell against each other and wept joyously. They didn't seem to notice the silent audience of two. Arms around each other, they staggered back into the Inn.

Jeff picked up the pistols. "That's as close to death as those two care to go. They'll love each other for a long time now."

Merrie sighed deeply. "You said they were from your camp. For your sake, I hope you don't have many more like them."

Jeff grinned. "They're no better nor worse than the rest. I'll take them back to camp, by Monday they'll be ready to put in twelve hours of hard work."

"Typical loggers?"

"Am *I* a typical logger?"

"Heavens no!" Merrie exclaimed. "You're too . . ." She squinted up at him thoughtfully. ". . . Too quiet. You're a gentleman."

Jeff grimaced. "Is that right? My dear girl, loggers are more or less like other human beings. They come in all shapes and sizes, they possess various degrees of sensitivity, courage, loyalty, cowardice, orneriness. There are fifty men in my camp and not one is a 'typical logger.' "

"I'll bet these two here give you more trouble than all the rest put together."

Jeff laughed. "McArvan and McChesney? As a matter of fact, they're less bother than most, because they save their cussedness for when they're off the job. I'd take four of them for one trouble-some youngster such as I have in camp right now."

Merrie said instantly, "Tell me about him."

"Still interested in stories, eh?" Jeff asked. "Stories that aren't true but sound as if they were?"

The memory of her first night in Jeff's cabin returned in a rush. The impression of Jeff seated by the bed, talking to her in a deep, quiet voice, had been buried by the weight of pain that fol-lowed. "True stories are always sad," Jeff had said, and she remembered replying, "Then tell me a story that *sounds* true. . . ."

The loneliness of the past months settled sud-denly in a lump in her throat. Jeff had been so close to her when she was in pain and in need. But when the need was gone and she moved to the Inn, the bond between them was broken. Now she knew that the need for him hadn't ended; she had missed him terribly. "A true story is fine," she said. "Oh, Jeff, it's good to have someone to talk to."

His gray eyes rested on her intently. "Let's not talk right here in the middle of the road," he said, "and let's not waste time discussing my trouble-some young logger. Not much of a story there, anyway. He got hurt again today, that's why he was on my mind. For the third time since he ar-rived in camp."

Merrie was concerned immediately. "Badly hurt?"

Jeff grinned. "That's what I always ask. No, he never gets badly hurt. But his injuries are always needless. I've almost decided that he wants to get hurt."

"What's the matter with him?"

What's the matter with Tony Marko. . . . Jeff said wryly, "So you're wondering, too, and you've never even seen him." He dismissed the injured logger with a gesture. "Merrie, you look tired. We'll go inside, and sit down in some nice, warm, comfortable place. Then we'll talk, or I'll tell you almost true stories, or whatever you like. Come on now."

In the kitchen Julie was watching the children. "Teacher went back to bed," she said. "I'll go finish the chores."

"I'll start the children's supper. . . ."

Jeff cupped his hands under her elbows, picked her up as if she were a doll and placed her carefully in the rocking chair. "They can wait a bit. Look at them. Fat and healthy, and you're thin and peaked-looking. We're going to have some tea."

"I'll make it. . . ."

Jeff said firmly, "I'll make it, if you please. It's the one thing I can cook that isn't fried."

It seemed as if she were back in his cabin, with all her troubles held at bay by Jeff's deep voice and quiet strength. But today there was a difference. When they first met, the circumstances of Joseph's birth had determined their roles. Jeff was the protector—strong, comforting, and kind. She had been his charge, as helpless and dependent as a child. No such crisis bound them together now. There was another sort of bond, invisible and undefined but as real as the crazy lurch of her pulse when she saw him walk toward her across the Bengston's barnyard. Suddenly there was more meaning to the looks they exchanged, greater depth to the feelings that flowed between them, more awareness of each other, whatever the term for the emotion from which the new awareness sprung. . . . Merrie leaned back in the rocker and closed her eyes. She had thought of Jeff so often, without realizing, as she did right now, how badly she missed him. What did he mean to her? What was the feeling that shot through her like an electric current when he picked her up in his arms and carried her to her chair? Why was she already feeling sad because his being with her would not last, that inevitably he would say goodbye and ride back to camp?

Jeff poured the tea, sweetened her cup and handed it to her. She sipped it slowly. She knew what they must talk about, so did he. But Jeff would know when to start.

Jeff set his cup down. "Merrie, Brother Bill found no trace of your husband."

"Oh . . ." Merrie's hands tightened on the arms of the rocking chair. Why be upset? Had she really expected that the minister would find Jim, when it was so clear that Jim did not want to be found?

"Bill got back to Gold Mountain only yesterday. He had been at Gilman for almost two weeks. He did talk to several men who thought they had seen someone answering Jim's description, but they all said he hadn't been in town for some time. Without a picture to show them, Bill couldn't be sure the man they remembered was your husband."

"Jim refused to have his picture taken. Even when we were married . . ." Her voice dropped. "Would you thank Bill for me?"

"Of course. But Merrie . . ." Jeff leaned forward so as to look directly into her face. "It doesn't mean we won't find him. I have never asked you before, and perhaps I shouldn't now. Do you, yourself, have any idea what could have happened to Jim?"

"I think he failed again, and couldn't face me, and went on to something else." It was a poor reply to give a man who had every right to a sensible answer. "I'm sorry," she added unhappily. "That hardly answers your question, does it?"

"On the contrary," Jeff assured her. "I'm sure you got right to the heart of the matter."

"There is so much to explain," Merrie said. "The kind of family Jim came from, his feelings about his father and his mother. He was always so . . ." She struggled for the right word, but it eluded her. She sighed. "He needed me."

Jeff's mouth tightened. For an instant Merrie thought he was angry, but the expression was gone almost as soon as it came. "You're happy here," he said, in his usual deep, controlled voice.

Merrie smiled wistfully. "If it weren't for the waiting, and wondering. It's like hanging up in the air. Everyone else is moving ahead, going someplace, building something. But I can't move or get my feet on the ground. It's like being half-alive. Of course, I'm warm, comfortable, I'm happy . . ."

"Half-happy," Jeff said, "half-alive."

Merrie smiled wistfully. "I wonder why I tried to explain to you."

Jeff slapped his hands on his knees and stood up. "What you need, my dear young lady, is a night in town. I'll bet you haven't been to Gold Mountain since the day you got off the train."

Merrie shook her head. "No, I haven't."

"All right. I'll come by here about five o'clock Saturday afternoon. You tie your hair up with that ribbon you used to wear and we'll see the sights. We'll get something to eat at Sam's Café, we'll talk with everyone we see, and I'll buy you a trinket at Nate Tarpee's store. Another hair ribbon, maybe. A green one, like your eyes."

Merrie laughed delightedly. "Do you suppose it would be all right?"

"What do you think?"

Merrie hesitated only an instant. "I think it would be all right."

Jeff nodded. "Then I do, too. Now I'm going to drag those no-good Irishmen out of here and take them back to camp. I'll be back Saturday afternoon."

That night Merrie went to bed with the feeling that she would sleep peacefully until morning. But the dream returned. Jim was coming, she fled from room to room, he was at the door . . .

She sat bolt upright. "You left me, I don't have to come with you now. . . ." At the sound of her own voice, she awakened fully. Joseph was in his cradle, there was no one in the room but the two of them. She lay down. She would think about Jeff's visit, every bit of it, from his first appearance in the barnyard to his parting words in the kitchen, "Don't forget that hair ribbon. . . ." She closed her eyes and began at the very beginning. She hadn't got as far as Saturday in Gold Mountain when she fell sound asleep.

6

ON SATURDAY AFTERNOON Merrie pressed her blue serge skirt and best shirtwaist, the one with ruffles at the wrists and throat. She examined her hair ribbon. It was a bit faded, a bit limp. She washed it, added starch to the rinse water, ironed it. . . . Holding it at arm's length, she squinted at her work. It would look fine, if it didn't get rained on. She was humming disjointedly as she went upstairs to dress.

Ruffled collar was buttoned, hair ribbon was in place, when Julie opened the door and announced cryptically, "He's here."

Merrie gave the ruffles under her chin a last pat. "Good, I'll come right down."

"Not Jeff," Julie said. "Lord Henry. Mr. Cowen."

Jim's uncle . . . The mood of the afternoon vanished. She confronted her image in the mirror. What will he think of me? she asked herself. What will I say to him? The face she was staring at had turned pale and the hair ribbon, stiff as a little girl's petticoat, now had a foolish look. "I'll come right down," the reflection murmured, echoing the Merrie who had been pink-cheeked and light-hearted a minute before.

"I'll tell him." Halfway out the door, Julie turned back. "He's a good man," she added, with a show of feeling that was unusual in Nils' quiet, half-Indian daughter. "Don't laugh at him."

Merrie shook her head. "Of course not, Julie."

Julie smiled and disappeared. Merrie followed her slowly down the stairs.

The man seated at the kitchen table looked so much like Jim that for an instant the notion sped crazily across Merrie's mind that he was in reality her husband. Aged, beaten out of shape by time and weather, but Jim Cowen, all the same. His hair was gray and grew to his shoulders; he kept it back from his face by tucking the long strands behind the ears. His skin was leathery, his eyes so deep-set they seemed to be peering at her from another era. But the shape of the head, the fine cut of nose and chin, were Jim's.

The man stood up, "I'm his uncle," he announced, as if her thoughts had been written across her face.

"I'm glad to meet you. . . ." The nicknames of "Hennie" and "Lord Henry" crowded forward on her tongue. She swallowed and added carefully, "You're Mr. Henry Cowen."

This sent the man into convulsions of dry, soundless laughter. "Who taught you to be so polite? Call me Hennie. Call me anything you like.

Though I must say, I don't really care for 'Lord Henry.' ''

He came toward her, hand extended. For the first time, Merrie noticed his costume. His trousers were tight-fitting cavalry pants, so bleached and worn that their original color was lost except for the yellow stripe down the side of each leg. Above and below this relic of a uniform he was dressed like an Indian. His feet were in moccasins; a red, gray and black blanket covered his shoulders and hung down below the belt line.

She took his hand. It was rough, dry and warm. His dark eyes looked down brightly as he said, "So you married Jim, and bore him a son, and he went off and left you."

Merrie was flustered by his directness. She withdrew her hand and walked quickly to the kitchen table. "Won't you sit down?" she asked unsteadily. "Would you like a cup of tea?"

Rather than replying, Lord Henry slapped his trouser leg soundly. "I was a member of the Yeomanry," he offered. "Volunteer cavalry unit in England. Paraded around in great style with all the other gentlemen, even if the rest of the Cowens were miners."

Merrie said politely, "I saw it was a uniform."

"Part of it," he corrected. "Just as I am only part of an Englishman. Mind you, there's not much left of either of us." He reached the kitchen table in two or three long strides, picked up a hat which he had left on one of the chairs. It was the gray, wide-brimmed hat of a Confederate officer. He raised it to eye level, flicked it with a snap of the fingers. "Hat went through the battle of Bull Run, but I wasn't under it, thank the Lord. Belonged to Harvey Smith's brother. Jeff Smith's uncle."

The mention of Jeff was like a glimpse of home. As always, Jeff meant safety, and peace. "Jeff's coming here this evening to take me to Gold Mountain. He's about due to arrive."

Lord Henry nodded slowly. "I know that. I've just come from the camp. And in a hurry. I want to talk to you before he gets here."

The remark and the urgency with which he delivered it made Merrie uneasy.

"Don't look so frightened," he said quickly. "Here, may I sit down?"

"Yes, of course."

"You, too."

Obediently Merrie took the chair opposite him. He sat up very straight, rested his brown hands on the table, palms down. An odor hung over him of smoke and pitch and wet earth. "Jeff told me how you came, and why," he said. "God loves you. You couldn't have fallen into better hands than Jeff's, and you couldn't have moved to a better home than Bengstons'." He threw her a look that was both wise and doleful. "Your bad luck is that you married Jim and that his uncle isn't much better than he is."

Merrie impulse was to defend Jim, no matter how pointless her argument might sound. But he didn't give her a chance.

"It's a dirty bird that fouls its own nest," he continued briskly. "I didn't come here to lay bare the devilish weaknesses of my own kin. I came with the money to send you and the baby back to Dakota, where you belong.''

"Oh, but I can't . . .''

He raised his right arm, straight out like an Indian salute. The gray and red blanket hung from it like a flag. "You can. This time out I collected a rather heavy sack of gold dust. Believe me, I have no better use for it than to buy your railroad ticket. Your pride about going back to your aunt and uncle? Oh yes . . .'' he smiled. "Don't look so startled. Jeff mentioned that feeling of yours. We discussed you pretty thoroughly, you know.''

"I'm getting along just fine.''

"I can see that.'' His expression changed. A look of sweetness came into his eyes. "You're a lovely child. That's why I advise you to go back to Dakota. You'll be happier, in the long run.''

"But Mr. Cowen, I don't understand. What makes you say that? Why are you so . . .'' she gestured helplessly, "so *sure* . . .''

"Because I know where Jim is.''

It seemed like a long, long time before either of them spoke. Merrie was conscious of the heavy pounding of her own heart, of the strange watchfulness in the man's weathered face. "Then tell me,'' she said in a hollow voice. "Where?''

"He's not five miles from here. He's been working in Jeff's logging camp ever since last September, under the name of Tony Marko.''

"Does he know I'm here?''

Lord Henry shook his head. "That,'' he said acidly, "is the beauty of it. I said that the Lord loves you. No one knows much of anything, except you and me. That fool stableman Kittinger is as stingy with words as he is with money. Anyone else would have spread it all over the Valley, who the girl was he drove to Jeff Smith's cabin, but he kept his mouth shut. Almost makes up for the fact that he's English. On top of it, good old Jeff gave out some story about you're a cousin of his from Kentucky, waiting to join your soldier husband at Fort Keogh. No, Jim doesn't know you're here. Praises be."

"Does Jeff . . ." Merrie's voice almost failed her. She steadied it and said again, "Does Jeff know who Tony Marko is?"

Lord Henry brought his hands together in a thunderous clap. "No, no, that's what I'm telling you. And a good thing, too. Jeff has been mighty all-fired patient with that nephew of mine, but if he knew this 'Tony' was the man who left you, I think he'd give him the beating he deserves. Jeff's an odd one, you know. He'll do anything for anybody as long as his own feelings aren't involved. Surprising to me that he's let himself take your part the way he has.

"No, believe me, I kept my mouth shut this afternoon in camp when I caught a glimpse of Jim, and luckily Jim didn't see me. If the sight of my fine nephew startled me, Jeff didn't notice. He was too busy telling me the trouble 'Tony Marko' has been causing him. Which doesn't surprise me. Except for Charles, we Cowens weren't meant to live with other people."

Merrie thought of Jim's father, dying on the parlor sofa with the railroad poster from England nailed to the wall above his head. Jim's restlessness had been inherited from his father—should he be blamed for it? "What are you telling me to do?" Merrie asked. "To go back to Dakota, with the baby, without letting Jim know I am here?"

"Exactly. And the faster the better."

"But we are married!" Merrie cried. "How can I leave him?"

Lord Henry looked at her sharply. "My dear child, didn't he leave you?"

"He may have tried to find me at the hotel in Seattle after I had gone."

Lord Henry shrugged. "Possibly. Belated concern, don't you think?"

"If I did go back to Dakota, would that settle anything? He is the father of my baby. I would still be married to him. What could I look forward to?"

Lord Henry's lips pursed together in an angry smile. "You could hope, as I am fervently hoping, that the next time Jim ignores the foreman's orders, the biggest fir tree on Jeff Smith's claim falls right on top of him."

Merrie stared into the face that was so like Jim's. "What a terrible, terrible thing to say."

The prospector's dark eyes were hard. "There should be no doubt left in your mind," he said curtly, "that I, too, am a Cowen." He leaned back and crossed his arms over his chest.

Merrie got up from her chair. His glance was too penetrating and his likeness to Jim only added to her confusion. "I'd better go right over to camp."

"To meet Jim?"

"Of course."

"You won't find him there. He was leaving when I saw him. By now, he's in Gold Mountain, trying to see how fast he can get rid of a week's earnings." He got to his feet, picked up the old gray hat, dusted it off lovingly with the back of his hand. "Well," he said, more to the hat than to Merrie, "I'm sorry I was up in the mountains so long. If Jim is what you really want, I could have found him for you months ago."

He walked to the back door.

Merrie followed him. "I'm sorry I was—rude."

He set the Confederate hat on his head, pulled it down securely over his ears. The thick gray hair bristled out from under the brim. "You weren't."

"Not even a cup of tea . . ."

"I hate tea," he said dryly. "Reminds me of England."

"Will you come again," Merrie asked, "sometime when the baby is awake?"

"We'll see," Lord Henry answered. Merrie offered her hand. He took it, and she was aware once more of the dryness and warmth of his skin. His voice softened. "You know, little Merrie with the big green eyes, I'm beginning to wonder about you. Are you so confounded anxious to locate your husband because you want to be his wife, or because you *don't* want to be? Are you wanting to pull all the miserable little bits and pieces of your holy wedlock back together again? Or maybe wanting to make sure he knows it's broken for good? You've got to find him before you can tell him to get lost—I can see the logic of that. Well, now . . ." He patted her hand and smiled. "So, when Jeff drives you to Gold Mountain, you're going to look him straight in the eye and in the name of honesty, truth, and the dear Lord our loving Father, you'll unload the whole story of your marriage to my rotten little nephew.''

Merrie nodded. ''I think I have to.''

''You're going to ask him to drive you fast as he can so you can find Jim?''

''What else is there to do? What else *can* I do?''

The old man shrugged. ''You'll do what you have to do. I mean, you'll do what you *think* you have to do. With a little more age on you, you'd know there's a difference. Meanwhile . . .'' He paused. ''Well, meanwhile, you might have a real man loving you, but you won't be able to see him.'' He touched the brim of his hat, and on moccasined feet slid soundlessly out the door.

II

It had rained heavily all day. Wagon wheels had cut deep ruts into the muddy streets of Gold Mountain, and the Saturday night crowd was keeping to the sidewalks. A dozen buildings faced each other along the main street; some were painted white, others were gray as the rain clouds overhead. Nate Tarpee's general store and hotel; the Gold Mountain Livery Stable where Martin Kittinger rented rigs and repaired harnesses; Sam's saloon on one side, Mark's on the other; the blacksmith shop, the Home Boarding House, the two-story farmhouse with Doc Adams' office downstairs, his home upstairs—these were the heart of the town.

Jeff held the team to a slow walk. "Might keep an eye out as we pass by Sam's," he said. "It's the loggers' hangout. The shingle weavers seem to have taken over Mark's place, just opposite."

It was the first time he had spoken in an hour. "Shingle weavers?" Merrie was grateful for relief from the long silence; the subject hardly mattered.

"The men who cut shingles. There are two mills south of town. The weavers do the actual cutting, the 'bolt haulers' move the big bolts of timber from which the shingles are cut. You wouldn't have used such expressions in Dakota."

"I've heard Nils talk about shingle weavers, I'd just forgotten . . ."

But Jeff wasn't to be drawn into conversation. "Your husband might be at the general store, up ahead to the right."

"I'm looking. . . ."

Once again silence fell over them like a cold fog. It had been a long, unhappy ride.

Jeff had been laughing when he arrived at the Inn. He was adjusting the hair ribbon more to his liking, teasing her gently about her "grown-up finery," when she began pouring out every detail of Lord Henry's visit. She had planned to hold back some of it. The prospector's suggestion that she return to Dakota immediately, without Jim's knowledge. His disdain for his own nephew. She had meant to sound grown-up, and tell Jeff simply that she had found her husband, that she would soon be reunited with him, that he and the Bengstons need no longer worry themselves about her future. But in Jeff's comforting presence, intentions dissolved. It all came out, helter-skelter, one word falling over the next. And when she was through, she realized that she had revealed, along with Henry Cowen's contempt for his nephew, her own dread of meeting him again. To make it worse, she had somehow driven Jeff away.

For the crooked grin was gone from his face. His

jaw was set, the understanding gray eyes were cold. Jeff had retreated as he listened, without moving a step.

Merrie stood before him helplessly. For the first time she realized that throughout her talk with Jim's uncle, confused and unhappy as she had been, she had felt sure everything would be all right once Jeff got here. Jeff would bring an end to confusion. Jeff would quiet her fear. But Jeff was silent. He seemed to be looking at her from a distance. Whether he was angry, or disapproving, or merely indifferent, she couldn't tell.

"I guess there's . . ." She faltered, waiting for him to help her. He didn't move. "I guess there's nothing more to say."

"You'd better get your coat," Jeff answered.

In silence they left the kitchen. In silence Jeff helped her into the wagon. And during the entire three-and-a-half-mile drive to Gold Mountain, they had scarcely exchanged a word.

The street was pocked with yellow-brown rain puddles, the mud was ankle-deep. Horses were tethered in front of Sam's saloon, more were tied up at Mark's. Another cluster of patient animals waited at the hitching post in front of Tarpee's store. Men in work clothes, women in rainy-day dresses with shawls over their heads, picked their way through the mud or from look-out stations on the high wooden sidewalks peered down into the street to identify this latest arrival from "out of town."

Merrie's gaze moved anxiously from person to person. Every man might be Jim. She looked for the slim figure, the dark hair, the quick, impatient gait. As they passed the cafés, the hotel, the taverns, she tried to see into interiors and by a supreme effort draw from the shadows the sight of Jim. She was tensed for it. Her fingers tightened on her purse, her pulse quickened until her throat ached.

They reached the far end of the main street.

"I don't see him," she whispered.

"Neither do I," Jeff said curtly.

Of course, he knew Jim, too. It was a fact she hadn't fully accepted until now. While she searched for her husband, Jeff, as silent and perhaps just as intent as she, was looking for a troublesome young logger named Tony Marko.

At the livery stable, Jeff reined in, jumped to the ground and tied the team to the hitching post. Coming around the wagon, he raised both arms.

Without a word, she leaned forward and let him lift her out of the wagon and set her down on the sidewalk.

"No use getting your skirts muddy," he said gruffly. Narrowing his eyes, he looked up and down the street. "We'll have to ask around. Let's start with the general store."

It had been natural to accept help from a Jeff who was kind. But from an indifferent, angry Jeff? "There is no need for you to look for Jim," Merrie said stiffly. "I'm sure you'd rather do something else."

"I'll stay with you until we locate him."

"You don't need to!" Merrie retorted. "I can take care of myself!"

For the first time since they had left the Inn, Jeff looked directly into her face. "I know that, Merrie Dooley," he said quietly, "but as long as I'm around, you don't have to."

The door of the livery stable opened and the wiry figure of Martin Kittinger appeared. "Hello, Jeff," he said, looking sharply at Merrie. "And you, how are you, Mrs.—uh—Cowen?"

Merrie murmured, "Fine, thank you." She was determined not to leave the burden of questioning on Jeff. "Mr. Kittinger, have you seen Tony Marko this evening?"

The stableman's thin face showed surprise. He turned to Jeff. "That young fellow who's been working for you?" he asked slyly. "The dark one?"

Jeff nodded.

Kittinger's pointed glance returned to Merrie. "*You* looking for him?"

Jeff's voice was as threatening as a clenched fist. "The lady asked if you'd seen him."

Kittinger shrugged. "I haven't been through the front door since noon. Wouldn't be out here now if somebody hadn't come running in to say the shingle weavers are getting ready to race." His bright little eyes focused on some scene at the far end of town. "By Harry, I think they are, too."

At the far end of main street, seven or eight men were mounting horses. The doors of Sam's and Mark's saloons stood open, and men, twenty or thirty of them, were moving out onto the sidewalks. A hoarse cheer sounded on one side of the street, catcalls and whistles answered from the other.

"Where's that old lion of a Dr. Adams?" Kittinger muttered. "He'll have work to do before the night's half started."

Merrie felt Jeff's hand on her arm. "This is not the place to be when the shingle weavers race," he said. "They come down this sidewalk, not the street. Safest spot would be inside Nate Tarpee's store. Or we could climb back in the wagon, if you want to get a good view of it all."

"I'll get up there with you," Kittinger squeaked, and hopped like a scared cricket into the back of Jeff's wagon.

Merrie hesitated. Men were spilling out of the buildings. Those on the south side were stepping down from the sidewalk and forming groups in the center of the muddy street. On the north side, the wooden walk was crowded, not only with men but with women and children taking up positions for a good view of the race. Somewhere in the crowd was Jim.

Jeff answered her unspoken question. "There's no use trying to look for him now. After the race."

The moment she had been bracing herself to meet had been put off, if only for a little while. Merrie sighed. "All right, Jeff, after the race," and she let him pick her up and swing her onto the wagon seat.

Jeff climbed in beside her. "You'll notice there's one big gang of men right in front of Sam's saloon. Those are loggers. Then there's a second gang, standing in the street closer to Mark's place. They're all shingle weavers. The weavers do the racing. No logger would think of breaking into their clan or challenging one of them. I'm thankful that Saturday night races are the shingle weavers' specialty. My men get banged up enough as it is."

Merrie was concerned immediately. "You mean someone might get hurt?"

Jeff pointed to the far end of Gold Mountain. "See where the riders are collecting? The race begins about there, two or three blocks the other side of town. No buildings or sidewalks there so they can ride six abreast. So far, so good, but when they get to the first building, the race course gets narrow, because they're supposed to make their horses follow the sidewalk, even when it runs under a porch where two horses can scarcely get through at a time. I've seen many a weaver bounce against those wooden pillars that hold up Tarpee's porch. And I've seen quite a few dumped or thrown before they got that far, down there where six, eight, ten of them are trying to get onto the sidewalk all at the same time."

"They *will* get hurt!"

Jeff answered with a wry smile. "Well, as the loggers say, shingle weavers live safe all week long, they might as well prove they're men one night a week."

"You sound as if you thought loggers were better than shingle weavers."

Jeff laughed outright. "I do. The weavers get higher pay for working under a roof than loggers get for heavy work outside in all kinds of weather. Maybe they should, to make up for all the fingers they send down the chute. You'll soon learn, Merrie Dooley, that loggers and shingle weavers aren't meant to love each other. You might have a good friend in the opposite camp but you don't make a show of it in public and you don't mix at box socials or square dances or baseball games. It's a tradition. I wouldn't try to join the gang of weavers at Mark's any more than I'd ride my horse down the street and try to get into the race."

"Looks like they're ready to cut loose," Kittinger broke in.

Jeff studied the line-up. "I see the champion got into it. Isn't that Emil Greene, on the pinto, second from the end?"

"That's Emil. If he don't race, then he figures they'll say the winner would have beaten him if he had been in it. So he races every time."

Merrie asked, "Who do you think will win?"

"The point of the race isn't so much who comes in first, but who finishes at all."

"Here they come!"

Kittinger's exclamation was drowned out by the clamor that broke out suddenly up and down the street. The loggers yelled, the shingle weavers yelled, the spectators who didn't belong in either camp added shouts and squeals and cheers.

"Oh, oh," Merrie moaned. "I can't watch . . ."

Jeff turned and looked down at her. Her eyes were tightly closed. "Well, well," he said. "I thought you were the girl who never liked to miss anything."

"I don't," she said, eyes shut.

"I also understood that you weren't afraid of the sight of blood. You told me that back in Dakota you once helped a doctor sew up a man who got caught in a threshing machine."

Merrie nodded. "I did. But he was already hurt. It's seeing someone *get* hurt that I can't stand. While it's happening, or I think it's going to happen, I keep wanting to do something to prevent it. It's a terrible feeling. Like running in a dream."

"I dare you to look," Jeff said quietly.

Merrie's eyes flew open. She swallowed hard and turned to watch the race.

The horses were coming at full gallop. Their riders, having drawn for starting positions, were already trying to edge to the right. At the end of the first block, one man dropped behind. At the end of the second, the remaining five were so bunched the riders' legs were touching. One horse pulled ahead, tried to cross in front of the horse to his right. His flying hoofs hit the pony behind him, the crowd gasped as the injured horse whinnied, reared, and dropped back.

Four left in the race, and the narrow opening of the sidewalk was only a hundred yards away. A man riding a pinto had the right-hand position and seemed to be holding it. "Emil Greene," Jeff said. "Notice how the other three are trying to crowd him so far to the right that when they reach the sidewalk he'll have to rein in or run his horse into the building. Beating Emil would be more of a triumph than winning the race. They're ganging up on him."

"Watch out, Emil!" Merrie cried, though she had never seen the man before.

Jeff grinned. "Don't worry about Emil," he said, "they won't squeeze him out."

Shouts from the muddy street accompanied the

struggle for the sidewalk. For an instant it looked
as if all four horses were going to charge the spot
despite the fact that there was barely room for two.
There was a flurry of horses' hoofs, waving arms,
slapping reins, and then at the final instant one
rider lost his nerve, pulled his horse up sharply,
turned and, with defeat at his back, raced in the
opposite direction to the starting point. Three . . .
One of the remaining ponies let out a shrill cry,
shied, his rider sailed into the air and landed on his
back in the mud.

The two horses still in the race thundered down
the sidewalk. Women shrieked as they tangled
under the porch, raced on and miraculously came
out, disentangled, on the other side. On to the
sidewalk in front of the livery stable. Merrie
gasped as the horses galloped past so close to Jeff's
wagon she could hear the heavy breathing of the
men. The hollow roar of horses' hoofs on wood
died suddenly as they came to the end of the sidewalk and an open stretch of mud. Emil and his
pinto were well ahead. There were shouts as he
crossed the invisible finish line, the east wall of the
blacksmith shop, the last building on that side of
the street. He reined in, guided the panting pony
back toward the center of town.

The crowd moved down the street to meet him.
A solid phalanx of shingle weavers got there first.
Only a few feet from where Merrie and Jeff sat in
the wagon, they surrounded Emil and his pinto.
The loggers approached slowly, hooting derisively
as they were expected to do. Winners, losers and
spectators—they were all in high spirits.

Merrie responded instinctively to the excitement. "It was fun!" she exclaimed, forgetting that without Jeff's dare she wouldn't have seen it. For an instant she even forgot it was time to resume the search for Jim. But only for an instant. The crowd of loggers was closer now. Her glance, casual at first, suddenly fixed itself on one of them. There he was. The figures surrounding him blurred, the tumult of voices seemed to fade away. There was Jim.

Jeff was watching her. He had seen Jim, too. The blood drained out of her face. Weak and helpless, she waited for Jim to see her.

He was the only one among all the loggers who wasn't laughing or shouting. Though all the others wore hats, his head was bare. His mouth turned down at the corners, he was looking up at Emil Greene with the moody, envious expression Merrie knew so well. He turned his head slightly, his petulant glance traveling over the crowd to which he so obviously did not belong. His head lifted slightly as he looked up into the wagon. He stiffened. He had seen her.

What will he do? Merrie thought numbly. She had feared this moment, but now that it had come she wasn't frightened at all. Uppermost in her mind was Jeff's presence. Whatever Jim might do or say, it would be easier to bear if Jeff were not here to see it.

Very slowly Jim came through the crowd. No one seemed to be looking. The men who were shouting continued to shout, the smiling women kept on smiling, the youngsters dancing around Emil's horse didn't slow down because she was sitting there feeling cold and sick—and Jim was coming. It was just like the nightmare. Step, step, step, Jim is coming. Bang, bang, bang, the shutter is banging in the cold wind. But the baby Joseph wasn't here. He was at the Inn with the Bengstons, safe.

Jim reached the wagon. He was standing right below her, close enough to touch. A sense of his nearness swept over her. The warmth rising from his body, the quick rhythm of his breathing, the anger and pleading in his eyes, his mouth . . . Every detail of his physical being demanded recognition. "This is where you've been," she whispered, "all the time."

"Merrie," he said huskily, "Merrie . . ."

Jeff stirred.

Jim's mouth hardened. "So you are the woman who lived in Jeff Smith's cabin." His voice was harsh.

"Please," Merrie begged. "Not here."

Jeff's voice behind her said, "Why don't the two of you go into Tarpee's store. It must be deserted right now."

"I'll manage my own affairs!" Jim's face was contorted with anger.

"I hope you can," Jeff said very low, "though I haven't been impressed so far. In any case, you're not welcome to use my wagon as a stage, not when it's standing in the middle of Gold Mountain."

"Jim, I'll come with you," Merrie said anxiously. "We'll go inside the store. . . ." Whatever was to happen, let it happen, but not here where Jeff would see.

Jim was looking past her, at Jeff. "The big

timber man, Jefferson Davis Smith," he said. His voice shook. "So this is your cousin from Kentucky. I'd like to beat you with my bare fists!"

Merrie cried out, "Jim!"

"How about now?"

Jeff said it so softly that Jim seemed to lean forward to catch the sound. But he had heard. Merrie knew from the sudden quiver of his lower lip and the dull black look in his eyes. He turned away from the wagon so quickly that Merrie thought he was going to run away. He moved only a few steps, until he was in the center of the crowd that had knotted around the pinto on which Emil Greene sat. "O.K., Emil," Jim shouted above the other voices. "I dare you to race down the other side of the street!"

The challenge brought silence. Disbelieving faces turned to study the young logger with such a crazy notion. Everyone knew that the north side of the street was too dangerous for racing. Wild as the shingle weavers might act of a Saturday night, they didn't admire foolhardiness, and to attempt the north-side course would be just that. More offensive than the foolish challenge was the idea of breaking tradition. Loggers had never raced shingle weavers. Who was this young man anyway?

The crowd's resentment was obvious. Jim reacted to it by shouting even more loudly, "Well, Emil, I said I'd dare you. I don't hear you saying anything."

Jeff stood up abruptly, jumped down from the wagon, and pushed his way through the crowd.

"Look here, Tony. That side's too dangerous, you know that. Sidewalk has three steps in it, in front of the old warehouse. Three steps up one end, three down at the other. A horse could easily break a leg. Then there's that slice of log in front of Sam's saloon. You know as well as I do that one of you is bound to hit it."

"You stay out of it!" Jim flashed at him. "I'll take orders from you at your logging camp, but I don't have to listen to you here."

"I'm not giving orders, I'm trying to appeal to your common sense," Jeff said grimly. "I told you once before that when you take unnecessary chances, you're not the only person to suffer. I see no reason why Emil should risk serious injury because of a childish dare."

Jim was too angry to speak. He broke through the crowd, ran down the street to the hitching post in front of Sam's saloon.

"Whose horse is he taking?" someone asked.

Another voice answered, "Looks like Joe's, and Joe ain't here."

And the first voice said mournfully, "It does seem someone ought to stop him. . . ."

But no one did. Jim mounted the strange horse, dug his heels into its flanks and cantered back.

The murmuring ceased.

"Are we racing, Emil?" Jim called defiantly. "Or are you scared of losing to a logger?"

There was a burst of protest from the shingle weavers. Emil Greene's simple face was puzzled. "I don't know you," he said slowly. "I don't think I ever seen you before in my life."

"Are we racing," Jim repeated, "or aren't we?"

Emil shrugged unhappily. "Sure, I guess so. As long as it's a dare."

Jeff spoke. The wonder of it was that with all the shouting around him, anyone heard. But they did. He spoke low, and they all stopped talking so they could hear him. "If you're bound to race, you can race. With me." In two strides he was standing next to Emil's horse. He gave Emil a commanding nod. "Get off."

Emil said, "Gosh, Jeff, you shouldn't do it. Gosh, I'll race him. . . ."

"Get down."

"Gosh . . ." But Emil dismounted and backed away, shaking his head. "It just don't seem . . ."

Jim thrust toe in stirrup and threw his long leg over the pinto's back. He held the reins lightly, turned the horse's head toward the north side of the street. "All right, Jim Cowen," he said. "I'm ready, are you?"

"Oh my God," Kittinger said fervently. "Where *would* that damned doctor be, at a time like this?"

Merrie stood up in the wagon. "Jim, please!" she called over the heads of the crowd. "Don't, don't . . ." Everyone in Gold Mountain was staring at her, she was making a spectacle of herself with her waving arms and frantic voice. It didn't matter. "Jeff," she sobbed, "don't race him, Jeff. . . ."

"Whatever got into Jeff?" Kittinger squeaked. "Him with such a cool head, whatever happens."

Jeff signaled to her. A nod of his head, that told her to sit down. She dropped to the seat. Her purse slipped from her hands but she was trembling too violently to pick it up. In desperation she turned toward Jim. Jim was laughing. He answered her pleading look with a toss of his head, a louder burst of laughter. "Let's go!" he shouted, lifting the reins high and riding forward so suddenly that a dozen men had to jump to get out of his way.

He reined in at Jeff's side. They were in position now, Jeff looking straight ahead down the deserted sidewalk, Jim, still laughing, turning to wave to the crowd.

Merrie covered her face with her hands.

"Mrs. Cowen," Kittinger's voice said, "let me take you inside."

With an effort Merrie dropped her hands to her lap and lifted her head. "No, I'll stay here," she whispered. "In case something happens."

The traditional shingle weavers' race had been accompanied by cheers. Part of the fun was the loud joking, the shouts of advice, the friendly insults exchanged by the loggers and weavers. For this race there was scarcely a sound. An uneasy murmur rippled across the crowd as horses and riders moved into position, but it died out the instant one of the loggers raised his arm to give the starting signal.

They were all too sober to ignore the dangers of racing on the north side of the street. The narrow steps were a hazard, but the spot in front of Sam's saloon might be deadly. Some years before, one of the largest trees in the area was cut down and Sam had acquired a slice off the butt end. If was fifteen feet in diameter and a foot thick; he had set it on edge between the sidewalk and the street, bracing it in position with a beam extending out from the building like a flying buttress. The chances of riding a horse under that plank without being killed . . . They knew it was crazy to try.

And what was it all about, anyway? They were puzzled. Loggers didn't race on the sidewalks. They didn't know this man Tony Marko or Jim Cowen or whatever his name was, but they did know Jeff Smith. Jeff had never mixed into something like this. If there was a brawl, he stopped it or he was on hand to take the losers to the doctor's office, but he held himself a little apart. Today he wasn't acting in character—that was as disturbing as the race itself, which was in defiance of all tradition and somehow not enjoyable to anyone.

So there were no whistles or cheers when the logger brought his arm down and the horses shot ahead. Only a whispered "Aahhh . . ." from a half dozen throats, and then tense silence.

The race was over quickly.

Jeff rode the pinto hard but carefully. Jim rode recklessly, waving one arm as if he were flying a banner. At the beginning, they were even. When they reached the first steps, both horses made the jump smoothly. They were neck and neck when they cleared the three steps down at the other end of the warehouse.

As they approached Sam's saloon, Jim's laughter died out. Jeff turned his head slightly, just enough to see Jim's face. He read in it just what he had expected to find. Jim was watching for the first movement of Jeff's hand that would show he was reining in. Jim was confident that Jeff cared less, and would not be as reckless as he.

There wasn't room for two horses to pass between the building and that great slice of tree. Even if one horse tried it, the rider was bound to be scraped off his back by the overhanging timber.

Jim was still watching him.

No, by God, Jeff thought to himself, no . . . He slapped the end of the reins over the pinto's rump. As the horse leapt forward, Jeff pulled the pinto hard to the left. Jim was cut off. Jeff caught his startled look as Jim reined in, turning the horse's head sharply and grabbing for the pummel.

Jeff was alone now, but to turn back before he'd ridden past the log would be to lose the race just as much as Jim had. He gave the pinto another quick slap with the reins, threw himself forward and sideways, arm around the horse's neck, one leg over the horse's back. He passed under the board safely, came out the other side. He righted himself, finished the course. Then he turned back and rode slowly toward the crowd.

Loggers and shingle weavers joined in the applause. Others laughed, with relief and surprise. Now that it was all over, it had been fun.

"Pretty fancy riding there, Jeff!" someone called as he approached, and someone else added, "That ought to hold him for a while, eh, Jeff?" Clearly, they were glad he had won.

At the hitching post in front of Sam's, Jim

was dismounting. No one left the crowd to console him, few looked his way. He looped the reins around the horizontal pole, turned on his heel and walked away.

Jeff returned the pinto to Emil. A boisterous group of loggers at his heels, he made his way back to the wagon.

Merrie was sitting up stiff as a wooden doll, her hands in her lap and her eyes fixed on the scene in front of Sam's. Without looking at Jeff she said "I've got to go and talk to him."

Jeff dismissed his noisy convoy of loggers with a grin and a gesture. When they were out of hearing he looked up at Merrie. "Is that what you want to do?"

Her face was white, she was fighting tears. "No," she said, shaking her head. "No. I . . . I dread it."

"Then why do you do it?"

"Because . . . Because he feels a fool, and they're all laughing at him. I can't just look the other way."

Jeff nodded. "That's what I thought. No one else will talk to him, so you must." Silently he extended his arms, lifted her off the seat and set her down on the rutted road. "Merrie," he said quietly, "Jim is the cause of his failures. Jim brings about his own unhappiness. Not you, not me, not that bunch of loggers who are laughing at him as they would expect to be laughed at if they had done something so damned foolish. Are you going to spend the rest of your life trying to make up for Jim's selfishness and foolish pride? Because if you do, he will destroy you, little by little, a little bit at a time. Merrie . . ." Jeff looked intently into the pale face and unhappy eyes. "Merrie, tell me honestly. Do you love him?"

"I used to think so. Now, I don't know. I don't honestly know what I feel. Except that this one time, I have to go talk to him. To settle things. To say . . . goodbye."

"Then go." Jeff released her. "I'll wait for you."

She didn't answer nor look at him. Skirts dragging in the mud, she hurried down the street after Jim. "I'll wait for you this time," Jeff added, but she was too far away to hear him. "But not forever."

Kittinger appeared at his shoulder. "Hey, she dropped this," he said. "You want it?"

It was the blue hair ribbon. The evening dampness had taken the starch out of it; it drooped like a faded flower. Jeff took it from Kittinger's hand and thrust it angrily into his pocket.

III

Jim turned at the sound of her running footsteps. She halted abruptly. Somewhere she had lost her hair ribbon, and her long curls were hanging loose about her shoulders. Her cheeks were hot and she was out of breath. It was a long time since they had seen each other, many questions lay between them, and the impulse that had sent her racing headlong down the street was already subsiding. With an awkward, absent-minded gesture, Merrie tried to straighten her hair, and then she walked toward him slowly.

They met in front of Doc Adams' barn. That end of Gold Mountain was deserted, everyone in town had collected at the far end of the street, where shouting and laughter billowed up every few seconds in successive puffs of sound.

Face to face, neither of them spoke.

Why, he hasn't changed at all. . . . As the

thought struck her, Merrie realized she had expected him to look different. Surely the experiences of the past months would have affected him as they had her. "I didn't want you to think . . ." she said at last, "I didn't want you to go away without . . ."

Jim's eyes were black in his handsome boy's face. He glanced at the empty barn. "Come in here," he said hoarsely, pulling her through the opening where a door had once been.

"What's this?" Merrie stammered.

"Old barn belongs to the doctor. No one will see us in here."

Dusk was gathering outside, but in the cavern of the deserted barn, night had fallen. Jim's face was indistinct, but his words echoed loudly. "Merrie, come here."

"I haven't seen you in a long time. . . ." Merrie objected. Her voice bounced against the darkness. Every sound came alive. Jim's heavy breathing, the whispering of rough cloth against cloth as he raised his arms and stepped toward her, even the throbbing of her own pulse. She backed away from him.

"You followed me."

It was true, oh, it was true. "I just wanted to talk to you," she whispered, shaking her head helplessly. "Nothing more, really, nothing more. There are so many things we must—settle."

Jim's hands grasped her arms and pulled her forward. "You followed me," he repeated very softly. His arms tightened, he forced her head back, his mouth was on hers.

The feeling of the kiss was still on her mouth as she pushed against his chest and sobbed, "What right have you got to touch me!"

His arms dropped to his sides. "I know, I left you," he said thickly. "Deserted you when you were going to bear me a child. Do you want me to recite the whole piece? By now you must know it by heart."

"I haven't talked about you with anyone." It wasn't quite true. With Jim's uncle, with the Bengstons, in her letters to her aunt and uncle in Dakota, she had remained loyal, and those who saw through the pretense had abetted her in it. But with Jeff, she had been truthful. Merrie felt the blood rush back into her cheeks. "I've always said we were separated because of a . . ." She choked, finished in a whisper, "Because of a misunderstanding."

"Too bad. If you had told them the truth you would have gotten twice as much sympathy. Or was it your pride? Didn't you want to admit your husband is a failure?"

"Jim . . ."

"I should say, a three-time failure. No good as a Dakota farmer, no good at Port Townsend, didn't have the guts to work in the mines at Gilman. But you'll see. I'm not going to quit this time. By the end of the year I'm going to know more about logging than all the worn-out old men in Jeff Smith's camp. Inside of five years I'm going to own more timber than Jeff ever dreamed of, and I'm going to run an up-to-date logging camp like none he's ever even seen."

No, he hadn't changed. The biggest wheat farm in Dakota, the biggest operator at Port Townsend, the richest miner in Gilman, and now, the best logger. And in his dreams there was still only one person, the "I," the confident, self-important Jim. Jim, who was about to triumph once and for all and had no need for her.

As usual, this triumph was to be over someone; Jim was to rise while the imagined adversary went down. In Dakota, it had been his father, who was dead, or perhaps his mother, who didn't care; Jim had set out to "show them." Now it was Jeff Smith, for Jeff had what Jim wanted and was, in so many ways, the man Jim wished to be. How Jim must hate him, Merrie reflected. How terrible that hate will be after losing the race. . . .

"Why don't you say something?" Jim said. "You don't believe me, I suppose, or you don't care."

"I hope everything works out as you want it to."

"You don't believe me."

"I *hope* for you," Merrie cried. "What more do you expect? What am I to you, after all these months? You left me, and you haven't explained why. We have a child you've never seen, but you haven't asked about him. Instead you talk to me about owning timber and running a big logging camp. Five years from now. But this is *now!*"

Her voice, low and choked at first, rose as the words tumbled out. To each echoing word was added the sharper echo of the next word until, when she had finished, the darkness trembled with her complaint.

She had never before defied him, never before refused to applaud his childish dreams. She tensed, dreading the violent outburst that had always been his way of coping with reality he did not want to face. After the storm, he would ask to be forgiven. He would plead that he needed her, that his insane fury was born of fear that he might lose her. Finally she would put everything out of her mind but the sense that this need was real, and she would put her arms around him and whisper reassurance. . . . But that was not now. Not today. "He will destroy you," Jeff had said, and she knew it was true. Today her impulse was to escape from him, not to give him comfort.

Jim broke the silence. "I tried to find you, Merrie. After I got the job at the logging camp, I began saving money. When I had enough for railway fare and to pay the hotel, I went back after you. But you were gone. The hotel manager said you hadn't lived there for two months. I figured you were in Dakota. I was going to stay with logging until camp closed down for the winter. Then I was going to go back and get you."

"Why didn't you . . ." Merrie stopped and shook her head wearily. If she must ask—Is it true?—what was the use of asking at all? Jeff would know whether Jim really had made a trip to Seattle at some time after he came to camp. Jeff could tell her whether camp truly did close down for the winter. But she didn't mean to inquire. She sighed. "You still haven't asked about the baby."

Jim reached out and pulled her forward so suddenly she nearly fell. "I love you," he said huskily, "I need you. . . ."

She let him kiss her, neither sharing nor resisting. But the pressure of his mouth, the demanding, groping movement of his hands stirred feelings she had thought were buried so deep they could not come alive again. She tried to free herself, but the strength had gone out of her.

"We'll go to the hotel," Jim said against her mouth. "I'll rent a room. . . ."

"I'm going back to the Inn."

"No," Jim said roughly. "You're coming with me."

Then she fought him, pushing both hands against his chest, sobbing wordlessly as she struggled to get free. He let her go. She stumbled through the dark to the open door and into the street.

He followed her, grabbed her with one hand and held her. "You're my wife," he said angrily.

Merrie winced as his fingers tightened on her arm. "We haven't settled anything," she gasped. "You say you love me, but I don't believe it. And I don't know how I feel about you."

"I'll show you. . . ."

The blood was pounding through her, it was hard to breathe. "I'm going back to the Inn," she said weakly. "The Bengstons are expecting me."

With an angry movement Jim turned her around, held her right arm tightly under his left, and forced her to walk beside him toward town. "I'll drive you to the Inn."

"But you don't have a buggy. . . ."

"I'll get one from Kittinger."

"But what will Jeff . . ."

"I'll tell Jeff!"

They walked toward the center of town. Relief flooded over Merrie as she saw that the crowd had dispersed and Jeff's wagon had left the spot in front of the livery stable. Along the quiet street horses stood at the hitching posts. Three or four women had stopped to gossip in front of the general store, here or there a man leaned against a building or clumped along the wooden sidewalk to disappear into a building. Pale yellow lamplight shone through the windows of the saloons and stores and hotels.

Merrie was grateful that night had driven people inside. Her arm ached where Jim held it, and all she could think as she walked obediently at his side was that Jeff might not see them, after all. He had probably gone into Tarpee's store. She prayed that he had, and that he would not come out until they were gone.

"Wait here!" Jim said when they reached the livery stable. She nodded and sank into the shadow of the darkened building.

Jim was back in minutes.

"Did you find Jeff?" she asked.

"Yes, I found him. The great Jefferson Davis Smith."

Touching for the spot that hurt most, Merrie asked, "What did he say?"

"Offered to loan me his horse and wagon."

"Are we . . ."

"When I want a rig, I'll hire it!" Jim said furiously. "And it will be better than his!"

In a few minutes Kittinger had been roused, a horse had been harnessed to the most costly buggy he had, and Merrie and Jim were riding away with the little Englishman's curious gaze following them.

Now, at last, Jim spoke of the baby. "I didn't really want to go to the hotel," he said, slapping the reins hard along the horse's back. "What I want more than anything else in the world is to see my son."

Merrie closed her eyes. Her effort to defy Jim had exhausted her. Let him claim the victory if he liked; she had defied him once before, though he didn't know it, and she had won. "I named the baby Joseph," she said quietly, "after my father."

Jim's voice lashed at her out of the dark. "We can change that," he said, "and we will."

7

JIM LEFT MERRIE at the Inn with little more than a curt "Good night." He wanted nothing in the world so much as to see his son, he had said in Gold Mountain, but when the long, silent ride was over at last, he made no move to get down from the wagon.

The Inn was dark except for the kitchen. There a circle of lamplight glowed in the center of the room, and Katherine Bengston was seated at the big table, her head bent over some kind of fancy work. Merrie shivered and looked longingly toward the warmth and safety of the familiar room.

"I'm not going to bother you," Jim said. "Not tonight. Go ahead, run to your friend."

Merrie picked up her purse and gathered her skirts. "Good night, Jim," she said unsteadily, groped for the step and carefully lowered herself to the ground.

"Good night." He lifted the reins, turned the horse around sharply, and was gone.

An hour before, he had kissed her passionately and silenced her protests with an angry reminder—"You're my wife. . . ." Now he left her alone, to sink or swim in the flood of emotions he had released. He hadn't even touched her. . . . Merrie turned away from the sound of the departing wagon and ran to the kitchen.

For a week Merrie moved blindly from task to task, her mind in confusion and a cold, helpless feeling in her heart. From their actions, she guessed there was little she could tell the Bengstons about Saturday's events. Katherine was studiously cheerful. Once or twice Nils came close to asking a personal question, but a meaningful glance from Katherine sent the big man loping out of the room. Again and again Merrie thought—they wonder what I'm going to do. I must make up my mind. How *do* I feel? Where can I go? What will I do? When these questions assailed her, the brief effort to think logically always ended.

On Sunday Jim returned to the Inn. He was in clean clothes, he was smiling, he wanted to see his son. Blood rushing to her face, Merrie let him in.

Nils and Katherine were in the kitchen. With a great effort Merrie found her voice and made the introductions. Katherine was tight-lipped but polite. Nils scowled but held out his hand and mumbled, "How do?"

Merrie stammered, "I'll go—go get Joseph. He's asleep upstairs," and she hurried from the room.

When she returned with the baby in her arms,

Jim was alone. The smile was gone and his mouth was set in an angry line.

"Where are the Bengstons?" Merrie asked. "What happened?"

"They decided to mind their own business." He crossed the room and looked at the baby.

Merrie was seized by an impulse to turn and run. It was the old nightmare suddenly come to life. *Where* were Nils and Katherine? . . . Her arms tightened convulsively around the baby.

Joseph's round face puckered and he began to cry. "Sssshhh . . ." she whispered contritely, looking down so that Jim would not see her unreasonable panic.

But Jim didn't try to take the baby from her. He touched Joseph lightly with one hand, his face softening and a dreamy look in his dark eyes. "So we have a son," he said finally, very low. "Have you got the proper clothes for him?"

"Enough," Merrie replied. "Enough to do."

Jim shook his head. "I'll buy him some more."

"I could make what he needs, if I had some cotton flannel and yarn from Tarpee's store."

Jim's face went white. "You expect me to go to Gold Mountain after the mess Jeff Smith caused last Saturday? I'll do my shopping in Seattle, and get the best."

The next week he returned with an armload of parcels. Nils and Katherine got up to leave the room, but he insisted they remain while the boxes were opened. Each contained baby clothing more elaborate, obviously more expensive, than anything the Bengstons had ever seen. At every exclamation the proud look set deeper into Jim's face. He scarcely glanced at the clothes—it was the faces of Katherine and Nils he was watching.

The expression brought to Merrie's mind the scene at the Providence depot when she and Jim had boarded the train for Seattle. Then Jim had been looking over the crowd so as to feed on the envy of people who would never ride on so fine a train as this, nor go so far. . . . Merrie turned away. "You've bought too much," she murmured, busying herself unnecessarily with string and wrappings. "I'm afraid Joseph will outgrow these things long before he wears them out."

"When that time comes, give them away," Jim said, "and I'll buy more."

Such a boast was as familiar to Merrie as his unpredictable outbursts and his long, black silences. But for the next hour he was cheerful and attentive, in every way the handsome youth who had once been able to excite her with nothing more than the touch of his hand. He seemed to have forgotten his furious promise to change the baby's name. Instinct whispered he was charming her deliberately, that his friendliness and apparent interest in his son were deceptions that would end in some kind of emotional storm. At the same time she was deeply relieved by the absence of the ugly moods; was the violent Jim the real Jim? Was it fair to say the "real" Jim was angry, violent, egocentric, and that Jim smiling, friendly and interested in the baby was a sham? In this emotional crosscurrent, attracted and repelled but above all grateful for being spared an ugly scene, Merrie agreed to leave the baby with Katherine and go for a walk. "It's a warm night," Jim said, "and I've got something to tell you."

They walked along the riverbank where a light breeze carried the perfume of the balm of Gilead trees. Jim set a fast pace; there was an air of excitement about him, yet he didn't speak. When they had gone some distance from the Inn, Merrie asked, "What did you want to tell me?"

"In a minute, in a minute . . ." He stopped and looked around. They were in a patch of meadow between a grove of alder and cottonwood and the sandy, sloping bank of the Snoqualmie. "Here," he said, "Here's a grassy spot," and he sat down.

Merrie hesitated. "It'll be getting dark soon."

"Not for an hour." He brought the palm of his hand down hard on the ground beside him. "Sit down."

Below the river coursed nosily over a series of riffles. Jim stared at the water, still without speaking. Merrie sat up stiffly, as if a straight back established her independence of him. The silence stretched on. All at once she couldn't bear it any longer. "Jim . . ."

He turned toward her. "Merrie," he said earnestly, "listen to me. I've done just what you've always wanted me to do. I've found a home. A home of our own."

Merrie caught her breath. It was as if her heart stopped for an instant and began beating again at a furious pace. "A home of our own," she repeated dully.

"A homestead claim, with a cabin already on it.

226

The man who built it left for the Yukon before he proved it up.''

''We've never even talked, you've never explained . . .'' Merrie was too shaken to look at him.

''Explain? I admitted that I'd failed, that I'd left you. That was almost a year ago. What is there to talk about now?''

Merrie shook her head.

Jim's hands fell on her shoulders. He turned her toward him and said roughly. ''Look at me, Merrie. I've left you alone. I've given you time to think. Now it's time to remind you that I'm your husband.''

Jim's face was drawn with the intensity of his feeling. His dark eyes burned. ''You're my wife,'' he said in a husky voice. ''I've found a home for you. I have a right to take you there.''

''Months and months have passed . . .''

Jim pulled her into his arms and kissed her. She tried to draw back, but his arms tightened and he kissed her again. No, no, no! her mind was crying. The kiss ended, he pressed his mouth against the soft hollow of her throat. ''No!'' she cried again, aloud this time, and jerked backward so suddenly that she broke free.

She sat gasping for breath, tensed to jump to her feet if he should reach for her again. ''How can you act as if nothing has changed? I was your wife, it's true. When you disappeared, I searched for you, that's true, too. But it wasn't because I thought that if I found you we'd be married as we had been. I looked for you because I had to know what had happened.''

"What happened is past."

She shook her head. "No, don't you see? We haven't been together. . . ."

"I haven't touched you," he said angrily. "Is that what you mean? I've seen you twice and I was polite and kept my hands off you. Do you think that makes you free of me?"

"Yes," she said.

In his absence, she *had* been free. Her mind still defied him. "You have no claim on me," she whispered, "not any longer. We haven't been man and wife for a long, long time,"

"We're going to be," he said hoarsely, "now . . ."

II

Later, when night had fallen, Jim said, "We'll go back now. But this is your last night at the Inn. I'll come for you in the morning and take you home."

Merrie didn't move.

"Stop your crying," he said impatiently. "The Bengstons might still be awake. I don't want them to see you this way."

Slowly Merrie got to her feet. Jim turned on his heel and began to walk toward the Inn. Merrie followed, but there was no stopping the tears. She cried for the debasement of making love with a man for whom she had no respect. She cried because she knew she could have stopped him if she'd fought harder. She cried most of all because she had come so close to being forever free of him, and now, and now. . . . Yellow lamplight shone from the kitchen window. She dried cold tears with a cold and trembling hand and walked slowly toward the light.

III

"Home" on Jim's lips sounded unreal, but Merrie took some hope from it the Sunday she left the Inn. In the back of the wagon he had borrowed from Nils was everything she owned. In her arms was the baby Joseph, everything she truly loved. Ahead—"home." Jim spoke of it with such enthusiasm that she was ashamed of not sharing it. Though it was almost a year since she had been at the mercy of Jim's moods, she returned instinctively to the old habit of cherishing the good ones and dreading the bad.

"It sounds wonderful," she said cheerfully, though she scarcely heard what he was saying about the land, the cabin, the stream that came down off the mountain to provide a water supply. If his heart was in it, then hers must be, too.

"You'll have what you want," Jim was saying, "and I will, too. One of the finest stands of timber in the Valley. It's the first step."

At those words, Merrie became fully alert. A

warning sounded as clearly as if a gong had been struck. The first step—toward what? "You hadn't mentioned the timber," she said cautiously. "Have you made some—some plan?"

Jim tossed his head. "Do you think I'm going to be a flunky for Jeff Smith all the rest of my life?" he scoffed. "In five years I'm going to own a bigger logging outfit than his. In ten years he'll be an old man, asking me for a job. In fifteen . . ."

A feeling of sickness swept over her. She bent her head quickly, pressing her cheek against Joseph's. Jim didn't notice. He was talking, and talking, and talking . . .

Merrie would not have seen the cabin if Jim had not prepared her to look for it. They had turned off the main road onto a trail that was almost obscured by underbrush. The sun was shining, but here the road was no more than a narrow path through the timber, and the world was suddenly dark but for the strip of sky directly overhead. Some years before, wagon wheels had worn ruts into the ground but now they were barely discernible. Alder had sprouted in the abandoned road; as Jim urged the horse forward, the saplings slapped against the animal's sides and scraped the bottom of the wagon. "There!" Jim exclaimed, pointing straight ahead. "We're coming to the clearing. You'll see the house right in the center of it."

Merrie had considered the squatter's shack to which Jim took her as a new bride the loneliest place in the world. But this "house" Jim pointed to so triumphantly was more dismal that anything she had seen on the barren Dakota plain. The clearing in which it stood was no bigger than her Uncle Mike's hay barn. Stumps taller than the cabin seemed to crowd against it, vying for space and for air. All around were the giant trees; she was in a hole, a black, damp hole in the forest, with blackberry vines and ferns five feet high and poisonous devil's-clubs closing in around her. The cabin was the only sign that a human being had once tried to make a mark here, and it was as overgrown as the rutted wagon road which led to it.

"We'll have to chop out some of this," Jim said, "right around the house."

Though Joseph was heavy, Merrie lifted him down from the wagon; she would not leave him alone in this dark and frightening place. With the boy in her arms, she followed Jim through the brush to the cabin.

It was one room, built of unpeeled cedar logs and roofed over with hand-split shakes. Two openings had been cut in the walls; they had never been filled with window glass, but the remnants of rough shutters hung on crude leather hinges. The floor was of packed dirt. At the far end of the room a battered tin stovepipe protruded through the wall, suggesting there once had been some kind of cookstove. The framework of a bunk bed was nailed against one corner. Beyond that, there was nothing but the leavings of rats and skunks, and cobwebs that swayed under their burden of dust.

Jim was too much absorbed by his own mood to be sensitive to hers. "I bought a mattress, a stove, a few other things. It was a stroke of luck. An old man who lives over toward Gold Mountain is moving out, and he was willing to give me everything he had for half what it's worth."

"Tools? Will there be tools?"

Jim shrugged. "Might be an ax, or a shovel or two. All we'll need."

Merrie had lived for many years in an area where the work men did, the tools they owned, in fact the pattern of their daily lives, was dictated by the requirements of the Homestead Act. The lonely rain-soaked spot had cast a spell over her, but only temporarily, for now her practical nature was aroused. "We'll need a great deal more than that," she said firmly, "or we won't be able to prove up this claim. This clearing isn't nearly as big as the law calls for. We've got to cut trees, and cultivate, and plant. Those stumps have got to come out, we'll need fence . . ."

Jim's angry glance warned her that she had said too much. "Don't you think I'm capable of running things?" he asked. "Are you trying to tell me again that I've failed before? *I'll* tell *you* what we're going to do. I'm not going to cut one tree. I'm not going to spend one cent. The timber won't be touched until I've saved enough money to buy the equipment I need to start logging. And then," he said, his voice rising, "I'm going to walk out of Jeff Smith's camp and go into business for myself."

"But the Homestead Act . . ." Merrie objected.

"There are ways!" Jim said, an odd grin twisting his mouth to one side. "It can be done, you'll see. . . ."

Merrie was suddenly too tired to stand. She turned away, crossed the room and sat down on the dusty framework where the bunk had been.

Jim followed her and dropped to his knees beside her. "It's all for you, Merrie," he said plaintively, "everything I'm planning is for you."

She nodded wearily. His face looked so white, his eyes had such a funny brightness to them. . . . To her surprise, she could look into his face, and for that instant, at least, feel nothing. Neither fear, nor pity, nor love. "Thank you, Jim," she said quietly.

"Love me!" he sobbed, throwing his arms around her and burying his face on her shoulder. "Love me, Merrie . . ."

Unwittingly, perhaps, he was pushing the baby out of her lap. She moved Joseph to the side, securing him with one arm. "Yes, Jim," she whispered, "everything's going to be all right. . . ."

IV

Work was her release, and it brought some rewards.

Jim stayed at the logging camp during the week; each Saturday when he returned, there was some improvement to show him. The old cabin emerged from its chrysalis of brush and vine, and the sun reached in and dried its mossy walls. The interior remained bare, for the pitiful collection of castoffs which Jim had bought contained very little they needed and more was stacked in the lean-to outside than ever got into the house. The "water supply" Jim had referred to ran down the hill a hundred yards or more from the clearing and no trail to the creek had been cut; every bucket of water for drinking or cooking or washing had to be carried through heavy underbrush, even over fallen logs. But this was a chore that required no mechanical skill, just dogged determination. Merrie preferred it to the other jobs that confronted her, such as building shelves or repairing the bat-

tered cookstove, for she had never attempted the
simplest bit of carpentry and had it turn out the
way she had planned it. To her, hammers and saws
were like knitting needles; she used them energetically but not skillfully. Eventually, though, the
cabin was clean. There was a bed, of sorts, a stove,
of sorts, and other things necessary for day-to-day
existence.

It was a long day's work just to keep clean and
fed. Merrie saw many ways in which the struggle
could have been made easier. If they bought pipe,
for example, the creek water could be brought
closer to the house. If they bought a pump, and dug
a well, the heavy chore of carrying water would be
eliminated altogether. If they had heavy tools, the
clearing could be enlarged, and there would be
space in which to plant a garden. If they cut trees,
there would be pasture, and they could buy a cow.
If . . . But such suggestions angered Jim. He
wouldn't cut a single tree, he repeated; every one
was to be saved for the day the Cowen Logging
Company began operations. He wouldn't spend a
cent unnecessarily; some of his pay check went for
dried beans and flour and canned milk, but no
more than was necessary to keep them from going
hungry. The expensive gift-clothes for Joseph
were only a memory.

When Merrie dared to remind him that they
were not complying with the Homestead Act, he
grew sullen. But he did ride to Gold Mountain and
return with a half dozen live chickens tied by the
feet to the back of his saddle.

"Improvements," he said, laughing at Merrie's

expression. "Keep them penned up for a few days, then let them loose."

"They're molting," Merrie said, appraising the hens with the expert eye of a Dakota housewife. "And they look too old to lay, anyway. We won't get any eggs."

Jim laughed. "What difference does that make? You wanted to abide by the Homestead Act, didn't you? We're going to."

Besides the chickens, he had brought a dozen saplings. "Apple trees," he said, throwing the wilted bundle to the ground. "Man on the homestead to the north just finished proving up, he let me dig them up."

"They won't stand more than a foot high!"

"They're apple trees," Jim retorted.

Jim's last concession to the Homestead Act was to cut a few of his precious trees. He felled a narrow strip along the edge of the claim. "There's your clearing," he said triumphantly, "one tree wide and a quarter-mile long, but multiply it out and you've got just what the law requires."

"But the point of a clearing is to plant a garden, to develop the land."

"I'm tired of you sounding so high and mighty," Jim said testily. "There's hundreds of people who have proved up a homestead without living on it at all. Hire some kid to stay on the claim, they live in a comfortable house in town. When the five years are up, they've got 160 acres of virgin timber. There are dozens of private land companies hiring kids to squat on their claims; then the minute they get the deed they sell off the land at high prices. If we didn't grab this timber, someone else would."

A "home of our own"—there was no longer any talk of that. For six days a week she and Joseph were squatters whom Jim had placed on his claim in order to obtain free timber. On the seventh day she was his wife, but even then there was no common purpose to draw them together. Jim moved about the place restlessly, calculating the amount of standing timber, then distrusting his figures and calculating all over again. He was silent, easily irritated by anything that distracted him from his private dream. He didn't need her. Until night. And then he would plead with her if she was reluctant, tease her if she was willing, and then fall asleep by her side like a sick child whose fever has just been broken.

Week by week the burden of loneliness grew heavier. The time came when she had done so much work—in the cabin, in the clearing, even along the trail to the creek—that there wasn't enough left to exhaust her. She was hungry for people. All kinds of people, for Merrie liked everyone and needed to be liked, actively, openly, in return. She thirsted for the sound of voices, for gossip and arguments and storytelling. She yearned for something to be curious about, to laugh at. Nils and Katherine came to see her once or twice, but Merrie sensed that there would be a bad scene with Jim if she returned the visits. Her mind turned again and again to Jeff Smith. The memory of his thoughtful gray eyes, his deep and gentle voice, made the loneliness so much worse that she had to think quickly of something else.

One Monday morning after a stormy week end with Jim, she came to a decision. If she earned money herself, she could make the improvements Jim refused to finance. How to earn money? She had only a vague notion when she started off toward Gold Mountain. She had to walk, for Jim had ridden his horse to camp. And she had to take Joseph with her. Undaunted, she made a kind of hammock out of burlap sacks, stowed Joseph into it Indian-fashion and hiked to Gold Mountain with the baby on her back.

Her decision didn't weaken during the four-mile trek. If anything, it grew stronger, and by the time she reached Gold Mountain she had a dozen plans. She might do laundry for Tarpee's hotel and the Home Boarding House. She could bake for those establishments, as well as for the café adjoining Sam's saloon. There must be families for whom she could sew, especially if she were willing to take payment in barter. If she exchanged sewing for groceries, Jim could save even more of his wages, which might cool the temper she was sure he'd be in when he discovered what she was doing. . . .

Nate Tarpee was skeptical, Sam was frankly amused, the owners of the boarding house thought she was joking. In the end she convinced them all. Every Monday she would pick up the washing and orders for bakery goods, every Friday morning she would make deliveries. On the subject of sewing she was less persuasive, for she was all too honest about her ability. But she had made a good beginning. No one asked her how she was going to haul laundry and pastries and bread and all the rest from the cabin into Gold Mountain. She didn't think of it herself until Bertha Tarpee surveyed the odd contraption in which Joseph was dangling, narrowed her eyes, and asked, "You *walked* to town?"

"Just this time," Merrie answered, her confidence shaken by the question she read in Bertha's shrewd little eyes. "I'm on my way to the livery stable right now."

"I need some kind of a cart, and a horse," Merrie explained to Martin Kittinger.

The wiry Englishman cocked his head to one side. "That'll be five dollars a day."

"I couldn't possibly pay that much!"

"All right, four, but at that price you'll have to take what you can get in the way of a rig."

"No, you see . . ." Merrie took a deep breath. "You see, I haven't got any cash. The reason I need a horse and cart is to earn some money. I was hoping I could buy one and work out the payment."

Kittinger said dryly, "I see you don't know much about the value of horses. What do you think you could do for me, that would pay off two hundred, two hundred and fifty dollars?"

For the first time Merrie was touched by serious doubt. "I didn't know it would cost that much. I can do sewing, or washing, or baking."

Kittinger chuckled. "So can my wife, or I'd be a single man."

The burlap sack in which Joseph rode was cutting into her shoulders. Merrie shifted the baby's weight, brushed her hair back from her forehead, and turned to go.

"Your husband and you settle on the old Brewer place?" Kittinger asked.

Merrie nodded.

"That's halfway around the mountain. See here . . ." His bright little eyes narrowed. "I'll make you the loan of a horse and wagon. Two dollars a week and you can pay me whenever you're able."

To Merrie a problem which awaited at some vague point in the future wasn't a problem at all. "Oh, that would be kind of you!" The boarding house had offered her a cow in exchange for baking and washing. Cream from the cow could be churned into butter, butter could be sold for cash, cash could pay Kittinger for the use of the horse and wagon. . . .

"Mind you, the wagon won't be much and the mare is so old you couldn't get her to trot if you used a goad stick."

"I don't need a fast horse," Merrie said earnestly.

"You won't have one. Well, this will work out fine. I don't mind waiting for my money."

"Thank goodness," Merrie breathed, so relieved that she didn't think to ask how long it would be before the stableman would start "minding."

The horse and wagon lived up to Kittinger's description, but Merrie climbed onto the seat, propped Joseph up against her side, and took the reins in hand. They drove slowly the full length of town, the mare selecting her own pace and her own route, the curious stares of townspeople following their erratic progress. At the far end of town, Merrie tried to turn from the main road into the narrower trail which led to the homestead. The mare seemed to dislike Merrie's choice. She snorted a few times and stopped.

Merrie urged her on with a slap of the reins and a soft "Giddap." That failing, she tried a louder "Giddap." People began to collect around the wagon Merrie felt herself flushing. "Come on, girl!" she pleaded, trying to sting the horse into action by flicking her rump with the ends of the reins.

The mare put her head down between her knees and backed up.

"Whoa!" Merrie cried, and a ripple of laughter went through the crowd.

Merrie was too intent on getting the horse to move to see where Jeff Smith came from. He appeared beside the wagon with a rifle in his hand, said something like, "Having trouble, ma'am?" She gasped, "No, I can take care of myself . . ." But he vaulted into the wagon, pushed her gently out of the driver's seat and took the reins from her hands. The murmur of comment and laughter subsided and the crowd dispersed.

Jeff grinned down at her. "Now, where to?"

For a moment Merrie was so overcome by Jeff's sudden appearance she couldn't answer. His nearness was like a hearth fire radiating warmth and driving out the chill. Where to? With Jeff beside her and Joseph cradled in her arms, it really didn't matter. She didn't want to think about it, but of course she had to. "Home?" With Jim she pretended it was home. She even pretended to herself that it was home, or could be, if she did everything in her power to make it one. But with Jeff, the word stuck in her throat. "The old Brewer place," she said, avoiding his curious glance.

"The old Brewer place," Jeff repeated. He did something magical with the reins and the mare moved forward obediently.

Merrie leaned back and closed her eyes. "Mr. Kittinger said the horse was old."

"Old?" Jeff snorted. "This is Jessie. She was famous in Gold Mountain when I was no bigger than Joseph here. Would I be presumptuous to ask how you are so lucky as to be driving her?"

Merrie poured out the details of her plan. Baking in exchange for a cow, butter to pay for the use of the wagon, washing bartered for groceries, and somehow, out of it all, cash with which to buy furnishings and tools and yard goods and everything she needed to turn the old cabin into a home.

Jeff listened respectfully. "Will Jim approve?" he asked finally.

"I don't know," Merrie said wearily. "It got so I had to try it anyway, and take that chance."

A tight look appeared around Jeff's mouth. "I don't believe you need to worry." There was an edge to his voice.

Merrie looked at him curiously. "You think Jim won't object to my working?"

"I know what his plans are," Jeff replied. "He told me once, in a fit of anger, that he intended to open his own camp. When he set out to prove up the Brewer claim, I began to put stock in what he had said."

"He is a dreamer."

Jeff said quietly, "When you tell him you're going to earn money, I think you'll see he has a practical side."

How Jeff disliked Jim! And how Jim disliked—no, hated—the tall, deep-voiced man who was in position to give him orders. If Jim knew Jeff was driving her to the homestead . . . In her excitement at seeing Jeff, she hadn't even thought of it.

"Jeff," she said urgently, "I can go on alone. You must have business in Gold Mountain. You must have left your horse, or a wagon, back in town. I wasn't thinking."

"My business can wait. I have to pick up a few supplies, and I thought I might have a visit with Brother Bill to see how he's progressing with the church. Mostly, though, this trip to town was foolishness." He gestured toward the rifle which he had laid in the back of the wagon. "My father's old Spencer," he explained. "Old .52 caliber with a hinged breech lock. I had Nate Tarpee send it into Seattle, got the worn parts replaced, have her all cleaned and fixed up. Main purpose in driving to Gold Mountain today was to pick up the gun. Truly, I've got time to see you home."

Merrie winced. "You mean you'd make the time, and then you'd have to walk four miles back to town."

"Why shouldn't I?" Jeff asked, without looking at her. "I know old Jessie here, you don't. I can make her move and I'm not so sure you can."

"I've got to learn," Merrie said, anxiety increasing. "I'll be driving her in and out of Gold Mountain every Monday and Friday."

"You're peaked-looking and about to fall asleep," Jeff said. "This once I'll drive for you."

"No, Jeff, really, you shouldn't. Jim would feel . . ."

Jeff reined in suddenly. "Of course." He turned to her and their eyes met, hers anxious and unhappy, his dark with resentment. "Merrie," he said, very low, "I'm going to suggest something I've never asked anyone to do before. In a very small way, I want you to deceive your husband."

"Oh, but I . . ."

"Wait," he said gently, covering her hands with one of his. "In a very small way. I want you to take this rifle, without mentioning it to Jim. We both know how he would feel about your accepting anything from me."

Merrie nodded. "Yes," she whispered, "though he has no reason . . ."

"He is your husband," Jeff said stiffly, "he needs no reason. I've been worried about your staying out there alone. With this new project of yours, there's the added danger of driving back and forth to Gold Mountain alone. It's not the animals. Even cougar will run from meeting a human, if given half a chance. It's people, the weak creatures Brother Bill thinks are worth saving. A wagonload of linen or bake goods is a big temptation. You need protection."

Merrie looked down at her lap, where Jeff's big brown hand was restraining her own hands from pulling nervously at each other. "You're always taking care of me."

"It's an old habit," Jeff said dryly, "dating back to the day Martin Kittinger delivered you to my doorstep and then ran for his life."

Merrie tried to smile but a lump formed unexpectedly in her throat. How strange, she thought. At the time, I felt that I was enduring the worst experience of my life. Abandoned by my husband, forced to give birth to my baby in a stranger's cabin—but looking back, those weeks under Jeff's care seem more peaceful than any I have ever known. "I don't even know how to shoot a gun."

"I'll show you," Jeff said firmly, "here and now."

He picked Joseph up, threw him over his shoulder, and jumped to the ground. The baby laughed delightedly. Jeff swung him forward suddenly and held him at arm's length. Another burst of laughter.

"Your mother used to do that," Jeff said to Joseph. "She used to laugh a lot. She could find things to laugh about that the rest of us were too slow-witted to see. Why doesn't she laugh any more, Joseph? Can you tell me that?" He set the child down on the ground and turned to Merrie. "Joseph says he doesn't know."

She smiled, but her eyes were sad. "I guess he's too young. You have to grow up to be unhappy."

"Look, Merrie . . ." Jeff's hand caressed her cheek, brushing back the curls that had escaped from the blue ribbon. His fingers rested under her chin, lifting so that she would have to look up into his face. "I've been staying away from you, Merrie girl, and I think you know why. But remember this. If you ever get to the point where you'll admit to yourself that you cannot live with Jim—that you have no obligation to live with Jim—then I'll be there. Not until then. Do you understand?"

Merrie nodded. "Yes, Jeff. I understand."

"Then understand this." Jeff's head bent, his mouth was on hers. The kiss was gentle, giving only as much of himself as he could and still hold back the storm of feeling that merely touching her aroused. He straightened up, stepped away from her, and said quietly, "Now for that lesson."

Jeff taught Merrie to load the gun, and afterward stood behind her, one hand steadying her arm as she learned to sight down the barrel. His hand over her hand, he tried to give her the feel of the trigger. They talked little, only as much as was necessary to the lesson. When Jeff touched her, it was nothing more than the gentlest pressure of his hand on hers, the briefest contact as his arm rested for an instant across her shoulders. Yet there was an intimacy between them such as they had not shared since Merrie lived in his cabin. He spoke about caliber and breechloading and bore, but in the circle of his arm it sounded like a lullaby. Merrie's attention wandered. "Yes, Jeff, I see," she said sleepily. "Yes, I'll remember. . . ."

"End of lesson one," Jeff said abruptly, withdrawing his arm. He helped her into the wagon and placed Joseph beside her. "This is a beautiful gun," he said, giving the rifle an affectionate pat, "but don't forget it's a deadly weapon. Never aim it at anything you don't mean to kill." He laid the gun in the back of the wagon. "Good-bye, Joseph . . ."

The moment was slipping away. Merrie took the reins in hand and the mare, suddenly responsive to the lightest touch, jerked against the traces as if the only pace she knew was a fast trot. "Good-bye, Jeff . . ." Merrie called, and tightened her hold on the reins. The wagon rolled forward, Jessie settled into a deliberate walk. Yes, the moment was gone. Merrie looked over her shoulder, half hoping that Jeff would signal her to come back. But he was walking down the road toward Gold Mountain. He was going one way, she another.

"Come on, Jessie," Merrie implored the old mare, "come on, girl . . ." She drew Joseph closer and tried not to think of the loneliness ahead.

All week Merrie prepared herself for Jim's return to the homestead. By Saturday she had delivered one load of bakery goods to the Home Boarding House and had picked up enough washing to keep her busy for several days. The Tarpees and the others would have work for her the first of the week. But she meant to minimize these things when she talked to Jim. The moment he rode into the clearing, he would see the mare and the wagon, and the bundles of laundry could not be hidden. So she would come out with it, all of it, except Jeff's gun, which she would hide in the shed while Jim was at home. . . . By the time Jim actually appeared she had rehearsed the scene so often in her own mind that she ran out to meet him and began talking before he was out of the saddle.

She had expected him to be angry. "Doing menial work, making a spectacle of yourself . . ." She was tensed for such comments and braced for the fury that was bound to go with them.

Jim said curtly, "I wondered how you got hold of that horse and wagon," and walked past her into the cabin. The room was littered with laundry in various stages of hand-washing—some in stacks, more soaking in a battered copper wash tub, some drying on a line strung across the cabin near the stove. Jim frowned distastefully, shrugged, and said "Well, the more money we save, the sooner I can start logging."

So Jeff's prediction was right. If there was money in it, Jim would show a practical side. Merrie thought bitterly—If there's money in it, Jim expects to take it all. He doesn't even ask what purpose I might have for earning it. He will not, or maybe he cannot, see things from a point of view other than his own. Jeff made me proud of working. Jim makes me feel like a dumb beast, a work horse who can pull a plow but never run in the races down Gold Mountain's street on a Saturday night. To Jim, I am a means to an end. To Jeff, a human being, a woman.

* * * *

Monday morning Merrie rose at sunup, built a hot fire in the cookstove and began heating water.

Once more there was work, a great deal of work. And in a few days, a trip to town, where there were people. People to talk with, even laugh with, though Jeff believed she had forgotten how.

For weeks Merrie throve on a new sense of accomplishment. Orders increased with every trip to Gold Mountain. The cabin, once barren and neat, was now full to brimming with the clutter of her activity. Soapsuds spilled over the rim of the washtub while fragrant red juice dripped from berry pies cooling on the sill. Merrie never attacked chores singly. Washing, sewing, baking, ironing were all begun at once, and the resultant tangle, with some things burning, some soaking, some boiling and some drying, kept her running until long after dark. Her workday ended when she was too tired to stand, but she was grateful for exhaustion as a person in pain welcomes a drug that will stop his suffering. Eyelids drooping, she would sag into a chair and survey the day's work. The finished laundry bore many a scorch mark, the loaves of bread were never quite the same shape or size as those in a previous baking. But they were a comforting sight; she sometimes went to sleep sitting up while she was looking at them.

She lived for Mondays and Fridays. At daybreak she was already loading the wagon. Bakery goods were wrapped individually and packed into barrels Nate Tarpee had given her. Laundry was stacked into big wicker baskets. Barrels and baskets were protected from dust or rain by a heavy canvas which she stretched over the top and secured to the sides of the wagon.

After many a false start, Merrie came to grips with some of the old hand tools Jim had bought, and made a special seat for Joseph. It was a small armchair with straps and was nailed to the wagon seat beside her. Thus Joseph could neither fall nor crawl along the seat and perhaps reach for the gun which she always carried beside her.

In time Merrie's wagon was as familiar a sight in Gold Mountain as shingle weavers on their ponies Saturday afternoon or the steam train pulling into the depot just before suppertime. The bareheaded girl, slapping the reins along the back of the notorious Jessie. The dark-eyed baby, teething happily on a biscuit. The lantern swinging from a nail near the driver's seat. The rifle propped up at the girl's elbow, its gleaming barrel pointing skyward . . . The picture changed slightly when it rained. In exchange for mending, Bertha Tarpee gave Merrie a big, black umbrella; the picture of Merrie with reins in one hand and the umbrella in the other moved Nate to fashion a stand in which to fit the long handle. On rainy days thereafter, Merrie opened the umbrella, propped it upright in the stand, and she and Joseph rode to Gold Mountain under a small black tent.

Jim asked her frequently how much money she had earned, and at first grudgingly accept her explanation that her work was still paying off their debts. But as the weeks passed and Merrie was still exchanging washing for groceries and bread for the wagon she used to deliver it in, he began to make angry demands. "When are you going to get cash out of this? Damn it, why don't you start asking for the money they owe you?"

Merrie couldn't answer, for she was never sure what was owed to her, if anything. The circle of customers widened, but the pay was usually in barter and when someone couldn't afford to pay at all, she was sympathetic to their reasons and made no effort to collect. She had been earning most of their food supplies, it was true, and the boarding house had presented her with a milk cow. But they had set the value of the cow so high it was going to take months to get out of their debt. Then there was the money due Martin Kittinger for the use of the horse and wagon, and the little Englishman had been hinting that he'd like a payment, and soon. Ask for the money due her? She couldn't, and sooner or later Jim would have to be told why. . . .

During her next round of calls in Gold Mountain, she made an attempt to straighten out her accounts. It cost her dearly. The trip to town had been her reward for days of hard labor. To Joseph's delight, she had always carried on imaginary conversations all the way to Gold Mountain, and on the return trip she dramatized the actual meetings, with imitations highly satisfactory to herself and to Joseph.

The pleasure went out of the trip when she knew she was going to have to ask her clients for money. It was a miserable trip, a miserable day, and nothing came of it, anyway, for when she tried to talk about money, she chattered so incoherently no one knew what she wanted. Or if they guessed, they found it very easy to pretend they hadn't.

Her last stop was the boarding house, and there

in the parlor she met Brother Bill. "Brother Bill," she exclaimed, "I haven't seen you in a long, long time."

She was obviously so glad to see him that the minister's long face broke into a smile. "Not since Joseph's christening. How is the boy?"

"Growing fast, getting into things." Merrie added proudly, "He's almost too big for me to carry."

"He's with you?"

Merrie nodded. "Strapped to his seat in the wagon."

Brother Bill's eyes rested on her thoughtfully. "Sit down a minute," he said, "you look worn out."

There was an awkwardness to the minister that wasn't like Jeff at all, but the words could have been Jeff's. Throughout the difficult day Merrie had wished the tall slender logger would appear suddenly at her elbow, like a good genie. In her mind Bill was associated so closely with Jeff that she turned to him eagerly. "I'm having some trouble over money," she confessed, leaning back wearily in the chair he had selected for her. As if he were Jeff, she poured out the story of payment due and barter and debt.

Bill listened, nodded solemnly. "I wish I had some good advice to give you," he said when she had finished. "But you couldn't find anyone in Washington who knows less about handling money than I do."

Merrie smiled. "You've done more for me than giving me advice. You've listened."

"That's usually better than being preached at." Bill cleared his throat. "Mrs. Cowen, I can't help wondering . . . That is, this business you've built up is taking too much out of you." His homely face was suddenly suffused with color. "Now I'm preaching, after saying I wouldn't. But don't you think you ought to give up all this baking and laundry?"

"Why?"

Now the minister was clearly in misery. Looking down at the floor, he replied, "A woman should make a home for her husband."

How could she explain that it was her desire for a home that had driven her into the unsuitable project? The thought struck Merrie that if this were Jeff, she wouldn't have to explain. "Yes, a woman should make a home . . ." Bill had always seemed old and wise, but for the moment the relationship was reversed. It was the minister who was unsure of himself, she who was old and world-weary. "But sometimes circumstances make it impossible." She stood up. "You'll find out," she added gently, for the look on his face convinced her she had been short with him. "You'll get married, you'll discover that what you 'should' do doesn't always work out."

"My wife's happiness will always come first," Bill said in a hollow voice.

Merrie was beginning to worry about Joseph. She had been gone too long. "I'm sure you'll be very happy," Merrie said, as if Bill had just announced his engagement. She gave the minister's arm an absent-minded pat. "Yes, very happy. Do you want to come out to the wagon and say hello to Joseph?"

The minister nodded mutely and followed her out of the parlor.

From the veranda they saw the old mare, the wagon, and Joseph standing on the wagon seat. Standing . . . Merrie hurried down the steps. He must have loosened the straps, for he was on his feet, wobbly but free. One chubby hand was clutching the back of his chair and the other was reaching for the loaded rifle.

The knowledge of impending disaster awakened such terror as Merrie had never known. "No!" she screamed, running down the walk. "No, Joseph, don't touch!" The explosion covered her second cry. Joseph was on the floor of the wagon, blood spurting from a gaping wound in his side.

The blood vessels in her neck and throat pounded, but she felt cold. Brother Bill was beside her. As he leaned forward to touch the baby, her mind cleared. "No!" she said, pushing him back. She slid her arm along Joseph's spine, lifted him carefully until she was holding him against her body. People were running out of the boarding house. A crowd knotted around her. There was Brother Bill's face, white and drawn. There were others, a mass of faces, blurred by fright. Somewhere a woman was crying.

"Please get out of my way," Merrie said. Her voice was husky but steady. "I've got to hurry to Dr. Adams' office."

Bill said, "Mrs. Cowen, let me."

Merrie shook her head. "I'll carry him."

"You're getting blood all over," a woman sobbed. "Oh, oh . . ."

Without a word Merrie walked from the stricken group.

"I'd of carried him," someone kept repeating. At her shoulder, Brother Bill's voice said, "John, run ahead and tell the doctor we're coming,"

The main street of Gold Mountain stretched ahead. Merrie walked with her eyes fixed on Dr. Adams' two-story frame house. She was only half aware of the mumbling crowd which followed. Her stride was long, but controlled; she dared not run. She began counting. One, two, three, four . . . The front of her dress felt damp but she did not look down. Five, six, seven . . . As she progressed down the street, the crowd behind her grew. Eight, nine, ten . . . The voices faded, only the sound of footsteps pursued her down the wooden walk. Eleven, twelve . . .

Dr. Adams was waiting on the sidewalk in front of his house. His mane of white hair was rumpled, his hands pulled restlessly on his unbuttoned vest. "Rifle wound?"

Merrie nodded.

"Give him to me," the doctor ordered.

Merrie relinquished the baby. A woman beside her exclaimed, "Oh, look at her dress!"

The doctor turned on his heel and disappeared into the house. Now that Merrie had given up the baby, the crowd dared to approach her.

One of the women was Nate Tarpee's wife Bertha. "Here, dear," she said, "come with me."

Merrie shook her head and followed the doctor

into the house. He hurried through the outer office and into the back room used for surgery. The door closed between herself and Joseph.

"Come with me," Bertha repeated, laying her hand soothingly on Merrie's arm. "There's nothing you can do but wait."

"That's right," the other women chorused. Someone held out a shawl. "Wrap this around you," she said, "cover yourself up . . ."

They sounded like chattering children. "I'm going inside to help the doctor," Merrie announced and walked toward the closed door.

"That's the operating room!" someone cried. "You can't do that!"

Merrie reached for the doorknob. Two women grabbed her arms and pulled her back. "Oh, no, dear," one of them said. "That's not for you to watch."

Merrie turned toward them blindly. She knew them well, she had chatted with them time and again during her trips to Gold Mountain, but at this moment she couldn't distinguish one from the other. "Let go of me."

"No, no, we won't let you go back there."

Merrie said quietly, "There aren't enough of you here to keep me out."

Their restraining hands dropped away. Merrie went through the door and closed it behind her.

Dr. Adams looked up from examining the wound. "It's a bad one, but we can fix it," he said matter-of-factly. "You want to help?"

"That's why I came in."

"You going to be all right?"

Merrie nodded. "Tell me what to do."

The doctor issued instructions in a brusque voice, Merrie followed them methodically. In twenty minutes Joseph was bandaged and put to bed in the crib the doctor kept in his back office.

The doctor turned his attention to Merrie. "Well," he said, "you going to be the next patient?"

Merrie shook her head indignantly.

"Not going to faint? It's the usual thing for a woman. Hold up fine during an emergency, fall apart afterward. I wouldn't blame you."

"How is Joseph?" Merrie demanded.

The doctor smiled. "He'll be just fine, just fine. Mean-looking hole, but it was a glancing shot. You'd better leave him in town for a few days, though, so I can change the dressings and look him over a couple of times a day. Too bad we don't have a hospital here, but Bertha Tarpee'll keep him for you."

"If only I could stay with him! But there's the cow to be milked, the baking orders I've promised . . ."

"I know, I know," the doctor said with an impatient gesture. "Go on home. We'll take care of the boy." His voice softened. "You were a good helper, Merrie. If I didn't know how young you are, I'd figure you must have done some professional nursing at some time in your life."

"I worked at Providence Hospital in Seattle for several months. And I've often taken care of sick people."

"I remember when you were Katherine

Bengston's nurse." He looked at her thoughtfully as his fingers ran slowly through long, white hair. "You wouldn't take a job, would you?"

"I've got one. That is, I do baking and washing."

"I know all about that," the doctor replied. "You've got the whole town of Gold Mountain watching for you and that wagon of yours. But I wonder . . ." He studied her face for a moment. "Which would you rather be, a washwoman or a nurse?"

"A nurse, of course."

"You should have formal training, work in a hospital. But with your knack, I believe I could teach you more than you'd get in school. Forget about baking pies for hotels and cafés and scrubbing other people's linen."

Merrie looked away. "There are reasons why I can't. The homestead to prove up, my husband's plans . . ."

"Those are your problems," the doctor said abruptly. "You have to work them out. But the job is yours, if you want it. Of course, you'd have to live in town. You're on the old Brewer place, aren't you? I couldn't have my nurse four miles away when I needed her."

"If I did take the job," Merrie said earnestly, "a lot of problems might be solved. . . ."

The old doctor interrupted gruffly, "Then work it out, my dear girl, work it out."

8

IT WAS THE ugliest scene of their marriage.

"Work it out," Dr. Adams had said, as if there were nothing more to gaining Jim's approval than to talk with him, freely and openly, as her Aunt Sal had always turned to her Uncle Mike or as Katherine Bengston sought out Nils. She had several days to plan what she would say. But as before, rehearsing a meeting she dreaded was no help to her when the time for it actually arrived. She told Jim everything the moment he walked into the cabin. About the gun she had been carrying in the wagon, about the accident, about Dr. Adams' offer of a job. And she told it all in one long frantic recital, hardly stopping for breath.

Even at first the very sound of her voice seemed to annoy him. "So the boy's still at Tarpee's," he broke in irritably, "with that creaky old doctor paying him a call every day? What's that going to cost?" She explained, and because she could see anger collecting in his face, she repeated her explanation, and with a growing sense of helplessness, repeated it again.

His eyes darkened. The familiar nervous twitch began to pull at the corners of his mouth. At the mention of Jeff's name, his anger broke loose.

She thought he was going to strike her, for he moved toward her, fists clenched, his face a deathly white. "Jeff Smith!" he screamed hysterically. "Jeff Smith's gun! He tried to kill my son!"

"Jim, no! He had nothing to do with it! And Joseph is almost well again. The wound has healed. . . ."

"Jeff tried to kill my son!" he repeated, advancing toward her.

Merrie backed away. He didn't follow. From the center of the room he lashed her with insults, shrieking the words in a high-pitched voice, gasping for breath now and again as if each phrase had been a physical blow and he must gather strength for the next one.

If she tried to speak, he would not hear her. If she turned away, he would surely hit her. She could not tell how long it lasted. A minute, perhaps, five minutes, maybe even ten. At last his fury was spent. It died with a hoarse complaint, so low she could not catch what he said, and he stood before her, shaking with a sudden chill.

His hands went to his head. "I'm sick," he groaned, "Merrie, I'm sick . . ."

If she doubted him, it was only for a second. This wasn't the man who had been yelling at her with a crazy look in his eyes. This was Jim, and he was ill. She went to him, put both arms around him. He was shivering violently. "Don't leave me," he begged. "Some day . . ." His voice was chopped off by the chattering of his teeth.

"Some day," Merrie crooned, "some day . . ."

She led him to the bunk. Here she had a job she understood. Hands that scorched the boarding-house pillow slips and kneaded the bread too long, were quick and gentle when it came to caring for the sick. She undressed him, washed him, covered him with a cotton flannel sheet so freshly laundered that it smelled of soap and sunshine. In a half-hour he was asleep.

Merrie sat down in a chair by the window. The shutter was open, so she could look at the mountain. Darkness was gathering. The forest at the mountain's base was submerged in purple shadow, the cliffs above were pink with afterglow. Her mind was numb; there was a heavy, helpless feeling about her heart. "It doesn't matter," she told herself, "it doesn't matter . . ." The shadows deepened around the mountain, the color faded from the barren cliffs. As night fell, the sky seemed to lighten, until the outline of the mountain stood out sharp and black against the pearl-gray sky.

"Merrie . . ."

Jim's voice startled her into wakefulness. She got up quickly and made her way to the side of the bed. It was very dark in the corner where the bunk bed stood; only his face was visible. She laid her hand on his forehead; the skin was dry and cool.

"Sit down, please."

She withdrew her hand quickly. "I'll light the lamp. . . ."

"No. Just sit down."

Every muscle in her tensed in resistance, but she lacked courage, or will, to resist actively and walk away.

It was his voice that held her. "I want to talk to you. . . ." There was a clear, natural ring to it, a note of appeal. . . .

Merrie sat down on the edge of the bed, back stiff and hands clasped primly in her lap. "Yes?"

"Did you tell me something about a job? A nursing job, working for Dr. Adams?"

Merrie started, forgot her prim posture and turned to look at him. She couldn't make out the expression on his face. "Why, yes. I told you all about it."

"Tell me again."

Once more she recited the story of the accident. Her voice moved mechanically from detail to detail, for she was frightened. Not of another outburst of temper; surely no rage of Jim's would ever again have the power to terrorize her. She was afraid of something else, something as formless and shifting as fog.

She finished her story, and Jim's voice said matter-of-factly, "We'd have to move into Gold Mountain. But we wouldn't lose the homestead. There are ways to prove up land without living on it."

"I suppose there are. . . ."

"You'd make more money as Dr. Adams' nurse than you can doing baking and washing and sewing."

"Yes, oh yes."

263

He was silent for a moment. Merrie looked across the dark room, wondering.

"I haven't made a good life for you," Jim said suddenly. "But I will. Merrie, believe me, I will."

"Yes, Jim . . ."

He said earnestly, "Once I own the timber, and can start logging, then I'll build you a home. And a fine one. The finest in the state."

All at once it was hard to talk. "No need," she whispered. "I don't want a fine home."

She heard him move, felt his hand on her arm. "Lie down beside me."

The question that was tormenting her burst from her mouth. "Jim, I had already told you about the accident, and the job. Why did you ask me to tell you again?"

His answer was a long time in coming. Neither of them moved. His hand remained on her arm, she sat up stiffly, looking straight ahead. She imagined that the sound of his breathing grew loud and rough, that she could hear the heavy pounding of her own heart.

He said slowly, "Because I couldn't remember what you said."

His fingers pulled nervously at her sleeve. "I'll leave you alone, if you'll just stay with me."

Merrie lay back on the bunk bed. Jim sighed deeply and withdrew his hand. They lay side by side, still as figures of wood.

Merrie stared at the black ceiling. She felt strangely chilled, not by the coldness of the room, but by a frozen core of hopelessness and misery deep inside. At every point where their bodies touched, her own quivered with revulsion. His shoulder against hers, the sharp hip bone, the muscle of his calf . . . This was the body that had continued to arouse her even after she felt injured and cheapened by what it made her do. Now, at last, she was free. She was still trapped, yet somehow the hateful bond—the bond she had put upon herself—had been broken. She lay dead still, listening for Jim's breathing to become slower and deeper. At last he was asleep. She closed her eyes, pretending she could see the long pendulum of her Uncle Mike's grandfather clock. She watched the slow swing of the pendulum, counted out the minutes . . .

At last she rolled over on her side and sat up. Once more she waited. Carefully she got to her feet. Jim didn't stir. Hand extended, she felt her way across the dark cabin, and sat down in the chair by the window, and looked out at the mountain.

"What will I do now?" she asked the great mound of rock. "What now?"

II

Another move. Another hurried leave-taking of everything that was familiar. This time the future was sure to be better than the present. The cottage Jim had rented in Gold Mountain was one of a cluster of small frame houses only a block off the main street. There were picket fences, flower gardens, back yards where little children played and washing hung on the line. The atmosphere was as neighborly as the homestead had been lonely, and the house was handy to Dr. Adams' office, besides. And yet when the wagon had been loaded for the last time and they were leaving for good, Merrie choked up and couldn't look back.

"I thought you hated the place," Jim said peevishly. "Now you're acting as if you were suffering a great loss."

"I can't help it," Merrie said, very low. "I'm always afraid of leaving a place, any place."

That was true. To make a change was to let go of something she had been clinging to. The future might be happy, but Merrie felt as if she were retreating into it.

"You said you liked the house in Gold Mountain."

"I will, once I'm in it."

And she did. In a week's time, she was completely at home in Gold Mountain. She knew every family in the block and had flooded her neighbors on all sides with pies and bread and free nursing care.

"You're running me out of business," was Dr. Adams' rueful comment, "patching everyone up, giving them tonics, dousing them with liniment. If you'd leave them alone, they'd end up coming to me. Of course, I have this consolation—these same people are eating your bakery goods. My practice won't disappear altogether."

On weekdays life was the cheery scramble Merrie liked best. Always more to do than time allowed, and a great many people involved in the doing. By eight o'clock in the morning she had left Joseph with Bertha Tarpee and was walking briskly down the street to Dr. Adams' office. Until six o'clock at night, and often later, she was occupied with other people's troubles. Most of them were physical, but many were not; in Gold Mountain the young man who had quarreled with his sweetheart was just as apt to consult Dr. Adams as was the woman with a pain in her side. When the doctor was in, Merrie was an assistant. When the doctor was out on a call, Merrie was accepted without question as physician-until-Doc-gets-back.

The doctor had been in practice for the better part of fifty years. He'd had the finest education available—eleven months in a medical school in New York State. He'd completed every course they had to offer and had never treated a live man or woman or studied the physical remains of a dead one.

In a half-century, he'd made up for the lack. He'd been the only doctor in a small town when half the population was wiped out by an epidemic. He'd treated wounded Yankees in a temporary Army hospital until the Confederate Army swept through the area, and then he'd treated wounded Southerners. He'd hung out a shingle in Ohio, then in Missouri, finally wrapped it in burlap, stowed it away in a Conestoga wagon with a big red cross painted on the side, and moved west to Oregon with an emigrant train. From Oregon City to the newly established Washington Territory to the town on Puget Sound called Seattle, and finally, when Seattle grew too big for him, to the village of Gold Mountain in the Snoqualmie Valley. "I've had thousands of patients," he sometimes said, "but never a one that wouldn't speak well of me. Those that might have reason to complain aren't around to do it."

He'd never married. Perhaps because of this there had never been any distinction between his domestic and professional affairs. He'd never held "office hours" in his life; in his experience people had never fallen sick on schedule. His home was the second floor of the rambling farmhouse he used as an office. If there was no reason to get up in the morning, he didn't. But he never locked the house. If someone needed him, all he had to do was walk in, yell up the staircase, "Hey, Doc," and the old man was on his feet, eyes clear and hand steady. As long as he could set a broken leg or sew up a knife wound or deliver a baby, what difference did it make that he was in his nightshirt?

At seventy, Dr. Adams felt no inclination to change his ways. But in Merrie he had a nurse with no intention of limiting herself to a nurse's conventional duties—in fact, she had no idea what those duties were.

The first morning she reported for work the office was empty. But it was cluttered with the overflow from the bachelor's quarters upstairs. A bit of laundry thrown into one corner. Used dishes, cups and silverware on the window sill— apparently the doctor had had a caller while he was eating, and had carried his supper downstairs. She could see that the tools of the trade—the shelves of medicine, the surgical instruments, the worn cowhide bag, the rolls of bandage—were clean and ready for use, but they were scattered around the room. She decided it would look nicer if they were in order. The bandages all in one place, the big bottles grouped together, the little bottles over on the other side . . .

Merrie worked up a good hot suds in an oddly shaped pan she found under the sink, and went to work. In an hour she had arranged the office to her liking. She was surveying the room, wondering what to do next, when an upstairs door opened and the doctor appeared on the landing.

About his massive figure flapped a red and white striped nightdress. "Someone sick?" he asked, running his hands through his mane of white hair.

"Not yet," Merrie replied cheerfully.

"Then what's all the banging about?"

"I've just straightened things up a bit. You'd better come right down and tell me what to do next."

He groaned. "I think I'm going to need a cup of coffee before I view the wreckage."

"You should have a good hot breakfast," Merrie said firmly. "I'll come upstairs and make it for you."

The doctor resisted weakly and not for long. Merrie was a good nurse. She learned quickly and took orders well, even when he issued them in a gruff, impatient voice. But there was no convincing her that doing his laundry, mending his socks and cooking his meals were not a part of the job he had hired her to do.

"I ought to fire you," he growled the day he discovered she had rearranged the books in his library (by the color of their bindings).

Merrie was cutting gauze for surgical dressings. She looked up. "Why? What did I do wrong?"

The doctor muttered inaudibly, shook his head, pulled at his long hair and finally grumbled, "You can't sew worth a damn."

Merrie exclaimed, "But I'm learning to be a nurse! You don't have to sew to be a nurse!"

"That's just it!" the doctor exploded. "That's what I've been trying to tell you!"

"Whatever it is, I'll sew it over again."

He shook his head. It wasn't the sewing that had bothered him, anyway. "Don't you pay any attention to me," he said, breaking into a smile. "You're doing just fine. Believe me, in fifty years I haven't had a nurse like you."

"Are you laughing at me?"

"No, no . . ." He paused and looked at her affectionately. "Merrie, you've found your calling. I'm serious. I'm convinced that the demands of nursing are heavy enough to make you happy. You are happy now, aren't you?"

Merrie nodded quickly. "Oh, yes, Dr. Adams . . ."

It wasn't entirely true. Merrie sensed that the old man knew it or would not have asked the question. During the week she approached happiness along a familiar route—she kept herself too busy to think. Even at night the job absorbed and protected her; she borrowed some of the doctor's books and incomprehensible as most of the contents were, she forced herself to read until she fell asleep. Happy? Almost. Jeff Smith had understood. "Half-happy, half-alive," Jeff had said, and it was still true. The almost happy days of the week were shadowed by doubt and fear. Every week end that Jim came home from camp, the shadow darkened.

She came to dread his arrival, for his moods came on him more frequently now and they seemed to be increasing in violence. In a good mood, he was gayer than he had ever been. He sang, he made her dance with him, he tossed Joseph into the air and burst into high-pitched laughter when the baby began to cry. His rages

were as wild. She learned not to listen as he
stomped back and forth across the kitchen, abus-
ing her with words, his voice rising in frenzy when
he couldn't make her flinch. Sometimes while he
was home, he would count the money they had
saved, and talk once more about his logging camp,
the camp that would beat Jeff Smith's in every
way. And sometimes often after a fit of temper, he
would come to her begging, "Love me, Merrie.
Help me . . ."

To Merrie's surprise, he did not thwart her the
first Sunday morning she dressed in her best and
went to church. She knew he would not go with
her. The memory of the day he dared Jeff to race,
and lost, had burned deeply into his mind; unless
he was riding high on the crest of a happy mood, he
avoided the main street of Gold Mountain. She did
expect that he might resent her going to church
alone. He had always been irritated by her friendliness and even more by the fact that people obviously liked her in return.

"Go ahead," he said diffidently. "I had planned
to ride out to the homestead. If you'd rather listen
to that raw-boned Methodist than come with
me . . ."

Merrie had an impulse to protest. When they
moved into Gold Mountain, Jim had "hired" an
old derelict bachelor to live on the homestead and
"prove it up." Having bowed to legal requirements to that extent, he had shown no interest in
the place, beyond riding past occasionally on his
way back to camp. She knew that he had just this
instant made the "plan" to spend the day at the

homestead. It was ridiculous to suggest that she and Joseph could accompany him; she had returned old Jessie and the wagon to Kittinger's stable and Jim was not the kind to ride ten miles, to the homestead and back, with Joseph in the saddle in front of him and herself behind holding on. But to point out that he was, in a sense, lying to her, would surely throw him into a temper. "All right, Jim," she said quietly, took the toddling child by the hand and started for church.

"I won't be here when you get back!" he called when she reached the door. "I'll keep right on to camp!"

His voice was rising. How many times had she heard that first warning of the tantrum to come . . . "As you wish, Jim," she said hurriedly, and closed the door. Joseph's hesitant gait would slow her down. She picked him up. Panting with the weight, she fled down the dirt road toward town.

After that Merrie went to church every Sunday. Jim scoffed, or ignored her absence, but only once flew into a rage and ordered her to stay home. At first, churchgoing was an escape. It gave her two peaceful hours, safe from the storm that threatened every minute Jim was home. And then Brother Bill asked the ladies of the congregation if they could do something to help the building fund, and all at once church became important in itself.

Services were held in the schoolhouse, just as they had been in the days when Bill was still an itinerant preacher and Gold Mountain was a point on his circuit which he reached only ten or twelve times a year. Bill was building a church, but had got no further than bare floor, walls, and a roof, when the funds ran out. His salary was gone; he had used it to pay the last bill from the sawmill in Three Forks. If the church was to be finished, they must order windows, shingles, finished lumber for the pews, altar and choir benches. The building plans called for a steeple; if they meant to install a church bell, then they must raise the money for that, too. They had talked about a big dedication service —but, Brother Bill reminded them solemnly, finishing the church building wasn't enough. To be dedicated, it must be free of debt. At this point he turned to the women. In other towns, he said, the ladies of the congregation had put on dinners and fancywork sales. Would those present be willing to work on such projects?

The last hymn was sung, the final prayer was said, Brother Bill nodded dismissal and walked stiffly to his position at the door. Sunday petticoats rustled as the women got to their feet. The men straightened up from cramped positions at desks too small for them, sighed, stuffed their hands in their pockets and waited for their wives to lead the way. The children bounded for the open door, throwing grins or guilty looks at the preacher as they raced toward freedom. Church was over—until the two-hour prayer meeting scheduled for seven o'clock that night.

Merrie approached Brother Bill eagerly. "I'll be glad to help," she said. "I'm not very good at fancywork, but I can cook and bake."

The minister took her hand, gave it a quick,

nervous shake and dropped it. "You're just about the busiest woman in Gold Mountain," he said. "Are you sure you have time?"

His manner puzzled her. Behind the pulpit, even the improvised pulpit here in the schoolhouse, Brother Bill had the dignity of an older man. But when he met her informally, as he had in the boarding house the day Joseph was hurt, he appeared unsure of himself. Merrie thought—poor man, he just doesn't know how to talk to women. Instantly she felt sorry for him and liked him better than she had before. "Of course I have time," she assured him.

"There's to be a business meeting Tuesday night. Perhaps you could come to that. . . ."

There was no hesitation in Merrie's reply. Jim would be at camp. "If the doctor doesn't need me. Week nights we sometimes work late."

Brother Bill said, "Perhaps Saturday or Sunday would be better. . . ."

Merrie felt the blood rush to her face. She leaned down quickly to button Joseph's coat. "Tuesday evening will be fine."

She felt the minister's gaze upon her as she hurried across the school yard and turned down the road toward the house where Jim was waiting.

III

On a Saturday in March Jeff hitched the big mare to the wagon and drove to Gold Mountain. It had been a long time since he made the trip. Not since Christmas, when he had spent the day with Nate and Bertha Tarpee. He'd never forget it, because he had thought all day, this is Merrie's birthday, and he kept wondering what sort of a celebration Jim Cowen was providing for her in their little rented house a few blocks away. He hadn't left camp for the rest of the winter; Mike Jessup or Dave Riley had hauled supplies for him.

"Years ago, a logger *had* to stay in camp for three, four months at a time," Dave had said. "And how we bellyached and howled and cussed. Here you can get to town every Saturday night, easy. What's itching you, Jeff?"

"Nothing," Jeff had replied curtly. "That's why I don't have to go to town."

"You'll turn into a hermit. A blind hermit, too, if you don't quit all that reading. Books, books. What you got against people?"

Jeff grinned. "Nothing. As a matter of fact, I like people very much. The books I read are all about people."

"Hrmph," Dave replied. "That's not as good as the real thing."

"Sometimes it's better," Jeff retorted. "You can close a book."

Dave didn't know his reason for staying in camp. If his good friends, Nils Bengston or Brother Bill, had guessed it, he would have lied to them deliberately. But he was honest with himself. He had avoided Gold Mountain because he did not want to see Merrie until the sight of her had lost the power to disturb him.

She is a married woman, he had reminded himself that day last summer when he helped her get old Jessie started on the road to the Brewer place. However hot-tempered or childish or cruel her husband might be, however hurt or disappointed she might feel, she went to him. That was the fact to remember. In that one lingering kiss, he had felt her respond to him. In her backward glance as she drove off he had seen her reluctance to leave him, or perhaps her reluctance to go back to Jim. Either way, the point was—*She had gone back*.

Again and again the afternoon he taught Merrie to use a rifle came back in vivid detail. Again and again he told himself not to think about it. Not about the sadness in her eyes. Not about how thin she had gotten. Not that the faded hair ribbon he'd intended to give back to her some day must have been the last she had, for that afternoon her coppery-brown hair had been tied back with a leather thong. "She went back to her husband," he repeated doggedly, saying it out loud so that the sound of his own voice drove the hurt even deeper. If he had to remember anything, let it be that.

In camp he saw Jim Cowen six or eight times a day. Here was the truth in flesh and blood. Merrie's husband. The sight of him would be a reminder, day after day, week after week—he would never turn away from it. In time he would stop hating Jim and stop loving Merrie.

Feelings die, he told himself, and I will be free. I *am* free. The timber can be sold, the camp can be closed. I'll go with old Henry Cowen when he heads north for British Columbia; I'll go farther, to the territory the prospectors are beginning to talk about among themselves, the Yukon. I'll leave the building of the Valley to others, and the high hopes and disappointments that go with it. Let Brother Bill erect a church, and Nils Bengston and Katherine fight for a new school. . . . All winter he hugged this dream. But he never put his property up for sale, never told Henry Cowen that he would go with him in the spring. He found that he couldn't even offer to sell the land that had been his father's. He couldn't even leave it.

This trip to Gold Mountain, his first in many months, was proof to himself that he had recovered the freedom he had known before Merrie came. Once more he was lonely, but at peace. "Permanently impermanent," as Brother Bill had expressed it. Jeff smiled. He'd look for Bill the minute he got to town, and see how the preacher had fared in recent battles with skeptical elders and penny-pinching parishioners. Perhaps, he mused, Bill has found a wife by now.

The main street of Gold Mountain was crowded even for a warm evening in March. There were families from the neighboring town of Three Forks and even from Black River, some ten or twelve miles away on the riverbank below the falls. The usual groups of shingle weavers and loggers had taken up their customary positions before their favorite saloons, but both groups were swollen with men Jeff had seldom seen out on the town on Saturday night.

Something doing, Jeff noted, and when he tied up at Kittinger's stable he found out what it was. Three large, brightly painted wagons stood in a row in the side street between the stable and Nate Tarpee's store and hotel. Several thin, large-boned draft horses were grazing in the field beyond. There were posters nailed to the walls of the store, to the side of the stable, to the wagons: *"The Logger's Sweetheart,* or *Revenge in the Forest,* The Greatest Sawmill Drama of All Time, a Tale of Death and Danger in the Deep Woods . . . Thrilling Action . . . The Most Authentic Sawmill Scene Ever Produced West of the Great Divide . . ."

So that was it. A traveling theatrical company had come to town.

In Tarpee's store the crowds were thicker and the posters more numerous than they were outside. Nate hailed Jeff from behind the counter. "Well, Jeff," he called over the heads of children who were selecting candy from a big glass jar. "So it took a bunch of live actors to bring you in from the woods."

Once this store had been the property of Nils

Bengston, and Nate had been only the manager. Then the counter was rough-hewn and the stock was confined to essentials. But when hard times hit the hop industry, Nils had lost the trading post along with ownership of the biggest hop ranch in the world, and Nate had bought it from the receivers. Nate was proud of the improvements he had made. Nowadays the shelves contained everything from loggers' boots to spring tonic to embroidery thread to those newfangled one-pound paper sacks of Arbuckle's coffee that came already roasted and ground. Some of the old hand-hewn counter remained, just as it had been when Jeff was a little boy, but a large section had been replaced by a glass-topped cabinet in which Nate displayed such oddly assorted items as cut-metal shoe buckles and mustache wax.

Jeff leaned on this cabinet and grinned at the balding storekeeper. Nate had given him his first taste of barley candy—Jeff touched the big glass jar affectionately, for it was just like the one he'd viewed so longingly as a little boy that Nate had invariably slipped some of the contents into his hand when his father wasn't looking. "The show seems to have brought everybody into town," he remarked. "Business ought to be good."

Nate answered with a wry nod. "Tonight I could sell the ache in my back, if there was any way to wrap it up."

"Then why do you look so worried? Bertha lay you out today?"

Nate chuckled. Bertha's scolding tongue was part of Gold Mountain folklore and was as generally accepted as her big heart. "If she didn't, I wouldn't know I was awake," Nate said. "No, I'm worried about how this night is going to end up. Seems to me everyone's expecting an awful lot. By the time the show starts some of them aren't going to be in a mood to get disappointed."

"You think they will be?"

Nate shrugged. "I seen the men who are going to act out this drama, as they call it. They're supposed to be loggers. If they're loggers, that little dried-up Kittinger across the street ought to be lifting weights in the circus."

Jeff laughed. "They're professional actors, Nate. They don't have to be loggers to know how to act like them."

"*Everybody's* in town," Nate objected, anxiety pushing his voice to a higher key. "Every logger and shingle weaver on the west side of the Cascades. And look at that poster . . ." He pulled one of them off the wall behind him, threw it onto the counter and pointed to the illustration. "Look at that, Jeff. Look at it yourself. That there is supposed to be a circular saw. It's different from any circular saw I've ever seen and I was born so close to a sawmill I've had a ringing in my ears all my life."

"It's the drama that counts."

"Oh, no," Nate said, shaking his head so emphatically that the few remaining strands of hair were dislodged from their fixed positions on his shiny skull. "Oh, no, not to me, it ain't. I've got to think about my store. I've been outside and I notice the loggers are lining up on one side of the street and the shingle weavers on the other."

"They always do that."

"I'd rather see them mixing," Nate said mournfully. "There'll be a fight."

"A fight?" Jeff chuckled. "They don't consider that trouble."

"Well, it ain't fun to me," Nate said, still shaking his head. "Sooner or later somebody will come in and ask to buy something I haven't got. While I'm trying to explain, they'll take the place apart looking for it."

Pessimism was as much a part of the storekeeper's make-up as his shiny pate and fear of his two-hundred and-fifty-pound wife. Nate was the central figure of several legends, many based on reports of what Bertha had done when he forgot to renew her stock of chewing tobacco. Another popular tale established Nate as the man who sold a bottle of bluing to an Indian on the customer's promise not to drink this special kind of firewater until he was a mile out of town.

"You'll know what to do," Jeff said, grinning.

"Sure," Nate retorted, "I'll yell for you."

"Then you'll have to make it loud, because I'm going to spend the evening with Brother Bill, if I can find him."

"You can find him, all right. Down at the schoolhouse, busier than a saloonkeeper on Saturday night."

Jeff stood up and stretched. "I'll walk over there. What sort of doings?"

"Church supper, biggest we've ever had. That nurse at Doc Adams' is behind it. Soon as she heard a theatre troupe was coming, she got the women organized and they've been cooking and baking and fussing all week long." Nate gave a dry chuckle. "That Merrie. She even got Bertha over there, dishing out chocolate cake, first church supper Bertha ever saw in her life. I got to hand it to that girl, all things considered."

"What do you mean," Jeff said, very low, " 'all things considered'?"

Nate looked at him shrewdly. "Do you know her husband?"

Jeff said roughly, "He works for me."

Nate shrugged. "Then you ought to know what I mean."

Merrie no longer had the power to disturb him. . . . Jeff had believed that, in the lonely security of his cabin or the logging camp. Yet hearing nothing more than the mention of her name, he knew it wasn't true. "Should be about time for the great sawmill drama," he said.

"Starts at eight o'clock, in Doc Adams' old barn." Nate pulled a large silver watch from his pocket, pressed the side with his thumbnail so that the top snapped open. "It's only five to seven," he said, squinting at the Roman numerals on the watch's face. "Full hour before the show."

"I'll go find the boys from my camp, make sure they aren't stirring up trouble."

"But I thought you were going to see Bill?"

"Tomorrow," Jeff snapped. Nate looked up quickly. "When he's not so busy," Jeff added, and tried to smile.

Nate studied him for a moment, then shrugged

and turned his attention to his watch. He closed the lid carefully, polished the watch front and back against his sleeve, returned it to his vest pocket. "Eight o'clock," he repeated, "in Doc Adams' barn."

Jeff nodded, made a gesture of farewell and left the store.

IV

It wasn't Cordray's or the New Seattle, but the barn next to Doc Adams' house made a passable theatre, at least for a company whose longest engagement had been three nights in Portland, Oregon and that five years before when their scenery was new.

A platform had been built at one end of the barn, and a faded red theatre curtain, property of the troupe, had been strung from the rafters so as to screen the improvised stage. What mystic preparations the actors might be going through behind that curtain, nobody knew. The audience had come from every corner of the Snoqualmie Valley. Many had never seen a "drama," many wouldn't have gone to a threatre in Seattle, on the grounds that all actresses are immoral and all such entertainment wicked. But *The Logger's Sweetheart* was about a sawmill and the environment, old Doc Adams' hay barn, couldn't have been less sinful. So, as it neared eight o'clock, the rows of benches began to fill. Farmers, their wives, and their children. Storekeepers, drummers, loggers, shingle weavers. They were all there in force, all waiting expectantly for the greatest sawmill drama of all time.

It was curtain time and the barn was filled to capacity when Merrie and Jim arrived.

Merrie had not wanted to come. There was work to do at the schoolhouse. Dishes to wash, accounts to be straightened, and then there was to have been a special meeting when the women (Bertha Tarpée had confided) were to present her with a gift in thanks for the work she had done. But just before eight o'clock Jim had appreared at the schoolhouse door.

"Come on," he said irritably. "The play starts in ten minutes. We'll be late."

Big colored posters had been displayed all over Gold Mountain for a week or more, but Jim had never before mentioned the show. "I can't leave now," Merrie whispered. "There's a lot to be cleaned up, and besides they asked me especially to stay for a meeting."

"What makes you think they can't get along without you?" Jim said. "Let them have their meeting. You come with me."

She knew instantly that Jim had learned the purpose of the meeting. But if she insisted on staying . . . She threw an unhappy glance at the women washing dishes on the other side of the room. Everyone was looking the other way, they were talking all at once and making an unnecessarily loud clatter with the dishes.

"You go ahead to the show," she said to Jim urgently.

"I want you to come with me!" His voice was shrill, the corner of his mouth twitched angrily.

"All right," she whispered. "Please, Jim, I'll come. But what about Joseph?"

Jim shrugged. "Bring him."

And so she had risked what the women might think of her for leaving, because she knew how much worse the humiliation would be if she stayed. She had offered them only the briefest explanation. "Don't worry, dear," Bertha Tarpee whispered hoarsely, and the other women kept talking and looking the other way. Jim turned on his heel and walked out. Merrie picked up Joseph and hurried after him, away from the schoolhouse and down the street to Doc Adams' barn.

The interior of the barn was dark, and crowded with the moving shadows of men and women stirring restlessly on the benches and standing along the walls. The only illumination came from a row of kerosene lamps which had been placed, like footlights, along the outer rim of the platform that was to serve as a stage. Every other lamp had been lighted; the yellow flames danced nervously before the wind that whistled through the cracks in the old barn's wall.

"Over here," Jim commanded, pushing past the men who were standing along the wall. Someone Merrie could not recognize in the darkness got up from the bench and said, "Here, lady, you and the baby can have my seat." Merrie took it gratefully, for her arms and back ached from carrying the boy. As she settled Joseph on her lap, she heard Jim speak to another man, there was an angry retort, a brief scuffle in the darkness, and then Jim was sitting beside her.

"What was that?" Merrie asked anxiously. "Did you take someone's seat?"

Jim said gruffly, "Watch the show."

Two boys emerged from behind the curtain and began to light the alternate lamps. They were local boys whom the company was rewarding with free tickets to the performance. Recognizing them, a dozen men whistled. From the rear of the barn one voice called out, "Say, Joey, what all's going on back there? You got that famous sawmill running yet?"

Everyone laughed, everyone turned to see who had spoken. Merrie did not know the man, but as her glance traveled over the crowd at the opposite side of the barn, she saw Jeff.

He was looking at her. Their eyes met, she knew he must recognize her and must know that she had recognized him. But he didn't move or speak. Her pulse jumped skittishly. She lifted one hand to wave. . . . Jeff was looking past her, at Jim. Her hand dropped to her side. Slowly she turned back toward the stage. Jim had not seen Jeff, and from this position she couldn't either. Neither man would know about the dull pain that had settled around her heart.

Grinning self-consciously, the boys finished lighting the lamps and disappeared behind the curtain. They reappeared in an instant and began to pull the curtain back by hand. This act was greeted with a burst of whistling louder than the first. But all sounds from the audience died abruptly as the scene behind the curtain was revealed.

This was no sawmill, such as everyone was prepared to see. According to a big white sign which one of the boys was holding over his head, it was "Home of Millionaire Lumberman Silas Schmidt." But this was only the first act. The audience sighed audibly, sat back, and waited.

They watched patiently while a story about a rich girl, a poor logger and the rich girl's millionaire fiancé unfolded slowly and awkwardly on the platform in Doc Adams' hay barn. The illusion of opulence of a rich man's home was created by a painted backdrop showing crystal chandeliers, marble columns, and other wonders which would have been more easily identified if the paint had not been so badly faded. A strong draft was blowing through some spot in the barn wall that needed a new batten, and the millionaire's marble house had a tendency to ripple. But everyone wanted to see the sawmill scene, and so they watched without a murmur as the first act was played out and the boys pulled the curtain back across the stage.

As the curtain opened for the second act, the audience watched expectantly and again sat back, disappointed. "In The Woods," the sign said this time, and sure enough, the backdrop was now covered with trees. All kinds of trees—larches, white birches, scrub pine, and several other varieties common to the woods two or three thousand miles to the east. Against this background the poor logger wooed the rich girl, the rich girl quarreled with the millionaire lumberman who was her fiancé, the millionaire blamed the estrangement on the logger. The audience was beginning to grow restless. Somewhere in the shadows a man burst out, "The board I'm sitting on is getting to feel kind of hard. How's yours, Joe?" Laughter rose from the benches.

"Quiet!" another voice commanded from the other side of the barn. Ordinarily that order would have released a flood of noise. Nothing happened. They were still waiting, still anxious to see that sawmill scene.

At last it came. The boys had hauled the curtain down, dragged it back again for the third time, and there it was revealed, the most authentic sawmill scene west of the Great Divide. Silence gripped the audience as man, woman and boy leaned forward on the benches and stared.

The saw stood in the center of the stage, and it was turning slowly, powered by a pitifully small gasoline engine. A log lay on the carriage, ready to be cut. It was a cull, a small, crooked discard such as any logger would blush to cut except for firewood. The carriage it lay on lacked every mechanical device necessary to turning logs into lumber. Nothing to hold the log in place as it went past the saw. No way to control the carriage. No means of turning the log over so that the saw could slash through the other side.

The poor logger and the rich girl recited their lines as loudly as they could, but the first, tentative burst of laughter grew rapidly into a steady roar. Loggers and shingle weavers alike began to give advice to the players as to how to get clear-grained boards out of that measly snag.

Rising shrilly above these professional comments were the voices of the hero and heroine, who by now were screaming endearments at each other in their attempt to be heard. The villainous millionaire lumberman charged onto the stage. Over loud protests from the other side of the footlights, he knocked the logger unconscious and turned on the girl.

A voice rose high and clear from that corner of the barn where the shingle weavers had gathered. "Now there's one logger that looks just as natural as can be, flat on his back with his hands folded real neat acrost his chest!"

The good-natured laughter died. A moment before, loggers and shingle weavers had been ready to move onto the stage and take the sawmill scene apart with joyful coöperation. This insult from the shingle weavers killed the project instantly. There wasn't a logger or a weaver in the audience who was even looking at the stage, though all three actors, including the unconscious "logger" on the floor, were pleading at the top of their lungs, "Quiet, please! Quiet, if you please?"

Merrie turned to Jim. "I think we'd better leave." Her thought seemed to be shared by others, for women were already getting up from the benches and hurrying toward the door.

Jim said curtly, "I'm going to stay and see the end of the play."

"But there could be a fight!"

"I paid for these seats!"

All around them people were standing. From the shadows men came forward, joining the group of shingle weavers on the one side of the barn, or the phalanx of loggers on the other. Merrie's arms tightened around Joseph, and she got to her feet.

"Sit down!" Jim's voice commanded. His hand fell on her arm and he pulled her down to the bench. "*I'm* deciding what to do," he muttered in a strange, thick voice, "*I'm* taking care of you."

The two groups of men surged across the room toward each other. With Jim's hand heavy on her arm, Merrie turned to look for Jeff. He was gone. She stared unbelievingly at the spot where he had been. Yes, he was gone, and this somehow was far more frightening than the blocks of angry, half-drunken men moving toward each other.

"Quiet, please!" the villain was repeating on the stage. The girl he had tied to the sawmill carriage a foot or two from the saw was now propped up on one elbow calling, "The show isn't over, the show isn't over, there's more, quiet, please!"

"You're right, sister!" a voice boomed from the audience. "The show is just now getting started!"

In the half-darkness men laughed, swore, pushed each other, leapt over the benches in their eagerness to get into the fight. In the center of the storm, Merrie sat with Joseph on her lap, still and cold as a stone. Women and children brushed past her as they escaped toward the door. "Jim," she begged, "Jim . . ."

Louder than all the shouting was the sudden sound of a bench hurled against the barn wall.

Jim released her arm and leapt to his feet. "I'm

going to get into it!" he cried excitedly. "Here I come!" He ran toward the tangle of fighting men, tripped against a bench, caught himself, and ran on, fists clenched. She heard his high, shrill laughter, and then he disappeared into the mob.

I've got to get out. . . . Merrie struggled to her feet. Panting, swearing figures jostled her on all sides. Frightened, Joseph clung to her and began to cry.

Out of the shadow someone reached out, took the baby from her. Even before she looked up, she knew it was Jeff.

"I'll carry the boy," Jeff said quietly. "You walk right behind me, close as you can get. Hold onto my belt, and don't let go."

Between them and the door was a howling, stampeding mob of men, some fighting to get out, others elbowing their way forward to join the battle. "Make room, friends," Jeff commanded in a low voice. He moved forward with Joseph in his arms and Merrie at his heels, and the human barriers melted away.

On the street clusters of people were chattering together excitedly. A child was crying, women looked back anxiously at the open door. Without a word Jeff strode down the street toward Merrie's cottage, and Merrie followed. He slackened his pace, and they walked side by side, neither of them speaking. When they got to the cottage, Jeff walked in and set the baby down carefully in the rocking chair. "Good boy," he said to Joseph, "good boy . . ." and then he turned to leave.

Merrie followed him to the door. "Thank you,"

she said. "Again, thank you for helping me."

She could not see his face, but his tall figure stood out clearly against the blue-black sky. "Jeff," she whispered, "oh, Jeff . . ." She reached out toward him. But he was gone. He had turned away from her; he was walking quickly down the street toward town.

V

Sunday morning sunshine broke over a town as
innocently peaceful as a sleeping baby. There was
some evidence that the great sawmill scene had
met with displeasure the night before. At some
point loggers and shingle weavers had tired of
fighting each other, and the survivors had banded
together to take the "theatre" apart. They had
removed the "stage" from Doc Adams' hay barn
and stacked it untidily against the wall of Nate
Tarpee's store. Benches had been reduced to splin-
ters and the painted backdrop to shreds, and then
the men had descended playfully upon the actors
themselves.

The actors, meanwhile, had taken refuge in their
rooms in Tarpee's hotel. The scuffle, Nate reported
to Jeff at breakfast, had not lasted long. The mob
had hustled the actors out of their rooms and
across the street to the livery stable. In a matter of
minutes, horses were hitched to the wagons, men
and women were lifted aboard and the traveling

drama troupe was on its way out of town. Total damage, Nate observed with relief, was a few broken door handles and splintered doors. Nothing to lose sleep over.

Jeff grinned. "I was upstairs, you know, while you were downstairs with your head under the pillow. Whose sleep are you talking about?"

"Just a fair-to-middling ruckus," Nate insisted, "but I'm going to make the boys pay for some new doors." He squinted up at Jeff. "That young hothead out at your camp, that Jim Cowen, or Tony Marko, or whatever he calls himself, he's one of them that's going to have to give me a few dollars for the fun he had here last night. You can tell him that for me."

"You'll have more chance of collecting if you tell him yourself."

Nate chuckled wisely. "Yes, I'll bet he don't like you much for showing him up so bad the day he pushed his way into the horse race."

"That's part of it."

Nate leaned toward Jeff confidentially. "Why do you keep that guy in camp, Jeff? He's a troublemaker; everybody knows that."

Jeff said curtly, "I'm short of help. He's a good logger."

"The hell you say," Nate replied, with a grimace.

Jeff stood up. "Well, I'm on my way back to camp."

"Going to stop by and see Brother Bill?"

Jeff nodded.

"You don't need to tell him where you heard

what people are saying—about wanting a married preacher, and about the church bell, and that."

"I won't even discuss it unless Bill tells me himself."

"And don't wait so long to come back to town, Jeff. You're going to get peculiar, keeping to yourself so much."

Jeff grinned. "There are fifty loggers in my camp. You can't say I'm alone."

Nate shook his head. "Boy, I've known you since you were born. You're the most alone man that ever was."

Jeff rode to the schoolhouse, where he knew he'd find Brother Bill preparing for church and Sunday School. The preacher greeted him warmly. "It's been a long time since you've come to town," he said. "Going to stay for the service?"

Jeff shook his head. "I've got to get back to camp. But I wanted to get the latest report on your battle with the forces of evil."

"It's not bad people who give me trouble," Bill said dryly, "it's the good ones."

Jeff chuckled. "I understand you're having difficulty raising money to finish the church."

Bill nodded.

"Does that surprise you?"

Bill's long face was intensely solemn. "Here, yes. I expected it when I was walking the circuit, because people were poor, and they lived far apart, and they couldn't see what their money was going for. But here I'm building a church. When they give, it's for something permanent, something they themselves will own." He shook his head.

"I'm going to have to go to work, if I want to finish the church and see it dedicated."

"Work . . ." Jeff smiled. "You're working all the time, or you've changed since I last saw you. You mean you're going to get another job?"

"On the railroad crew. They're putting in some bridges about ten miles down, near Gilman."

Jeff said, "I didn't know you were an engineer."

"I'm not," Bill said, "and I told the foreman as much. Sixteen, seventeen years ago I was loading schooners on the Seattle waterfront, though at that time I was a cooper by trade. Foreman said he didn't need a stevedore, a cooper, *or* a preacher, but if I knew how to run a jack plane and would plane some heavy timber by hand, I had a job. I start tomorrow."

"Then Gold Mountain won't have a preacher for a while?"

"I'll come back for services every Sunday."

"Work at Gilman until Saturday night, back on the job at Gilman on Monday morning—you're going to walk twenty miles to give a sermon?"

Bill said gruffly, "If I thought it would improve my preaching, I'd walk farther than that."

Jeff grinned. "Your sermons never last longer than fifteen minutes. How could you improve on that?"

Bill's solemn face broke into a smile. "What's been keeping you at camp? It's been a long time since we sat down and talked."

Jeff ignored the question. "Any problems developed here in Gold Mountain?" he asked lightly. "I like to hear about your troubles, Bill, you've always got so many of them."

Bill frowned. "There's been a fuss about a church bell. Mark offered to buy one and donate it to the church, I turned him down. Some of the congregation are saying I shouldn't have refused."

"Mark, the blacksmith? Man with the shop right next to where you're building the new church?"

Bill nodded. "That's the man. But he also runs a saloon. I can't preach against the use of alcohol and then accept money for the church that comes from the sale of beer and whiskey."

"Forget about the saloon, think about the smithy."

Bill snorted. "That's what some of my good people are telling me, but they aren't joking."

Jeff laughed. "If that's your only problem, I'd say your situation in Gold Mountain is pretty peaceful."

"I'm right about the bell," Bill said stubbornly.

"Oh, I'm sure you are," Jeff agreed. "But what a terrible burden it is, to know so surely what's right, and what's wrong."

Bill looked at him curiously. "What's on your mind?"

Jeff stood up. "My logging camp. I've got to get back."

Bill followed him to the door of the schoolhouse. They smiled at each other, shook hands. "I almost forgot to ask," Jeff said. "Remember our long conversation, back in the fall of '93, when you first decided to settle down in Gold Mountain?"

To Jeff's surprise, Bill's pale face flushed suddenly. "I remember," he said, "the day the girl came."

"Yes." Jeff looked into Bill's anguished face and found his own poise shattered by a new realization. "You said that day that as a permanent minister, you might consider marriage. I've been wondering if you'd found someone. . . ."

"Yes." Bill said. "But she isn't—she isn't for me."

Dear God, Jeff thought. He loves her, too. Hurriedly, he said good-bye and rode back to his cabin, Merrie's face, and Bill's face, were before his eyes everywhere he looked.

9

SPRING RIPENED INTO summer. The meadow larks sang in the open fields, dust rose behind the wagon wheels, wild cucumber vines climbed the fences and hung from the lower branches of the swamp maple trees. Gradually the days grew shorter; the air was clear, the sun bright, but when darkness fell, mist rose from the ground and settled over the meadows. September, October—and all at once Joseph's second birthday was only a few days off.

It would come in the middle of the week, when Jim was at camp. "We'll have a party, you and I," Merrie told the little boy. "With a big cake, and candles, and a present from the store."

The present was a small cast-iron wagon drawn by a pair of sturdy cast-iron draft horses, the whole painted in shiny yellows and reds and browns. The cake was big, as Merrie had promised, and well illuminated, for the only candles in Nate Tarpee's store were the large, white, practical variety townspeople and homesteaders kept on hand against the moment they ran out of kerosene. They made great holes in the cake and sent quantities of smoke spiraling toward the ceiling, but Joseph was delighted.

"Blow," Merrie instructed the boy. "Like this, see? Blow. Blow *hard*."

Joseph blew, tentatively at first, then with increasing gusto. The twin flames bent away from him, flickered, and were gone. Laughing, the boy grabbed a candle in each hand, pulled them out of the cake and began licking the frosting that clung to the butt ends.

"Happy birthday," Merrie sang, "happy birthday, Joseph. . . ."

Two years in the Snoqualmie Valley . . . All day long that thought had haunted her, but what was the use of looking back? Perhaps it was Aunt Sal's letter that made her so broody. "It's a comfort to hear what a fine boy Joseph is, and to learn that you are busy and happy. . . ." Busy—yes. Happy? Of course, she had written that she was, and at such a moment as this it was almost true. Whenever Jim was gone . . . She stopped herself. Jim was not here to spoil Joseph's birthday; she must not let her feelings about him spoil it, either.

She slept fitfully that night, awakening again and again with a sense of having narrowly escaped some terror which her dream was about to reveal. Her body was rigid, her heart was pounding, her fists were clenched so tight the fingernails cut into her palms. Coming fully awake, she would take a deep breath, open her hands out flat, palms down. The big aluminum alarm clock ticked loudly in the darkness. Joseph slept peacefully in his bed. The dream receded—what was there to be afraid of . . . ? Then she would close her eyes and tell herself to think about her work for Dr. Adams. Patients received yesterday, patients expected tomorrow, and what she would cook for the doctor's dinner . . . The first pale light of the new day was edging its way into the bedroom when Merrie came upon the idea of founding a hospital.

She was in Dr. Adams' office an hour ahead of the usual time.

The doctor growled from the top of the stairs, "Emergency case?"

"No," Merrie said briskly. "I have a plan I want to talk to you about."

"No doubt it has to do with what I'm supposed to eat or what I'm to wear or something else I used to be able to decide for myself?"

"No."

"Then come upstairs and make some coffee and tell me what it is."

When the doctor was settled at the kitchen table with a cup of coffee, the sugar bowl and a pitcher of cream before him, Merrie began. "Dr. Adams, I did a lot of thinking last night." -

His keen eyes rested on her briefly. "More thinking than sleeping, it looks like to me."

"And I decided we ought to have a hospital in Gold Mountain."

The old man lifted his coffee cup to his mouth, sipped noisily, carefully set it down again. "A hospital," he repeated. "You know, my dear child, you're the type of female that always gets big ideas when she's tired out or coming down with a fever.''

"Gold Mountain *needs* a hospital. You've said that yourself.''

"Oh, yes,'' the doctor agreed. He picked up a spoon, stirred the coffee vigorously. Then he grasped the cup by the rounded side, secured the spoon handle between his index and middle finger, and took another long, slow drink. "Yes, indeed,'' he said as he set the cup down. "When I first came to Gold Mountain, the nearest hospital was in Seattle, and the only way to get there in a hurry was by wagon. I drove many an injured man that forty miles to town without knowing whether he'd be alive by the time I got him on the operating table. Prayers for me, a quart of whiskey for him—it's surprising how many lives I saved with generous doses of both.''

He let out his breath, chuckling and sighing at the same time. "When the railroad was finished in '89, Seattle wasn't so far away. When the coal mines opened up in Gilman and they built that little hospital, things were even better. But it's still a long ride to a hospital, and there's only one westbound train a day. I haven't had a patient yet who arranged to get hurt or sick just at the right time so we could catch that train.''

"Of course,'' the doctor continued, "there's been many a time when the section foreman took me and a patient to Gilman on a handcar, but the blasted old coot is getting greedy. Remember the night that logger jumped out of a second-story window in the boarding house and broke both legs? The foreman was willing to take us to Gilman, all right, but he slowed the handcar down every mile and held out his hand for another quarter.''

The old man leaned back in his chair and ruffled his mane of white hair with both hands. ''Yes, it would be good to have a hospital. Like the time poor old Tom Stump come running in here holding his ear onto his head with one hand. He'd been stealing cord wood from his neighbor, the neighbor got tired of it and planted a half dozen rifle cartridges in the wood. When he put it in the stove, they went off. I don't know whether it was a bullet that hit Tom, or part of the stove, but anyway he was in bad shape. And Tom's excitable. It wasn't easy, holding him down and pushing chloroform under his nose and sewing him up, all at the same time. I pulled him through, but his left ear still has a slant to it. . . .''

The doctor smiled to himself, and then sat up straight and brought himself back to the present. ''So you think we ought to have a hospital in Gold Mountain,'' he said. ''That calls for expensive equipment, and for extra help. Where's the money to come from?''

Merrie said uncertainly, ''I haven't worked out *all* the details.''

The old man sniffed. ''It also calls for a building.''

Merrie brightened. ''Oh, *that's* no problem. We'll use this house.''

''This house?'' the doctor exploded. ''My house?''

''We'd have to start small, I know that,'' Merrie

explained quickly. "Your bedroom is plenty big enough for three hospital beds. The sitting room would hold four beds. The kitchen should be the surgery, and the spare room could be a nursery or a supply room or something like that."

The doctor's big hands flew up in a gesture of helplessness. "My dear girl, where are you going to put me, after throwing me out of the building that's been my home for fifteen years?"

"Oh, Dr. Adams, don't you worry about that!" Merrie assured him. "I'm going to fix up that little room downstairs for you."

The doctor was silent for several minutes. He finished his coffee, wiped his mouth on the back of his hand, and looked at Merrie thoughtfully. When he spoke, his voice was unusually gentle. "My dear girl," he said, "what are you trying to do?"

"I don't understand . . ."

"I always knew what I wanted to do with my life, and I've come close to it. Do you know what you want to do with yours?"

Merrie looked at him squarely. "You can't always do what you want to do."

"You like nursing."

Merrie replied instantly, "Oh, yes, very much. I plan to continue as your nurse. But I thought of the hospital because that would be . . ." Her voice broke. Determined as she was to be firm and businesslike, she could not meet the old man's wise and probing gaze. Looking down at her hands, she said, "Because that would be building something, doing something."

"It could be done," the doctor put in. "Whatever I said at first, the truth is that I have most of the equipment we'd need, and if we used this house and didn't try to get too fancy all at once, the costs wouldn't run too high. A younger man would have thought of it himself.''

Merrie looked up. ''Then you agree?''

The doctor shook his head. ''I'm not worried about the cost. I don't even mind being shoved into that blasted little back pantry you say you're going to fix up for me. What I'm concerned about is you. How long are you going to stay in Gold Mountain?''

Merrie's eyes widened. ''What do you mean? I love it here, and you know my husband's plans. As soon as he's saved enough money, he's going to open his own logging camp, on our homestead. We have no thought of leaving Gold Mountain.''

The doctor sighed. ''*He* told me different.''

''He must have been joking! This is—this is home, the only home I have. . . .''

''I don't think he was joking,'' the doctor replied. ''He said he hated logging, that he was going to sell the homestead and go north with his uncle, when Henry goes prospecting in British Columbia. He sounded very . . .'' the doctor hesitated, searched for the word, and added carefully, ''very confident.''

Despite herself, Merrie's eyes filled with tears. ''I don't understand,'' she said, ''I just don't understand . . .''

The doctor reached across the table and patted her arm. ''I had an idea, when he talked to me, that you might not know anything about it. I didn't ask you about it because I didn't want to upset you. You like to stay in one place."

"That isn't it, exactly. I want a place that is mine, wherever it is. Just one spot where I *belong*."

The old man nodded. "Jim's plan sounded to me like a great big wonderful dream. He's probably forgotten it by now. But I had to mention it, for this reason. I'm an old man. Cranky, set in my ways. I can help you build a hospital but I can't do it alone. Naturally I don't want you to start tearing this house apart if right in the midst of things you're going to pick up and leave."

"I don't want to leave."

The doctor said quietly. "What was it you were telling me just a few minutes ago? 'You can't always do what you want to do'?"

"But it's useless!" With a helpless gesture Merrie wiped her tears on the back of her hand. "What was the point of getting the homestead . . . saving every cent of money we could? It was because he wanted to be a logger. A bigger camp than Jeff Smith's, more timber than Jeff Smith has . . ." She stopped abruptly, ashamed that she had said so much.

The doctor's face was sad. "Merrie," he said softly, "has it ever occurred to you that Jim is not well? I don't mean physically, I mean sick in mind."

"Yes," she whispered. "I've thought of it many, many times. . . ."

Silence fell. Slowly the old man withdrew the hand that had been patting her arm so reassuringly. "Just one more question. If Jim does go north, would you go with him?"

"He probably wouldn't want me to."

"That's not the question, Merrie," the doctor said quietly. "I meant, would you go with him, if he wanted you to?"

It was too much. All night she had fought against formless fears. Fleeing her dreams, she had embraced daylight eagerly, and created a new plan from which she could take new strength. Suddenly the cup of strength was emptied. She covered her face with her hands. "I don't know," she cried, "I just don't know. I'll have to think . . ."

"Did you eat any breakfast?" the doctor interrupted gruffly.

She shook her head.

"Then get busy and fry up ham and eggs and potatoes. For the both of us. If you've got to think about something, think about that. Ham, eggs, potatoes."

He had given her the time she needed. She uncovered her face, sat up straight, and managed an unsteady smile: "You shouldn't eat so much fried food at your age."

"Move me down to the pantry, take my house away from me, run my life for me, but don't tell me what to eat for breakfast!"

His scowl was so black that Merrie began to laugh. By the time they had finished breakfast, she was trying to decide what the name of the hospital should be.

II

For the third time in an hour Jeff picked up the sheets of paper, read the columns of figures, threw the papers back on the desk and walked outside.

All but two or three of the men were in the woods. Hands in pockets, Jeff surveyed the peaceful scene. A furious outburst from the kitchen shattered the quiet. The cook. His complaint, a torrent of Swedish epithets and American swear words, was aimed, as usual, at the flunky. Across the clearing the blacksmith was shoeing an ox. The great animal was suspended from the ceiling of the shed, his bulk cradled by wide belts under his belly and hoisted a foot off the ground by a Spanish windlass. As the smithy shaped the plates, two for each cloven hoof, the rhythmic sound of his hammer added exclamation points to the cook's remarks. Jeff grinned. The scene hadn't changed in fifteen years. Did he want it to change? That was the question no columns of figures nor descriptions of equipment could answer for him.

Should he sell the oxen and send the bull-whackers on their way? He thought of Dave Riley, and a picture came sharply to mind of the big bull puncher as he was and always had been. Dave standing head and shoulders above the other men. Dave roaring at the oxen with the goad stick over his shoulder like a gun. ("Longest goldanged stick in the county," Dave bragged, and there might be some truth to it, for the length of the stick was determined by the height of the man.) Dave in such a fury that he leapt onto the animals' backs with calked shoes. Dave at ease, with his thumbs hooked under the old Irish-green galluses, the old felt "Boss Raw Edge" hanging on the back of his head . . .

A fun-loving timber stiff had once stolen Dave's hat, selecting the one time of the day or night when it was off his head, the Saturday night cleanup before the men rode in to Gold Mountain.

Dave had lifted his head from a tin washbowl of soapy water, noted his loss, and let fly with some of the language that had commanded the respect of other bullwhackers in Washington for more than twenty years. The men in the bunkhouse listened admiringly while the Saturday night wash water dripped down on his galluses and Dave, without a second's pause in the flow of words, wiped soap out of his eyes with the hairy backs of his hands.

All at once he stopped. Whether it was soap or exhaustion, no one could tell, but at any rate, to their amazement, he began to sob.

"My hat!" he choked. "I can't go out in the woods without my hat. Why, if I was ever to get lost and run out of grub, I'd cut it into pieces and chew it!''

Ridiculous as he looked and sounded, nobody laughed. The bunkhouse was gripped by a dreadful silence as the men rolled their eyes toward the guilty logger. If a word was said, it was no more than a whisper; if anyone stirred, it was with a barely perceptible, sideways movement. When Dave Riley had turned around, his hat was on his bunk. . . .

Sell the oxen? Several times Jeff had put the question to the blacksmith.

''You keep the bulls,'' Smitty always replied. ''Sure, the ox is slow. The good Lord don't ask his creatures to be strong and fast, both together. And the ox got dignity. Why, over on the Sound, at Edmonds . . .''

''Yes,'' Jeff had said quickly, ''yes, I know, you told me. When they had to get up a petition for a town charter, they were short two signatures, so one of the town's leading citizens signed the names of his two oxen, Bolivar and Isaac. Their names are on the town charter.''

''That's it,'' the smithy had agreed, nodding violently. ''Oxen got dignity. That's what I tell you.''

The blacksmith's view was narrow and sentimental. But Jeff asked himself, is my view any broader? Do I want to bring in steam engines, and blocks and lines, exchanging for men like Dave Riley the new brand of loggers, the hook tenders and donkey punchers and head riggers? The change would go down to the lowliest job in camp. If he built a logging railroad to connect with the existing line from Gold Mountain into Seattle, there would be no need to float the logs downriver to the mill, no need for the skid road from the woods to the river. The fifteen- or sixteen-year-old boy who traditionally began life in the woods as a skid greaser would now start his career as a whistle punk, signaling to the donkey puncher when it was time to let in the steam and drag the log out of the brush.

New methods would result in more production—even Dave Riley admitted the oxen were slow and Mike Jessup had said a dozen times, "Look, Jeff, if it's worrying about us old-timers that's holding you back, forget it. We can learn something new. If we can't, there's plenty of camps that's still using bulls. In fact, I'll lay you my gold watch against your ten dollars that some of the small outfits hereabouts will be logging with bulls for the next eight, ten years. But you don't have to stay small. You've got the timber, you're young, by the billy blue gollies you *oughta* bring in steam!"

Jeff turned around, walked back into his office, resolutely picked up the sheets of paper.

He need not make the change all at once. Start with a Dolbeer donkey engine and a line horse, just for getting logs out of the brush to the skid road, let the bulls drag the logs down the skid road to the river, as they were doing now. It wouldn't be as big a commitment, as final a promise that he would stay in the Snoqualmie Valley for years to come. . . .

Once more Jeff threw the papers down and

walked out of the office. Mike Jessup and his men were falling trees only a short distance from camp. He'd stay with the falling crew for a while, then he'd follow Dave Riley and the ox teams to the booming grounds. There, where he could visualize expansion in terms of men, and not as a column of figures, there was the place to come to a decision.

Having made up his mind to that extent, Jeff was impatient to get there. He walked rapidly, listening for familiar sounds. Long before he had reached the clearing in which the men were working, he heard their axes. One, two. One, two. One, two. The sound stopped. The fallers were tipping the water bottles up to their mouths, drying sweaty palms on their pants, getting a firm grip on the ax handles. Again he heard the axes. One, two. One, two . . .

At the edge of the clearing, Jeff stopped. The men hadn't seen him. He was in the secure but uncommitted position he liked so well—on the outside, looking in.

The fallers finished the undercut, put down their axes and picked up the long crosscut saw. Back on their springboards, they began sawing through the tree from the side opposite the undercut. Once or twice they stopped, and adjusted white oak wedges so as to keep the sawblade free.

This won't change, Jeff reflected, even if I bring donkey engines into the woods. Engines can drag logs away, and hoist them onto flatcars, and hurry them out of the woods to the sawmill, but it takes men to cut the trees. Fallers who can drop a tree on a dime, buckers who cut it into lengths. The cool head, the sharp eye—there was no way to improve on a man like Mike Jessup. . . . At the thought, Jeff's attention focused on the men. Mike was setting a wedge in the back cut. The man at the other end of the saw was Jim Cowen.

Merrie's husband . . . That was the way Jeff had trained himself to think of Jim, and the two words shot to the surface of his mind as he identified the dark, slender figure. You came out here to make a decision, Jeff told himself angrily. If Merrie Dooley Cowen has something to do with that decision, then welcome the sight of her husband. But that's wrong. The question of expanding, of exchanging bull teams for steam engines—the answer should be in those columns of figures, not in my feelings about another man's wife. . . .

The tree was almost ready to go. Mike was signaling to the other men to move back. When they were safe, he would strike the last blow and the big fir, already leaning away from him, would fall within a foot or two of the spot he had chosen.

Jeff stepped into the clearing, inner conflict swept aside for the moment by his admiration for Mike. Every movement was strong, but precise as a woman doing fancywork. Mike could be daring, but in the woods, with the lives of other men involved, he was cautious as a loving grandmother. No, there would never be machines to replace a man like Mike. . . .

"Timmm—berrr . . ."

It all happened in the space of seconds. Mike's crew had retreated to safe postions behind the falling tree. All but Jim Cowen. Jim was walking away from the tree, but too slowly. Mike shouted at him, Jim shrugged. For an instant the tree seemed to hang in the air. Then there was a loud, cracking sound as it gained momentum. At just that moment, Jim caught sight of Jeff. He stopped, his head went back in a defiant gesture Jeff could read from across the clearing—I'm not afraid, see? I'm not running. . . .

Another shout from Mike. Mike was running toward Jim. Jim was looking toward Jeff. A thunderous tearing sound as the tree ripped through the smaller trees, a deafening crack as it hit the ground. They were safe from the big tree, but the tricky, unseen limb, the vicious "sidewinder," shot out of nowhere. A big limb, torn loose by the force of the tree's fall, dropping from the sky like death's own hammer . . . Mike threw himself against Jim. Jim fell forward clear of the branch, but Mike was pinned to the ground.

Jeff ran. From out of the brush the men of Mike's crew ran forward, too. Swearing, praying, they tugged at the limb. "Easy," Jeff cautioned them, though his own hands were pulling on the killer limb as if he meant to strangle it.

Someone was crying, "Mike! Mike!"

"Ready?" Jeff said thickly. "All right, now, all together, lift it off easy. . . ."

The muttering and the calling stopped. Mike lay on his face, his body in a strange cramped position as if it had been broken in the middle. The limb had caught him across the back. Not a mark on him, but he was dead.

Behind them Jim moaned. The men looked up,

but no one moved. Jim sat up slowly, and his hands went to his head. "I'm hurt. . . ."

Jeff was seized by anger so great he couldn't speak. He walked away from Mike's body and the silent loggers surrounding it. He leaned down, one hand clamped on Jim's shirt just below the throat, he jerked the young logger to his feet. "I'm hurt!" Jim cried.

Jeff's big hand released him. He dropped to the ground and lay in a heap, groaning. Again Jeff reached down and pulled him up with such furious strength that Jim lost his balance and clutched at Jeff's arm to keep from falling.

"You killed Mike Jessup," Jeff said, very low. "Get out of my camp."

Jim let go of Jeff's supporting arm and backed away. "You owe me a week's wages."

"I'll pay you." Jeff's throat and shoulders ached with the furious pounding of his pulse. He was blind to everything but Jim's white, scared face, bobbing in front of him like the distorted, grimacing, disembodied face in a nightmare. He moved toward Jim, his hands reaching for him hungrily.

"I'm hurt . . ." Jim repeated dully, turning toward the other men. There was no response. The loggers remained impassive, watching.

Jim ran toward them as Jeff advanced. "I need a doctor," he whimpered. Jeff's left hand caught him. Jim screamed as Jeff's right hand, knotted into a murderous fist, swung forward to his jaw.

As he dropped, the red haze of anger cleared. Jeff looked down at Jim's unconscious form, then up at the silent loggers. They hadn't moved. "Take him to Gold Mountain," Jeff said quietly. With anger gone, he felt cold, cold to the bone. "I'll take care of Mike."

"Want me to use the wagon?" one of the men asked.

Jeff shook his head. "Throw him over the back of your horse," he said. "I'll need the wagon."

One of the men picked Jim up and left the clearing. Jeff knelt on the ground, slid his hands under Mike's body and gently lifted him up into his arms. The men waited respectfully, with their old felt hats in their hands. Still bareheaded, they formed a single line and silently followed Jeff down the trail toward camp.

III

It had been a quiet day, and since the doctor had spent most of the night delivering a baby in a homestead cabin six or seven miles east of town, Merrie sent him upstairs about three o'clock with orders to take a nap.

"The females of today are weak and helpless," the old man complained. "Twenty years ago that woman would have saddled up her horse and ridden to town, and saved me the long ride. Forty years ago she would have birthed the baby without any doctor and that way spared both me and the horse."

"Another reason for making the second-floor rooms over into a hospital," Merrie said positively. "Then you wouldn't have to make these long rides into the country. The woman would come here."

"Go to a hospital to have a baby?" the old man exclaimed. "My dear girl, you've got some crazy notions. They'll never do that."

Merrie laughed. "Then you'd better go get some sleep, because Faith Carlson is about due, and the Carlson place is halfway to the Pass."

"Weak and helpless," Dr. Adams muttered as he went obediently to his room upstairs. "All of them weak and helpless, except you . . ."

Merrie was alone in the office when the quiet was broken by a noise at the front door. She was startled, for Dr. Adams' patients were seldom put off by a closed door. They walked in, called, "Hey, Doc!" and settled themselves in one of the old oak chairs to await the doctor's arrival. This wasn't the sound of knuckles rapping on wood— someone was kicking the door with a heavy boot. Dr. Adams was bound to be disturbed. . . . Merrie ran across the office.

"Don't wake the doctor!" she scolded as she opened the door. "He's been up all night. . . ." Her voice died. One of the loggers from Jeff Smith's camp was standing on the doorstep, with Jim in his arms.

Again and again Merrie had shown a cool head and a strong stomach, no matter how bloody the injury or how sickening the disease. But for an insant she thought she was going to faint. She grabbed the doorframe, steadied herself, swallowed hard as the wave of nausea broke and receded.

"He's not dead," the logger said bluntly. "Where do you want me to put him?"

Merrie stepped aside. "In the back room." Her voice shook, but she managed to close the door firmly and walk to the bottom of the staircase. "Dr. Adams? Would you please come down?"

The door at the head of the stairs opened and the doctor's voice rumbled, "That Carlson woman already?"

"No," Merrie answered. "It's . . ."

The doctor appeared at the top of the stairs. "It's what? Who tried to kick in the front door?"

"It's . . ." Merrie choked. "Please," she said unsteadily, "would you come, quickly. . . ."

The doctor was down the stairs and at her side. His long white hair was uncombed, he was in his stocking feet, but his hand on her shoulder was firm. "Your husband, eh," he said gruffly. "Bound to happen, sooner or later. All right, Merrie, you're the nurse. Let's go in and have a look."

The logger was standing in the middle of the room, holding Jim's unconscious body as if it were a useless object he had made up his mind to discard. "Where?" Jim's head rolled like a dead weight as the logger moved his arm. "On that table there?"

The doctor nodded. The logger deposited his burden, straightened up, dusted one hand off against the other. His final glance at Jim was heavy with disgust. "So long," he said, without looking at Merrie or the doctor, "you don't need me no longer," he walked out of the room.

"Now," said the doctor, "we'll estimate the extent of the damage."

"You didn't ask what happened at camp!"

The doctor threw her a sharp look. "I don't need to. Someone was careless, probably this husband of yours. What happened? That's Jeff Smith's business. I'm a doctor. I'm going to find out how bad hurt this young man is, and I don't intend to go into it any deeper than that.''

The old man bent over the examination table. His fingers moved quickly along Jim's legs, arms, body. Jim's head had rolled to one side; the doctor turned it gently, exposing the other cheek. "Hmmm," he said, "so that's it."

From cheekbone to jaw line, this side of Jim's face was bruised and skinned. The lips were badly swollen and there was a cut in the corner of the mouth, in which blood had thickened and dried.

"He must have fallen," Merrie whispered. "Or he was hit by a limb. . . .''

The doctor said ruefully, "Maybe. But if I had any money on it, I'd bet those are the marks of a fist, not a tree. The wonder of it is that whoever was mad enough to hit him so hard only hit him once."

"He's hurt, and you're joking. . . .''

"He's not bad hurt," the doctor said, his voice softening. "And I'm not joking. It's a fact—two blows like the one he got could have finished him."

"Who would have done a thing like that?" Merrie cried. "Who?"

"Don't think about that," the doctor said wisely.

"Poor Jim . . .''

The doctor cleared his throat. "And don't feel sorry for him. His face is messed up a bit, but there are no broken bones, no cracks in his skull. I can't understand why Jeff sent him into town. For this kind of trouble Jeff's as good a doctor as I am. Patches up his own men, nine times out of ten."

His hand shot out suddenly and gripped Jim's shoulder. Jim's eyes flew open. "Why *did* Jeff send you into town?" the doctor demanded. "Let's hear it from you."

"Dr. Adams!" Merrie stared at the old man. "An unconscious man . . ."

"Hhrmph . . ." the doctor snorted. "He came to an hour ago. Maybe before that. All I know for sure is that he hasn't been unconscious for one second since he's been in this house."

"Merrie," Jim murmured. "Take me home. . . ."

Merrie turned to the doctor. He shrugged. Confused, she looked back at Jim. All at once it was important to assemble the facts and face them squarely. Whatever Jim might say, the truth lay in the manner of the logger who had brought him in from camp, and in the doctor's shrewd appraisal. If Jim had been injured in a logging accident, it was because of his own carelessness. If he had taken a beating from one of the other men, he deserved it. On top of it, Jim had been pretending—wasn't that proof? She was repelled—and yet Jim, lying on the examination table, looked frail and helpless. His dark eyes were pleading with her, he was like a sick child, begging her to make him well. . . . "Shall I take him home?" she asked the doctor.

"By all means," Dr. Adams replied gruffly. "And don't let him lean on you too hard. His head might ache him but there's nothing wrong with his legs."

Jim raised himself to a sitting position. Merrie

reached out to help him, but he pushed her aside. He got to his feet slowly, with an unsteady, lurching gait walked through the office to the front door.

The doctor made no attempt to help; motionless as a rock, he watched Jim's effort with a cold, unblinking gaze.

Merrie felt a flash of anger. "Are you sure you won't need me for the rest of the day?" she asked, wrapping her shawl around her with a quick, impatient gesture.

The doctor crossed the room. "My dear child," he said, so softly she knew he did not intend Jim to hear. "My dear child," he repeated, shaking his head. "You know, and I know, that your husband comes ahead of all other considerations. But I wish . . ." He hesitated, which was unlike the positive, all-knowing doctor, and there was a troubled look in his eyes such as she had never seen before. "I want you to take care of yourself, too. Don't let him . . ." He stopped, cleared his throat loudly. "He's not dangerous, as far as I can judge. But I might be wrong. If he ever—that is, if you ever need help, let me know," he concluded irritably, turned away from her and walked to the other side of the office.

"Merrie!" It was Jim's voice, weak (or feigning weakness?), calling her from the next room.

"Good night, Dr. Adams," Merrie said hurriedly and followed her husband into the street.

Jim walked slowly, looking straight ahead, not speaking. Merrie adjusted her own step to his. The doctor's remarks buzzed around her head like a swarm of stinging gnats. When they were well out of sight of the doctor's house, Jim turned to her and said, "Help me, Merrie, give me your arm. . . ." She could see the look in the old man's eyes as clearly as if he were there watching them. She put her arm across Jim's back. With a sigh, he leaned against her, and they continued down the street.

As if to answer the doctor's invisible presence, Merrie asked, "Tell me, Jim, what happened at camp?"

"Take me home," he moaned, closing his eyes. He seemed about to stumble. . . . Merrie put both arms around him. "All right, Jim, all right. We're almost there. . . ."

He opened his eyes. "I need you, Merrie," he said hoarsely. With her arms around him, he began to walk again.

When they reached the house, Jim staggered into the bedroom and sank onto the bed. Merrie laid a cold, wet cloth on his forehead and covered him with a quilt. In a few minutes he was asleep.

"I'll go to the Tarpees and fetch Joseph home," she whispered, but he didn't stir. She left quietly, closing the door with only the faintest click of the latch.

It was several hours before Jim awoke. She had brought Joseph home from his daytime "nursery," the back end of Tarpee's store. She had cooked his supper, bathed him and put him to bed. Daylight had faded into dusk, dusk had deepened into a black, threatening night. The wind had come up; sudden gusts from the east shook the little cottage.

Merrie was about to blow out the lamp and

prepare for bed, when Jim appeared at the bedroom door.

Merrie looked up and started to speak but the words stuck in her throat.

Jim's face, red, swollen, bruised on one side, deathly pale on the other, was contorted by anger. He advanced toward her, weaving as if he were drunk. "I'll tell you what happened!" he shouted. "Jeff Smith tried to kill me!"

Merrie knew Jim's moods; they lay on her memory like scars. But a fit of temper had never before erupted so suddenly; it was as if the fury had been collecting within him while he slept, to come spilling out the moment he awakened, dark blood from a half-healed wound that consciousness reopened.

"Did you hear me?" His voice rose to a womanish scream. "Jeff Smith tried to kill me! I got away from him. I got out of camp. He wouldn't dare follow me. I'm safe here. . . ."

He took two or three steps toward her.

Merrie knew the pattern of the scene by heart. She would simply wait, neither replying nor backing away. He would shout, threaten her with his fists, gradually expel from his tortured mind the hatreds and fears and suspicions that possessed him. Once rid of them, he would grow quiet as suddenly as he had become angry. She would be able to lead him back to bed, he would fall asleep quickly. . . .

But this spell was worse, much worse. Sometimes his attack was aimed at her, the next moment he was pouring verbal abuse on an invisible person at his side. He strode blindly around the room, bumping into furniture, once brushing against her so roughly that she lost balance and had to catch at the back of a chair. He mentioned Jeff Smith again and again; Jeff who had caused the accident, hoping to maim him or kill him; Jeff whom he had escaped by fleeing to Gold Mountain; Jeff who had pursued him all the way from camp, with a gun . . .

"I can't go back, he'll kill me!" His voice threw a challenge to the wind outside.

He fell silent. Merrie tensed—surely this was the end of the spell. She thanked God that Joseph was a healthy baby; he must have slept peacefully through it all, for there wasn't a sound from the bedroom. A heavy, quivering silence pressed down on the house. Jim stared at her with blank eyes. She clenched her fists, lifted her chin, forced herself to return the gaze. Outside, the wind tore at the trees and whined against the window.

In a flat, strange voice, Jim asked, "Where is my son?"

Merrie's throat constricted. This wasn't the pattern. In anger or in triumph, Jim never thought of Joseph—in fact, he seldom paid attention to the boy, no matter what his mood. "He's asleep."

Jim frowned. He was looking at her but without any recognition. "Where is my son?" he repeated. "Don' try to hide him. I'll find him, whatever you do."

The door to the bedroom in which Joseph slept was directly behind him, but Jim moved away from it toward the front door, as if he were lost in a strange house. Merrie stepped aside and Jim walked past her. "He's not dangerous," Dr. Adams had said, "but I might be wrong."

With her pulse beating hard in her throat, Merrie moved cautiously along the wall toward the bedroom. Jim turned around suddenly. She stopped, praying he wouldn't guess what she was trying to do. He didn't seem to see her. Muttering angrily, he addressed someone who wasn't there. She took another step toward the bedroom door. Jim began waving his arms, threatening the invisible someone. His voice rose in the bitter argument. . . . Merrie took a deep breath and ran into the bedroom.

The room was dark. She stumbled against the bed, and a sharp pain shot through her leg. Biting her lip, she continued blindly to Joseph's bed. The warmth, the sweet and soapy odor of a sleeping baby, reached her even before she had touched him. Until that moment her only thought had been to get to him. Simply to hold him, to stand between him and Jim. Now, instinct signaled the new move. She must take him away.

In the parlor Jim was stomping around the table, his voice growing louder as he tried vainly to catch the person he was chasing. Merrie's senses were alert for the moment Jim would give up the crazy pursuit and come after her. She was cold, though her heart pounded and her skin tingled. She picked Joseph up in her arms, pulling most of his covers with him. He murmured sleepily.

"Go to sleep, go to sleep," she whispered into the little boy's ear. "This is your mama, everything's all right. . . ."

The only way to leave the bedroom was by the door through which she had entered. If she dared do that, she could turn sharp right into the kitchen, run from there into the woodshed, and out into the back yard. The only alternative was to remain here in the dark bedroom, waiting for Jim to come. . . .

She tightened her hold on Joseph. Her eyes had grown accustomed to the dark; she made her way across the bedroom quietly and quickly. At the door she halted abruptly, aware that the sound of Jim's voice had broken off. She waited. He was walking back and forth. Quick, restless steps. He approached the bedroom door. Heart in her throat, she backed into deeper shadow. For a minute or two she could hear his breathing. Rough, gasping breathing, very near the bedroom door. Then he moved away. In a moment he began talking once more, and now his voice was coming from the other side of the room. Merrie closed her eyes in silent prayer, then lowered her head, darted out of the bedroom and around the corner into the kitchen.

"Merrie!"

He had seen her. It was a shrill, desperate call. She ran blindly, out of the kitchen, into the shed. She heard his footsteps; it seemed as if he were right behind her. She must not let him catch her with Joseph in her arms.

The shed was dark, but desperation sharpened her mind so that she felt as if this were a scene she had always planned. The cradle in the corner. The cedar cradle Jeff Smith had fashioned when the baby was born. It was too small for Joseph, but it would hold him for a while. She laid him in it, straightened up, listened. . . . Jim's stumbling footsteps were nearer.

Instinct told her to get away from the crib. When Jim found her she must be on the other side of the shed. . . . She groped through the blackness until her outstretched hands touched the opposite wall Rough cedar siding, split by hand many years before. Her fingers slid down the wall and fell upon the smooth wooden stock of Jeff Smith's rifle.

She knew it was here—she herself had stored it here, not knowing how to return it to Jeff without hurting him or angering Jim. At the feel of it she began to tremble.

Jim must be very close, for the sound of his footsteps had stopped. He must be waiting, listening, somewhere in the darkness, perhaps at the entrance to the shed, only a few feet away. Joseph stirred. The sound was faint, like the whisper of dry leaves scattering before the wind. She drew in her breath, held it, listening, until she could hold it no longer. If Jim were inside the shed, that restless movement of Joseph's would lead him right to the cradle.

Her hand closed over the rifle's stock. Carefully she lifted it off the two long nails on which it had been resting. Jeff Smith's warning came back to her, "A gun is a deadly weapon. Never aim it at anything you don't mean to kill. . . ." She could see his deep gray eyes as he said it to her that day he gave her a lesson on the wagon road to their homestead. She hesitated. A gust of wind hit the shed, tearing a shingle loose. Broken twigs, leaves, a small branch dropped onto the roof from the overhanging trees. The sound of Jim's breathing or his footfall on the dirt floor would be drowned out. He could be standing right in front of her. . . .

The wind died. In the silence the sound of Joseph, moving restlessly in cramped quarters, was as sharp as a crack of thunder. "It is a deadly weapon," said Jeff's deep and quiet voice. . . . Trembling, Merrie fitted the rifle butt against her shoulder and aimed the long barrel at the darkness between herself and the shed door.

Joseph whimpered.

Her hand tensed. The finger poised over the trigger was cold as ice. Not a sound. She waited. Minutes passed. Across the shed Joseph found a comfortable position and slept peacefully. The wind returned occasionally, each burst quieter than the last. The darkness which had been impenetrable and threatening, now seemed to thin out—she could feel that it was empty. Still she waited. She was shaking with real, physical chill; now that the wind had died, a cold mist was settling. Five minutes, fifteen minutes, a half-hour . . . She could not guess how long she had been standing there with the gun at her shoulder. Slowly she lowered it, felt along the wall until her hand touched the protruding nails, and returned it to its place. Then, for the first time, she realized how futile her stand had been. The day Joseph had been wounded by this rifle she had removed the shells; the gun hadn't been loaded for a year.

Merrie moved cautiously across the shed. Every few steps she stopped and listened. Silence. The kitchen was lighter than the shed, for the parlor lamps were still burning and their pale yellow light shone through the open door connecting the two rooms. Merrie crossed the kitchen one step at a time, planting each foot carefully, heel down, then rolling her weight forward, balancing for a breathless instant while whe listened, then another step. She was tensed for a sound she could identify—a footstep, Jim's voice, a door closing or a piece of furniture pushed roughly across the floor. At the parlor door she heard it. Jim's breathing. Heavy, rhythmic breathing. She slipped around the corner into the bedroom. In the half-darkness she could see him, with his arms out to each side as if he had thrown himself down with great force and frozen in the position in which he fell.

Merrie retreated into the parlor. At last she had lived the nightmare that had awakened her so many times since Joseph's birth. She had known every part of it. Jim pursuing her, the feeling of the baby in her arms, the flight from one room to another, the final terrible moment when she was trapped in a cold, windy room and a shutter was banging in the wind and Jim's footsteps were growing louder and louder . . . It was over, she was exhausted. But reality did not end where the dream had ended. Joseph was safe—but for how long? There was something more to do.

She glanced at the parlor clock. It was after midnight—she had been hiding in the shed for two hours or more. If she took Joseph to Tarpee's at this time of night, all of Gold Mountain would start whispering. Bertha was a loving friend, but she had a malicious tongue. There was only one place she could leave Joseph without explaining why, one place where even curious, quick-tongued Bertha would expect Joseph to spend a few days. Bengstons' Inn. It was five miles away and Jim's horse had been left at camp when the logger brought him to town after the accident. Wake Martin Kittinger and ask for a horse and rig? No . . .

This was the way the dream ended. This was the slow, hard part of the nightmare that waking had saved her from enduring. She found her heavy shawl, wrapped it around her body and knotted it at her waist. She picked up one of the parlor lamps, walked through the kitchen into the shed, there found the old burlap hammock in which she had once carried Joseph from the homestead to Gold Mountain. She lifted Joseph out of the cradle, talked to him softly and rapidly, comforted him as she slid him, blankets and all, into the strange homemade contraption she had never been able to throw away. He whimpered sleepily, then lay still, chewing on the corner of the blanket. ''Bless you,'' she whispered. She found matches, a barn lantern, and when the flame was bright and steady, she blew out the parlor lamp and set it down carefully in the corner of the shed. With the lantern in her hand and Joseph cradled on her back, she set out on the long walk to Bengstons' Inn.

10

THE BACK DOOR of Bengstons' Inn was never
locked. Merrie's cold hand grasped the doorknob
as if it were a hand extended to save her from a
black and icy sea. She turned it slowly, pushed—
the door opened so easily that she lost balance.
Mindful of Joseph on her back, she fought to keep
from falling. For a fraction of a second she clawed
at the darkness, and then she was down, a cold,
exhausted, crumpled heap, on the kitchen floor.
Joseph began to cry. She was too weary even to
pull herself to a sitting position so that she could
take him off her back. The baby's frightened
whimper grew to a wail. She was here. This was
Bengstons' Inn. She was safe. . . . Merrie began to
cry.

There were quick footsteps, the darkness was
dissipated by a sudden flood of lamplight, and Nils
Bengston's voice burst out, "Well, what have we
got here! Kate, never mind the gun. It's Merrie and
the boy."

Nils' big hands picked her up. Through her tears she saw Katherine Bengston's small, anxious face, and felt the brush of the little woman's heavy red braids as Katherine's arms went around her. "Lift the baby out," Katherine instructed Nils, "and put him in the rocker."

"Quit your bellering, Joe," Nils said gruffly . . . and then the weight was off her back, and the baby's crying subsided, and Katherine was murmuring, "There, there, Merrie, there, there . . ."

Katherine led her to a big armchair. "Sit down, dear. . . ." Merrie sank into it, shivering.

"Nils, get that afghan from the front room. Her clothes are damp, she's chilled to the bone." Nils was back in an instant, the soft woolen cover enveloped her, she was warm. . . . Merrie dabbed at her eyes with the corner of her shawl. "I just can't stop crying," she sobbed. "I want to, and I can't."

"Go ahead and bawl," Nils said hospitably.

"Stir up the fire, Nils. We'll have some good hot tea."

"*Tea,*" Nils muttered, "tea . . ."

Katherine pushed a handkerchief into Merrie's hand. "The baby's fine," she said softly. "You just rest and pretend we aren't here."

"I can't stop crying," Merrie repeated helplessly.

"I know, I know," Katherine said, patting her shoulder. "It's a terrible feeling, isn't it? But it will go away."

Merrie opened the handkerchief and covered her face. The sobbing stopped, but the tears continued to roll down her cheeks. "She walked the whole way," Katherine was whispering to Nils at the other side of the room, "and with that child on her back. Why, he must weigh thirty pounds."

"What could of happened?" Nils asked, in his own hoarse version of a whisper. "After the trouble at camp today, I would have thought . . ."

"Sshh, Nils, sshh. She'll tell us, when she's ready. . . ."

The handkerchief smelled familiar. Soap, and rosewater, and the faintly burned smell made by too hot an iron. All at once the crying was over and the room came into focus. Joseph was making soft, sleepy sounds from his nest of blankets in the rocking chair; she had first rocked him to sleep in that chair when he was only two months old. Katherine was setting out the familiar cups, the blue and white cups Merrie had filled, and drunk from, and washed and dried a thousand times. Nils was standing in a position she had seen him take again and again—the big, blond giant with arms folded across his tremendous chest, watching his efficient little wife with a look of love and wonder. . . . Suddenly Merrie laughed. "You'd think I was still doing the ironing around here," she said. "This handkerchief is scorched."

Nils and Katherine turned around quickly. "You're feeling better," Katherine said, bustling across the kitchen with the teapot in her hand. "Come sit down, Nils, and we'll have our tea."

They didn't ask questions, but Merrie knew they were waiting. She sipped the hot drink slowly, wondering how to begin.

Nils cleared his throat, opened his mouth,

closed it hard when he saw the expression on Katherine's face.

There was only one way to tell them what had happened. "This afternoon there was some kind of trouble at the logging camp . . ." she began, and told them the whole story, beginning to end, from the moment the logger had kicked the door of Dr. Adams' office to her arrival at the Inn almost twelve hours later.

They nodded from time to time as if she were repeating a tale they had already heard. Occasionally Nils growled wordlessly, or Katherine murmured in sympathy. When it came to describing the hours of terror in the woodshed, Merrie hesitated—it was hard to tell them about the gun. She forced the words out, watching their faces anxiously. But they were not shocked. Nils looked grim. Katherine was tense, her eyes on Merrie's face until Merrie reached the point where she returned the gun to the wall; then Katherine sighed and looked down at her hands.

Only once did Merrie's story seem to startle them. "Jim said Jeff had tried to kill him. His face was cut and bruised, and he's afraid to go back to camp. . . ."

A small, explosive sound burst from Nils' throat.

Katherine's hand fell on his arm. "Wait until she's finished," she said, her small face very white in contrast to the frame of red braids. "Please, Nils, wait . . ."

And so Merrie continued. The realization that she must take Joseph away, the long walk with the child on her back and the lantern in her hand. The cold lakes of fog that lay in the open fields, the black vacuum of the forest, where the flame inside the lantern quivered and seemed about to die for lack of air. The night sounds, sharp, lonely, in the impenetrable blackness through which she walked. The almost unbearable relief she had felt when she could see the great dark bulk of the Inn, the last, desperate effort it took to stumble across the barnyard, and walk up the steps, and turn the knob of the kitchen door . . .

She had finished. In the silence she looked at them uncertainly, realizing for the first time how badly she needed their approval.

Nils cleared his throat.

Again Katherine's hand restrained him. "Merrie, my dear, have you thought what you will do now?"

"I haven't thought at all, beyond getting Joseph away and bringing him to you."

Nils burst out, "You'll stay right here with us. And if that no-good, rotten-tempered husband of yours wants to know why, I'll be glad to explain it to him."

"Wait, dear . . ." Katherine said to Nils, and turned to Merrie. "Please move back to the Inn. You know how welcome you are."

Merrie shook her head. "How much I'd like to. You *know* I'd like to. It's home. But right now, with Jim hurt . . ." She spoke carefully, her throat aching with the effort to speak. "Don't you see? I can't leave him while he's hurt and can't take care of himself. He's got to have someone with him. Who else is there but me?"

"I don't give a damn!" Nils bellowed. "No, by God, you won't go back to that man!"

Katherine murmured, "Nils, dear, please . . ."

Nils brought both fists down hard on the kitchen table. "Don't try to hush me, Kate." His blue eyes, bright with anger, were fastened on Merrie's face. "You think that because Jim's your legal husband, you've got to go back and play nurse. You think he's going to be nice and helpless and all full of gratitude. Where'd you get this goddamn stubborn idea of yours that it's your duty, or something else just as stupid, to stand by when the going's rough? Huh? That's what you think, is it? Now look a-here. You ran to us with Joseph in your arms through the worst storm of the year because you thought Jim would hurt his son. How about his wife? You knew enough to save Joseph from harm. For God's sake how about yourself?"

"Now listen . . . No, Kate, I'm not through yet. So Jim Cowen comes home to you and says Jeff tried to kill him, that he doesn't dare go back to camp. Well, I promise you little girl that if Jeff Smith tried to kill him, he'd stay killed. I'm going to tell you what really happened. Because Jim is a show-off and a fool, one of the best loggers in Washington was killed this afternoon. Mike Jessup. A decent, smart, hard-working man, a good friend of mine and a good friend of Jeff's. Worth ten Jim Cowens, and I'll say it to you even if you are Jim's wife."

"So Jeff tried to kill Jim, did he? By God, I'll bet he wanted to. But all he did was hit him once and then order one of the falling crew to take him in to Gold Mountain. That's the truth for you, Merrie

Dooley, and you'd better think about it before you go back to Jim."

In a small voice, Merrie asked, "How do you know all this?"

"From Jeff Smith. He carted Mike's body in to Gold Mountain, talked to Brother Bill about the funeral service and getting the undertaker out from Gilman. He stopped by here on his way back to camp."

Katherine said softly, "Jeff doesn't lie. . . ."

And Jim does . . . Merrie was overwhelmed by a sudden wave of loneliness. "No, Jeff wouldn't lie. . . ." Her voice trembled and broke off. There was so much more to be said about Jeff. The door to her memory burst open and she was too exhausted to close it. "Jefferson Davis Smith is my name, my father came from Kentucky. . . . Will you take my arm, Mrs. Cowen, let me help you into the house. . . . Don't you worry about the noise you're making, here's my hand, hold on tight, I'll look the other way. . . . Tell you a true story? But they are always sad. . . . Joseph, you're a good boy. You're laughing. Your mother used to do that, a lot. . . ."

Nils' angry voice brought her back to the Bengston kitchen. "I've done some bad things in my lifetime, and I don't look down on people who are worse than I am. I've known men who killed other men, and I couldn't hate them. Men steal from each other, and I can't honestly say I'm better than they are. But there's one kind of man I can't tolerate, and that's the man who lies."

"Nils, please, you're not helping . . ."

Merrie's back stiffened and her chin went up. "That's all right," she said firmly. "Nils is saying what he believes, and he's right. Now I'll say what I believe. My husband is not well. I know it, and I think Dr. Adams knows it, too. Lying is part of—part of his disease. I wouldn't desert him if his back were broken, or if he had a bad fever. How can I leave him just because his sickness is not quite, not quite . . ." She stopped, swallowed hard, and finished in a whisper, "Because he's not right in his mind . . ."

Nils uttered a tremendous sigh. "I want to help you, Merrie, not make things harder than they are already. Okay. Go back if you have to." He turned to Katherine. "Kate, if I open my mouth again, stuff a couple of sofa cushions into it, will you? It might take three."

Katherine took her husband's big hand in both of hers. "This ought to suffice," she said primly, but she was smiling.

"*Suffice,*" Nils muttered. "Oh, what an awful thing it is, living with a schoolteacher."

Katherine studied Merrie's face, her head tilted to one side. "You said Jim was asleep when you left the house?"

Merrie nodded.

"Is he likely to sleep through the night?"

"Yes. After one of these spells . . ."

Katherine interrupted briskly, brushing aside the explanation. "Then wouldn't it be wise to go home right away?"

Merrie felt blood rush to her cheeks. How well Katherine understood, how much she must have guessed. "Yes, there will be far less trouble if I'm home when he wakes up."

Nils' face was fiery with his effort not to speak. He pushed his chair back, stood up and growled, "I'm to hitch up, Kate, is that it?"

Katherine nodded. "Yes, please, dear. While you're doing it, I'll heat up some bricks. It's a cold night, they'll feel good under your feet."

Merrie said apologetically, "Nils, I'm sorry. I hope you understand."

"I don't have to understand," the big man replied gruffly. "Kate seems to, and that's good enough for me. Wrap her up real good," he said as he went out the door toward the barn. "I don't give a damn what happens to Jim Cowen's wife, but I'd hate to see old Doc Adams lose his nurse."

II

A lamp was still burning in the parlor when Nils and Katherine drove up before the little house in Gold Mountain. Other than the carriage lamp, it was the only light they had seen. All along the way, the homestead cabins, the farmhouses, the houses along Gold Mountain's rutted streets were peacefully dark. By contrast the lamplight shining through the windows of her own house was a symbol of the trouble within. No peace here, the pale light seemed to say. Here there is something wrong. . . .

Merrie threw back the quilt in which Katherine had wrapped her for the long ride.

Nils said quickly, "Here, let me help you into the house."

"Please stay where you are." She climbed down, walked around the wagon to Nils' side. "There's no way I can thank you."

"Yes, there is." Holding the carriage lamp in his hand, Nils leaned down so that the light would fall on her face. "I want you to promise me you'll turn to us when you need help."

"I promise."

"I mean it," Nils insisted. "Swallow your pride. Face the truth, girl—there's only just so much that a woman, or even a man, can take. When you get to that point, come to us."

"I will. . . ."

Nils sighed, straightened up, and replaced the lamp on its hook at the side of the rig. "Or go to Brother Bill. I can't stand preachers but he's all right, he used to be a stevedore. Doc Adams would help you. Better yet, go to Jeff. He's the smartest man in the Snoqualmie Valley, as long as it's other people's problems that have to be solved. Besides, maybe you haven't noticed, but he'd do anything for you."

"I can't presume. . . ." Her voice broke.

Katherine went to her quickly and put both arms around her in a loving hug. "Enough talk for tonight. Just remember—there are so many who truly love you. You are loved, and admired. And you are strong. But don't exhaust that strength. Your heart is big. What you need is more backbone. Loyalty is a virtue, Merrie dear, but at some point it becomes a fault, and a foolish fault. Goodnight now. Bless you."

"Goodnight," Merrie echoed, and ran up the path to the house.

Merrie opened the front door so slowly that her hand cramped on the knob. The door squeaked. She stopped, heart pounding, and waited. Not a sound. Hardly breathing, she stepped into the house and pulled the door closed behind her. Still no sound. She took several steps toward the bedroom, letting her weight down carefully each time her foot went forward. The loose floorboard creaking under her weight, Jim's querulous voice calling her from the bedroom were so real to her it didn't seem possible they were sounds she hadn't yet heard.

She reached the table on which the lamp stood. Cupping her hand over the top of the globe, she blew out the flame. In the protective darkness, she moved more daringly. She stopped at the bedroom door, listened and released her breath in a long sigh. Jim was sleeping, she could hear the even rhythm of his breathing. Quickly she felt along the bedroom wall to the corner where her clothes hung on a row of pegs. She found her nightdress, undressed quickly, drew it on. Her bare feet made hardly a sound as she walked around the bed; there was the faintest rustling, no louder than a sigh, as she lay down on the bed and pulled the quilt up to cover both herself and Jim. He stirred, turned on his side. Merrie stiffened. . . . He murmured sleepily and lay still.

She prayed for sleep. Several times it was about to claim her. Warmth enclosed her like a cocoon, she was sinking deeper, sinking . . . And then Jim would move, or mutter in his sleep, and she would awaken instantly, so tense that breathing was difficult and her throat ached.

She had learned to put herself to sleep by making plans. Trivial plans, perhaps, confined to that area of her future into which she dared to look. The kind of curtains she would make for the parlor, the Christmas gifts she would send Aunt Sal and

Uncle Mike, the sweater she would knit for Joseph. But for the moment the future did not exist. She could not look ahead, even to the smallest, most trivial matter.

"Your first obligation is to your baby," the sister at Providence Hospital had said even before Joseph was born, sensing, without meeting the father, that there was a conflict between them. But Merrie hadn't chosen between Joseph and Jim. She had simply obeyed a strong instinct to protect the child. How long would Joseph stay with the Bengstons? She didn't know. He was safe, and she must cope with the larger question—Were Jim's neurotic need for her and her sense of obligation to her marriage vows enough to live on for the rest of her life?

"Such a waste of love, such a waste of loyalty"—that had been Henry Cowen's parting remark the first, and the last, time they had talked about Jim. In his words, and in those of the Catholic sister, were contained the excuses she needed for leaving Jim. But what comfort were excuses offered by other people, no matter how reasonable they might be?

She watched the sun rise, listened to the first sounds of day from houses nearby. A door slammed, a rooster crowed, someone was chopping wood, a dog barked, a little child cried . . .

Jim opened his eyes. He stared up at the ceiling, then slowly turned his head. For long minutes, he remained motionless, looking at her. She lay very still, her body rigid. His gaze was steady; the opaque, muddy look that had clouded his dark eyes the night before was gone. His face was pale, but the swelling was gone. The wild anger, the tormented raving—the night had erased all telltale signs but one. She saw it in his eyes; he was frightened.

"Merrie . . ." He moved toward her.

His fingers touched a strand of hair that had fallen across her cheek, brushed it back gently.

She drew away.

"Merrie . . ." he said huskily, "don't go away. Not right now."

She hesitated, her body tensed for the action she had been about to take. She would turn her back to him, sit up, put her feet on the floor, stand up, walk away. . . .

His hand slid from her cheek to her shoulder. It was trembling. . . .

Merrie took the hand between her own. "Just for a minute."

Jim's fingers tightened around hers, as if he were saving himself from falling. "After you brought me home from the doctor's office, did we talk? Did anything happen?"

Merrie felt a lump form in the pit of her stomach. "Yes, Jim, quite a bit—happened."

Looking fixedly at the ceiling, he said, "Tell me. I don't remember."

"Better not . . ."

"Tell me!" Jim's hand pressed hers convulsively. "I want to know."

She did not refer to Joseph, nor her flight to the woodshed, nor her desperate trip to Bengstons' in the middle of the night. But the earlier scenes—his accusations of Jeff, his furious pursuit of some unknown person he imagined to be there, to the moment he threw himself down on the bed and fell asleep—these she described to him faithfully.

When she had finished, he was still staring at the ceiling. His hand was no longer trembling; it was cold, and she sensed that his body was as rigid as hers. He spoke as if he were choking. "I suppose you know I was lying to you. Jeff didn't try to kill me. A branch broke loose and fell on Mike Jessup. It killed him. Jeff blamed me, he knocked me down."

Jim withdrew his hand, threw back the quilt and stood up. "I've had enough of logging," he said irritably. "I'd open my own camp, but the homestead isn't proved up." He thrust his hands into his pockets and began to pace back and forth with short, nervous strides. "I'm going north. To British Columbia. Maybe the Yukon."

Merrie sat up. So the terror of the night before was to end with a scene so familiar she could recite his lines as well as her own. "I'll own the biggest wheat farm in Dakota . . . the biggest logging camp in Washington . . ." and now, the richest gold mine in the Yukon. Last night she had seen tragedy in the disintegration of this man's mind, the man she had loved, married and once even believed in. The morning light reduced Jim to a spoiled child, spouting excuses for another flight from failure. She felt ill.

"I've been talking with Uncle Henry," Jim said, pacing and gesturing with his hands. "Forty years ago they took a lot of gold out of British Columbia, but they aren't running into anything big nowadays and they aren't likely to. But farther north, along the Klondike River . . . Oh, my uncle isn't the only prospector who's talking about it. There are signs of gold up there, no matter how loud some miners laugh at the idea. Someday someone will hit a really big strike. Then they'll be talking about the Yukon all the way from here to Boston, and every tub in Puget Sound will take on a load of prospectors and head for Alaska. I'm not going to wait. I'm going to get there first, I'm going to be there when the big strike is made. . . ."

Merrie drew the comforter closer. The moment of nausea had passed. She might protest against this new dream, as she had when he decided to abandon his homestead in Dakota, and again when he left to work in the coal mines in Gilman. But how useless to reason with him. She would speak her lines, he would speak his. . . . "No," she whispered, answering her own question; with a gesture of utter weariness she covered her face with her hands. Her sense of obligation had brought her back to him; surely she was not obliged to watch him strutting and waving his arms.

"Our savings are all I need for a grubstake. I can buy supplies in Seattle. There's a steamer every week for Skagway. At Skagway they light you in on a scow, two miles to Taiya on the mainland. That's where you pick up the trail to Chilkoot Pass. . . ." His voice rose as he described this new vision. "You go through the Pass to Lake Bennett. Chances are I can find some freighter to sled my packs through the Pass and ferry them across the lake. Then, I'll be in the Yukon. . . ." He sat down on the bed beside her. His hands closed around her wrists, he pulled her hands away from her face. "Look at me," he demanded. "Talk to me."

His face was very close to hers. His eyes were bright, there was a nervous twitch pulling at the corner of his mouth. As she looked into his face, the dark pupils of his eyes seemed to dilate. Merrie shook her head. "If you have decided to go north, what is left for me to say?"

Gripping her wrists, he lifted her hands from her lap and shook them fiercely. "You're coming with me."

Her wrists hurt, but she looked at him squarely. "No. I will stay here."

He dropped her hands. For a moment his eyes blazed and she thought he might strike her. Instead, he threw himself down and hid his face in her lap.

Minutes passed. Such gestures had often won her over. How many times had he begged her to love him? When had pity become the only emotion that bound her to him? Her hand moved mechanically to smooth his long, dark hair. "Merrie, Merrie," he moaned, and began to cry. With an empty heart, she held him, a weeping child, and waited.

Her glance fell on Joseph's crib; at the sight her pulse began to race. Jim had walked past the crib a dozen times. Blinded by the glories of his latest vision, he hadn't noticed it was empty. The vision would fade, it was fading now. With each racking sob he was falling back to reality. When he discovered that the boy was gone . . . Merrie closed her eyes, gathering strength for the ugly scene ahead, thinking—Thank God Joseph isn't here. So pity was, after all, the only feeling Jim had left her. With Joseph safe at Bengstons', she wasn't even afraid.

Gradually Jim grew quiet. Like a man who is physically exhausted, he sat up, rested on the edge of the bed for a moment with his head in his hands, then slowly got to his feet. When he walked toward the door, Merrie slid out of bed quickly, putting on her robe. When he reached Joseph's crib, and looked down into it, she was ready. "I took Joseph to Bengstons'," she said very distinctly.

Jim stared at her as if he hadn't understood.

"It is the best place for him," Merrie continued more loudly. Whatever fury she was unleashing, let it come quickly and be done with. "They're glad to keep him there."

To her amazement Jim burst into boyish laughter. He bounded toward her, swept her up into his arms. "Just you and I," he exclaimed. "Merrie, my darling, just you and I . . ." His arms tightened around her, he lowered his head to kiss her.

Anger was an emotion Merrie rarely experienced. When it struck, it was very quickly diluted. But she felt no sympathy now. Jim cared nothing for Joseph—was, in fact, glad to be rid of him. She was seized by such fury that for a moment she didn't muster the strength to free herself. The anger began in the very center of her body, a hot, pulsating knot. It spread out quickly, racing through her blood stream, until her cheeks were hot, the blood was pounding in her throat and neck, she was looking right into Jim's face and couldn't see him. The moment of helplessness passed. With all her strength she put her hands against Jim's chest and pushed with such force that he stumbled backward.

"That's all!" Her voice throbbed with the furious beating of her pulses. "I never thought I'd feel this way, I never expected to say the things I'm going to say. But you listen to me, Jim Cowen. I loved you, but I don't love you any more. *I said, I don't love you any more!* I married you, and now I know it was a terrible mistake. You have been a coward, a liar and a brute, and I've known it better than anyone else, and felt sorry for you. I don't any more. Only one good thing has come of the past two years, and that's Joseph. I'll stay with Joseph. You go to the Yukon. I'll give you our savings, I'll pack your clothes, but you get out of here today. Today! Right now!"

They faced each other in silence, only an arm's length apart. Merrie was shaking so hard her teeth were chattering; her stomach contracted with a sudden flash of nausea. Jim seemed to be paralyzed; his mouth had fallen open, but he didn't speak. Eyes flashing, jaw clenched, Merrie stared him down.

"You always were a stick-in-the-mud. . . ." There was a whining quality to his voice. "I wanted to better myself by coming out to Washington, but no, you cried and fussed, you had to stay in Dakota. I knew I could make money in the coal mines, but you were afraid of Gilman, you stayed in Seattle. You didn't want to leave Bengstons' Inn and move to the homestead, then you didn't want to leave the homestead and move to Gold Mountain.'' He shrugged. ''What kind of a wife have you been to me, turning balky every time I made a change?''

The blinding wave of anger was receding, but there was enough left to carry her through an answer. ''Part of what you said is true. I've often been ashamed because I dreaded moving from one place to another. I was afraid of change. I didn't understand the feeling and I did my best to overcome it. Now I know why I hated each move we made. It wasn't because I wanted to stay put. It was because I never felt safe. You never gave me that feeling, so I tried to find it in a house, in a home, in a place. I was wrong. Places can't make you feel loved. Only people can.''

''You're quite a talker, aren't you?'' Jim said, his mouth turning down in a frown.

He wasn't angry. He was shocked, as a child might be whose gentle mother had suddenly slapped him without cause. The frightened look in his dark eyes was clearer than ever. He stepped toward her, raising one hand in a pathetic parody of a threat, hesitated, turned and walked away.

Merrie's anger ebbed quickly. She felt tired, and more than that, thoroughly confused. Twice in a day she had been jolted by emotions such as she had never known before. Complete animal terror, as she had raised Jeff's rifle to her shoulder and aimed it at Jim. Overpowering anger when the woman within had emerged to lash him with truths she had never expected to voice or even admit to herself. "If you would please leave the room," she said wearily, "I'd like to get dressed."

He stood at the door, his mouth working silently as a storm of words brewed in his unhappy mind. "Remember that poster my father brought from England?" he asked suddenly in a bright, gay voice. "I remember when he nailed it to the wall of that miserable little squatter's shack we lived in. 'This is Charles Cowen's declaration of independence,' he said, and my mother said, 'Charles, I shouldn't have given my table linens to your sister-in-law. What's this table going to look like without a cloth?'"

Jim sucked in his breath and shook his head as if he were trying to clear it. "Then he died. . . ." His face contorted with a grimace of pain. The eyes darkened, the lips pressed together, the color drained from his cheeks. Then he laughed. A high-pitched, unsteady laugh, sharp with rising hysteria. "Remember when he died? Were you there? Out by the pump in the barnyard? He was saying, 'Look, Jim, there is no finer place than Dakota. I've taken out a homestead claim in your name, it'll be yours when you come of age, and if you work as hard as I have, it will one day be as fine a wheat farm as my own.'

"I told him he couldn't chain me to Dakota. What did I want with a homestead as good as his? That wasn't good enough, and I told him so. He stopped pumping water, he stopped and looked at me, and while he was looking at me, it happened. His mouth turned down at one side, spit ran out of the corner, he rolled his eyes up and reached straight out, and fell forward, into the watering trough." Jim lifted his head proudly. "I carried him into the parlor and put him on the couch."

Merrie said quietly, "I remember." She could see the picture in her mind. Charles Cowen's body, lying in state below the worn and faded poster. "Cheap and fertile lands are open for settlement in sufficient quantities to furnish freehold farms for all applicants. . . ." And below, the rugged face of the Englishman who had sworn never to go down again into the mines, but whose cheeks, even in death, seemed to be streaked with coal dust. Sitting beside him, weeping brokenly, the little brown figure of Jim's mother, who had wanted to bring her table linens and who liked her breakfast biscuits sweet. Mrs. Cowen had known her son. "Has he hurt you, dear?" she had asked, and her bright little eyes were sad. . . . "Yes, I remember," Merrie repeated, though she knew Jim hadn't wanted an answer.

Jim laughed again. Then he sobered abruptly, and his gaze went all around the room, finally settling on Merrie. "I heard what you said!" Once again he began to pace, back and forth, from the door to the crib, back to the door. "You think I don't know what's going on. But I do. All this church work you've been doing. You and Brother Bill. Church suppers, church meetings. Now this big affair at the falls. You thought I wouldn't find out, didn't you? An excursion train coming out from Seattle, a parachute jump over the falls, and lunch for everyone on the train—see, you couldn't keep it from me, could you?''

"Keep it from you?'' Merrie exclaimed. The "plans'' he spoke of were nothing more than a hope. Word had reached Gold Mountain that the railroad was organizing a series of Sunday excursions to Snoqualmie Falls, the first to take place in the spring. Searching for some means of reducing the church's debt, the Ladies Aid had voted to serve lunch to the trainload of city folk, whenever, if ever, such an excursion was made. The parachute jump over the falls? That was no more than a rumor; Bertha Tarpee had relayed a third-hand report that the railroad was going to arrange some kind of entertainment. It might be a tightrope act over the falls, such as had been staged years before as part of the celebration when the line into the Snoqualmie Valley was first completed. Or it might be something new and even more exciting, a parachute jump. Half of Gold Mountain had heard of these "plans'' by now; Jim had been one of the first to know, for Merrie had told him herself.

"You look surprised,'' Jim said, a crooked smile turning up one side of his mouth. "You and Brother Bill. You and Brother Bill!'' he repeated shrilly, walking toward her. "I know what's going on. Do you hear me? You and Brother Bill are trying to get rid of me. I know, I know!''

She must not back away. Her body strained with the effort to remain still, but her mind was clear. He might hurt her, and she dreaded it. But this was a simple emotion, compared with the fear and revulsion and pity these spells of Jim's had caused in the past.

He advanced toward her, muttering unintelligibly. A few feet in front of her he halted, narrowed his eyes, and said shrewdly, "I heard that. I heard what you said."

Merrie shook her head. "I didn't say anything."

He threw his head back and laughed wildly. "What a fine pair you'll make. The cheap little Irish orphan from Chicago and the Methodist minister with rheumatism in his back. Ha, ha . . ."

She lifted her arm to strike him, but as quickly dropped it to her side. "You're sick," she said quietly.

He sprung on her so quickly that she hadn't time to back away or to run past him. She struggled, but he was stronger than she was. His arms encircled her, pinning her own arms tight against her sides. The only movement she could make was to turn her head away from him.

He laughed. "You were going to hit me, weren't you?" he said thickly.

She froze, her head turned away, her eyes closed.

"I know what you said! You think I didn't hear it!" Laughter burst from his mouth and rose like a scream. In fright, she opened her eyes and looked into his face. He wasn't laughing at all. The eyes were black, his lips were drawn back from his teeth, his breathing was rapid. His fingers tightened and he began to shake her viciously, muttering, "I'll show you!"

Despite herself, she cried out.

As if her voice had paralyzed him, Jim let go. But it wasn't her cry, it was another sound. A loud, insistent knocking at the front door.

Merrie stepped back cautiously, but Jim didn't follow. He was staring at the front door, listening, his head tilted to one side. "Just a moment, please," Merrie called. Jim didn't move as she walked past him, across the parlor to the front door. Dr. Adams was standing on the step.

"May I come in?" he asked gruffly.

"Of course . . ."

The old man walked into the parlor. His glance rested briefly on Jim. "Patient looks all right."

Jim scowled. "I'm to believe you came here to find out how I'm feeling?"

"If you like." The old man turned his back to Jim, walked purposefully across the parlor to the largest rocking chair, and sat down.

"More likely, you came to spy on your nurse."

The doctor shrugged. "That might be. I wouldn't want anything to happen to her."

Jim's lip curled. "It seems to me it's too early in the morning for a nurse to go to work."

The doctor rested his elbows on the arms of the chair, knitted his big hands together, studied them for an instant, and then looked up at Jim and said pointedly, "It's not too early for a logger to be on his way to camp."

Jim burst out angrily, "You have no business here!"

The doctor turned to Merrie. There was an all-knowing look in his eyes, and yet he seemed to be saying, if you don't need me, I'll go.

But she needed him. A break had to be made. She had reached the point Nils Bengston had seen ahead, the point beyond which her own strength could not carry her. "A person can only take just so much. . . ."

It was, in a way, the biggest decision of her life, and yet the actions and words which accompanied it were so simple that it was all over before she was fully aware of what had happened.

Merrie said, "Dr. Adams, Jim has decided to go prospecting in British Columbia and the Yukon."

Jim didn't move or speak. The doctor pursed his lips together, nodded slowly. "I knew he had been considering it."

"He is leaving today."

The doctor's eyebrows rose, then dropped. "I see."

Merrie turned to Jim. "You know where the money is. I'll go pack your clothes."

The doctor cleared his throat. It was as definite a signal as if he had spoken out loud.

"I won't be long, Dr. Adams," she said quickly. "If you'll wait, I'll walk to the office with you."

Jim's voice rose in a complaint. "Look here, Doc. I want to say good-bye to my wife. I'm going into dangerous country, I'll be gone a long time. You don't need to wait around."

The doctor pressed thumbs and forefingers together and studied them thoughtfully. "I'll wait."

Merrie said, "I just remembered. Two of your good shirts need to be ironed." She went toward the kitchen.

"Morning train for Seattle leaves in forty minutes," the doctor said.

Merrie nodded. "Yes, I know," she said simply.

This was the drama of the end of love. Tragedy, heartbreak, the death of hope. What remained between them? She could pack his suitcase and iron his shirts. She went into the kitchen to heat the iron.

11

IN THE OPINION of Dr. Adams, it was a right good thing Gold Mountain was growing; the present population didn't have enough troubles to keep Merrie happy for more than a year or two. She was concerned about his problems, though he often reminded her that he hadn't known they existed until she rushed in to solve them. Then there were his patients. Merrie sympathized with them to the point of sharing their symptoms; her forehead felt hot and dry after he had treated someone for a fever, she invariably had an ache in her side after an appendectomy, and whenever the patient was a child, she left the office early and hurried to Tarpee's to see if Joseph was all right.

"Merrie's Burdens," the doctor called them. After the last patient had left in the evening, Merrie stirred up a hot fire in the cookstove, boiled a fresh pot of coffee, and the two of them, the white-haired doctor and the girl who was not yet twenty years old, sat down at the kitchen table to discuss them. The doctor listened gravely, Merrie talked. Bertha Tarpee's heart, Brother Bill's various feuds with the tavernkeepers, Jeff Smith's lonely life in the woods, the neighbor who had to shoot an ailing dog, or the girl who was disappointed in love. "Don't ever let people know how much of their worrying you're doing for them," the doctor often remarked, "or they'd get to be more shiftless than they already are."

It was understood, without their saying it aloud, that they would not talk about Jim. His departure had been observed by many curious townspeople, for old men and little boys, in particular, always gathered at the depot when the morning train was getting ready to pull out for Seattle. They came to see who all was going to town, and to guess, by the luggage they carried, what their business was in the city and how long they intended to stay.

When Jim Cowen walked into the depot, flanked by Merrie and Dr. Adams, the sociable chatter faltered. They knew what had happened to Mike Jessup and where to place the blame; the logger who had carried Jim to the doctor's office had made the rounds of the taverns before he rode back to camp. And they remembered the horse race; Jim's crazy challenge and Jeff's victory had made good depot and post office talk for two years.

They didn't like this young man, and their faces showed it. One by one they stopped talking; heads turned toward him, keen eyes appraised his good suit and white shirt and wide-brimmed hat, and measured the capacity of the straw suitcase he was carrying.

The steady gazes moved to Merrie and the doctor, and then their antagonism wavered. They were embarrassed. They had trusted the doctor for thirty years—or, more accurately, he had trusted them, for many had owed him money for that length of time. That nurse of his with the big eyes was still a *cheechaco* but already she was accepted as an old-timer, as if she had lived here for many years. Their eyes moved back to Jim.

"One way to Seattle," Jim muttered through the brass grillwork which separated the waiting room from the ticket and telegraph office.

"What was that?" the depot agent asked, in the strained, polite voice of the very deaf.

"One way to Seattle!" Jim snatched the ticket from the agent's hand, threw the coins on the oak counter and strode out of the depot without waiting for his change.

It was raining, a steady, gray drizzle foreshadowing the winter months ahead. The other passengers had already bought their tickets and boarded the coach; they had passed scrutiny and stirred no speculation exciting enough to draw the crowd outside. But when Jim, Merrie and the doctor left the depot, the silent watchers abandoned their comfortable benches as if by common accord. One by one they stood up and in solemn procession filed out into the rain.

The asthmatic voice of the steam engine was the only sound. The onlookers pulled up their coat collars, stuffed their hands into their pockets, and surveyed the scene from under the brims of hats pulled down hard over the ears.

Jim threw his suitcase into the car, put one foot on the step, one hand on the railing.

The doctor murmured, "I'll wait over there," and backed into the crowd.

The whistle blew, the children on the platform jumped, kicked, stared. Merrie and Jim faced each other. It was the time for good-bye, but neither of them spoke. The whistle blew again, the train jerked forward, and Jim jumped onto the first step.

The only spoken farewell came from a man Merrie didn't know. A big man, in logging boots, stagged work pants and mackinaw, as the train rolled forward, broke free of the group of spectators and ran along beside the coach. "Too bad you can't stay for Mike's funeral!" he shouted, shaking his fist. "But good riddance! You don't never need to come back!"

Dr. Adams was at Merrie's side. "Let's head for the office," he said sternly, but his hand on her shoulder was gentle as he led her away from the depot and the last glimpse of Jim's dark, fear-ridden eyes.

"He's got plenty of money," the doctor reassured her. "And he's old enough to take care of himself. No use to worry about him."

Merrie said dully, "You were right. He had been planning to go north."

"If he hadn't left you, he would sooner or later have forced you to leave him. This is a better way for it to end."

"End?" Merrie repeated it wonderingly, waiting for the word to strike some response. She felt nothing. "End . . . Yes, I suppose it is." She sighed. "We'll be late at the office."

"You're not going to the office," the doctor growled. "Jeff brought Jim's horse in from camp last night. You're to saddle up and ride to Bengstons' and bring that child of yours back home. . . . Oh, don't look so startled. I know all about it. That big Swede woke me up at four o'clock this morning, right after he left you off at your house. He didn't like your trying to handle Jim alone, and I didn't either. Why do you suppose I was knocking on your door at quarter to seven in the morning, with my shirttail tucked in and my jaw sticking out?"

Merrie's heart bounded. "Really? Will you get along all right if I go to fetch Joseph?"

"What a modest young lady you are," the doctor said dryly. "Since I have been practicing medicine for fifty years, more or less, I'll try to take care of minor injuries, and such as that. If anything really serious comes along, I'll tell 'em to keep breathing until you get back."

Merrie burst into delighted laughter and broke into a run. The doctor followed slowly. They did not talk about Jim again.

Much discussed, however, was one of Merrie's favorite burdens, the conversion of the doctor's house into a hospital. He protested every change, including those he had agreed to, even applauded as "sensible," when Merrie first presented them over the coffee cups.

"You really mean to start a hospital, don't you," he grunted, "in spite of me?"

"Oh, no, not in spite of you," Merrie replied

earnestly. "You'll have to pay for it."

And so the big old farmhouse became the office-home-hospital which Merrie called the Adams Memorial, though the doctor protested loudly that he wasn't dead yet and the name wasn't to be breathed to anyone as long as his body was warm or twitched.

It wasn't a hospital in the conventional sense, any more than Merrie was a conventional nurse. New hospital beds and the usual white enamel miscellany were shipped out from Seattle and installed upstairs, but by the time Merrie had finished decorating the rooms, their resemblance to a standard hospital was hardly noticeable. Merrie didn't like white ("Nothing in nature is white," she explained. "Everything is blue or green or purple or brown or red. How can you get well looking at white?") and she was repelled by blank spaces. She liked bright colors, or better yet, combinations of several bright colors. She liked pictures, illustrated calendars, embroidered daisies, ruffles, potted plants and clocks.

"Looks like the spare bedroom in my Aunt Rebecca's house in Ohio," Dr. Adams grumbled.

Merrie scented an interesting story. "Really? Did you have an aunt in Ohio? What was the spare room like?"

"Like"—the doctor gestured helplessly toward the row of wildflower prints Merrie had tacked to the wall, above a table of geranium plants in lard buckets, below a heavily embroidered motto about Home and Mother—"like this."

"It must have been a nice room."

"Well," the doctor admitted, "as a matter of fact, it was."

"You see?"

"Yes," the old man nodded, "I see."

The Adams "Memorial" opened with the simplest of ceremonies. The section foreman on the railroad carried in a member of his crew who had, under the spell of Saturday night festivities, mistaken a moving flatcar for a boxcar parked on a siding. After setting the broken bones and sewing up the major cuts, the doctor said, "This man ought to have hospital care for a couple of weeks. Well, Merrie? Do we send him to Gilman or do we keep him here?"

"Oh, yes, indeed, we'll take care of him here." Her eagerness faded. "Dr. Adams, how in the world are we going to move him up those stairs?"

The doctor's bright eyes twinkled beneath the shaggy white eyebrows. "I've been wondering when you'd think of that. I'll move him like I've been moving patients for fifty years—I'll carry him. Until you figure out a better way," he concluded with a chuckle. Then he picked the unconscious man up in his arms and carried him up the flight of stairs without stopping to rest or catch his breath.

"We'll have to install an elevator!" Merrie called after him.

"If the 'we' is me," the doctor retorted over his shoulder, "then the kind of elevator we've got right here is good enough."

Merrie ran up the stairs. "But some patients will be bigger and heavier than this one."

"You'll take one end, I'll take the other," the old man said cheerfully, entering the room that had once been his parlor. "Now get busy, nurse. Turn down that bed. Your hospital has just been opened for business."

Other problems developed as the hospital went into operation, many of them because Merrie had planned to do all the work herself. She worried because she couldn't; at the doctor's insistence she hired women to do the cooking and cleaning, and then she worried that they might not be doing it right. Problems that had not arisen troubled her, too.

"There are three rooms with three beds apiece," she said to the doctor over their evening coffee. "What will I do if we have seven men patients and two women patients?"

"A very grave situation," the doctor replied, "but my business is medicine, not morals. You'd better consult your good friend Brother Bill."

"I'm *concerned* about him." Merrie's mind leapt nimbly from one worry to the next. "The debt on the church hasn't been paid off, and he has his heart set on dedicating it before Easter. We've been getting twenty-five cents a plate at our Ladies Aid dinners, but we've had so many of them I don't believe anyone in Gold Mountain would come to another. Of course, there's that excursion train from Seattle to Snoqualmie Falls. It's coming for sure, and we'll serve a big dinner, but that won't be until after Easter. . . ."

"My dear girl," the doctor interrupted, "you're never prettier than you are when you're floundering in a sea of other people's difficulties. Sickness and disaster—they bring a wonderful color to your cheeks."

Merrie flushed. "You mean I thrive on other people's troubles?"

The doctor shook his head. "Absolutely not. I mean that you thrive on digging them out of trouble. I wish you had a life of your own."

It was as close as they had come, since that rainy morning at the railroad depot, to discussing Jim's departure.

Bertha Tarpee had been less tactful. "You're neither a wife nor a widow," she had exclaimed several times. "Where is that husband of yours, anyway?"

"I've never heard from him," Merrie admitted. "By now he must be in Alaska or the Yukon."

"And how long does he expect you to wait?" Bertha snorted, biting furiously into a plug of tobacco. "Until he gets good and ready to come back?"

"He won't come back," Merrie said quietly, "and I'd rather not talk about it, Bertha."

"You're young," Bertha muttered, "and you're kind of pretty. Preacher Bill would marry you in a minute. The way some people are talking, he'll have to get a wife if he's going to keep the church. Not that that's the reason he'd marry you. I've seen him when you're around. Neither a wife nor a widow. It don't seem fair. . . ."

Merrie cupped both hands around the mug of coffee, and looked down into the steaming liquid. There was no answer to the doctor's comment about a "life of her own." Bertha's inept outbrusts were closer to the truth than anything she could say herself. "Do you realize," she said, turning the cup in her hands, "that Christmas is next week?"

"I've thought of it. You're going to take the day off, young lady, whether you like it or not. If there's anyone upstairs, those women you hired can take care of them. It will be your first rest since . . ." he hesitated, for as they both knew Merrie hadn't spent a full day at home since Jim had left for the Yukon. "Since November," he finished gruffly. "I don't suppose you'll know what to do with yourself."

"I'm going to give a party."

The doctor's eyebrows lifted. "No doubt you picked that idea at random out of that crazy collection you've got stuffed into your head?"

Merrie laughed. "Just this minute. What do you think of it?"

The doctor spread his hands out on the table, palms down and studied them for a moment before answering. "Sounds like as good a way as any to keep from being alone."

"You're invited," Merrie said quickly. "Most people will spend the day with their own familes. But I'll ask Brother Bill, and Jeff Smith, and maybe . . ." She stopped. Another name, another face, came to mind. "Is Mr. Cowen, Henry Cowen, in the Valley now? Have you seen him lately?"

"Lord Henry? His mules were tied up behind his cabin when I rode by yesterday afternoon."

"Then I'll invite him, too," Merrie said impulsively. "That'll make four. . . ."

"The lonely ones," the doctor murmured . . .

With four guests, herself and Joseph, Merrie made preparations for ten, and the week preceding Christmas was the happiest she could remember since she had moved to Gold Mountain. She knitted a gift for each of the men. She baked fancy cookies, decorated in blue and yellow frosting, Nate Tarpee having run out of green and red coloring. She moved all the furniture so as to reveal corners it had hidden from view; having scrubbed these corners until they were fit for exhibition, she moved the furniture back in place. When she was finished, the house smelled like a tub of hot soapsuds and the curtains were so stiff with starch that they rattled when the wind blew.

Then she began to decorate. A Christmas tree, yards and yards of green and red paper chains, strings of popcorn, wreaths of holly. As she worked, the little house in Gold Mountain took on the color and fragrance of the Bruner farmhouse in Providence, North Dakota. She realized, as she made paste out of flour and water, that it was her Aunt Sal who had taught her how to mix it. Dabbing the sticky mixture on a strip of red paper, she could see all the little Bruners, as she had organized them at the kitchen table, one cutting the paper, another applying the paste, a third pressing the ends together to form another link in the chain. Once they had mastered the operation, nothing could stop them (or Merrie) until they ran out of paper. Red and green chains had covered the

Christmas tree; they had hung in festoons from the ceilings; they had been draped over picture frames and mirrors and the parlor organ. . . .

Merrie jumped up and ran into the bedroom. Joseph had been napping in his crib and was still half asleep. He blinked at her and smiled. "Come sit with me," she said, picking the child up in her arms. Back in the kitchen, she settled Joseph in a chair next to her own, and began to hum contentedly as she went to work on another length of red and green paper chain.

"Everyone coming?" the doctor asked a few days before Christmas. "You got word to Lord Henry and to Jeff?"

"Brother Bill rode out and invited them for me. They're coming."

"Good. That crazy Englishman belongs in the hills, but Jeff ought to get out more. It seems like a year since I've seen him. Not since . . ." He ran his fingers through his hair in a gesture of frustration. "Dammit, not since Mike Jessup's funeral."

Merrie lifted her chin. "Dr. Adams, let's stop *not* saying things. You haven't seen Jeff since Mike Jessup's funeral, and that was the same day Jim left Gold Mountain."

The doctor muttered, "All I meant to say was that I'm looking forward to seeing Jeff."

"So am I," Merrie said simply. "I've thought about it all week."

"You didn't have to tell me that," the doctor muttered, and walked out of the room.

Because of Bertha Tarpee, Merrie had a new dress. "What you going to wear?" Bertha asked the moment Merrie confided her plans for a Christmas party. "Not the poor little scraps you go round in every day, I hope."

"I'll put a little extra starch in when I wash my good blouse."

"Starch!" Puffing indignantly, Bertha pulled herself out of her armchair and wobbled across the store to the shelf of yard goods. "Starch won't make it new." She squinted at the stack of bolts, drew out the one of her choice and threw it down on the counter. "It's only calico, but it's blue. Men like blue, How you going to put marrying ideas into Brother Bill's head if you don't pretty yourself up once in a while?"

"I have no intention—I mean, it isn't right . . ." Merrie stamped her foot. "Bertha, you know better than to talk about Brother Bill marrying me. And I don't want the yard goods. I haven't got time to make it up into a dress, anyway."

"Neither a wife nor a widow," Bertha keened. "I'll make the dress for you."

Merrie awoke early on Christmas morning and rushed into the final preparations. By the time her guests arrived, the turkey was roasting in the oven, the bread was rising in the warming oven and Joseph was teething on some of the tastier Christmas tree decorations. Hearing footsteps on the front porch, Merrie ran to the mirror. A hasty, absent-minded glance told her that the dress Bertha had made for her was pretty, that her cheeks were pink as fall apples and that her hair was falling into her eyes. She brushed back the unruly curls and tried to tuck them under the strip of blue calico that was serving as a hair ribbon. Her fingers flew from the ruffled collar to the rows of wide ruffles on the skirt; Bertha *had* used starch, for the skirt ruffles flared out like the petals of an open flower, low in the front, then swooping up along the line of her hips to a spot at the small of her back where the layers of ruffles were massed into a bustle. When she walked, the dress rattled like the kitchen curtains—it was a pleasing sound. Merrie sighed happily and felt her cheeks with the backs of her hands. Someone knocked. She waved gaily at the mirror and ran to the front door.

The doctor was at the door, wearing the suit he had steadfastly claimed was "too fancy" even for weddings and funerals, and he was carrying two packages. "Where do I put these darnfool things?" he grumbled.

The thin, stooped figure of the Methodist minister followed him up the walk. "Merry Christmas," Bill said awkwardly, looking at the doctor.

Jeff and Henry Cowen arrived together a few minutes later. "I can't believe you meant to invite me," was Lord Henry's greeting as he stepped through the door. "Though I've known you to do crazier things than that."

Merrie laughed and turned to Jeff.

"Merry Christmas . . ." His deep voice, the thoughtful gray eyes, released a flood of memories. She held out her hand; he accepted it with a gesture that had the touch of formality she remembered so well. The other men turned to admire the Christmas tree. Merrie looked up into Jeff's face. With a funny feeling in her throat, she said the first thing that came to her mind, "Your hand is cold."

"Happy birthday, Merrie Dooley . . ." he said quietly.

She clung to his hand, forgetting that she had meant to shake it politely. "Oh, Jeff," she whispered, "seeing you is like coming home."

A sudden exclamation from Henry Cowen kept her from hearing Jeff's reply. "See here, young man, are you supposed to eat the candles?" The men laughed. Jeff inclined his head, almost in a bow, and withdrew his hand.

"I'd better go—look at the turkey," Merrie stammered and hurried into the kitchen.

Expectation had kept her happy all week long. She wanted to please the doctor, and Brother Bill, and Jim's eccentric uncle. But it was Jeff's opinion that she valued most and she had imagined, down to the smallest detail, what it would be like to have him here. Jeff knocking at the door, Jeff smiling as she asked him to come in, Jeff's firm handshake and thoughtful gaze . . .

It all happened just as she had pictured it.

The cottage came alive. Voices intermingled in laughter and argument. The windows fogged over with steam, the kitchen was redolent with the odors of sage and freshly baked bread and the sweet spices of hot pumpkin pie. The men praised her cooking and even managed to sound appreciative of the pink and blue bed socks she had knitted for them. Cheerful noises, a confusion of jobs to be done, and in the background, Jeff. Jeff watching her light the Christmas candles. Jeff smiling as she tied a bib around Joseph's neck. Jeff catching her as she stumbled over her ruffled skirt and nearly dropped the turkey platter. All week long she had imagined what it would be like to see him again—Jeff the quiet thoughtful one, her protector. But her happiest day dream hadn't prepared her for the feelings his actual presence unleashed. At some time in her struggle to survive, Jeff had become far more than a comforting presence. She was deeply, uncontrollably excited by having him so near.

She knew when he was watching her as surely as if he had touched her. When she turned to meet his eyes, she saw something in them that made her pulse skip. And then suddenly, when the party was gayest, her imagination produced a picture of Jeff saying goodbye and going out the door. The warmth of the moment chilled with the thought of his leaving. A silly, indefinable panic surged through her because he would be gone before she could talk to him alone, though she hadn't the least idea what it was she wanted so badly to say.

Dr. Adams had produced his box of dominoes and he, Henry and Brother Bill were seated at the table with Jeff their silent observer. Merrie rejoiced at the thought that the game would keep them here longer. So, perhaps, would some fresh coffee and another round of applesauce cake. She jumped to her feet. "I'll put on the coffee pot," she said a little too brightly, and hurried into the kitchen.

The doctor and the minister were in spirited argument when Merrie returned with the granite pot of steaming coffee and a plate of cake. Jim's uncle was sitting a little apart from the others, arms folded across his chest, eyes half closed. At Merrie's approach, his eyelids snapped open and he sat bolt upright, every gesture saying "What do you know! I must have fallen asleep. . . ."

"Bill," the doctor said, "we'll never get the salvation of man settled tonight. Our stomachs'll be too full."

They had finished both coffee and cake and were about to leave when Lord Henry cleared his throat and said crisply, "This has been a fine day. I'm going to prove my gratitude by telling the hostess something she won't want to hear."

The other men glanced at him sharply. Lord Henry hesitated. With a crooked grin, he asked, "Well, Merrie?"

Merrie looked directly into his bright, dark eyes. "If there is something I ought to know, please tell me."

"What, if anything, have you heard from my daring young nephew?"

Dr. Adams snorted loudly, "Henry, I had no idea you cared what happened to him."

"Right!" the prospector nodded energetically. "I would be overjoyed at the news that he had fallen down a mine shaft, but to all his lesser adventures, I am completely indifferent."

Brother Bill threw an unhappy glance toward Merrie. "No need to upset Mrs. Cowen."

Lord Henry snapped, "I know what I'm doing."

"*You* do, Henry," Jeff said, "but I don't. You'd better explain."

"I happen to know Jim Cowen didn't go to Alaska. Or to British Columbia, for that matter, and I thought that might be of interest to his wife." Lord Henry added pointedly, "And to some of the rest of us."

Merrie said steadily, "I'd like to hear whatever you have to say."

The prospector shrugged. "Only this much. I've been prospecting hereabouts for a good many years. Between the trips I made and the trips I only talked about, I've gotten to know the Seattle waterfront like a crawling infant knows its crib. Jim talked about going with me. When I heard he'd lit out of Gold Mountain and was headed for the Yukon on his own, I got curious, partly because he picked a crazy time of year to head north. You don't leave in the fall, you leave in the spring so as to get there right after the breakup, make the trek inland and build winter camp before everything freezes up. So I wondered which way Jim went, and where he was headed. Not that he's worth the trouble, but he is my brother's boy. . . ." He shook his head. "I asked questions all over Seattle, and I satisfied myself that he hasn't bought supplies and he hasn't bought passage on a boat."

The doctor's gruff voice was the first to break the heavy silence. "You figured this information would be a comfort to Merrie?"

"I'm not concerned about comforting her," the prospector snapped. "I'm trying to warn her. That handsome young nephew of mine, who was going to brave the wilds of Alaska in the middle of the winter, has undoubtedly been risking his life in a comfortable hotel room in Seattle. So be it. If some one of his associates sees fit to dump him in Elliott Bay, so much the better. The ugly truth is that so far no one seems to have taken the trouble, and once brave Jim runs out of money, he'll be back here."

The minister leaned forward, his hand raised in an awkward protest.

"It's all right, Brother Bill." Merrie looked squarely into the face of Jim's uncle. "Mr. Cowen, have you seen Jim since he left Gold Mountain?"

"Of course I have," Lord Henry said irritably. "Do you think I'd make you miserable if I didn't have to?"

"Where?"

"What difference does it make? He shouldn't have been there, and neither should I, let's leave it at that. It wasn't the King County morgue, the more's the pity." He stood up. "I told you to go back to Dakota," he said, an incongruous show of affection softening his face, "But I'm glad you didn't. You will find what you want right here in the Snoqualmie Valley. Someday, somehow . . ." He picked up his wide-brimmed Confederate hat, set it down gently over his long gray hair. "Time to go."

One by one they thanked her. She accepted the thanks numbly, shook hands and said good-bye. Jeff was the last to leave. "Merrie," he said quietly, "I've been happier today than I've ever been in my life." One finger under her chin, he tilted her head back and looked into her face. "You are beautiful. More beautiful to me than any other girl in the world."

"Jeff . . . Don't leave me. . . ." The words rang

in her head but she hadn't said them out loud, for Jeff was turning away, following the others and the flickering light of Lord Henry's kerosene lantern. The circle of light grew dimmer, the voices floated away from her and melted into the darkness. . . . Merrie closed the door. She had known all along that the day would come to an end, and that when it did loneliness would hurt more than ever. There was the clean-up to do. Time, too, to see that Joseph hadn't kicked off his covers.

Without needing to light her way, Merrie moved swiftly through the cluttered kitchen to the stairs leading to the tiny bedroom with the dormer window which was hers and Joseph's. He was sleeping peacefully, as she had expected he would be, but instead of going downstairs immediately she went to the window and rested her forehead against the frosted pane. Perhaps in the silent darkness she could force her mind to regain some control of her feelings, or at least help her sort them out. "Know your heart from your head, Merrie Dooley," uncle Mike Bruner had often said. "You need the both of them. You also need to know when it's time to let one be stronger than the other."

At the sound of footsteps, she whirled around. Jeff was standing in the doorway, his tall figure outlined by the pale light of the kitchen lamp at the foot of the stairs. "I came back," he said quietly.

He crossed the room as softly as a mocassined Indian, and stood just inches away from her. In the velvety shadow she could just make out his dark eyes and the curve of his mouth. The warmth of his body seemed to reach out and enclose her. "I just came up here for a few minutes," she said unsteadily. "Just to make sure Joseph was covered up."

"And he is."

"Yes."

"But you're standing by the window, looking out where there's nothing to see. You were thinking."

Merrie felt blood rush to her cheeks. "Yes," she said, just above a whisper.

"Tell me the truth, Merrie. Were you thinking about me?"

She wanted to cry out "All the time! All day long! When I wake up in the middle of the night, and I can't get back to sleep. . . ." Instead a small strangled voice answered "Yes. I was thinking of you."

Jeff's hands moved and came to rest on her shoulders. His deep voice said "That's what I needed to know." Merrie scarcely moved, it was more like falling, but she was in his arms.

He held her tightly and she clung to him, eyes closed, face pressed hard against his shoulder. She could feel his heavy heartbeat. "Don't leave me," she whispered.

"I wouldn't be holding you now if I intended to let you go."

She clutched his shoulders in wordless expression of the longing she had been trying for many months to suppress or ignore. She lifted her head. "Jeff . . ."

"Love me," he breathed, and bent his head to kiss her.

The kiss was long, and flowed through her like a

warm current lifting and carrying her. It ended abruptly as Jeff released her, stepped back, and held her at arm's length. "Merrie, understand this. I love you. I want you, right now. And you want me. I know it by the way you are trembling. It's there, in your kiss. But is it *just* for now? Because some day Jim will come back, Merrie. I think you know that as well as I do, except that you won't allow yourself to face it, and I know that I must. If caring for me is to last only as long as you are alone and deserted. If pity and loyalty and wanting to be needed by someone weaker than yourself are some day going to be stronger than what you feel for me, you must say so right now. I won't stop loving you, but I can live with that, as I have been for almost two years. But if we make love, you are my girl. *My girl,* and I'll never give you up or stand aside."

"Jeff . . ." Merrie said urgently. "Jeff. Don't leave me. . . ." and this time she said the words out loud.

The shadowy figure loomed over her but did not move. "It can't be both ways, Merrie. You cannot be all things to all people."

"I don't love Jim. Maybe I never did. Or else . . ." Her voice broke off. "Or else it was another kind of love. It . . . it made me less of a person. Sometimes it made me ashamed."

"He'll come back to you."

"No!"

"Oh, but he will. What will you do, Merrie, when he does?"

Merrie shuddered involuntarily. "I don't know.

I do try not to think of it, but that's because it frightens me."

"But little Merrie Dooley, you are the most courageous woman I've ever met." Jeff's fingers touched her chin, gently tilting her head until she had to look up into his face. "It's very simple. As simple and as basic as love itself. If you love me, you're my girl, and you will not go to another man's bed."

"I know," Merrie whispered. "I don't want another man. With all my heart, I want you."

For a long moment, neither moved and the only sound was Jeff's barely audible exhalation of breath. Then he swept her up into his arms and carried her to the little bed in the corner. His fingers moved rapidly but gently until her new ruffled dress and her petticoat and chemise lay on the floor beside her shoes. The lamplight from the kitchen penetrated the darkness, drawing the small white figure out of the shadow. Slowly, his eyes never leaving her body, Jeff undressed.

"Merrie," he murmured. "Oh my God, Merrie . . ." Her arms lifted, encircling him and drawing him down. "Only you," she said against his mouth, and then every undecided issue, every doubt and fear for the future were swept away by the tide of their yearning for each other, everything forgotten except the hungry joining of their bodies.

II

Brother Bill tried to convince himself that this weekend in April would be the most memorable of his preaching career. Ever since Christmas, he had been working towards the dedication service; now that the time had come, it even looked as if Saturday's sunshine would reappear on Sunday to smile on him, his congregation and the elder from Seattle. This was the eve of his triumph. And yet, he was uneasy.

It seemed to Bill that he had never had a successful conference with any presiding elder. The elder who was coming out from Seattle today was a milder man than many of those with whom he had differed. He would most likely take Bill's side in the controversy which gripped the Gold Mountain congregation. Nevertheless, Bill was nervous, and his discomfort increased as the hours before the meeting slipped away.

It was a feeling rooted in long experience, for Bill had been in the ministry only ten months when

384

he suffered his first failure in the eyes of his superiors, many years before. The setting was burned into his memory. . . .

He thought back to a grove of trees on the south bank of the Nooksack River, in the sparsely settled north corner of the state. A beautiful spot for a camp meeting, and Bill was proud that so many of his people had come—settlers from all corners of his circuit, and a hundred and fifty Indians as well. Such attendance was to his credit, the elder would be impressed at what he had accomplished in less than a year. So he met the party eagerly, the presiding elder who had come by horseback from Blaine, two missionaries from British Columbia, a minister from the Skagit and Island County circuit, and other preachers who came by canoe and horseback from districts still farther away.

The elder was a man with scowling eyebrows and a thin, high voice, not at all like the genial elder Brother Bill was to meet in Gold Mountain today. In his presence Bill's confidence had melted; he felt like a boy who can't make his coat sleeves come down to his wrists.

"Have you taken up the benevolence collections?" the elder asked.

Bill shook his head. "The people were poor. I didn't like to ask them."

The elder frowned. "How much have you received?"

Bill's temper had been more of a burden to him then than it was now. It stirred dangerously as he answered, "In ten months I've taken in twenty-five dollars."

"And turned back four times as much," the elder snapped in his high-pitched voice: "A poor record . . ."

Bill had fled into the woods. For an hour he had planned to roll up his blankets, go over into Canada and never tell anyone he had hoped to be a Methodist minister. It was a thought that assailed him many times afterward, but never more strongly than it had as he stomped up and down the bank of the Nooksack, Bible in hand, but so consumed by rage that he hadn't the strength to open it. The appearance of an old woman called Grandma Peters had kept him in the ministry. Grandma's cabin was miles from the camp site. There was no road out from it, only a blazed trail, and Grandma was far too feeble to walk. But she had wanted to go to one more camp meeting before she died, so her four sons had slashed and cut and worked until they made a sled road all the way from her cabin to the riverbank. They built a sled, loaded it with bed and blankets, seated Grandma on top of it all and with a yoke of yearling oxen for a team they brought her to the meeting, singing and shouting all the way.

They passed Bill on their way to the camp ground. Grandma was on top of the sled, her eyes peering out brightly between the shawl that covered her head and the worn comforter she was lost in from the chin down. The four sons were singing; it was a hymn, but they were shouting it like a cavalry charge. As the sled skidded past, the old woman caught sight of Bill. "God bless you, Brother Bill!" she chirped. Bill hadn't moved from the spot until she was out of sight and the voices of her sons echoed back so faintly he could not make out the words of the hymn. Then he followed them back to camp. . . .

Now Bill reminded himself that a church in Gold Mountain in 1896 was far different from a camp meeting in the wilderness of Whatcom County in 1878. This was a permanent post. He had built a fine church, and thanks to some unexpected donations, it would be dedicated tomorrow. He could make a good report. . . . These thoughts sustained him as he met the afternoon train.

The elder was a white-haired, pink-cheeked man, with pale blue eyes and a small, round, flexible mouth. He seemed pleased with everything Bill told him as they walked from the depot to the church. It wasn't until they were standing directly in front of the church that the elder's tone lost its geniality.

With a nod of his head, he indicated the blacksmith shop next to the church. "I understand that the owner of that establishment has offered to donate a church bell."

Bill stiffened. "Yes, sir." In the elder's manner he could detect the plan of battle. An old battle, Bill thought wearily. "Yes, sir," he repeated. "I refused to accept it."

"So I understand." With another nod, the elder directed Bill to continue into the church.

Bill led the elder into the tiny room behind the choir loft which was to serve as the minister's study. He made no effort to talk while the older man selected a chair, sat down, and squinted critically at the bare walls and meager furnishings. The elder would talk when he was ready; besides, Bill thought with a twinge of the old bitterness, I know what he's going to say.

"You refused to accept it," the elder repeated, still maintaining the air of deliberate patience. "Many members of the church are badly disappointed."

"I know that," Bill said. "I expected it."

"They told me the reason you had given them, but I'd prefer to hear it from you."

This was a matter of conviction, and conviction for which Bill had fought stubbornly for many years. His awkwardness disappeared. "The owner of the blacksmith shop is also the owner of a saloon. If liquor put a bell in my church, how could I get up in the pulpit, with the bell ringing in my ears, and tell people they shouldn't drink?"

The elder sighed. His pink face was suffused with a look of genuine kindness. "You may think that you are the first minister who has ever faced such a situation." He shook his head several times. "But of course you aren't. Over and over again, we are called upon to decide when, if ever, the questionable means justifies the worthy end."

Bill said flatly, "I can't compromise."

The older man spread his hands on the table and studied the stubby fingers. "A bell would be a fine addition to the church. Your people feel you have no right to deprive them."

Bill's jaw tightened. "I'm not taking anything away from them," he said angrily. "I'm trying to give them something: conscience and the love of

God. Those who complained to you don't want the bell because it will beautify their house of worship; they want it because it would make the Gold Mountain church the first in the Snoqualmie Valley to have a bell.''

"They're human," the elder said, smiling.

"Of course they're human, and so am I! But if I'm going to set myself up as a minister of the gospel, it's my job to discourage that side of being human which is greedy or selfish or materialistic. As long as I'm the minister in Gold Mountain, we won't accept a saloonkeeper's bell!''

"Sit down, Bill," the elder said quietly, "and stop waving your arms."

Bill dropped into his chair.

"There is no issue between you and me," the elder said, "nor between you and the church, so far as the bell is concerned." His short fingers began to drum on the arms of his chair. "The debt on the church has been paid off, that's fine. I understand that some generous donations cleared it up."

"So generous I've been worried. I can't find out who made them."

"Donors often wish to remain in the background." The elder cleared his throat. "I also understand that the women of the church have been active. What's this about serving dinner to an excursion train?"

Bill described the project, but it was clear he wasn't holding the elder's attention. The elder had something else on his mind and was simply letting Bill talk while he decided how to launch a subject which he found difficult or unpleasant. Bill didn't have to wait long. He was in the middle of a sentence when the elder raised his hand and said crisply, "Very interesting. Now, there is another matter we must discuss." The elder's round mouth pursed as he gave himself one last second before delivering the blow. "The congregationtion feels that a permanent minister should be a married man."

He hesitated, obviously waiting for Bill to speak. Bill remained still as a rock. The elder fidgeted, cleared his throat, and went on. "I understood when you accepted this appointment that you might be, uh, thinking along those lines."

Bill said bluntly, "I didn't deceive you. But you didn't tell me that the appointment depended on my going out and finding a wife."

"No one expected you to marry immediately, nor even within the year. But they want some assurance that you—well, as I said, that you have some—plan."

Bill's jaw tightened as he held back an angry retort. What should he say? "Yes, sir, I've been thinking along those lines. But I've run into a little difficulty. The girl is married. . . ." He could see the elder's round mouth fly open with shock, the elder's pale eyes harden with disapproval. . . . Suddenly Bill felt tired. The elder didn't want to hear such things. No doubt he had assembled the usual arguments—a wife is a necessity, she can direct the Sunday School, play the organ, make the parsonage a suitable place for missionary meetings, a minister can't do his job without a wife. Solid reasons, but they hardly applied to a preacher who coveted another man's wife. . . . "Yes, sir," Bill said quietly, "I have thought about marrying. I can't say more than that at the present time."

The elder looked vastly relieved. "Fine," he exclaimed, "very fine! No need to, uh, rush your plans. When a date has been set . . . Well, I'll hear from you. . . ." His hands fluttered and came to rest on his stomach. "Now," he said, retrieving his air of authority, "now, let's discuss the dedication service tomorrow. I'm pleased that you've asked me to deliver the sermon. . . ."

The more formal the occasion, the deeper was Brother Bill's fear of failing. The Gold Mountain church was the work of his own hands. Earnestly as he had prayed that it might be dedicated properly, and soon, he had dreaded the ceremony itself.

But the service progressed smoothly. The opening prayer, the first hymn, the reading of the Scripture, the collection, the second hymn—Bill's relief grew as he led the congregation toward the point where the elder would take charge and his own responsibility would end. There were so many chances for error, for Bill was never more clumsy than when he was trying to follow a carefully prepared plan. At last he introduced the elder. The elder rose, his pink face glowing with a paternalistic smile.

Bill sank into his chair, covered his mouth with his hand and gulped for air; he was as winded as if he had climbed a mountain, and his back ached.

The elder's voice rose to the high, sweet pitch he always used when he was reading from the Bible. It sank to its natural level as he began his sermon. It would be an hour before Bill would have to stand and remember the correct and proper thing to do. A full hour, Bill reflected, for the elder wasn't the kind to underrate an occasion with a thirty-minute sermon.

Bill's gaze traveled over the congregation. How often he had looked down into the upturned faces and wondered what these people were thinking. In the light of yesterday's conference with the elder, the question took on new meaning. Someone down there had wiped out the church's debt at the lumber yard. Someone had paid for the pews. Someone had complained because he would not accept the bell, others—many others, the elder had hinted—were dissatisfied because he was not a married man. Who? Who was against him, who was with him? Or was it that simple? Bill reminded himself that it was not. The man who paid for the lumber could be the loudest in demanding that he accept the bell. The men and women who wanted Bill to remain as their minister would see nothing inconsistent in demanding that he leave, or take a wife. . . .

Bill's glance sought out Merrie. She was sitting next to Bertha Tarpee, with Joseph in her lap. The question the elder had raised could not be put off. Jeff Smith had predicted this crisis long ago; Bill knew he had been guilty of deliberate self-delusion when he retorted that as long as he was a good enough carpenter to build them a church, the people of Gold Mountain wouldn't notice whether he had six wives or none at all. Now the church was built, and in an hour would be formally dedicated. They didn't need a carpenter any more. They needed a settled man, a man with a wife who could do all those things the elders had been reciting to him for sixteen years or more. And they were right. Gold Mountain was a town, not an outpost. The job called for a minister, not a wandering preacher, retired because of the ache in his back. . . .

The elder's voice rose in exhortation. Bill jerked to attention. Something about conscience . . . Conscience, Bill mused, the heaviest yoke God hung on man. Conscience and the necessity of making his own decisions. It would have been easier to accept the church bell than to refuse it. It would have been simpler to listen to Nate Tarpee's warning that his temperance lectures were embarrassing several townspeople who could do him some good. But he'd listened to his conscience, and conscience told him to double the number of temperance lectures. When the attendance dropped to three, he had filled the benches by canvassing the saloons and carrying out bodily the customers he thought would benefit most from a good, loud bawling out.

Conscience had been a burden even when he was a little boy. The nearest settlement then was ten miles from his father's homestead; he had often walked twenty miles in order to attend Sunday School. One morning he was on his way to church, two dogs trotting along at his side, when he was confronted by a black bear. The dogs flew at the bear, the larger running near the bear's head and barking while the smaller dog bit at the bear's heels. Concerned about his dogs, Bill had picked up a club. He ran toward the howling, snarling trio and with all his strength brought the weapon down on top of the bear's head.

He had meant to hit and run, but as he tried to get away one foot slipped on the dry pine needles and he fell, bear and dogs on top of him. For an instant, Bill recalled, he thought he was dead. Miraculously, he got free of the bear and dogs, and ran. He hadn't gone far before he again thought of the dogs. He stopped in his flight, looked around quickly for another chunk of wood, found one and advanced.

The big black beast was lying on his back, battling the dogs with teeth and claws. Bill thought of the way they always killed salmon, by hitting them on the nose. Gritting his teeth, he raised the club, brought it down with all the strength that fear had given him. There was a dull, cracking sound, the dogs fell back panting, the bear was dead.

He had saved the lives of his dogs, but he had killed a bear on Sunday. Heart beating hard, Bill hung the bear in a tree and continued on to Sunday School. He said nothing about the bear to his parents. Monday morning he took out his rifle, announced he was going hunting, and returned that night with his kill. It had seemed right, until it came time for the spoken lie.

"A big fellow," his father had said. "Lucky you got him with your first shot."

"I didn't shoot him to death," young Bill had confessed, pouring out the whole story of the Sunday encounter.

His father had looked at him quizzically. "You killed him yesterday, you went back and shot him today?"

Bill nodded unhappily.

Bill's mother had said, "I'm sure you've learned a lesson."

And Bill's father had smiled and said, "Yes, when you want to kill a bear with a club, hit him on the nose and not over the head."

"I'm talking about keeping the Sabbath," Bill's mother had corrected him firmly. "It's not the time to joke."

"Sorry, Miranda," his father had replied. "But while you're working so hard on the boy's conscience, don't neglect his sense of humor entirely."

There had been very little humor in his life, Bill reflected, but an awful lot of conscience. Then let conscience lead me to the answer, Bill thought now; it's the only part of me that doesn't ache.

This congregation wanted him to marry, and he had convinced himself that there was nothing he wanted more, once the church was built. He looked down at Merrie's upturned, eager face. Her wide eyes were following every gesture the elder made; as she listened, one hand stroked Joseph's cheek. He worshipped this girl, knowing he could not possibly marry her. Her husband was an obstacle—but did he want that obstacle removed, or was he hiding behind it?

Two years ago he'd told Jeff Smith that he wanted to settle down, and for two years he had believed it just as sincerely as he had believed that he would love Merrie, if only she were free. What did conscience say to these things now? Bill covered his face with one hand. Under cover of the elder's sermon, he whispered a short prayer.

In a moment the truth came to him. He considered it, not with surprise, but with relief and recognition. Like finding an old friend among strangers. He uncovered his face, and sat up straight. The elder must be getting on toward the end of his sermon. It would be his turn at the pulpit; only a few minutes left in which to decide what he was going to say.

It came to him easily; his best sermons had always been those he had delivered without preparation. The elder sat down. In the silence the eyes of the congregation turned to Bill. He stood up, walked slowly to the pulpit, grasped it firmly with both hands, and began to talk.

"Brothers and sisters, what I have to say won't take long. Two years ago I left my circuit and came here to Gold Mountain because there was work here for me to do. That work is finished. Now there's a different job to do, and I know in my heart that another man could do it better than I can. The Conference will find you a real good minister. As soon as they do, I'm going back to walking a circuit. If my rheumatism gets too bad, I might buy a horse.

"You people built this church. Most of you did, anyway. But you don't own it. It isn't like your houses or your stores or your barns, it belongs to God. The minute you forget that, it's nothing but a building.

"I'll put the siding on the east wall before I leave. Now let's sing a hymn—'A Mighty Fortress Is Our God,' that's one tune I can carry. You better start raising funds for an organ. There's a lot of preachers that don't have any more of an ear for music than I do."

He saw shock and disbelief on their faces; the muted sputtering sounds at his back told him that the elder was surprised, too, and was not enjoying the sensation.

One face stood out from the rest. Merrie was looking up at him with a puzzled expression; there were worry lines between her eyes and she was forgetting to sing with the rest.

"God bless you, Merrie," Bill said, though he knew she couldn't hear him. "You never would have loved me, anyway."

12

BY THE TIME the excursion train arrived from
Seattle, three hundred men, women and children
had collected at the picnic site above Snoqualmie
Falls. The sky was gray, and darker clouds were
gathering over the mountains to the east. Some
pessimistic members of the Gold Mountain Ladies
Aid looked over their shoulders apprehensively as
they arranged the food on the long tables. They
were not the only group who had a stake in the
weather. An enterprising family of Snoqualmie
Indians had set up a shop on the riverbank. An old
squaw wearing a blanket and a man's felt hat was
standing beside an up-to-date but badly battered
card table. Her daughters, in white shirtwaists and
blue serge skirts, were helping to arrange the stock
of Indian baskets while the menfolk, father and
sons, leaned against a nearby tree and with expressions of sullen indifference appraised the food
the church women were setting out.

There were steep grades between Gilman and
Snoqualmie Falls, but at the top of the falls the
track leveled out, following the course of the river

to Three Forks and Gold Mountain. Here the excursion train was to stop; a hill rose above the track to the right, a strip of meadow sloped down to the river at the left. Here the coaches would discharge their loads of city folk who (the Ladies Aid fervently hoped) would be hungry after the three-hour ride. Here, and perhaps from vantage points along the railroad track where the view of the falls was better, they would witness a daring parachute jump arranged for people who otherwise wouldn't make the trip to see a 268-foot waterfall.

A platform had been built on the south rim of the falls, extending out over the great chasm. For a week, residents of Three Forks and Gold Mountain had been speculating if this man could satisfy the customers and still come out with his life. Jeff's wagonload of loggers argued the question all the way from camp.

"Five, six years ago they stretched a tightrope over the falls," one of the men recalled. "Man got out on it, with a chair in one hand, umbrella in the other, and did quite an act. He come out of it all right. Remember that, Jeff?"

Jeff laughed. "I remember . . ." It was true, the tightrope walker who had been hired to entertain an excursion train some years before had completed his repertoire. But when he had reached the safety of solid ground, he had fallen into the arms of the nearest spectator. Teeth chattering as if they had all come loose in his head, knees too weak to hold him up, he had mumbled over and over, "Bring me a beer, quick, just bring me a beer." As time passed by, more and more settlers claimed to be the spectator who had as good as saved the poor man's life. It appeared, after six years, that he had fallen into the arms of upward of thirty men. . . .

"I suppose the poor fool knows what he's doing," Jeff said. "He came out here a few weeks ago and looked at the falls before he agreed to make the jump."

Dave Riley shook his massive head. "I got a feeling we're going to a funeral."

"The man's professional. He's made a dozen jumps."

"What's so dangerous about it, anyway?" another logger put in. "That umbrella thing holds him up. Daredevil, hrumph. I bet he'd be scared purple if he had to fall a 250-foot fir."

"I'll stick to logging," Dave Riley concluded solemnly, spitting over the side of the wagon. "It don't seem right to work on Sunday. . . ."

On the fringe of the picnic ground Jeff tied his horse to an alder. The grove looked like the main street of Gold Mountain on the busiest Saturday night of the year. Buggies, wagons, pony carts, riding horses, even a mule with an old Army saddle on its back—Jeff grinned as he recognized the animal. For all his scoffing, Lord Henry Cowen had come to see the parachute jump, too.

The loggers raced toward the crowd. On the edge of it they wiped the eagerness from their faces, thrust their hands in their pockets, and proceeded at a leisurely pace.

"You here too, Jeff?"

Jeff turned. It was Brother Bill, sitting on the end of a railroad tie above the swarm of people.

Jeff waved and walked up the bank to the track. "I'd sit down next to you, if only I knew what time that excursion train is due."

"It won't come this far."

"Trust in the Lord, eh," Jeff said as he sat down. "But keep your ears open for a steam whistle."

"I've been wanting to talk to you."

"*I've* been wanting to talk to you." Jeff clapped his hands on his knees and gave the preacher a long, quizzical look.

"What about?" Bill said defensively.

Jeff grinned. "You know as well as I do. You didn't see me, but I was in church the day it was dedicated."

"I saw you."

He replied too quickly. Jeff shook his head. "You didn't act like it. You stood up and fired that farewell address of yours like a man who's got one charge of powder between him and the grizzly. You left in kind of a hurry, too, didn't you?"

"I finished what I had to say."

Jeff gave him a wry smile. "So I judged. I also had the impression that the elder from Seattle was not pleased. I hope you really want a rough circuit. You're bound to get one."

An unusually boyish smile broke over the preacher's face. "I'll get a hard assignment, all right, but it won't be in Washington. I've put in a request for missionary work in Alaska."

Jeff looked at Bill curiously. There was a change in the preacher, and it had taken place since that dedication service. In the past year Bill had become solemn to the point of being morose. Little as they had seen of each other, Jeff recognized that Bill was finding every decision more difficult, every solution less satisfactory. At times he had wondered if the preacher were physically ill. Now Bill was talking about missionary work in an area more desolate than the loneliest circuit in Washington, and he sounded happy.

"Bill, you astound me."

The minister, ordinarily so solemn, laughed outright. "Then you're not lost," he retorted. "I didn't think anything could."

"As for the good people of Gold Mountain . . ." Jeff looked down at the clearing in which the Ladies Aid had set up picnic tables. Twenty or thirty women buzzed around the tables like bees bringing in honey. Bertha Tarpee, even Martin Kittinger's wife. And Merrie. He had been looking for her, of course. It was the chance to watch her, if only from a distance, that had brought him to the falls; the loggers didn't really need him to drive the wagon. If she were in a crowd of a thousand people, Jeff thought, I'd see her. Of all the faces—dignified, or pretty, or handsome, only one would come in focus. . . . Jeff turned to Bill and saw that the minister was watching her, too.

"Bill, you love that girl, don't you?" Jeff said quietly.

The preacher started and frowned. "She's a fine girl, but you know as well as I do that she's married."

"Tell me the truth, Bill. Your decision to leave Gold Mountain was a surprise. I remember our talk a couple of years ago, when you and I were

402

sitting on the front step of my cabin and Merrie rode by in Kittinger's rig. You were all for settling down, you even admitted you'd like to get married. You worked for sixteen, seventeen years to get a church of your own, and now you're throwing it away. Is it because of Merrie?"

"There's no use . . ."

"Bill, I want to know."

The minister sighed. "No, not because of Merrie. All during the dedication service I fought this thing out with myself. I looked back over the past two years in Gold Mountain, and I tried to look ahead and imagine what it would be like to stay another two years. I've been feeling restless for a long time, and trying to call it something else. Truth is, I don't want to stay in one place. Say I'm scared of women, but I don't want to get married, either."

"This is the truth, Bill?"

"It's the truth."

Jeff said quietly, "I used to feel sorry for you. Now I envy you. You look to me like a happy man."

Bill shook his head. "I'm missing something, and I know it." He turned toward Jeff, and seemed about to say something more.

"Well?"

"There's been a few times that I wondered if you didn't love Merrie, yourself."

Jeff's jaw hardened. "You wondered right," he said curtly.

"You got me to confess like a regular papist. Would you care to try a little of the same?"

"No."

"I'm here to listen."

Jeff retorted savagely, "What could I tell you that you don't already know?" As soon as he'd said it he was sorry for the outburst. "I beg your pardon, Bill. But why talk about it, what's the use?"

Bill stood up slowly, one hand pressed against the small of his back. "There isn't any, I guess. I'm going down to the Ladies Aid tables. Come along?"

Jeff got to his feet. "No," he said with his usual grin, "but I'm getting off the railroad tracks if my divine protection is going to wander away and start sampling the potato salad."

"Don't make light," the preacher cautioned him automatically, as he had a hundred times.

The distinctive figure of Lord Henry, in Indian blanket and Confederate hat, eased itself away from the crowd and scurried toward the grove of alder. "I'll talk to my neighbor," Jeff said. "You go count the pies."

The prospector greeted him by saluting smartly and sweeping the gray hat off his head. "I'm sick of my fellow man," he announced. "Did anyone stay home today? I never could stand people, more than four or five at a time." He pushed strands of long gray hair behind his ears and carefully replaced his hat. "Crying children and fat women with chocolate cake. If they have picnics in the Klondike, I won't stay long."

Jeff laughed. "I can't understand why you came today."

Lord Henry's bright eyes narrowed. "It wasn't to see a parachute jump," he snapped.

Like a hound dog picking up a scent, he turned suddenly on his heel and squinted down the track toward the falls. "I hear the train. Come on . . ."

Jeff was about to ask him why, if he disliked crowds, he was so anxious to charge into the throng that was gathering to meet the train. But the prospector was already loping along the track, the Indian blanket flapping at his heels.

Jeff caught up with him just as the excursion train came into view. The steam engine was puffing hard as it came around the bend. Like a fat woman reaching the crest of a hill she'd never expected to climb, the locomotive exhaled mightily. "Look what I've done!" the gasping engine seemed to say as it rolled to a wheezing stop.

Through the open coach windows heads protruded, two or three at each window. The sticklike arms of little boys shot through the openings, waving red and blue banners in frenzied circular motions. Men plucked visored caps off their heads and flapped them erratically at the waiting crowd. The pink and white faces of young ladies appeared at the windows, framed by the scarfs they had tied under their chins to keep their hats from blowing off. Giggling, they grasped the ends of the scarfs and waved them with both hands. The coaches seemed about to burst with the cargo of excursionists.

Lord Henry's eyes darted from face to face. As the doors were opened and the passengers began to spill down the steps, he gripped Jeff's elbow.

405

"Listen, Jeff, there's a bigger crowd than I counted on. You go down to the other end of the platform, I'll stay here. Keep a sharp eye out."

Jeff's amusement at the prospector's odd behavior died quickly as he understood its cause. "Jim? You think he's likely to be on this train?"

"I know that boy pretty well."

"What will you do if he is?"

Lord Henry's eyes didn't leave the train. "How do I know?" he retorted. "I never did worry what to do with the pelt when I wasn't close enough to start skinning."

Jeff walked along the track to the other end of the train, skirting the groups of chattering, laughing excursionists. So shrewd old Henry thought his nephew would select this moment to return to the Snoqualmie Valley. He would be one among the well-dressed city folk—that would satisfy his desire to show off before the rough-cut loggers who had disdained him. And Jim knew that the Ladies Aid was to serve dinner to the train; he would know, too, how earnest Merrie was about the project. If he appeared suddenly, right at the peak of activity . . . Yes, Jeff thought angrily, Lord Henry knows the boy. Jim Cowen would relish such dramatics.

Jeff strolled among the first excursionists to get off the train, and satisfied himself that Jim was not among them. Hands in pockets, he took a position from which he could watch the last two coaches.

One by one the passengers descended, the children with whoops of joy, their elders more cautiously, trying out the ground with a tentative step or two before they stopped to survey their surroundings. Jeff sought the familiar face, the familiar strutting gait. The coaches were almost empty. Just a few stragglers now. A man leaning on a cane. A mother carrying a child, whose white, tear-streaked face rested wearily against her shoulder. And finally, the conductor, dusting trousers and sleeves as if he'd been at the bottom of the heap. He began to close the coaches.

Jeff called, "That's all? No one left inside?"

Despite the thorough grooming he'd given himself, the conductor looked ruffled. "Not that I can see. If there is, they're in for a while. We're running up to Gold Mountain to take on water and turn her around."

With two precise movements he dropped the metal platform into position and slammed the coach door. He stepped into the next coach and repeated the process. Up ahead, the locomotive's big brass bell began to toll a warning. The conductor waved and swung himself onto the rear car as the train rolled forward.

The crowds were converging on the Ladies Aid picnic tables. Jeff followed, glancing briefly at every face he passed.

The excursionists seemed to be falling into line. As he neared the tables, he saw why. Merrie was organizing. The church women were at their stations, spoons in hand and nervous smiles on their faces. Cheeks pink with excitement, Merrie was riding herd on the city people. "Follow the line down this side of the table," she kept repeating, gay as sunlight. Then she slipped a dinner plate into each person's hand and steered him firmly toward the food.

Jeff had gone to many picnics in the Snoqualmie Valley, but this spread beat everything he'd seen, even on the Fourth of July. Baked hams, stewed chicken bobbing in pots of steaming hot dumplings, roasts of venison, platters of fried trout, crocks of baked beans and side pork, potato salad, dill pickles, cottage cheese, sliced onions in vinegar, apple pies and chocolate cakes and four kinds of homemade bread. The members of the Gold Mountain Ladies Aid had been vying with each other; the church would have an organ, and soon.

Brother Bill was in the background, looking both willing and useless. His long face shone with relief when he caught sight of Jeff. "You look calm enough," he breathed as he joined Jeff. "But don't go over there and try to help. You risk getting knocked out with a gravy ladle."

Jeff grinned. "You haven't seen Lord Henry?"

"Not since the train pulled in." The preacher sighed. "But I'd be glad to go find him, if you're sure he's got three, four miles away by now."

"When duty calls, or danger, be never wanting there," Jeff said in mock piety, quoting one of the preacher's favorite short sermons. "Besides, you ought to stay and see the parachute jump."

The preacher shook his head. "I don't know. I met the man who's going to do it. He said this is an easy jump, but he didn't look as if he believed it."

Jeff said casually, "You haven't seen Jim Cowen, have you?"

Bill's joking manner dropped like a mask. "Is he here?"

"I don't know. Henry thinks he might be."

"Poor Merrie," the preacher muttered angrily. "He was sure to come back sometime, I think she realizes that. But he couldn't have picked a worse time."

"Jim would figure that out. . . ." Jeff said gruffly. "Let's hope he hasn't thought of it, wherever he is. I'd better find Henry."

Jeff began a systematic search of the picnic ground. The crowd had divided into two camps. The local residents—loggers, shingle weavers, farmers, storekeepers, Indians and old men and children in overalls—were scattered all over the hill above the railroad track. Some were eating box lunches, others were simply sitting and watching. The excursionists from Seattle had drawn together on the lower ground near the picnic tables. They were making a great deal of noise, and rather pretentiously ignoring the quiet audience up above.

A dozen young men, wearing identical caps and striped blazers with a club insignia on the pockets, had closed in around a short, muscular man in a baggy canvas suit. The parachutist, Jeff guessed, for the youths' faces were either worshipful or studiously indifferent.

"If it rains," Bill said, "maybe they won't have the jump."

"It would have to rain hard and fast. It's almost two o'clock."

"No sign of Jim?" the minister asked uneasily.

Jeff shook his head. "No, but I just caught sight of Henry. Way down at the end of the clearing, near the falls." He took two or three steps,

409

stopped, and came back. "Bill, stay right here for a while, will you?"

"What should I do?"

He'd asked Henry the same question, but there was no use repeating the old prospector's evasive and sarcastic answer. It was an ironic, perhaps ridiculous, situation. Three men appointing themselves to guard a legally married wife from her legally married husband. "Watch and stay near," Jeff said, and hurried across the picnic ground.

He passed Nils and Katherine Bengston, the Carlson family, Nate and Bertha Tarpee, a gang of his own loggers, Emil Greene and his cortege of shingle weavers, the schoolteacher, in earnest conversation with Sam the saloonkeeper, and many others. But when he reached the spot where he had seen Lord Henry, the old man was gone.

Puzzled, Jeff turned back, studying the groups of people he had just passed. The prospector with his long hair and bright-colored blanket was not easily lost even in a crowd. He couldn't have retraced his steps, he must have gone ahead. Jeff continued up the slope.

At the edge of the clearing, he saw Lord Henry. He was on the ground with his back to a tree. Seated right next to him, so close the two might have been attached, was Jim Cowen.

"Halloo, Jeff!" the prospector said cheerily. "We're just resting a bit, my nephew and I. Jim's telling me what a fine life he's been leading in Seattle."

Jeff saw at once that Jim had dressed up in his finest for this excursion trip. His suit, his dark red brocaded vest, his fawn-colored, pointed shoes, the derby that lay at his side were the trappings of a wealthy gentleman. But the picture was out of kilter. Several strands of Jim's wavy hair had fallen across his forehead—he hadn't removed his hat himself. Bits of leaf mold and fir needles clung to his neatly pressed trousers, and one of the fancy brass buttons on his vest had been torn loose.

Jim looked up at Jeff, his eyes blazing and his mouth working with some unspoken curse. He made a quick forward lunge, as if he meant to jump to his feet, and as suddenly fell back, panting.

"Not yet," the prospector said. "I told you, Jimmy boy, you're not going down there while she's still busy serving that dinner. You'll get to show her your fine new clothes, don't you worry. But not yet!" he said, emphasizing the order with a series of sharp jerks on Jim's imprisoned arm. *"Not yet!"*

Lord Henry looked up at Jeff. "Thought he could throw me," he explained pleasantly.

Jim said hoarsely, "You have no right . . ."

"No, I don't, indeed I don't!" Lord Henry agreed. "I must be breaking twelve laws, at least. But I'm holding you here until it's time for the parachute jump. The dinner will be over by then, and this little surprise visit of yours will be slightly less humiliating than it would be right now."

Jeff looked ahead uneasily to the moment when the prospector would release Jim. The boy's face had gone white; he was gasping with the pressure of fury he had no means of releasing. Later Merrie would be the target for the unbearable load of anger and humiliation. Jeff knew his presence was only adding to it. "I'll go back down. . . ."

"You do that." Lord Henry gave Jeff a meaningful nod. "We're getting along fine, just fine. . . ."

Brother Bill hadn't left his post near the picnic tables, but he was pacing back and forth as if he were at the end of a chain. "He's here," Bill blurted out the moment he saw Jeff's face.

"Old Henry's sitting on him up in the woods so Merrie won't see him until after the dinner." Jeff shook his head grimly. "Sometimes I think Henry hates the boy more than I do. Other times, like on Christmas Day, when he said, 'He's my brother's boy . . .' " Jeff sighed. Henry didn't hate Jim. The point was that sharp-tongued, eccentric hermit that he was, the old prospector had grown to love Merrie. Was there anyone who didn't?

"He wants to protect Merrie," Brother Bill said.

"Yes, and from his own kin . . ." Jeff stopped and glanced quickly toward the platform over the falls. "They're getting ready for the jump. It must be close to two o'clock."

The short, square man in the canvas suit walked to the edge of the platform and looked over. Whistles and bells would not have had as strong an effect on the crowd. The picnickers on the hill jumped to their feet and ran down the slope to the tracks. The last customers at the Ladies Aid tables set their plates down hurriedly. Mothers began calling to their children, men knotted into groups, clusters of tittering girls and self-conscious youths bobbed along merrily on the current of people flowing toward the falls. The church ladies seemed to feel it would not be proper to watch a parachute jump with their aprons on; they were removing them hastily, dropping them here or there as they bustled after the crowd.

Merrie was the last to leave. Jeff watched from a distance as she circled the picnic table, replacing the lid on an uncovered roaster of chicken, spreading a clean towel over a platter of rolls, brushing crumbs, stacking dishes. With a last worried frown at the unfinished chores, she turned her back to the picnic tables and began to walk toward the falls.

Jeff hesitated. Jim was in that crowd Merrie was approaching, and there was no way to foresee what the boy's sick mind would direct him to do when they met. Would the moment be worse for Merrie if he were with her, or better? Jeff's feelings told him to run after her, to pick her up bodily, if necessary, and carry her away. His good sense retorted that the meeting between Merrie and her husband was inevitable and it was useless—in fact, even from his own point of view it was unwise to try and prevent it. For a second Jeff didn't know what to do, and then a little thing dissolved the paralysis of indecision. Merrie was wearing the hair ribbon he had given her at Christmas. He hadn't noticed it before, but there it was, nestled at the nape of her neck, bouncing a little as she quickened her step. Plain as a signal flag. Jeff ran to catch up with her.

"Why, Jeff!"

It pleased but hurt him to see her open, unrestrained delight. "Look, Merrie," he said, "I'm sick to death of people telling you things you ought to know. Now I've got to do it myself. Jim is here. He came out on the excursion train.''

The color drained out of her cheeks, the little-girl eagerness vanished, she closed her eyes. The change in her was so sudden he thought she was going to faint and grabbed her arms to keep her from falling.

She opened her eyes. ''Thank you, Jeff. I'm all right now. You told me he'd come back sometime. But it's a shock anyway.''

Jeff continued to hold her, hungry to touch her, hungry for so slight a contact as his hands on her arms.

Her mouth trembled. ''Jeff, really, I'm all right.''

He withdrew his hands, but neither of them moved. Looking down into Merrie's troubled eyes, twin waves of love for her and anger against Jim Cowen swept over him. ''I know you have to do this, Merrie. I hate it, but I recognize it. Meeting Jim today is something I can't protect you from nor help you with. But this is your last meeting, Merrie. It will be unpleasant, maybe worse, but you won't be tormented as you have been in the past by trying to decide between loyalty to your husband and happiness for yourself. That decision has been made, Merrie. You made it on Christmas day, willingly, in an act of love I believe was more deeply moving to both of us than anything we'd known before. Now your loyalty is to *me*, Merrie. You're *my* girl. I'll let you talk to Jim alone because I know you must, but I won't be very far away.''

"Your girl," she repeated unsteadily.

"Now we'll go watch the parachute jump," Jeff said, placing a guiding hand on her elbow. "You and I, together."

In silence they crossed the picnic grounds. As they neared the mob of spectators, Merrie drew closer to Jeff, and she began to walk with a stiff, determined step. Jeff tightened his hold on her arm. They passed many of his friends, loggers from his own camp, townspeople like Dr. Adams whom he had known for as long as he could remember. He smiled, he waved, and a voice that sounded much too loud and too deliberate to be his own exchanged greetings all along the way.

They reached a spot on the hill from which both the falls and the platform were visible. "Here," Jeff said quietly.

Merrie's eyes were fixed on the parachute jumper, who was standing in the center of the platform, head thrown back, arms folded across his chest. She wasn't letting herself look into the crowd.

A second man climbed the ladder and joined the parachutist on the platform. He was wearing a dark suit and with a worn and moldy look to it, and his face was red and puffy. "Ladies and gennu-men . . ." he wheezed, lifting a megaphone to his mouth. "Your attention, please . . ."

"It won't be long," Jeff said.

Merrie repeated mechanically, "No, it won't be long. . . ."

The announcer pivoted slowly from side to side, sweeping the crowd with his voice. "You have come here today . . ." faintly, because the megaphone was aimed upriver, "to witness one of the most *thur-illing feats*. . ." very loud now, as the megaphone was pointed directly at them, "*that has ever* been attempted in the entire . . ." softer, softer, for he had wheeled to address the people to their left, "in the entire Yew-nited States. . . ." The last was indistinct. "This man that you see beside me, this man who is taking his life in his hands . . ." Slowly the volume of his voice increased as the big red megaphone swung back.

Brother Bill was standing with Dr. Adams, only a few feet away. The Bengstons were grouped a little to the left. Jeff's gaze moved on methodically. Nate, to the right. Excursionists. Below them the old Indian squaw and her daughters . . . Lord Henry, and Jim.

"This, the great falls of the Snoqualmie," the announcer was shouting, "this wonder of the world is one hundred feet higher than Niagara in New York State. Yes, one hundred feet taller than the famous Niagara Falls . . ."

The two of them were standing in the shadow of the platform. Jim was staring at the men above, his face flushed and his body leaning forward as if he were about to leap up the stair and join them.

"Merrie," Jeff said gently, "I see Jim."

"Where?"

"To our left . . . No, turn back a little. There. By the platform, right at the foot of the ladder."

He heard her quick intake of breath, and knew she had seen him. "Should I—Jeff, do you think this is the time to . . ."

416

"For this moment, you'll stay right here," he said quietly, "with me."

The announcer's voice came and went, now loud, now muffled. The parachutist bowed. An excited murmur rippled across the crowd as he stepped to the edge of the platform. But he wasn't ready to make the jump. Shoulders twitching under the weight of the curious object strapped on his back, he looked down, straightened up quickly, backed away. "Oh . . ." said the crowd. Jeff watched with a sense of utter detachment. All faces and figures but those of Jim Cowen and his uncle were only half-seen, like the incomplete, blurred images glimpsed out of the corner of the eyes. He was prepared for, and recognized, the moment when Jim looked up the hill and saw Merrie.

They waited, motionless as images, while Jim pushed his way through the crowd, the old prospector at his heels. They faced each other, and still no one spoke.

Even now, Jeff thought of Jim as a boy. His face was sullen, not angry. The weak mouth, the defiant but frightened look in his eyes—he is a child, Jeff thought, a child deranged by self-pity. Lord Henry's face was at his shoulder; old and lined as it was, there was strength to it the nephew's didn't have. And a deep sadness in the eyes, an expression which seemed out of place in the prospector's shrewd face.

Jim glared at Jeff. Jeff returned the gaze evenly, waiting for the boy to speak, for the inevitable moment when he and Merrie would have to be left alone.

Lord Henry muttered something. Jim started and threw a quick glance over his shoulder. The prospector gestured curtly. Jim hesitated, his handsome face twisted by a petulant frown, but he wheeled around so that his back was to Merrie and Jeff, and he was standing next to his uncle. Strange, Jeff thought—that boy is afraid of me, but he is far more afraid of his uncle.

With half his mind Jeff noted the progress of the celebration. The announcer finished his introduction. The parachutist circled the platform, bowing at intervals. A burst of applause greeted each bow. Clapping and shouting stopped abruptly when he completed the circle and moved cautiously to the outer edge of the platform. He adjusted the parachute, ran his thumbs under the shoulder straps, bent his knees two or three times, but he'd done these before. When was he *really* going to jump? . . . Now he was leaning over the edge. Now? Was it now? a guttural "Ah . . ." rose from the crowd, a lonely scream marked the moment of hesitation as he seemed to hang in the air. He jumped! A dozen shrill cries pierced the air as he went down like a stone dropped into a well. The parachute opened. The white silk billowed out, filling with air. The man's body seemed to be jerked upward as his fall was broken. The cords were out, he dangled at the end of a dozen strings, his body swinging from side to side.

The crowd might have been frozen as he floated gently downward. He had done it, they had seen it, the most breathtaking feat ever performed in the Yew-nited States. . . . No one moved. No sound but the steady roar of the water as it tumbled over the precipice and dropped two hundred and sixty-eight feet to the river below.

Jeff heard someone mutter "Downdraft . . ." Exclamations burst from a dozen throats. Something was wrong. Up on the platform the announcer was clutching the railing as he peered over the edge. Spectators elbowed each other in their effort to obtain a better view. The announcer had sunk to his knees. The big red megaphone dropped from his hand, rolled over, came to rest against the railing.

"He's just lying there! He's not moving. . . ."

"Downdraft," a deeper voice repeated. "Threw him against the rocks."

Somewhere a little child began to cry, a high, lost sound, mounting above the panicky murmur that rose from the crowd like steam.

The little world of the four of them was shattered. It was Jeff who said, "Someone's got to go get him. Henry, you stay here with Merrie. . . ."

Jeff turned and began to push his way through the crowd. He heard Jim's loud cry. "I'll rescue him! *I'll* carry him up. . . ." But Lord Henry was there, no need to go back and try to reason with the boy.

Some spectators were losing their heads. Jeff had to fight crosscurrents of men running toward the falls and men and women rushing the other way. Jim's voice, crazed with excitement, was shouting, "I know the path! *I'll* do it. . . ."

Out of the corner of his eye Jeff saw Jim race ahead, his uncle trotting doggedly behind. But Jim wasn't running toward the path. . . . Jeff hurried on.

It was a steep trail to the bottom of the falls, dangerous and little used. The lank figure of Brother Bill appeared at his side. "You might need help," the preacher panted, loping along at his side.

"Know the path?"

"Like my own face. But there's a short cut."

Jeff shook his head. "Too dangerous. The regular trail will take us five minutes longer, but we'll be alive when we get there."

Once again he thought he heard Jim's voice. It came from the left as he and Bill began their slow descent to the foot of the falls. The boy wouldn't be crazy enough to try the short cut. . . . "Confound it, Bill, do you hear anything?"

They stopped. Stones hurtling down a slide, twigs snapping, wind whining through the tops of the fir trees . . . But the sounds were smothered by the rumbling of the waterfall.

Jeff frowned. "Henry will stop him," he said grimly.

Bill looked puzzled.

"I mean Jim. Come on, I'll explain later."

They moved carefully, for there were no switchbacks in the lower trail; it dropped down an almost perpendicular embankment to the river's edge. Years before, someone had chopped crude steps into this precipice; this section had been cleared recently and some of the thickest underbrush cut away. To make it easier for the parachutist to climb back to the top of the falls, Jeff reflected. Ironically, this careful preparation would certainly make it easier for him and Bill to carry the parachutist's body to the top.

The short cut joined the trail at the bottom of the cliff. Below, giant boulders of basalt jutted black and wet from the foaming pools at the foot of the falls. Bill threw a look over his shoulder. "I see why you didn't like the idea of taking the fast trail. It's nothing but a dry wash. One slip . . ."

"That would be enough."

They lowered themselves carefully, seeking secure footing on the slippery rocks. The force of the falling water beat the pools into foam; the chasm at the foot was a caldron of swirling white mist. Hands, faces, hair were wet almost at once; drops of water collected on their eyebrows and made it hard to see.

Jeff shook his head and rubbed his eyes. "He should be right about there. . . ."

Bill said, "I think I see him. . . ."

"Point him out. . . ." Jeff's eyes narrowed as they focused on the spot indicated by the preacher's long arm. "Yes, there he is. Let's go."

And then they saw Jim. He was lying almost at their feet, on a ledge of rock above the river.

Brother Bill muttered, "Jim Cowen. How did he, why . . ."

Instinctively Jeff looked from the crumpled form on the rocks to the abrupt ending of the short cut directly above. "The poor crazy kid," he said softly. "He was bound to be the hero. He took the fast trail, he was going to beat me to it."

Jeff slid along the ledge toward Jim. A sound

from the hill above made him stop and look back up the trail. A single large stone was rolling down the suicidal short cut. It bounced end over end, catapulted over the bank, came to rest against one of the basalt boulders. A big stone. Something like a human foot might dislodge it. Lord Henry? Was the old man trying to follow his nephew?

Jeff cupped his hands around his mouth. "Henry?" he shouted. "You coming down? Henry?"

But there was no answer. Jeff lowered his hands. "He was trying to keep up, but I guess the boy was too fast for him. Henry knows these trails better than I do, he'd know when to give up and turn back."

Jim was curled up on his side, knees drawn up slightly, head bent forward, like a sleeping child. Jeff pressed his fingers into Jim's wrist, looked into the half-open sightless eyes.

"How bad hurt is he?" Bill asked hoarsely.

Jeff straightened up. "We'd better go get the other one, there might be some hope for him. Jim's dead."

Without speaking, they made their way from rock to rock to the spot where the parachutist lay. He was unconscious and blood oozed from the corner of his mouth, but he was alive.

Above the roar of the water, Jeff shouted, "We'll get him up the hill first. I'll come back for Jim. . . ."

With the sagging broken body of the parachutist between them, they began the slow ascent. Half-way to the top a group of loggers met them.

Big Dave Riley was in the lead. "I knew it," Dave moaned, "I knew it. I *said* we were going to a funeral. I could of told you. . . ."

"You carry him the rest of the way," Jeff said, silencing the big bullwhacker with a curt nod.

"Sure, Jeff . . ."

"Easy, real easy . . . There, now one of you fellows take over for Bill. . . ."

Gently they transferred the burden. "I'll bet that Doc Adams is waiting right there at the end of the path. . . ." Dave nodded, and Jeff turned to go down.

"Hey, Jeff!" Dave exclaimed. "Where you going?"

"There were two of them down there."

"Two!"

"Jim Cowen. He tried to get down there fast, to pick this fellow up. He must have fallen."

"Now ain't that a shame," Dave growled. "A shame and a pity . . ."

"That'll be enough!" The words burst from Jeff's mouth. Dave's big face turned red. "Sorry, Dave," Jeff said quietly. "The boy's dead."

"I'll go down with you," Brother Bill said.

"No need. He doesn't weigh much. It would be better if you'd go up and find Lord Henry and tell him what happened. Someone will have to tell Merrie. . . ."

Bill said hurriedly, "Look, Jeff, I can tell her if I have to, but I'll be no comfort to her. You would be. You'd know what to say."

Jeff nodded. "The fact is that neither of us should go down there alone. Too much chance of getting hurt. Come on, Bill, we'll bring him up together."

Jeff lifted Jim's body as carefully as if he were trying not to hurt him. Bill uttered a wordless exclamation. "Look there," the preacher said, pointing to the side of the boy's head. "He must have taken a terrible fall. It almost looks . . ." the preacher's voice trailed off. "Here . . ." and he turned Jim's head so that Jeff could see.

Jeff felt as if there was a hand at his throat. The skull in the area of the temple had been crushed. He knew what Bill had meant to say. This *had* been too hard a blow. Jim had been struck deliberately—struck by someone who had picked up a sharp rock, brought it down on his head with one furious, shattering blow . . .

The truth was shouting at him, it was no use closing his ears to it. Jeff thought of Henry's face when he talked of his nephew, a face that was fierce with hatred. Just as fierce was the old man's protective love for Merrie, and the family pride that made him say, even as he denounced Jim, "After all, he is my brother's boy." How terrible the conflict must have been when these emotions clashed!

Now Jeff understood Lord Henry's strange behavior today. His appearance at such a celebration, though he hated and ordinarily avoided people. His dogged pursuit of Jim when the young man raced down the hill to the short cut . . . It was a bitter decision the old man reached when he and his mad nephew were alone in the woods. The single stone, rolling down the hill . . . Jeff knew now that a human foot had dislodged it.

Jeff looked directly into the preacher's troubled eyes. There was a moral responsibility to knowing how Jim had died. Should he ask Bill to share it? The answer came to him instantly. No. The "right" and the "wrong" of Henry's act was not as simple as the laws against it. Bill would see that, and would suffer, whether his conscience directed him to report the truth or to hide it.

"Yes, he must have taken a terrible fall," Jeff said quietly. "I wouldn't want Merrie to see his face. When we get to the top of the hill, I'll cover it with my handkerchief."

As they labored up the slope, Jeff asked himself—What shall I say, whom should I tell? I have made my decision about Bill, but there will be others. Even Lord Henry might be in the crowd above the falls. If so, I'll have to face him. Shall I conceal my knowledge from him as he will doubtless conceal his deed from me, or will we read the truth in each other's faces? Jeff's jaw line hardened. I'll know what to do, he thought. My conscience might plague me worse than Brother Bill's plagues him, but I do know what I have to do.

Neither Bill nor Jeff spoke until they reached the picnic grounds. There the crowd engulfed them. Curious, horrified faces were all around, a dozen voices asked, "What happened?"

The words came easily, because the decision had been made at the foot of the cliff. The truth was a burden he could carry alone. "He fell and hit his head against a rock," Jeff said. "Where is Mrs. Cowen?"

Nils Bengston broke through the circle. "Merrie's over there, helping Doc Adams. They're about to take that parachute jumper to the hospital." He looked at the figure in Jeff's arms, at the head covered with a handkerchief, then into Jeff's face. "Fool kid," he muttered. "I saw him run down the hill, with old Henry tagging along like a rooster with two broken wings. He was bound to take a fall. Fool kid."

"Where is Lord Henry now?"

Nils shook his head. "I don't know, that was the last I saw of him. Somebody's got to tell him about this, though, and he's going to take it a lot harder than you'd think." He frowned. "There's somebody else that's got to be told. Jeff, you leave Jim here with me. You go talk to Merrie before she sees him."

Jeff laid Jim on the ground, and the tight circle of silent, curious people opened for him as he went to tell Merrie.

She was sitting in the back of Bengstons' wagon, with the head of the injured man in her lap. Dr. Adams was climbing into the driver's seat. They both saw him coming, both turned their heads. The details of Merrie's face became clearer with each long step. The long, coppery hair, hanging loose about her shoulders. The sensitive lips, parted now with apprehension. The tilt of her chin . . . my girl, Jeff thought, my girl whatever happens. Jim's death had severed the last tie.

He reached the side of the wagon, and looked up into Merrie's face. With a quiet voice and simple words, he told her what had happened.

II

It was July of 1896. A man named William Jennings Bryan was bringing delegates to their feet at the Democratic convention in Chicago. Congress had satisfied itself that Mormons would confine themselves to one wife, and Utah, the forty-fifth state, had joined the union six months before. American sugar interests were growing uneasy about the rebellion in Cuba, and some newpaper editors were filling their pages with specific descriptions of Spanish atrocities. The Democrats were denouncing the Supreme Court, and the Republicans were raising the biggest campaign fund in the history of the party. . . . And the Syrian peddler called Joe was arriving in Gold Mountain.

It had been a hot day. Jeff Smith was expecting a shipment of supplies by the evening train, but it wasn't due for a while; he was passing time with the old men who daily commandeered the chairs on the porch of Nate Tarpee's store. They had known his father; fault-finding, affectionate, they were as good as his own kin. For thirty minutes they had been recalling incidents in which the son of Harvey Barrington Smith from Kentucky had played a part.

They quarreled over every detail. One squeaky voice claimed Jeff was only ten years old when he shot three cougar in two days; another retorted hotly that he wasn't ten, he was nine, and it wasn't three cats, it was four. Jeff was laughing and wondering when they would consult him, if at all, when he saw the peddler coming into town.

The nostalgia the old men's stories had awakened was suddenly doubled. Joe hadn't come to Gold Mountain of recent years; it was generally assumed he was dead, and Jeff had regretfully locked memories of the peddler's visits into the cupboard of events past and never to be relived. But here he was, just as he had always been. Walking right down the center of the main street, his wiry little body bent almost double with the weight of the incredibly large wooden box on his back. Puffs of brown dust rose at his heels—hadn't he always arrived on a hot, dry day: The dogs ran out to bark at him; he spoke to them softly in a strange tongue; magically, they fell into line behind him, wagging their tails.

Jeff had seen this happen a dozen times. The scene was plucked from his boyhood, to be reënacted, not in the old men's stories but right on the street in front of him. He began to predict what Joe's next move would be. He would come abreast of Tarpee's store, doff the tasseled red cap in a deep, ceremonial bow to the townspeople on the steps. He would replace the cap, turn sharply on his heel, and go direct to the Gold Mountain jail, a little weather-beaten building on the other side of the street. . . . He did all this, and Jeff found himself wishing Joe would perform the rest of the routine exactly as he remembered it.

The peddler rose on tiptoe so as to peek into the jail's interior. It was empty—Gold Mountain's judge did his biggest business on Saturdays and election days. The jail leaned against a somewhat larger shack which bore the sign, ''COURT HOUSE. Justice of the Peace.'' The peddler took a few steps and rapped politely on the door.

The judge was an old friend. Their mutual admiration had been born during Joe's very first visit to Gold Mountain. The judge had cast a suspicious eye on the peddler's dark skin and curious burden and arrested him, on grounds that weren't clear even at that time. Joe had spent a happy week in jail, rewarding the judge with a number of glittery trinkets for his wife and a large bottle of highly potent cough syrup for himself. After that, Joe was always the guest of the jail. Jeff could remember his own mother sending chicken broth (to be drunk hot) and goose grease (to be applied to the chest) to the jail the year Joe came in the winter and took sick. . . .

Jeff felt light-headed with relief as he saw that the peddler's performance wasn't going to vary from the pattern he remembered. The judge opened the door, greeted Joe with a roar of pleasure that could be heard all over the block. He disappeared briefly into his office, returned with a key ring as big around as a pie tin, and in a few minutes had unlocked the jail and ushered Joe through the door. Later Joe would set up his box on the sidewalk in front of the jail. But he was fanatically clean. He never opened shop until he had bathed and changed his clothes.

"Well, well," said the oldest man on Tarpee's porch, "I see Joe the peddler is still making his rounds. I figured he'd died of old age."

And someone retorted, "He don't look no different than he did twenty years ago. Nothing changes in this here town."

Jeff strolled away from the men. Nothing changes? The old man would know better than anyone in the Valley that it wasn't true.

Once the captain of the riverboat had said folks always would travel by river, but someone else had built a railroad, and the captain and his boat rotted on the riverbank below the falls.

Nils Bengston had owned the largest hop ranch in the world, and now he ran a hotel.

Brother Bill was going to stay in Gold Mountain for the rest of his life. Two years after he'd settled here, he had stood behind the Gold Mountain pulpit for the last time, directing the funeral service for Jim Cowen, and now he was at some outpost along the Stikine River in Alaska, trying to convince prospectors that there are things more important than gold.

Change? Most of Gold Mountain's townspeople had come to the Snoqualmie Valley to log or to farm, or to provide necessities for loggers and farmers.

Now, after rumors of gold in Alaska, every third male in the Valley was talking about mucking and drifting, about ground-sluicing and shoveling-in. Several men had left for the North, many more were talking about Forty-Mile River as if it were a branch of the Snoqualmie.

Change? Let news of a big strike up north reach

these people, and there would be change. Not that they expected it. Brother Bill hadn't expected to leave his church, Jim Cowen hadn't expected to die. . . .

Nor had old Henry Cowen. He had disappeared after the parachute jump, no one had seen him since. His mule had been tethered near the picnic ground until late that night, when Jeff untied the animal and led him to the old prospector's cabin. It was deserted. If Henry had been there and gone, there was no way of knowing it for sure. Jeff had fed the mules; after four or five days he had moved them to his own homestead.

Jeff guessed that the old man had finally gone to Alaska. In less than a week the Seattle newspapers proved him right. On April 6, 1896 the steamer *Willapa* had left Seattle for Cook's Inlet, with thirty-seven passengers and a crew of five. She had hit a storm and gone down; old Henry's name was on the list of those who had been lost. His full name was George Edward Henry Cowen. Many people in Gold Mountain had never known what it was. Many had been astonished to learn some days later that the old man left a will. It was short, written in a beautiful hand, and it bequeathed his property and belongings to Merrie. The judge in Gold Mountain had received it two or three days after the parachute jump; it came in a sealed envelope, enclosed in a larger envelope mailed in Seattle. . . .

The door to the jail opened. Joe the peddler stepped outside, appraised the commercial possibilities with a long glance that swept slowly from one end of the town to the other. Actually there was no one in sight except the watchful old men in the chairs on Tarpee's porch. But he seemed satisfied, for he darted back into the jail and reappeared with his box.

Legs sprang from the bottom, the lid parted like a morning-glory facing the sun, a series of shelves burst through the opening. This miniature store—and Jeff knew from memory the endless wonders it contained—was no more like the dusty black box the peddler had carried into town than Joe, with damp hair, shining face and a suit of sparkling white cotton, was like the bent and weary little man who had trudged into Gold Mountain with the dogs at his heels.

Jeff thought, "I'll go buy something . . ." and then, because she was always in his mind, he decided to buy something for Merrie.

It was a crazy, impulsive thing to do. He knew it, even as he hurried across the street toward the display which Joe's instinct for effective merchandising had impelled him to place right in the middle of the sidewalk.

"Hello, Mr. Joe," he said, and it seemed natural to address the old Syrian just as he had been taught to do as a little boy.

The little man beamed. "Something nice for you today, Jeff?" he asked, as if no more than a day or two had elapsed since their last meeting. "Nice watch? Pretty thimble, solid gold? Needles? String beads?"

Like swallows, his swift, dark hands swept down on the display and flew up with some treasure held daintily between thumb and forefinger. Glass beads, cameo brooches, silken coils of embroidery thread, boxes of perfumed rice powder, a brush and comb with silver backs, celluloid collars, cuff links and collar buttons, velveteen pillow covers on which scenes from Seattle's Jim Hill Carnival of three summers before had been painted in oil, napkin rings cut from a walrus tusk . . .

"Something very pretty?" the old man pleaded. "Something maybe for your wife?"

"No," Jeff said recklessly, "something for my girl . . ."

Two minutes later he was loping down the street toward Merrie's hospital with Joe's entire stock of hair ribbons in his pocket.

He opened the door without knocking. The doctor was leaning back in the examination chair, eyeglasses perched on his forehead and hands folded comfortably across his stomach. He sat up, lowered the glasses, and grumbled, "What do you have to come busting in here for and wake me up? You don't look sick."

"I'm not. Where's Merrie?"

"Upstairs. First door to the left. Open the wrong door and you'll fall into a nestful of expectant mothers. Can you imagine that? Coming to a hospital to have a baby. My feet hurt," the doctor growled as he went out.

With his pocket full of hair ribbons and heart beating so hard it hurt, Jeff bounded up the stairs to the hospital floor and knocked on the door the doctor had indicated.

The door opened. Merrie stood in front of him, wearing an apron that had apparently been designed for Bertha Tarpee, for it wrapped around her twice and was tied in the front. A wet cloth dangled from one hand, soapy water was running down her arm and dripping from her elbow.

His arms went around her and he held her tightly, deeply moved by the naturally sweet smell of her skin and the eager pressure of her body. "Merrie," he said at last, "Merrie, Merrie, I want to love you, right now, right here, with that damned wet soapy washcloth of yours dripping down my back. But I promised myself when I came up those stairs that the loving would have to wait."

She stepped back, a worry line deepening between her eyebrows. "Yes, Jeff?"

"I've been doing some serious thinking. With you close enough to touch, I'll never get it out." He turned away from her and walked to the window. "You know that I've been undecided for a long time as to what I ought to do with my logging camp. Whether to stick with ox-logging, or go into debt so as to buy donkey engines and such. The old way or the new way, that's what it amounts to. We used to talk about this. . . ."

"Yes, we did," Merrie said. "When I was living in your cabin, right after Joseph was born."

"Yes." Jeff felt as if his heart had constricted. That was a memory he cherished but it would always evoke some of the bitterness and frustration he had felt over Merrie's loyalty to another man. "I have finally come to a decision," he said carefully. "I plan to go into Seattle next week to place my order."

Merrie said warmly, "Jeff, that's fine. I'm glad."

He made a quick deprecating gesture with one hand. "It's the logical thing to do."

"I'm sure it is."

He cleared his throat. "Now the significance of this decision . . . Merrie, this means I've given up the idea of going away. I've always been 'permanently temporary,' as Brother Bill used to put it, but it won't be that way any more. I'll have financial commitments, a big project I'll have to see through. That is . . ." He stopped, turned toward her, and shrugged helplessly. "Merrie, it means I'm going to have to stay right here for the rest of my life."

She nodded solemnly. "For some time, at least."

She was still holding the dripping cloth—he could see she had forgotten it completely. The shiny look in her eyes was disconcerting, but he stuck to his purpose doggedly. "I have always been satisfied with the cabin my father built when he first took out the claim. As long as I didn't add onto it, or change it, it wasn't a real home; there was no tie I couldn't break easily whenever I wanted to leave. Now I realize I've kept the cabin just as it was simply because it was home as I had always known it. It belongs to my childhood, to the days when Joe the peddler came to Gold Mountain every year. . . ."

All at once his pocket seemed to be bulging out with its cargo of hair ribbons. Hand pressed against the pocket, Jeff said rapidly, "Merrie, have you been looking ahead? Do you know what you want to do, now?"

"Do you mean now that I'm a widow?"

"No," Jeff said huskily, "now that you're free."

"Yes, I do. Well, no, not exactly . . ."

"You used to talk about going back . . . Do you still want to go back to your aunt and uncle in Dakota?"

She shook her head firmly. "Jeff, their home isn't my home any longer."

Jeff's hands tightened into fists. Two steps forward, one quick movement, he would be holding her in his arms. Desire for her was almost unbearable.

"Then you think you could be happy here?"

She looked up into his face. "I could be happy anywhere with you."

"There are several factors to be considered. Changing the logging operation will cost money; I'll be in debt for several years. I may fail—that possibility has to be considered. I may be a bad risk personally. I'm older than you are. . . ."

"Jeff!" Merrie exploded, stamping one foot, "stop *reasoning* with me!"

He caught his breath, hesitated for a second while logic made a last stand and retreated in disorder. "I love you, and I want to live with you. That's all I've been trying to say."

"You've been taking too long."

Jeff covered the distance between them in one long stride, and swept her up in his arms.

"You used to say I was your girl," she gasped, clinging to him. "You said I was pretty."

"I did not. Your hair flies every which way. You've got freckles." He held her close. "Not pretty. Beautiful."

She laughed, with the gaiety of a child to whom a new and deeper note had been added—the warmth of a woman. "If you were to kiss me," she whispered, "you could close your eyes, you wouldn't have to look at me."

"That's no solution," Jeff retorted. "I'm going to have to get used to you." But he kissed her, anyway.

About the Author

CHARLOTTE PAUL is a native of the Pacific Northwest, though she is a graduate of Newton High School (Newton, Massachusetts) and Wellesley College, and for twenty-five years of her very active and creative life she has lived east of the Mississippi, one spot being as far east as Dresden, Germany, where she studied dance with Mary Wigman. She says her writing career began the day she learned to read and that her first (and unpublished) story was written in the attic cubbyhole of the Paul home in Longview, Washington, a niche designated as her "study".

After graduation from Wellesley with a B.A. degree and honors in English Composition, she became assistant foreign news editor for the Chicago Daily *Times* and later that paper's roving correspondent in the Caribbean. For three years she served in an editorial and re-write capacity for *Esquire-Coronet* in Chicago.

Twenty-five years as a freelance writer produced countless articles and short stories for national magazines, as well as five books—three novels including the best-selling *Gold Mountain,* and two works of non-fiction. Most of her work has been translated into several foreign languages, and several of them have been book club selections.

In 1962, Charlotte Paul took up a new career when the governor of the state of Washington appointed her to the Washington State Board of

Prison Terms & Paroles, the only woman on a five-man board. Two years later, after appointment by President Johnson, she moved to Washington, D.C., and began a six-year term as the "eighth man" on the U.S. Board of Parole. She has calculated that in six years of conducting interviews with federal prisoners, she has spent 24 months in men's penitentiaries.

Retiring from government service in the fall of 1970, she and her husband, Robert W. Reese, a long-time writer and public affairs officer for the Treasury Department, settled in the San Juan Islands, off the northern coast of the state of Washington, and Mrs. Reese went back to her first professional love—writing, particularly writing of fiction. The highly successful result of her first two years back at the typewriter was *Phoenix Island,* which has sold close to a million copies.

Charlotte Paul claims that her only hobby is work, but she admits to spending her leisure time hunting wild mushrooms, collecting edible weeds, and hauling driftwood for the two big fireplaces in the Reeses' sprawling cedar house where the front windows look out towards the Pacific and the snow-covered range of the Olympic Mountains. She also plays a mean piano, 1940s style, and occasionally gets together with a local bull fiddler and local guitarist to lift the roof off the local pub. She has three sons—Hiram Paul Groshell, public defender, John Paine Groshell, pro and part owner of a golf course outside Seattle, and Robert J. Reese, investigator for an insurance company. And three grandchildren.

AND two bassets and one cairn terrier.

There are a lot more
where this one came from!

ORDER your FREE catalog of ACE paperbacks here. We have hundreds of inexpensive
books where this one came from priced from
75¢ to $2.50. Now you can read all the books
you have always wanted to at tremendous
savings. Order your *free* catalog of ACE
paperbacks now.

ACE BOOKS • Box 576, Times Square Station • New York, N.Y. 10036